VALENTINA ON THE EDGE

Evie Blake

headline

First published in Great Britain in 2013 by
HEADLINE PUBLISHING GROUP

1

Cataloguing in Publication Data is available from the British Library

ISBN 978 0 7553 9889 8

Typeset in Sabon by Avon DataSet Ltd, Bidford-on-Avon, Warwickshire

Printed and bound in Great Britain by Clays Ltd, St Ives plc

Headline's policy is to use papers that are natural, renewable and recyclable
products and made from wood grown in sustainable forests. The logging and
manufacturing processes are expected to conform to the environmental
regulations of the country of origin.

HEADLINE PUBLISHING GROUP
An Hachette UK Company
338 Euston Road
London NW1 3BH

www.headline.co.uk
www.hachette.co.uk

For S.L.

In my dreams, I dance

Louise Brooks

Maria

1955

LAST NIGHT SHE DREAMT OF PARIS AGAIN. SHE WANDERED the alleyways of Saint-Germain-des-Prés at dusk – that time when they used to come out to play, the city still raw, still edgy from its recent liberation. She was searching for him. In the fading light she saw mauve shadows flitting this way and that, leading her on a false trail. She rushed down the streets, slipping on the smooth cobbles, desperate in her need to find him.

Yet he could not be found. She hunted for him in Le Flore, but the café was practically empty. Only Monsieur Boubal stood behind the bar, drying glasses with a white linen cloth, surveying her coolly.

You don't belong here anymore, she read in his haughty glance.

1

She looked for him in all the clubs, the violence of the jazz accelerating her heartbeat as she pushed through the hot throngs of young Parisians and the new Americans, the guys with the scruffy little beards, the girls with long, lank hair and blunt fringes. They all stared at her blankly.

What are you doing here? She knew they were thinking. *You are not a part of us anymore.*

She was back in the dark streets, running, running. The abbey loomed in front of her as she turned a corner and she spied their hotel. Relief coursed through her. Surely she would find him there? She ran through the lobby, ignoring Madame Paget and her resentful stare.

Get out, she imagined her saying. *You are not one of us.*

Up, up, in that rickety cage lift. How could she ever forget it? And down the dark corridor she ran. She flung the door of their room open, her heart in her mouth, but it was empty. Devastated, she stepped inside. There were the tousled bed sheets, the three dead geraniums in the empty wine bottle on the windowsill, the empty case on the floor and, sitting on a chair, as if it was expecting her, was his camera. And yet he was not there. She stepped inside the room and picked up his camera, cradled it in her hands. He will come back. He must. She sat down on the chair, destitute, and her memory came back to her in the form of flickering images projected above the bedstead like one of the films they made. She sees her breasts and his hands caressing her nipples, she sees their lips meeting and his body upon hers, within hers. All is grainy and soft focus, yet the images slice her heart open like knife blades. She had surrendered every part of herself to their love. She had been possessed by it. How could she live without it?

Maria woke up on fire, her mouth parched, her body bathed in sweat. She was pulsing with need. There was a deep ache inside her womb and she began to reach down with her hands, to put them between her legs, to touch herself. No! She tore the sheets off herself with vehemence and lay on her back, letting the air of their bedroom cool her until her heart rate slowed and she was back inside her body – a body that had almost forgotten the darker side of passion. Carefully, she climbed out of bed. The cool floor beneath her hot feet pulled her back down to earth as she stumbled out of the bedroom into the hallway. Their apartment ticked in silence and there was not a sound from the streets outside. Milan had not awoken yet. She looked up at the cross above the hall table. She squeezed her eyes shut, clasped her hands tight and prayed to Jesus, her sweet saviour, to give her peace. Yet even He could not console her. On these nights, there was only one thing she could do to comfort herself.

She opened the door of her daughter's bedroom and tiptoed inside. A lamp glowed in the corner, for her daughter was afraid of the dark. The room was a golden sanctuary. The shelves were full of books and dolls; pictures of fairies and magicians were pasted on the wall: the fairy-tale dreams of a little six-year-old girl. She sat down on the chair next to her daughter's bed and gazed down at her. She felt a twinge of guilt at disturbing her, as she stroked the hair away from her forehead and leant down to kiss her. The child's eyes fluttered open and she looked up at her mother, sleepy-eyed and confused. Maria climbed into the bed with Tina and held her in her arms. She pulled her child in so close to her that it was almost as if their two hearts beat as one. The child whimpered. She was tired, grumpy at being woken. Maria whispered into her tiny shell ear. She told her stories of a great romance. But this was not Maria's story. No. She told her own mother's tale: Belle and Santos; a love born in the majestic city of Venice; a star-crossed couple, destined never to be. A story that made the little girl cry and yet it was a story to believe in – that one day your prince will come. Maria squeezed Tina tighter. Better to fill her head with such nonsense than tell her the truth about love, of how it could turn a girl's soul inside out and take her to such a place of liberation that it was terrifying. For once you had tasted this kind of love, experienced such abandon and bliss, it was hard to settle for anything less. And yet, what if the man you loved could never be yours? Then you were in prison for the rest of your life.

No matter how many princess tales she tells her daughter, Maria knows it is to no avail. As her daughter grows older, she sees it. Every time she looks into Tina's unblinking eyes, she detects the fire of the spirit that burns in them all: her mother; herself; her daughter. And she sees more besides, for she recognises the child's father – an echo of him – within the outlines of her face. And, when she sees that, she is afraid.

Valentina

2012

VALENTINA LIES ON HER TUMMY, TURNING THE PAGE OF her book. She inhales the comforting scent of the paper as she rereads the paragraph again. Anaïs Nin is describing a Brazilian dancer, who is painting her sex with red lipstick. The woman is surrounded by her admirers, none of whom is permitted to touch her, only watch. The image plants itself firmly into Valentina's creative imagination. Anaïs Nin goes to town describing the red luscious lips of this dancer's labia, like a ripe tropical flower, and Valentina can't help but feel affected. She finds herself squirming on top of the bed covers and crossing her legs, yet even still she can feel her insides warming. She has an irresistible urge to paint herself, see how it makes her feel.

She hears a rustle of paper, as her companion turns the

page of his book. She twists round to look at him, leaning against the bedstead.

'What are you reading?' she asks.

'Edgar Allan Poe,' Leonardo replies, blinking at her from behind his glasses. '"The Murders in the Rue Morgue".'

'Oh, I've read that,' Valentina says, remembering that this was one of Theo's favourites. 'It's supposed to be the first ever detective story, isn't it?'

Leonardo nods, lifting his head and taking his glasses off. 'How is Anaïs Nin?'

'Steamy.'

He cocks his head, his eyes mildly amused. 'Is that so?'

She watches him regarding her body, his gaze resting on her backside. Leonardo has told her a thousand times she has the perfect bottom for a submissive: curvaceous, yet firm, plump and ripe for spanking. She knows he is teasing her, but the truth is she has grown to adore their games. It helps her to forget about Theo.

It is only five months since Theo and Valentina were in Venice together; only five months since their passionate reunion. And yet, the following day, it all fell apart. She remembers how close she had been to giving him her all, to admitting her love for him. Theo had spent months showing her how much he loved her, how he accepted her for who she was and never wanted her to change. Of course, he needed her to give something back to him; it was only fair. Yet something had stopped her from telling him she loved him. She still cannot reason why. It took just this one moment of hesitation to destroy their whole life together. For, despite her insistence that she could not even be called his girlfriend, they *had* shared a life in Milan. Until Theo was gone for good, she had not realised just how much he was a part of her.

After he had walked out on her in Venice, she decided she was going to win him back. Yet, when she returned to Milan, he was already gone. How did he manage it? To pack up and leave within twenty-four hours, the key to the apartment sealed in a blank envelope in her postbox. Not one word did he leave for her. Had he gone back home to America? All she knew was that his parents lived in Brooklyn. She had no address, and no phone number.

Of course, Leonardo knew where he was. They were old friends, after all. Much to Valentina's shock, he told her that Theo had indeed left Italy. But rather than returning to his native New York, he was living and working in London now. She had been furious at first. Theo had given her no chance to win him back. He had given up in the end. He had told her he loved her, but how could he, really? Surely he would have tried a little harder?

And yet, deep down, Valentina knows that Theo did try everything apart from begging. He had his pride. That was surely why she was attracted to him in the first place: his self-reliance and strength. He was never going to plead with her.

During those first few miserable weeks, Leonardo told her to go to Theo. 'You love him; he loves you. What are you waiting for?' her friend told her.

Yet she was adamant. 'No, it will only end badly. It is just as well,' she told him. 'It was never going to work. Even if we were to try for a while, what's the point? Because,' as she kept lecturing Leonardo, 'no relationship can last forever.'

She knew she was echoing her mother's words. She had wanted so much not to be like her but it seemed she was a carbon copy of her: a woman unable to commit to any man.

'Do you really believe that, Valentina?' Leonardo asked her.

'Of course; don't you?' she said.

Leonardo looked wistful. 'I am like you, Valentina. We are the same.'

'Friends who fuck.' That's what Valentina and Leonardo call themselves. No ties to each other. Leonardo has Raquel, for a start – his glamorous hourglass girlfriend, who has invited Valentina to join them for a threesome on many occasions. Valentina just isn't turned on by the idea. Despite the fact that Raquel and Leonardo have an open relationship, Valentina can't help thinking that Leonardo is Raquel's, so to speak. She prefers the idea of a more disparate threesome: herself, another unattached woman – like her new dancer friend, Celia – and Leonardo. All three of them are the same to each other. No ties. This is a get-together that has long been promised. However, Celia is on tour in America, and won't be back for weeks.

Leonardo is spiralling circles on her stomach now with his finger tip, creeping lower and lower. She puts her hand on his to stop him in his tracks, and turns to face him.

'No,' she says.

'Are you sure?' he asks.

She kisses him gently on the lips. 'You are such a conscientious friend, but no. It's time I got up.'

'Why? It's Sunday.'

He is right, yet she can't stay in bed any longer. Sundays were days she and Theo spent lazing in bed all day – making love again and again, only emerging for food and drink, before diving back under the covers. She knows that Leonardo has to go soon. He is expected back at home, since Raquel has her family coming over for the day. She can't bear to be left in bed on her own all day, reading Anaïs Nin and getting more and more frustrated.

'Are you coming into the club tomorrow?' he asks her.

Valentina has been spending more and more time in Leonardo's nocturnal hideout – the exclusive private-members-only fetish club he runs in Milan. She is there primarily on professional grounds: to construct artistic and tasteful erotic compositions with some of the consenting club members. Occasionally, on those nights when she misses Theo the most, her own sense of guilt, of anger, motivates her to try to block her feelings for him out and distract herself with

S&M games. Yet always she plays with Leonardo and no one else. He is the only one she trusts.

Leonardo sits now on the edge of her bed, pulling on his socks. She looks at the back of his head, his dark curly hair that is so long it is almost to his shoulders.

'You need a haircut,' she says, prodding his back with her finger.

'Raquel likes it long.'

'Well, she's making you look like one of those greasy gigolos!'

Leonardo whips round and in one deft movement pins her to the bed. 'Are you calling me a sleazeball, Signorina Valentina?' He begins to tickle her under her arms.

'No, no . . . How could I?' She stifles a laugh, looking at him in mock wide-eyed innocence. 'When I think you're the hottest man in Milan.'

Leonardo sits back on his heels and, for a second, Valentina imagines she sees a flicker of regret in his eyes.

'Only Milan? Not the whole world?' he challenges her.

She shakes her head. And they look at each other in silence. And for a second she wonders if they are doing the right thing, being such good friends and having sex together.

'So,' asks Leonardo again, 'are you coming in?'

'Tomorrow? Sure; Antonella wants to come with me.'

Leonardo groans. 'Oh, God; she's a maniac.'

'Yes, it seems she's found her dominatrix calling,' Valentina teases.

Leonardo is in the doorway, putting on his jacket. Suddenly, she is filled with an urge to stop him from leaving. She doesn't want to be on her own all day. Not again.

'Would you like some coffee before you go?' she says, pulling on her kimono dressing gown and walking over towards him.

'Sorry, darling; have to go.'

'Are you sure? I can make you a quick espresso.'

Leonardo steps forward and gives her a brief hug. 'I can't. Raquel is expecting me.'

After he is gone, Valentina wanders the corridors of her apartment. Sometimes she imagines leaving this place. She has spent her whole life here. It belonged to her mother before her and, when she moved to America, she told Valentina she could have it – sell it, even. She knows it's worth a fortune. She could buy somewhere amazing, somewhere else, in another country. She doesn't *have* to live in Milan. She's a photographer; she can work anywhere in the world. And yet the memories that haunt her also sustain her, and sometimes she imagines she can still hear Theo in his study, typing away on his computer, with the strains of an obscure cello concerto wafting out into the hall.

Valentina stands facing the study door and opens it slowly. She steps across the threshold and takes in the bare walls, the gaps in the bookcases where Theo removed his books, and the empty desk.

She feels the ache inside her heart, yet she grits her teeth as she walks into the room. She will not cry. She has to get over Theo, move on. She is a free spirit and Theo wanted commitment. Yet, despite his needs, he understood her. He did everything he could to show her that. She walks around the room, the marble floors cold upon the soles of her bare feet. She approaches the desk, sits down in the chair, lifts her feet and spins slowly. She can smell him in here: that crisp, dry tang of Bulgari that catches in the back of her throat and turns her on, even now. She closes her eyes and slowly stops spinning. She places her bare feet back down on the floor and parts her legs. At first, she imagines she is Anaïs Nin's dancer, painting herself and exposing herself to her admirers. Yet gradually the watching eyes fade away and there is only one man looking at her: Theo. She pushes her finger inside herself.

'Theo,' she whispers. Here, inside the privacy of his office, she can say his name. Oh, in these moments she sees herself leaving Milan, taking a plane to London and getting back her man. She circles herself with her fingertips, pushing deeper, further, imagining the touch of Theo upon her. She could never forget how he feels upon her body. She arches in the chair, summoning him to her.

'Come back. Oh, please, come back,' she begs, as she falls forward, climaxing and, within a split second, moving from release to devastation. She bends over, hugging her knees. She knows what this is. This is grief – different from her first heartache over Francesco, for that was a perverse, vengeful pain. No; this feeling is different – as if she has let drop the most valuable thing she ever owned. It is cracked forever; unfixable.

She sits bolt upright, squeezes her fists tight, and stands up. She has to pull herself together, get on with her life.

She marches out of the study, slamming the door behind her, and heads into the kitchen to make some tea. She has to push Theo out of her head. It is *over*. He has not called or written to her once in five months. She has to find the Valentina she was before Theo came into her life. She'll call Antonella and they'll go bargain hunting along the Navigli Canal. She has been spending a lot more time with Antonella since Marco moved to New York and Gaby is expecting a baby.

Gaby's pregnancy had shocked them all. Valentina hadn't even known her old schoolfriend had met someone else, after the break-up with her married lover, Massimo. Valentina had been so busy trying to forget Theo – which had involved a great many escapades in Leonardo's club – that the first time she met Gaby's new boyfriend, Angelo, was the very night they announced her pregnancy.

It had been Christmas Eve, and the friends were all out together. Marco had been the first of them to recover from Gaby's unexpected news.

'Brava, Gaby!' he said while at the same time slapping Angelo on the back. 'That is wonderful. Congratulations!'

Valentina was struck dumb. She stared at her friend, who was positively beaming with joy, and then at Angelo, who didn't look quite as happy, but still had his arm protectively around her shoulders. She guessed he must feel like he was facing the inquisition: Gaby's oldest friends.

'*Mamma mia*!' Antonella cried, articulating Valentina's thoughts. 'Are you crazy? You have only just met.'

Gaby glared at Antonella. 'We've been together two months. Besides, it doesn't matter how long we've been going out.' She picked up Angelo's hand possessively. 'When you know he's the one, you just know. Isn't that right, Valentina?'

Why was she asking her? Gaby knew how she felt about babies, marriage – the whole commitment deal.

Valentina took a sip of wine and looked away from her friend. What could she say? Gaby was heading for disaster. She just knew it.

'You know, girls, we're nearly thirty. Now's the time we should be thinking about having kids, settling down . . .' Gaby began.

'Are you for real?' Antonella exclaimed. 'My God, if I ever "settle down", please shoot me.'

Marco stifled a giggle, while patting Gaby's hand comfortingly. She coloured; her boyfriend, Angelo, looked at Antonella in horror. But Valentina could have said much the same as Antonella. She could have told Gaby what she really thought – that it would all end in tears. How could Gaby possibly think she could have a baby with a man she had only known a couple of months? Had she any idea of the hardship she was about to head into? Of course, Valentina said nothing. She loved Gaby. She had to make herself be happy for her.

Even so, since the announcement, their friendship has drifted slightly. Now it seems that Gaby goes everywhere with Angelo. Valentina has only seen her once on her own recently, when they went to a Matisse exhibition. Her old schoolfriend had been a nightmare, complaining that she felt sick every few minutes and telling Valentina that she had no idea how bad the nausea could be in early pregnancy. Of course, Valentina did know. But she wasn't going to tell Gaby that. There is only one person in the world who knows she was pregnant once. And she is never going to see him again, right? That had been the other thing that drove her mad that day with Gaby. Her friend kept bringing up Theo – trying to get her to talk about him, telling her to call him, advising her not to let him slip out of her life.

In the kitchen, Valentina makes herself a cup of English breakfast tea before sitting down at the table. She hasn't heard from Gaby in a couple of weeks. She should call her – check everything is OK. She should care that her friend is pregnant, and yet she doesn't want to think about it. In fact, if she is honest with herself, she hates the fact that Gaby is having a baby. She will lose her, too, just like she lost Theo.

Valentina opens up her laptop. She hasn't checked her emails for a couple of days. She likes not being available all of the time. Sometimes she imagines having the courage to throw her mobile off the top of the duomo and watch it smash into tiny pieces on the piazza below, but she knows that would be professional suicide. There is quite a lot of mail, mostly boring, but one item in her inbox grabs her attention. She looks with interest at its subject: 'Exhibition of Erotic Photography.'

When she clicks on the message, she has to read it twice before she actually takes in the content. She is being offered a place in a group show of erotic photography, in the Lexington Gallery in Soho, London, at the end of next month. Finally, all of her focus and drive is paying off. Last winter, during the weeks following her break-up with Theo, she had spent days putting together submission packages and sending them out to galleries in London. She had reasoned that she had always wanted to exhibit in London, although, if she is really honest with herself, it had also crossed her mind that this same city is Theo's new home. Without hesitation, Valentina grabs her phone. To hell with Raquel's family dinner, she needs to speak to Leonardo, now.

'Leonardo, guess what? I'm in a show at the Lexington Gallery in London!' she announces before her friend even has time to answer his phone properly.

'Valentina, that's great, but I can't talk right now.' Leonardo sounds unusually uptight.

'Oh, sorry . . .' She feels a little hurt; she cannot help it. She imagines Leonardo and his voluptuous wife, Raquel, at the dinner table, entertaining her family: the aroma of home-cooked food, wine liberally splashed into glasses, chat of young and old, children hiding in between the adults' legs underneath the table. A scene she has never, in her whole life, been a part of.

'I'll call you later.' His voice warms. 'Well done; it's really great news.'

At last, something else is happening in her life to take her away from her heartache over Theo. Finally, her profile as an art photographer, rather than a fashion photographer, is beginning to build. It takes her out of her mother's shadow – Tina Rosselli was Milan's iconic fashion photographer of the sixties and seventies – away from comparisons with her mother and into a world that is hers alone. Maybe that's why she keeps taking those photographs.

Her episodes in Leonardo's club make her feel better. She is not herself, disguised in some costume with her camera. She is a stranger watching strangers, taking pictures of them as they reveal the most nocturnal part of themselves, their secret desires, their shadow selves. The honesty of these scenes never fails to move her. And these are the only times she can hide away from her hurt. So she just keeps on snapping, consumed by this mission: to make something aesthetically otherworldly, beautiful and luscious out of sex.

She sits back against her chair, her heart rate quickening. It takes her less than a second to make up her mind. She quickly types a reply to the email, accepting the invitation.

Finally, she can get away from Milan for a while and all the memories of her and Theo that haunt the rooms within her apartment. In London, she can reinvent herself. And yet, the truth is that Valentina knows it is not just the idea of the exhibition that is exciting her. She now has an excuse to go to London, a huge city, of course, with a population of millions, and yet, even so, it is Theo's new home. In London, she will be closer to him.

$\mathcal{M}$aria

1948

THE DAY SHE LEAVES, IT IS RAINING – THE WAY IT ONLY can in Venice – a penetrating downpour, barrelling down upon them as they walk towards the ferry. The lagoon sloshes over on to the pavement to merge with pools of rainwater. Her feet are wet before she has even set out.

The ferry is already there. Maria grips her suitcase handle, feels the stiff leather burning her palm. Her breath is tight in her chest. Finally, she is leaving.

Her mother places her hands on Maria's shoulders, squeezes them tightly and looks intently into her eyes. She is hatless and her hair is stuck to her head like a shiny black helmet.

'Never forget who you are,' she says to Maria.

She looks away from her mother's gaze. It is too intense

and makes her frightened. She is beginning to have regrets. She is safe here in Venice. Why would she ever want to leave?

'It will be very different in London,' her mother continues. 'It's a very big city; much bigger than Venice. And it has been crippled by the war. Things will be harsh.'

Pina reaches forward and places her hand on Maria's mother's arm in reassurance. 'She will be fine, Belle,' she says gently.

Her mother drops her arms and, instinctively, Maria folds into the embrace of the two other women. She inhales deeply her mother's scent of crushed roses and Pina's more comforting aroma of burnt sugar and vanilla.

The bell rings for the ferry to depart and Maria knows that it is now, or never. If she doesn't get on the ferry today, she will never be able to extricate herself from her mother's love. It is so painful, this separation, and yet she has dreamt of this moment for many years – throughout the dull grey fear of the war, when she spent hours dancing on her own in the deserted palazzos of Venice, watching her young, supple body shimmering in the tarnished mirrors and dusty windows. She knows that, logically, her mother wants her to leave as well. She has always encouraged her to dance, reminding her again and again that her paternal grandmother was a Spanish dancer – that dancing is in her blood.

'It is your calling, my darling,' her mother had told her.

Her mother's faith, though, was all words, not action. It was Pina who had given her the practical skills to pursue her dream. It was she who had found the right dancing teacher for Maria: a French-American Jew, called Jacqueline, who they hid throughout the war, and who tutored Maria not only in dance, but also in French and English. Jacqueline had left them over a year ago. They had not heard from her until two months ago when she wrote to Belle and Pina, telling them that she had a teaching position in the Lempert Dance School in London. Upon Jacqueline's recommendation, the director of the school, Bruno Lempert, had a place for Maria. It was an opportunity Maria couldn't possibly turn down: to actually train with the Ballets Jooss, one of the most cutting edge contemporary dance companies in Europe. Her chance had been handed to her on a plate.

'Remember to work hard,' Pina says, her expression earnest, and Maria knows she is trying to hide her emotions, for Belle's sake.

'Oh, I don't know . . .' Maria begins to say. 'Maybe I should stay . . .'

Her mother shakes her head, fiercely, although tears are sprouting in her eyes.

'No way, young lady,' she says, picking up her case, and almost pushing her daughter on to the ferry. 'You are doing this, not just for yourself, but for all of us.'

Now they stand apart, her mother and Pina on the quayside and she on the edge of the rocking boat.

'Be careful,' Pina instructs her.

Maria frowns. 'Of what?'

'She means be careful of *men*,' her mother says, smiling despite the tears. 'She is right, my darling; don't let yourself be taken advantage of.'

'Of course not,' Maria says roundly, gripping her suitcase to her chest. She means what she says, for she tries to have no interest in men. Although her mother idolised her father – never said a bad word about him – as far as Maria is concerned, he abandoned them. He never met his own daughter. Belle tells her that he is dead but, when Maria asks where or how, she is unable to elaborate. If she doesn't know for sure, then it's possible that he could be alive, somewhere, couldn't he? It's possible he just never bothered to come back and is letting them all believe he is dead.

Pina has always been there in her life. Maria has been perfectly content living in the home of her mother, and her lover. It seems the ideal relationship: two women who of course completely understand each other. 'Such harmony, and no patriarchal mess.' That's what Pina was always saying. If only she liked women, but Maria has to admit that she is not attracted to other girls and, sometimes, she finds herself casting her eyes at a man – usually a lot older than herself for some reason – before she pulls herself together and looks away. She knows that if she is to succeed as a dancer then she must dedicate her life to her dream. Falling in love with a man could destroy her purpose. And yet, as much as she convinces herself that she doesn't want it, Maria can't help but sometimes fantasise about how it must feel to be in love, and to be loved. How is it to be one man's princess?

The ferry begins to pull away and she waves goodbye. Her throat tightens and she is not sure whether she is crying or not, her face is so wet from the rain. Her mother and Pina link arms and wave back, blowing kisses across the water. Maria catches them in her heart. My mother's kisses will protect me, she thinks. She is frightened of the world she is walking into: London, a city devastated by the war, its people tough and proud. And she is an Italian. Not as bad as a German, yet still the enemy until Mussolini was got rid of. She bites her lip and inhales sharply the damp air of the lagoon as she watches the city shrinking in front of her and the figures of her mother and Pina receding. The magic of Venice is unravelling around her as if she has been wrapped up in a magic carpet all these years. She shivers. The new sensations of her own life, her independence and her beginning, course through her veins.

'She is so innocent,' Belle whispers as she watches her daughter disappearing before her eyes, the wide lagoon swallowing her up.

'As were we all, once,' says Pina pulling her lover close to her side. She kisses Belle's damp cheek, places her hand upon her lover's heart and feels its quick, hurting beat. 'Let's go home,' she says.

Yet Belle can't stop a dark thought entering her head – that

Maria is too young to go to London, that maybe she is not ready to live this big ambitious dream of being a dancer. She can't help thinking that she shouldn't have let her go. Her daughter is too innocent. Will she ever return to Venice the same?

Valentina

'CAN I COME TOO?'

Antonella pins her with a pleading gaze, leaning forward and taking hold of Valentina's hand. She is literally squeezed into her latticed corset and her ample cleavage is brushing Valentina's own chest, the ends of her talon nails digging into the palm of her hand.

'I'm only going for a few days,' Valentina says, trying to put her off.

'Please, Valentina,' Antonella begs. 'It's so boring in Milan now Marco has gone to New York and Gaby is all loved up.'

Valentina hesitates. She had imagined herself alone in London – a time to reinvent herself.

'Please,' Antonella pushes, batting her false eyelashes at her friend.

'I don't know . . . I'm not even sure where I'm staying yet . . .'

'My aunt has a whole house in Kensington we could use.

It's really posh,' Antonella says smugly, knowing full well Valentina has no such useful relative in London.

'You have to let me come with you. I can help you curate your show . . . you know how good I am at that. Besides –' she licks her lips – 'there are some really cool clubs in London. We could have so much fun.'

Valentina cannot refuse her friend; maybe it would be good to have someone else there with her. If Antonella is by her side, distracting her, she might not be so tempted to contact Theo. And this is something she really mustn't do. She can't go back to all that pain.

'OK,' she says, 'but let's talk about it later. Don't you think we'd better go in?'

Antonella stands up and stretches. Despite the fact she is wearing spiky stilettos, she is still shorter than Valentina. She tugs at her corset, repositioning her breasts. She is wearing such a tiny red lacy G-string, she may as well not bother. Valentina still finds it bizarre seeing her friend dressed up this way and even more so taking pictures of her when she is in full flight in her dominatrix personna.

'No harm to keep him waiting . . . I *am* in charge tonight,' Antonella declares, as she saunters out of the reception area of Leonardo's club and down the black marbled corridor.

'Well, now, that is debatable,' Valentina counters, catching up with her, 'since this is my scenario you are a part of.'

'Oh, yes, one of your erotic compositions.' Antonella spins

around, her eyes gleaming. 'You see you *have* to bring me to London, seeing as I am one of the stars of the show!'

Inside the Velvet Underworld, all is as Valentina left it this afternoon when she set up the shoot, apart from the fact that the hammock she constructed is now occupied. Tonight she is extending her pictorial study of the dominatrix, using Antonella, as usual, as the main protagonist. She managed to persuade Leonardo to let her create her own version of a harness-cum-hammock, hung above the four-poster bed. She has removed all elements of crimson or purple from the area around the bed, covering its surface with a pristine white sheet. She's taken down the heavy drapes and replaced them with mosquito netting that flutters in the candlelight. She has two arc lights positioned at either corner of the room, throwing dramatic shadows of the hammock across the walls and ceiling.

She has spent weeks finding the right material for her hammock. This picture is so important in the series because she is finally managing to get over her aversion to the whole dominatrix scene. Although she has learnt to respond to various levels of pleasurable pain herself as a submissive, she still struggles to find the inflicting of pain on someone else erotic, despite the fact that Leonardo tells her she is being selfish about it – that those participating want to feel these extreme sensations. She still shudders when she remembers the first time she went into the Velvet Underworld. It has only been through Antonella that she has been able to understand a little about the turn-on of being a dominatrix.

'It's not just about power,' her friend told her. 'It's about control. It's a big responsibility to know how far to go, especially if they are wearing a gag and can't speak. You have to be able to read their bodies . . . You need to be incredibly sensitive.'

'But how do you find it erotic?' Valentina had asked her. 'It just doesn't turn me on.'

'Well, that's you, and that's OK. What I like about it is that I can design my own fantasy. It's not about hurting men, Valentina. You know I love men. It's about seeing the vulnerability inside a man – his fragility. I love that.'

It was when she explained it like this that Valentina began to get it. And so she set about creating a scene that revealed the fragile core of a man's sexuality, rather than his masochistic side. She wasn't sure how it would turn out at all.

She made her hammock out of sheaths of ivory silk. Antonella's partner for tonight is already lying within, face down, the contours of his naked body visible through the silk.

'Oh, nice, Valentina . . . It matches you,' Antonella whispers, indicating Valentina's backless ivory all-in-one, tied with a single silk ribbon.

Valentina picks up her camera from where she left it earlier; the weight of it in her hands calms the frantic beat of her heart. She cannot help it but, every time she is in this room, she feels a little frightened. Maybe it's looking at all the paraphernalia on the walls: the whips and riding crops, the chains and heavy, rough ropes.

'Remember what I told you to do?' she whispers to Antonella.

Her friend nods. 'Sure, but I am free to go with my instincts, right?'

Valentina nods in resigned agreement. Antonella sometimes stretched the artistic limits of Valentina's photography.

Antonella strides over to the bed and stands on top of it. She is a little shaky at first – her heels are incredibly high, after all – but she manages to regain her balance quite quickly. She is now standing over the man in the hammock, looking down at him. It is her current lover, Mikhail, another artist and experimental spirit, just like Antonella.

Valentina takes a shot of her just regarding him, contemplating what she is going to do. She says nothing yet, and Valentina prefers this. She finds most of the taunting phrases of the dominatrix are cliché and frankly not sexy at all.

Mikhail is face down in the hammock. Valentina watches Antonella as she strokes his naked back and bottom, her fingers pushing through his leg hair. She begins to massage his buttocks with her hands, pushing into his firm flesh and circling again and again. She takes her finger and draws it up and down between his two cheeks and then she pushes them apart, and begins to massage him more deeply inside. Valentina hears Mikhail groan, she guesses, in pleasure. Antonella stops abruptly.

'Do you know what I am going to do to you?' she hisses at Mikhail. She climbs off the bed and circles the room, inspecting some of the whips and crops hanging on the wall. Mikhail is straining to see her, but he is hardly able to move in the tight hammock. He doesn't even acknowledge Valentina's presence.

Antonella finds what she wants and climbs back on to the bed. She totters on the mattress, clutching in one of her hands a long rubber toy, with a curved end, and in the other, a tube of gel. She squirts some of the gel on to Mikhail, and begins to massage his buttocks while, very carefully, very slowly, she begins to insert the instrument into her lover. Mikhail inhales sharply and Valentina watches Antonella working away, bringing her lover closer and closer to the edge. It is beginning to affect her, watching this woman controlling this man, and Valentina can feel herself soften. She wonders if this is something she and Leonardo could try, and the thought surprises her since she has been thinking of no one but Theo since she found out about the exhibition in London.

Antonella has brought Mikhail as far as she wants to, and she removes the plug, leaving him begging for more. She bends down and kisses him on the lips.

'Oh, no, my sweet,' she says to him. 'You have to watch me now.'

Antonella begins to pull at the silk hammock and, just as Valentina planned, the sheaths of material part so that she is able to pull his nipples free, pinching each one with her long nails, before freeing his cock. It is hard and ready for her, and she bends down and presses her lips to it as Mikhail shudders.

Antonella lets go of him and drops to her knees. She crawls under him and lies on her back on the bed right beneath him. The hammock is slung low and he is so close to her, yet not close enough. His cock is just centimetres away from her pussy. She pulls her red G-string off and opens up her legs, completely lost in her persona. Such a performer, Valentina's friend is. She begins to touch herself and, as she does so, Mikhail manages to free his arm, so that he brings his hand around to grip his cock. Valentina snaps away as her friend and her lover masturbate together. She is trying not to get too turned on, but it is hard not to feel it. She suppresses her primal urge to join them on the bed. Really, it would just be far too complicated to sleep with Antonella as well.

The two of them climax in synchronicity and Valentina catches a shot of Mikhail's seed as it marks her friend, gleaming in the spotlight, like stardust on her stomach.

Valentina gathers her things and backs out of the room. Now she should leave them in private. Her last glimpse is of Mikhail tumbling out of the hammock on top of the bed, as Antonella shrieks with glee.

She steps into the corridor at exactly the same time as Leonardo walks out of the Dark Room, the most sacred chamber inside the club where Leonardo's clients are able to act out those deepest fantasies. He is naked, apart from a black satin mask over his eyes. His skin is shiny with oil and sweat.

'Been working hard?' Valentina nods towards the steel door, finding it hard not to sound cheeky.

'As always,' her friend answers. 'How did that go?'

'Well . . . yes . . . I think it went well.'

'Did you join in?'

She can sense that her nipples are still erect against the slightness of her silk all-in-one.

'God, no. I have no desire to sleep with Antonella, for some reason.'

'Talks too much,' Leonardo says.

The two of them stand in the corridor and Valentina knows she should move, but she can't help noticing Leonardo's reaction to her near-naked presence.

'It did turn me on, though . . .' she whispers.

'Maybe we can try that some time,' Leonardo says, taking a step towards her, and she feels his naked cock brush against her stomach. 'Would you like to dominate me?'

'I think I prefer it the other way around,' she says, bringing her hand down to touch him. He takes his cue and pulls the string of her all-in-one so that it slides off her body. She is naked and all his as he puts his hand between her legs and touches her.

'Ah, my dear Valentina; always ready for me,' he says stroking her tenderly before suddenly spinning her around and pushing her up against the wall.

One of the club rules is, 'No sex outside of the safety of the rooms.' As Leonardo himself has said countless times, his club is not a brothel or some Berlinesque fetish club. His place is distinctly Italian: explicit yet always with some decorum; always behind closed doors. And yet right now he is breaking his own cardinal rule and Valentina wants him to. She is in such a state about going to London, and confused over whether she should try to contact Theo, that she needs to abandon all normality, even if for an instant. She pushes her backside against him and he takes her wrists in one hand and holds them tightly behind her. She presses against the cool wall and her body begs for him to fill her. She wants him to go so deep inside her tonight.

Leonardo slams into her, and she answers with a groan. She realises she was more turned on by Antonella and Mikhail's game than she thought. She is already quivering around Leonardo, aching for him to go further and further. Their coupling doesn't last for long, but it is intense and primal – outlawed sex. Leonardo thrusts in and out of her and she responds in beat to him. She is climbing, climbing, and together they come suddenly, sliding down the wall as one and collapsing on to the floor, curled up around each other.

Valentina leans over and removes Leonardo's mask. His eyes are closed and he is breathing heavily.

'What was all that about?' she asks. 'We're not supposed to do it here.'

He opens his eyes, looks apologetic.

'I know . . . I don't know what possessed me . . . Sorry . . .'

She kisses him on the cheek. 'Don't be silly; I wanted to do it as much as you.'

He pulls her up to her feet. 'Let's take a bath, drink some mint tea and calm down.'

Valentina reclines in the bubbling waters of the hammam pool. She lets fragrant steam waft over her body. She hasn't felt this relaxed in weeks. Leonardo is opposite her in the water. He turns to pour some mint tea out of a little teapot balanced on the side of the pool, and offers her a steaming glass. She takes the glass in both hands and sips delicately, watching her friend closely. There is something wrong, she can tell. His hands are shaking as he hands her the tea and he is refusing to look her in the eyes.

'What is it, Leonardo?' she asks.

He sighs and looks up at her, pushing his hand through his thick curly hair and away from his forehead so that she can see tiny beads of perspiration glistening on his skin.

'I'm thinking of closing down the club,' he suddenly announces.

Valentina is so shocked that she almost chokes on her tea.

'You can't be serious!' she exclaims, still coughing. 'You're doing so well.'

'That's the problem; too many people know about it.'

Valentina thinks instantly of Antonella. Ever since her

friend was introduced to Leonardo's private club, she hasn't stop telling people about it every time they go out in Milan.

'I'm sorry about Antonella; she's got such a big mouth,' Valentina says.

Leonardo puts down his tea and sinks lower into the water, so that only his head is bobbing above the bubbles. 'I wanted to keep it exclusive but now more and more want to join—'

'You could expand,' Valentina interrupts, putting down her glass of tea and sinking beneath the bubbles as well.

'I don't want to . . . It's too complicated.'

'It's such a shame. It's good for Milan to have somewhere like this . . .'

'I am sure someone else will fill the gap.' Leonardo pauses as if he wants to say something else. Yet, instead, he submerges himself under the water, so all Valentina can see is his unfocused outline waving beneath her. She can't believe that Leonardo wants to shut down. What will she do, if she can't come here?

He emerges from the water, shaking his head like a wet dog and spraying Valentina with droplets of water. She splashes back, but she can see Leonardo isn't in a playful mood. He looks serious.

'There's more, isn't there?' she asks instinctively.

'Raquel wants to have a baby,' he says bluntly. 'So you see, this place is not the best environment for a child.'

'You're going to have a baby!'

Valentina feels a surge of disappointment. She can't help it. Not another one of her friends 'settling down'! And Leonardo, of all people.

'She's not pregnant yet,' he says. 'We're just trying at the moment. You see, she's thirty-six now. She's worried she'll run out of time.'

'My God, she doesn't look it.' Valentina thinks of the last time she saw Raquel's perfect figure and cellulite-free thighs. She had assumed they were about the same age.

Leonardo takes Valentina's hand and pulls her towards him through the water. 'She says that she has always dreamt of being a mother.'

She floats in the water in front of him. She cannot think of what to say.

'You look shocked,' Leonardo says finally. 'Do you not think I'll make a good father?'

'I think you'll be brilliant. Look at the way you've taken care of me . . .'

He smiles ruefully. 'Mmm, that sounds a bit perverse, Valentina.'

She can't be happy for him. She can't help it. She knows she is being selfish but she doesn't want Leonardo to have a baby with Raquel.

'But what will you do if you close down the club?' she says, trying to cast some doubt upon his decision.

'Believe it or not, I do have other skills outside of the sex industry.'

37

'I never doubted it,' she says softly.

He grins at her. 'I am a skilled masseur . . . which of course you know all about. I've also got into yoga lately. I think I'd like to train to teach.'

The last thing Valentina imagined Leonardo might be interested in is yoga. He just doesn't seem the meditative type. She can't picture it at all: Leonardo standing on his head.

'Isn't yoga a bit chilled out and slow for you?'

'It depends what kind of yoga you are doing, Valentina. There is nothing slow about an ashtanga class, nothing chilled out about bikram yoga . . .'

Valentina can't quite believe him. Gaby practised yoga for a while and tried to teach her some postures, but Valentina found the whole thing boring. She had no patience for it.

'If you say so . . .' she mutters, drifting away from him in the water, letting its scented ripples caress her.

'You should try it sometime. It's really great for your sex life,' Leonardo says.

'My sex life is doing just fine, as you know.'

Valentina's fingers are pruning. She stands up in the pool, letting the water slide down her supple body.

'So, when are you off to London?' Leonardo says, but he is not looking at her face, he is looking at her body.

'Monday.' She cautiously steps out of the pool, turning her back to Leonardo. She doesn't want him to read her expression. 'I've been meaning to ask . . .' Despite herself, her voice has a slight tremble.

'Do you have Theo's phone number in London?'

Leonardo says nothing for a second. She hunts around for a towel, confused by her spontaneous question. She is not going to actually call Theo but, just in case she changes her mind, there's no harm having it in her phone, is there? She hears Leonardo getting out of the water. She decides not to turn around. For some reason she feels a little shy, even though they know every inch of each other's bodies.

'Sure,' Leonardo says finally. 'I'll text it to you later.'

She wraps her towel around herself, ties it tightly and turns around to face him. Leonardo is wearing a white towelling robe. His black curly hair hangs in wet locks. She takes him in. When he is a father, he will never want to play with her again. She doesn't need to ask him that to know. Yet it doesn't matter anyway, does it? They have never been a couple, and they can still be friends after he has a baby. Even so, she knows that she will never be able to make demands on his friendship in the same way that she has until now. All of a sudden, she wishes it were Leonardo, not Antonella, who was accompanying her to London. If he were by her side, then surely she wouldn't be tempted to call up Theo?

'Will you come over to London for the opening of the exhibition?' she asks her friend tentatively.

Leonardo looks surprised. 'Maybe. If you need me, I'll come.' He steps forward. 'Don't worry, Valentina.' He hugs her tightly. 'Why do you always look so sad?'

She hides her face in the safety of his towel-clad chest and breathes in his scent. 'I don't know.' Her whisper is muffled by their proximity. She feels so protected inside Leonardo's hug that a part of her wants to hide in Milan and not face the test of London and her dilemma over whether to contact Theo or not. Surely her ex-lover has moved on by now? To call him would be pointless. And yet there is an ache inside her heart that tells her otherwise. Could a love like theirs die so fast?

Maria

THE LIGHT OF VENICE IS GONE. EVEN WHEN IT RAINS, Maria feels there is a luminous quality to her home city. She didn't notice it until she left it behind her, but she has been thinking of it on her long journey, all the way to England.

It is spring in London, yet the sky is a dank grey and the air smells empty. The salty scents of home have evaporated. She walks alongside trees thick with cherry blossom, yet she cannot smell them. She is assaulted by noise. Cars: she is not used to them. The sheer aggression of them: honking, screeching to a halt, accelerating down the road. And the choking pollution of their fumes fills her lungs, making her feel poisoned. She hates them. Her mother had compared the boats of Venice to cars, but they aren't the same at all. The boats are at one with their surroundings, gliding down the canals, rocking along the waves of the lagoon. These cars and trucks and buses, they are in opposition to any nature there might be in the city.

Still, for all of its intimidation – the noise, the crowds and the sheer vastness of this city – London excites Maria. Even walking down a bomb-ravaged street seems like such an affirmation of life.

They had been lucky in Venice, the treasures of the city protecting them from any significant bombing raids. She remembers only once seeing an attack on the docks. She, her mother and Pina had climbed on to the roof of their apartment, despite Pina's reservations. Yet they had been perfectly safe, just like her mother told them they would be. The bombers dived almost vertically, pinpointing two big ships down at the docks. It had been like watching a spectacular firework display as the ships exploded, the only damage to the city a few broken windows.

London is a different story. Maria can see quite clearly how the city has suffered. She tries to imagine what it must have been like, hiding down in the filthy underground night after night to come up one morning and find that your house, street, neighbours have disappeared. And yet the people she sees on the streets of London in 1948 do not appear broken. They won the war. The spirit of the British got them through the Blitz. Maria finds this national pride fascinating; she remembers from her childhood the hatred her mother and Pina felt towards Mussolini, and their shame at Italy's alliance with Germany. They said that this was not *their* Italy, especially when Jewish people started to be victimised.

'Italians were never racists!' her mother had declared roundly. 'What is that idiotic man dragging us into?'

Her mother had done everything she could to undermine Mussolini and, after him, the Germans, but never openly, always covertly. She helped as many Jews as she could – not just Jacqueline – either to escape or hide. She risked all of their lives by doing so, yet they were lucky. Not once did Maria's mammas fall under suspicion for the Germans never took Belle and Pina seriously. They were just two middle-aged women, dressed up in eccentric costumes, taking pictures of tourists – and, during the war, countless Nazis – enjoying the sights of their city.

Maria pauses at the crossing. She takes the envelope from her coat pocket and unfolds it. She looks up at the sign on the street corner: Ebury Bridge Street. The directions her mother wrote for her describe a little street off this one. She is nearly there, at last. Her back is aching from all the long hours of travel, and she is sure she must smell a little. She is longing for a wash.

She turns down the street and begins to count the house numbers. Jacqueline lives at number eighteen. The street is so very different from the wavering passageways of Venice. It is a straight line of red-brick houses, all more or less the same.

She stands outside number eighteen: her new home. The building is much grander than she expected. Well, from the outside at least. Its red-brick façade is punctuated by tall

43

windows. She counts four floors. The front door is faded dusty blue, with a black lion's head as the door knocker. A lion, how English, she thinks. She walks up to the front door, her lips a little dry. She hopes that Jacqueline is home. She has no idea who else lives in this grand house.

A few seconds after her third knock, the door is opened by a scrawny-looking young man, with wild, wiry hair. He looks at her suspiciously, not a hint of a smile, his face obscured by his round spectacles and thick moustache.

'Yes?'

Maria coughs, composing her best English into a sentence. 'Good afternoon,' she says formally. 'I am looking for Miss Jacqueline Mournier.'

'She's not home,' he says. 'Who are you?'

'I am . . . I am . . .' she stutters, unnerved by his directness. 'My name is Maria Brzezinska.'

'Polish?' His tone is interrogative. 'You don't look Polish.'

Maria begins to feel a little annoyed. What right does this young man have to question her?

'Can I come in, please? I can wait for Jacqueline inside.'

The young man cocks his head on one side and continues his ponderings on her nationality, as if she hasn't spoken. 'You're not English,' he says, 'I can tell. So, where are you from?'

Maria sighs inwardly. Already she is being asked her

country of origin. She has not even been in London twenty-four hours.

'I am Italian.'

All of a sudden, much to her surprise, the young man flashes her a smile. It transforms his face. If he were to lose the spectacles and the moustache, he could be quite handsome, Maria thinks.

'Me, also,' he says in Italian. And, leaning forward with a flourish, he takes her case from her and ushers her into the house. 'Welcome, Maria Brzezinska,' he says. 'Let me introduce myself. My name is Guido Rosselli and I am a neighbour of Jacqueline's.'

Despite the grandeur of the exterior of the house, inside it is another story. The hallway is lit by one bare bulb that flickers intermittently, making the place seem creepy and uncared for. There is no carpet in the hall, just brown linoleum, much worn, and the wallpaper is peeling with damp. There is an odious smell, not just the damp but something rotten and penetrating. Maria can't help but take out her handkerchief and bring it up to her nose.

'Sorry about the stink,' Guido says. 'I am afraid it is our only English resident, Mrs Renshaw. We have asked her not to boil her cabbage for too long but she seems immune to the smell. I think she is trying to boil every last bit of goodness out of it. I cannot imagine what it must taste like.'

Guido leads her up three flights of stairs before pausing on the third landing and pointing to a door behind him. 'This is where I live,' he tells her.

She nods, waiting, not knowing what to say. She is suddenly overwhelmed with shyness. She is not used to talking to boys.

'Jacqueline is not here at the moment. But she said, if you turned up while she was out, to let you in.' He takes a key from his trouser pocket and waves it above his head. 'Come on,' he says. 'Just one more flight of stairs to the top.'

On the top floor – Jacqueline's landing, Maria supposes – the gloom of the house seems to have lifted a little. She can see a small skylight above their heads, with a square of sky above them. It is a tiny pocket of blue and yet it is some colour, at least. The boiled cabbage smell is not so strong up here, either.

Guido unlocks the door of Jacqueline's apartment and leads the way inside. They are right under the eaves of the house, and Maria immediately walks over to one of the windows. Below her is London, ravaged and ruined from the Blitz and yet still thriving. She can feel the industrial hum of it below her and it excites her. Such a different energy from Venice, a city that floats in and out of time; London feels like it is marching forwards, wounded and yet heroic.

'Would you like a cup of coffee?' Guido asks her stiffly, in English.

'What about some English tea?' Maria ventures.

Guido shakes his head apologetically.

'Sorry, I believe Jacqueline has run out of tea at the moment. Everything is still strictly rationed here. Tea is actually a luxury and it is easier to get hold of coffee, as it's not so popular with the English.'

'In that case, thank you; a cup of coffee would be lovely.' Maria takes off her hat and places it on the sideboard, along with her gloves and handbag.

Guido disappears through a side door, Maria guesses, into the kitchen. She looks around her mentor's living room. It is quite bare – unsurprisingly, since Jacqueline is a refugee. On the run for most of the war, her childhood home had been destroyed when she finally made it back to Bordeaux. Yet, despite the room's sparseness – one table, two chairs and a shelf of books – Jacqueline has managed to add something a little exotic to her flat. On one of the walls is an impressive painting, vibrant with colour. Maria wonders if Jacqueline knows the artist; that would be just like her. On the other wall is a series of black and white photographs of dancers. Maria studies them, scrutinising their faces. In all of them, the dancers are in costume and heavily made-up, and she struggles to recognise Jacqueline. Their postures are in opposition to any traditional ballet pose. In one image, she sees a woman in footless tights, barefoot and wearing a long top, her head hidden by a scarf, adopting the pose of a tree, both her arms hanging out from her body, one with the hand pointing down, one with the hand pointing up. On the floor in front of her, two other dancers are on their backs, legs in the air, bare feet flexed, reaching out for the tree figure with their arms. It is almost ugly, the images of the women earthy and vulgar compared to the pretty photographs of ballerinas Maria is used to seeing.

The door behind her clicks open and Guido returns with a coffee pot and two cups on a tray. He carries it over to the sideboard, the cups clinking on the saucers. Maria watches the tray shaking in his hands, and she struggles not to rush over and grab it off him, but she doesn't want to insult him. He places the wobbling tray down and Maria can't help noticing that his hands are still shaking. She looks up at his face again, fixed in concentration now he is pouring the coffee. Despite the moustache, he only looks about two or three years older than her. She wonders what he is doing here in London.

'So, where are you from?' Guido asks her as he hands her a cup of coffee with shaking hands.

It sploshes over the side of her cup, but she politely says nothing, sitting down on one of Jacqueline's chairs and holding the cup and saucer in both hands. 'Venice.'

Guido's eyes light up. 'I went to Venice as a little boy,' he says, 'with my mother and my father . . .' He pauses, looking away. 'Before the war.'

'And where are you from?' Maria asks him.

'I am from Milan,' he says. 'But right now I am a student at the university of London.'

'What are you studying?'

'Physics. My father sent me to England before the war . . . He was a scientist himself and he could see that my passion lay in that direction, so he sent me to school here in

England. And then the war broke out and I couldn't get home.'

'And have you been back since?'

He takes a large gulp of his coffee and scowls at her. 'No.'

The fierceness of his response silences her. Maria can feel herself colouring with embarrassment. She doesn't know what to say to this young man. She wishes he would leave her alone to wait for Jacqueline.

'She told me to welcome you.' Guido suddenly says, as if he is reading Maria's thoughts. 'We are friends,' he adds, by way of explanation.

'Thank you,' Maria replies curtly, still not knowing what to say. Guido Rosselli's eyes are blinkered behind his glasses, impossible to read.

He gets up suddenly and slides his cup and saucer on to the tray. 'We understand what it is like to be a stranger,' Guido says, 'Jacqueline and I. We are the same.'

He turns his back on her, walks over to the window and clasps his hands behind his back. Maria can see how narrow he is – his shoulders, his back, his hips – as if he has not fully broadened into a man yet.

'No family left –' he spins around – 'so we make our own family here. Everyone in this building is some kind of abandoned soul . . .'

The words flow out of him, now.

'Mrs Renshaw, for instance: her whole family was taken out one night during the Blitz. Husband, mother, children . . . She still can't understand why she was spared. That's why we don't really mind about the cabbage. You have to make allowances, you know, if you live here.'

Maria nods. The intensity of Guido Rosselli makes her feel uncomfortable. She doesn't want to know about the other people in this house. She doesn't even want to know about him. She has a feeling he has a sad and sorry past and she is not ready to hear his tale of woe. She is tired and dirty. She just wants a bath and some rest while she waits for Jacqueline. She wishes all of a sudden that she had stayed home in Venice. She isn't like her mother, Belle, although she had thought she might be. She is no adventurer. She is more like Pina, keeping the home fires burning.

'And, on the second floor, there is Monsieur Leduc.' Guido gives a short hard laugh. 'Wait until you meet him!' he exclaims, thrusting his hands in his pockets and pacing the room. He seems to have forgotten that she is still there as he races on. 'He loved his France so much he sacrificed all, and yet he has to live in London. Explain that to me?' He puts his head on one side and stares at Maria, yet he is not looking at her, but through her.

She shifts in her seat. 'Excuse me, Guido, but where is the bathroom?'

'Oh!' He jumps as if awoken from a dream. 'You have to go back down the stairs to the next floor. It's the door next to mine.' He shoves his hand through his thick hair, looking distracted.

'Thank you.'

Maria picks up her handbag and escapes down the staircase and into the bathroom. She feels a little queasy. She holds her belly and breathes in deeply, trying to steady her fluttering stomach. She is desperate to take a bath or wash, but she can't be too long, so she cleans up as best she can. There is only one small towel and she has no idea who it belongs to. She washes her hands and splashes water on her face before reapplying her make-up. She puts too much rouge on her cheeks and scrapes it off again with her handkerchief. She glances up at the mirror. She looks tired and hot.

Her mother and Pina are always telling her how beautiful she is, how like her father with her dark blue eyes, pink cheeks and curly hair. But she thinks she looks like a scarecrow today. She would rather she had inherited her mother's chic – her silky black hair and porcelain features – not these wild locks and rosy cheeks. She doesn't want anything from her father, she thinks bitterly, since he never seemed to have had any interest in her. She has never expressed these feelings to her mother, for Belle talks about her father as if he was some kind of God. But Maria has often seen the way Pina's expression hardens when there is mention of Santos Devine, and her face tells Maria that her father was not such a great man.

Maria pulls out her comb and attempts to tame her hair. It just will not obey her, no matter whether she tries to straighten it or curl it into a style of some sort.

* * *

As Maria climbs back up the stairs to the apartment, she can hear voices. Her spirits lift immediately. Jacqueline must be home. She opens the door and, sure enough, there is her dance mentor, the woman who taught her to dream.

'Maria!' Jacqueline exclaims, sweeping her up into a tight embrace. 'My darling Maria.' She showers her cheeks with kisses as Maria looks over her shoulder at the curious expression on Guido's face. 'Welcome, my dear. Welcome to London.'

Jacqueline pulls away and surveys her protégé. 'Oh, you have grown so much more striking since I last saw you. Isn't she such a beauty, Guido?'

Maria feels her cheeks flaring deep crimson. She casts her eyes down at the floor. 'Really, Jacqueline. I am the same; just a little bigger.'

'Yes; it has been how long? One, nearly two years, my darling, since I last saw you. But you are no bigger – not at all. You have lost all your puppy fat. Now you really look like the dancer you are.' Jacqueline stands with her hands on her hips, smiling with satisfaction. 'I cannot wait to present you to Lempert.'

Maria feels a knot of apprehension inside her stomach. 'I haven't had a proper dance teacher since you left, Jacqueline.'

'He will understand,' she says, patting Maria's shoulder and speaking confidently. 'He trusts my judgement.' She whirls around the room, collecting up Maria's abandoned cup and saucer and placing them on the tea tray. 'Now, you must tell me all about your darling mother and Pina. How are they? They must have been sad to let you go.'

Maria feels awkward in front of Guido. She doesn't want to talk about her mother and Pina in front of this stranger. 'They are well,' she says. 'They send their love.'

Jacqueline nods happily. 'You know, Guido –' she turns to the young man – 'I owe my life to Maria's mother, Belle, and her friend, Pina. They hid me during the war.'

Guido narrows his eyes at Maria. He doesn't look so impressed, although he says, 'That was very brave of them.'

'Yes, it was . . . but you should meet these women. They are . . . just . . . incredible.'

Maria is mortified. 'They did what any decent person would have done.'

'But there are not so many decent people in the world,' she hears Guido say under his breath.

'Now, my dear,' Jacqueline says, bustling Maria across the living room, 'I'm afraid I am a little short on space, so your room really is in fact the old airing cupboard, but it was either that or the living room floor, and I thought you would like some privacy.'

Jacqueline opens up a little door to reveal a tiny room, no longer than her height. It is empty, apart from a mattress on the floor, made up with sheets and blankets. There is a slatted shelf and, above that, a tiny skylight.

'I left it uncurtained. I thought you'd like to see the stars at night.'

'It's perfect, Jacqueline,' Maria says politely, although she is a little horrified by her confined quarters. She has always disliked small spaces.

'Excuse me,' Guido speaks up, 'but I must say goodbye for now. I have some work to do.'

'Oh, yes. Thank you, Guido, for entertaining Maria for me. Would you like to eat with us later?'

'I am afraid not,' his face is earnest with regret. 'I have a paper to write . . .'

As soon as they are alone, Maria finally feels herself relaxing. Why does the company of men always make her tense? As soon as she is with women, she is at home.

'Who was that man?' she asks Jacqueline.

'Guido Rosselli. Did he not introduce himself to you?'

'Oh, yes, he did . . . but . . . he is Italian; I was so surprised . . .' She trails off, feeling a little foolish.

'He may seem a little odd, Maria, but it is just because he is lonely.'

'Why doesn't he go back to Milan?'

'He can't, for the moment. His parents are dead . . . London is his home now, until he finishes his studies.' Jacqueline pauses, looks sad. 'He is like me: a war orphan.'

Maria feels a raw stab of pain for her friend. 'I am sorry Jacqueline . . . I didn't mean to upset you.'

But Jacqueline interrupts her, shakes her sadness from her shoulders and hugs her, showering her cheeks with kisses yet again. 'Oh, I am so happy to see you,' she says. 'I have missed you all so much.'

Maria leans into Jacqueline's neck, inhales her scent, and it brings back so many memories: times of her and Jacqueline dreaming as they drifted down the Canal Grande in a boat, the two of them lying on their backs, hidden from all, talking about dancing. She remembers how it made them feel. Yes, Maria thinks, fingering the memory of that time, the revelation of what dance turned her into.

For, when she danced, Maria felt free. Not the war, nor the suffocation of her mother's love, the reasoning of Pina or the abandonment of her father could restrain her. Jacqueline had given her that gift, told her that, when she danced, she became a bird. And when they danced together, they were two birds soaring in sky.

As she and Jacqueline talk about dance together, Maria remembers why it is she has come to London. It is not just about learning to dance. It is about finding her liberation.

Valentina

THEY ARE LEAVING FOR LONDON TONIGHT. FOR ONCE in her life, Valentina is packed and ready, with the whole day to spare. She sits with her cup of coffee on the windowsill beside her, watching Milan busy itself in the street below.

Again, she has the urge to cancel her trip to London and stay here in Milan, where she can continue her life undisturbed. Surely they can exhibit her work without her presence at the opening? In an ideal world, she would like to take part in the curation of the show, but it is not strictly necessary.

Valentina chews her lip, thinking. Of course, she must go. She should not let fear of the unknown, because that is what she is feeling, get in the way of her career. This is an exciting opportunity. London is huge and, unless she actually calls Theo, she won't even see him.

Yet this is what she is afraid of: her own curiosity, her need to hear his voice again, to find out what he is doing. Has he got over her? He had told her he loved her, and not just once.

She could not do the same for him. That is what had broken them up: the fact she couldn't say, 'I love you.'

She had been so close to opening up to Theo in Venice, if only he hadn't stormed off. Now it feels as if she has buried her feelings so deep inside herself that she may never be brave enough to express them. And yet her decision to go to London, made within a heartbeat, is not just because of the opportunity of the exhibition, but because of Theo. She has to admit it to herself. Hope, for some bizarre reason, beats inside her like a frantic bird – an insane sense that everything will be OK.

Valentina takes a sip of her coffee. The hot liquid calms her as she wraps her hands around the warm cup and breathes in. Could she get Theo back? For the first time, she lets the possibility occur to her. She shakes herself, reminds herself of her motto: nothing lasts forever. Look at her own parents, for example: their union hadn't lasted, had it? Her father had left her mother when Valentina was a little girl, and she hasn't seen him since.

Thoughts of her father remind of her something – an uncomfortable pinprick of memory that has been irritating her ever since it was revealed to her. Back in Venice, all those months ago, the police inspector, Garelli, had told her that her father would be proud of her. Garelli was the first person she had ever met who claimed to know her father, apart from her mother and brother, of course. She has always been adamant that she doesn't want to know her father. After all, he has never made the effort to contact her, so why should she try to find him? Her mother says she has no idea where he is, as does her brother, Mattia. And so Valentina had not thought about her father much, not until that strange conversation with Inspector Garelli in Venice the night she and Theo had last been together.

Valentina puts down her cup of coffee. She gets up and walks over to her desk, pulling open the top drawer. She shoves her hand inside the mess of papers, pencils, rubbers and Post-it notes. The last time she saw it, she was sure it was in here. She bends down, pushing her hand right to the back of the drawer until she fingers a crumpled piece of card. She pulls it out and, sure enough, there is Garelli's business card, somewhat moth-eaten but with his details still clearly printed on it. She glances at the clock on the wall. She is not meeting Antonella for six hours. She has plenty of time to call Garelli, talk to him before she goes. Of course, she could do it when she gets back from London, but now, all of a sudden, she just has to know what Garelli meant by his comment. How does he know her father?

Valentina taps her heels on the floor of Bar Magenta as she waits. She smoothes down her black-and-white striped dress with her hands, smiling inwardly at her choice of outfit. There will be no possibility of Antonella not finding her in the airport. As usual, she stands out: the dress is full length and figure hugging, with a long split on one side, all the way up to her thigh. She is wearing it with her black Carl Scarpa wedge-heeled boots and her tiny black leather biker jacket. The dress once belonged to her mother, who, in Valentina's opinion, took more care of her clothes than her children. It looks as good as new. She sweeps her hand across her brow nervously and takes a sip of her Negroni. Maybe this is a bad idea. After all, less than six months ago, Garelli was after Theo, who was under suspicion for art theft. She hasn't seen the policeman since, and assumes the case has been dropped. Still, it is a risk to stir it all up again. Could she be accused as an accessory, since she transported the painting from Milan to Venice? Maybe she should just leave it.

However, just as she is knocking back her drink and preparing to gather her things, Garelli comes into the bar. His eyes alight upon her immediately and he gives her a broad smile as if they are old buddies.

'Valentina,' he says, bending down and kissing her on both cheeks. 'You look as pretty as a picture, as always. Let me buy you a drink.'

'No, thank you. I'm fine.'

'But you've just finished yours . . . I insist.'

Valentina takes a big gulp of her fresh drink. Now that Garelli is actually sitting opposite her, looking at her expectantly, she doesn't know quite where to begin. In her confusion, she says nothing, scowling down at her drink instead.

'Well, Valentina,' Garelli finally says, obviously impatient. 'How can I help you?'

She looks up at him, trying to summon the words. For some reason, she feels intensely embarrassed, ashamed almost, to ask this man, practically a stranger, where her father is.

'Do you have more information on your Signor Theo Steen, perhaps?' he says, cocking his eyebrow at her. 'Although, I believe he is no longer in Milan . . . so not, strictly speaking, our problem anymore.' He looks at her benignly.

Valentina feels a flash of annoyance. How dare he be so patronising? 'No, I don't want to talk about Theo,' she says.

'Oh?'

'When I saw you in Venice, you said something to me . . . about my father,' she splutters.

Garelli says nothing, just watches her squirming in front of him.

'You said that he would be proud of me. And that you knew him.'

'Yes,' Garelli nods, 'I did know him.' He looks puzzled.

'How did you know him?'

'Why, we worked together, of course.' Garelli takes a sip of his wine. 'Has he never mentioned this to you?'

Valentina looks down at the wooden table and grips the edge of it with one of her hands. 'I don't know him,' she whispers, her embarrassment paining her.

'Really?'

She looks up. Garelli is staring at her in astonishment. She plunges on. 'He left when I was six years old. I haven't seen him since.'

Garelli frowns. 'That is not the behaviour of the kind of man I knew,' he says.

'Well, tell me, please, what kind of man he is,' Valentina says, suddenly annoyed by Garelli's sanctimonious manner, 'because I have absolutely no idea.'

She takes too big a swig of her drink and almost chokes.

'Philip Rembrandt is one of the good ones,' Garelli says simply, scratching his head. 'I knew him when your brother, Mattia, was small. Philip was devoted to him.'

'But how do you know him?'

'Did,' Garelli corrects her. 'I haven't seen him in years. Not since he left Milan.' He sighs. 'I never meant to lose contact, but you know how it is . . .' He looks wistful before gathering himself. 'Valentina, we worked together—'

'Was my father a policeman?'

'No,' Garelli says. 'Not Phil. He was an excellent investigative journalist. He helped me out on a couple of big Mafia cases.'

She sits back against the wooden bench. This is news to her. Her mother had told her that her father was a professor at the university. There had never been any mention of him being an investigative journalist. The image she always had of a pipe smoking, rather disorganised arty writer is being turned on its head. Her father was an investigative journalist. She thinks of Dustin Hoffman and Robert Redford as Woodward and Bernstein in the film *All The President's Men*, uncovering the Watergate scandal. They were hyperactive, brave, clever and daring men. It is just too hard to believe that her own father had been like that. Surely her mother would have bragged about it, for a start?

'Are you sure? I mean, it's just not what I was told.'

'Of course, I am sure,' Garelli says. 'We took down a guy called Caruthers together. It was a famous case at the time. He was one of the top Mafia heads, based in New York but operating here in Italy as well.' Garelli looks up at her hesitantly. 'What can I say, Valentina? Your father saved my life.'

Valentina is speechless; she stares at Garelli in astonishment.

'Last year, I was just keeping an eye on you, for your father's sake . . . I wasn't sure about Signor Steen.'

'You were trying to protect me?'

Garelli chuckles. 'I suppose. Although you obviously didn't need my help.'

She fiddles with one of her rings, nervous of asking her next question. 'Why did you say my father would be proud of me?'

'Because of your spirit, Valentina; you are just like your mother . . .'

She scowls at the mention of her mother. 'If he liked her spirit so much, why did he leave her?'

'I believe it must be more complicated than that,' Garelli answers enigmatically. 'Although, by then, I wasn't working with your father anymore. I was living in Spain at the time and I hadn't seen him since before you were born.'

'She drove him away,' Valentina growls, 'just like she drives everyone away.'

Garelli pauses, his voice softening. 'I don't think that is quite the case.'

Valentina scrutinises Garelli. She has a feeling that he is holding back, but the inspector's expression is impassive. He finishes off his drink. Valentina senses that she has revealed too much of herself to this man – a person she hardly likes. She feels exposed, awkward. She wishes now that she had never called him up. She should just forget all about this father thing. Her logic is screaming at her to let it go because, surely, if her father wanted to know her, he could easily contact her. Even so, she just can't smother her curiosity.

'I have to go,' she says, indicating her suitcase and standing up. 'I'm flying to London. Can we meet again when I get back? Will you tell me all about my father?'

'Of course we can, but you know you could ask him yourself?'

She freezes. 'Do you know where he *is*?'

She assumed that, since Garelli hadn't been in contact with her father in all these years, he would have no idea where he is now.

'We had to keep tabs on him . . . because of his history. As far as I know, he hasn't moved.'

'So, where is he?'

Garelli holds her gaze. She sees a smile spreading across his face.

'London.'

Maria

'MY INTENTION IS TO GIVE AN IMAGE OF THE VARIOUS forces of life in an ever-changing interplay.' Bruno Lempert speaks like a textbook, and she is finding it hard to follow his English. 'To recreate these forces of nature requires a purified and polished reflecting instrument.'

Maria is aching to scratch her back, but all the dancers are sitting completely still. It is as if they are listening to the very word of God himself. Lempert raises his eyebrows and stares at them. His eyes are round with heavy lids but, despite their rich, deep-brown colour, they appear cold to Maria. She is a little frightened of her new dance teacher. He speaks in riddles.

'That is what I need you, the dancer, to be. I need you to reflect, with your body, these different elements. When you are dancing, you cannot be yourself.'

He is staring, now, right into her eyes and Maria feels her cheeks colouring. She has an urge to flee the dance studio, but she can't. All the trouble her mother and Pina have gone to, to get her here – and Jacqueline, too . . . How she wishes *she* were her teacher, not this austere man. But it seems that Jacqueline's job is to travel to schools and teach the schoolgirls of London the new ballet: the bread-and-butter work. Maria's teacher is none other than Lempert, the principal and founder of this new dance school, and colleague and friend of Kurt Jooss himself. He has danced in Jooss's ballets. He knows what he is talking about and this small group of twenty young women and men are the chosen few. And yet, inside Maria, there is a small voice rebelling; for, when she is dancing, it is the only time she feels she *is* herself. If he asks her to give up that, then there is no soul left in her dance.

'There is, of course, a process to go through to achieve this,' Lempert continues. 'To reflect these natural elements, we have to study their dynamic within your body, your mind and your soul. Then, through movement, we will externalise them.'

A blonde girl next to Maria sneezes and takes a hankie out from the sleeve of her leotard to blow her nose. Maria glances over at her. The girl is beetroot with embarrassment, and Maria immediately feels a wave of warmth towards her. They glance at each other and smile, before directing their attention back towards their teacher.

'But first of all,' he says, walking around them in a circle, so that Maria does not know whether to twist around and watch him as he moves or sit still, 'we have to begin at the beginning, and that requires breaking down your body, freeing you from all habitual gestures.'

He is in front of them again as he claps his hands and, after a slight hesitation, the group rises. Maria shakes out her stiff legs.

'Please raise your hand if you have already trained in classical ballet.'

Everyone puts up their hand apart from Maria, the blonde sneezing girl, a woman with a short black crop, who looks slightly older than the rest, and two out of the four men in the room.

Lempert grimaces, and again Maria feels her face heating up. The first class, and she is already embarrassed by her lack of training. How could she possibly think she could be of a similar pedigree to the others? She glances over at the blonde girl and they smile at each other again, in sympathy.

'Please,' Lempert says, directing the small group, 'come and stand on this side of the room.' He then ushers the other dancers to the back of the studio and, to her surprise, Maria finds herself standing, with her companions, in front of the others.

'Now,' Lempert says, hands on hips and directing his speech to the group of ballet dancers. 'You are going to have to do a lot more work than these dancers because, with a classical dance training, your bodies have certain habits. Some groups of your muscles will only coordinate with other given groups. We are going to have to get your bodies to that degree of relaxation that you do not give in to your classical habits.'

'Are you saying that classical ballet is wrong?' A girl with red curly hair speaks up from the group of ballet dancers.

Lempert shakes his head. 'Of course not, Alicia. How can anything be that simple? But classical ballet is entrenched in years and years of tradition. We at Ballets Jooss are trying to do something different. For instance, if you look at the subject matter of our ballets, how would you describe them?'

'Revolutionary,' says the short, dark-haired lady, standing next to Maria.

Lempert whips around. 'Indeed,' he says, 'they are political, social, humanist . . . They combine the intellect and the heart. That is what we are trying to do here: combine spirit, mind and body. People, we want to *communicate*.'

Maria's head is beginning to pound. This is all too much theory. She just wants to dance.

She has a flicker of memory: she is in the deserted ground floor of the palazzo with her mother, Pina and Jacqueline. Jacqueline is playing a tinny old piano that Belle had somehow unearthed, and Maria is dancing for them. It is like a golden loop of memory. The Venetian winter sun is streaming through the half boarded windows as dust motes spin up into the air around her bare feet. And her mother and Pina are watching her; yet, despite their looks of appreciation, it is not for them she dances, but for a ghost sitting beside them – her father, Santos Devine: adventurer and sailor.

To her relief, Lempert claps his hands, signalling for the group to come together again.

'Now,' he says. 'Enough talk. Let us begin.'

To her surprise, Lempert makes them take off their dance shoes. The wooden boards are cool beneath her bare soles.

'No dance,' he instructs them. 'I just want movement.'

He nods towards the pianist, up on a rostrum under a small gallery at the end of the studio.

'On the count of four, I want you to start to walk around the room. No eye contact – eyes to the floor, please. One, two, three, four . . .'

Maria begins to walk, not looking at her fellow dancers, wondering what they are all thinking. Part of her is terrified of making a fool of herself, and yet another part of her is excited. She is beginning to grasp what her teacher is saying.

'I want you to walk with the emotion of hesitation,' he calls out.

The piano slows down and, in response, Maria begins to shuffle around the studio.

'Walk with contentment.'

She ambles along; for some reason, she has an image of herself as a large man with a big belly, well fed, heavy with satisfaction. She pushes out her stomach, puts her hand on it.

'And with joy.'

Now she is a black cat of Venice, jumping between rooftops, prancing in the spinning light, pausing to lick the cream off the tip of her nose.

'With freedom.'

She is gliding on an icy river. She imagines what it must feel like, for she has never skated in her life, yet the image is magical to her – that sense of moving on ice – all grace, speed and perfect balance.

As she is sliding around the room, she can't help noticing her blonde friend, who is tiptoeing around the studio. How different their versions of freedom are!

Despite the fact it is the first day of class, Lempert works them hard. After two hours of breaking down their bodies, everyone in the group is breathless and steaming. Maria's black leotard is stuck to her body with sweat.

'Enough!' Lempert suddenly announces. 'Every morning, we will have technical class and each afternoon we will study other related subjects such as dance notation, theory, stage practice, make-up and life drawing. This is a rounded education in dance – an organic approach.'

There is a rustle of surprise among the dancers.

'We will take a break now for lunch. Be back here at two for theoretical class.'

The girls crowd into the tiny changing room. There is no window in here and the dank room is lit by a single bulb. Despite the bustle around her, Maria takes her time. She has a packet of sandwiches with her that Jacqueline made for her that morning: some kind of grey meat paste between two precious slices of the coarse rationed bread. She has no idea where to go for her lunch, and she is too shy to ask anyone else. Gradually, the changing room empties out until she is the last left.

She hangs up her black leotard, damp with sweat, and is glad that she has a fresh one with her for this afternoon. She puts on her skirt and sweater, buttons up her coat and picks up her bag. Well, she should get some fresh air, at least; surely she can find a park to sit in. She is not hungry at all. Maybe she will give the London pigeons her sandwiches, although she knows – with food shortages and rationing – that would not be a very moral thing to do.

She walks out of the dance school – an old red-brick house, not dissimilar to Jacqueline's house – and stands for a moment on the pavement outside, pondering which way to go.

'Hello there,' says a voice behind her.

She turns around to see the blonde girl from class, adjusting her hat as she approaches her. The girl sticks out her hand. 'Joan,' she says.

'Maria.'

'Pleased to meet you. And where are you from, Maria?'

The girls begin to walk down the street. They seem to be heading away from the river.

'Italy,' Maria mumbles, waiting for the hostility. Joan, after all, sounds very British.

'Oh, Italy!' Joan surprises her by sounding impressed. 'Oh, lucky you. Where are you from in Italy?'

'Venice.'

'No? Really? Oh my gosh; I have always dreamt of going to Venice. Is it as beautiful as they say?'

Maria thinks about her home city as they walk down Kennington Road, cars and trucks passing by them, belching out fumes. It couldn't be more different from this urban jungle. 'Oh, yes,' she enthuses. 'It's a magical place.'

Joan giggles. 'Oh, I do so love the way you speak English. It's so sweet. You sound a little American.'

Maria feels a tweak of annoyance. 'I learnt from Jacqueline . . .'

'And she's half American, isn't she? That explains it,' says Joan. She stops suddenly and puts her hand on Maria's sleeve. 'I say, now I know who you are! Are you the daughter of that amazing Italian woman Jacqueline is always talking about? Belle?'

'Yes, that's me.'

'She sounds so brave, helping all those Jewish people escape during the war. You must be proud of her.'

'Yes, of course I am.' But all Maria remembers of that time is not how brave her mother was, but how tense she was. She couldn't stop herself from helping people, and yet there was always this fear they would be discovered. If she thinks about it, Belle risked her and Pina's lives to save strangers. She knows it is not very noble to think this way, but it is the truth.

'I say, let's go for a cup of tea and a bun. Do you fancy that? There's a café just down the road.'

Joan is a chatterbox, but Maria likes it. She is so friendly and warm, quite unlike any of the other English people she has met so far.

'So, what do you think of Lempert?' she asks Maria.

'I am finding it hard to understand his approach, to be honest . . .'

'Oh, don't worry; you'll understand soon enough, once we start dancing properly.' Joan's eyes shine. She opens up her cigarette case and offers Maria a cigarette. 'Of course, I am in love with him,' Joan says dramatically. 'But I am also in love with countless other men, as well.' She sighs with panache. 'I fall in love too easily, you see.' She removes the cigarette from her mouth while taking another sip of her tea.

Maria looks at the red lipstick stain left on the end of it. 'I have never been in love,' she says, all of a sudden, shocked at her admission to her brand new acquaintance.

'Oh, but you are so young, you are only just beginning. How old are you?'

'Eighteen. But you don't look much older than me,' Maria protests.

'Twenty-two, my dear, and that makes *all* the difference, I can tell you.' Joan pauses and stubs out her cigarette before taking a bite out of her currant bun. 'Although, I fell in love for the first time when I was seventeen. Still, that was the war. You grow up fast during the war. Things are different.'

'In what way?'

'Well, surely you must know? I mean, you were living in occupied territory and in so much danger . . . hiding all of those people like Jacqueline, and helping them escape.'

'It wasn't me. It was my mother who did that. I was too young, really, to know any different. Most of the time it was quiet. They only bombed Venice once and that wasn't even the city.'

'Well, it wasn't quiet here, I can tell you. I wanted to study dance, and I was down at Dartington Hall with Lempert and Jooss.' Joan tears her bun into tiny pieces and eats them one at a time, savouring each mouthful.

'Where's that?' Maria asks.

'It's this fabulous place in Devon – a performing arts school. Oh, I just loved it there.' Joan sighs, picking up every last crumb on her plate with her fingertip. 'But then, you know, it was wartime so I came to London to make myself useful. I wanted to be part of it, you know.' Joan's smile begins to droop. She shakes her head. 'God, I certainly was a part of it then . . .'

She pauses, takes another sip of tea and picks herself up again.

'But, you see, when the Americans came, we would have these terrific dances. That's where I met Stan. He was an American bomber pilot. He looked like Clark Gable, I promise you he did. He was so dreamy and I fell for him hook, line and sinker, so I did.'

'And what happened?' Maria asks.

Joan clasps her hands to her breast and says dramatically, 'He broke my heart.'

Maria is enjoying this love story. Her life with Belle and Pina had been devoid of male romance, and talk of the American pilot, Stan, has her excited. Did he die in combat? Did he go missing? 'What happened?' she asks, breathless.

'The scoundrel was married, back in Ohio. Only told me that after he popped my cherry.'

'Excuse me?'

Joan giggles. 'You know . . . took my innocence away . . .' She winks at Maria, who immediately colours. 'Oh, I know it sounds like I was cheap, but it was so different during the war. When you met someone and you felt a connection, well, you just acted on it. I mean, they could be dead the next day.' She drains the last drop of tea from her cup. 'So, I gave Stan the best thing I could. Like a talisman, I hoped it might keep him alive, and I guess it did – but not for me; for his little wifey back home in the US of A.' Joan grimaces.

'I don't think I can see you living as an American housewife,' Maria pipes up, wanting to make her new friend feel better.

Joan flashes her eyes at her. 'Exactly, my dear; you are so right. I am certainly not ready to settle down yet. I want to have fun.'

Maria nods, not knowing how to respond. Her life so far has been sheltered. No dances with American soldiers or romance of any sort.

Joan glances at her watch. 'I say, we had better get back.'

The girls gather up their things. As they scuttle out of the café, Joan grabs Maria's sleeve and squeezes her arm tight. 'I am so glad we got talking. All the other girls are so stuck up. It's going to be nice to have a proper girlfriend.'

Maria looks at Joan in surprise. They have only just met; how could she call her a girlfriend already?

'What are you doing tonight?' Joan asks Maria, ignoring her expression. 'Would you like to come out dancing with me? Meet some men?'

Valentina

THEIR TAXI WEAVES THROUGH THE CHOKED STREETS OF London and the city appears like a huge metropolitan beast, exhaust fumes steaming in the rain, the heartbeat of the city even more urgent than Valentina's dear Milan.

'Mikhail wants me to go to Russia with him,' Antonella is saying to her as they sit side by side in the back of the black cab.

'Does he want you to meet his family?' Valentina is only half listening to her friend; the other half of her is looking out of the cab window at the rain beating down upon the Londoners scurrying along the streets.

Despite this city's bleak aspect, her heart is pounding with excitement. She is here, in London. And so is Theo. He could be just around that corner right now. She imagines him walking in the rain, a large golfing umbrella held aloft and shielding him from the dismal weather, an English newspaper tucked under his arm. She knows it is a ridiculous thought.

Millions live in London, and yet she can't help hoping she will see his figure emerge out of the curtains of rain.

'Oh, no, of course not,' Antonella is saying. 'He wants to take pictures of me in Russia. Naked.'

'Why can't he do that in Milan?' She turns to her friend, giving her more attention. 'And, besides, I didn't know Mikhail was a photographer.'

'It's a new avenue for him. He says he is bored with painting,' Antonella huffs. 'I think it's because of you, and your pictures. I think you have inspired him.'

Valentina can't help feeling a little pleased about this, despite the fact her friend is piqued. She glances at Antonella, appreciating how stunning she looks. She is in her best gear for the trip to London. Her lustrous red hair is piled on top of her head, tendrils spilling in all directions; her eyes are made up smokey; her lips a red to match her hair colour. She is wearing a black military-style coat, unbuttoned, her ample bosom accentuated by a red silk shirt. Her nails are no longer talons, but have been cut short and painted such a deep crimson they could be black.

'OK,' Valentina says, 'but why Russia?'

'He has this idea of having me naked in nature, near where he is from.' She scratches her head. 'Oh, where is it now? Not too far from Saint Petersburg, I think. There are lots of forests, he told me, and he has this little wooden cabin in the middle of nowhere. He wants me to pose outside the cabin, naked apart from a large axe in my hand.' She grins mischievously.

'He has lots of ideas. He wants me to straddle a sawhorse, my ass in the air, and ready for the taking!' she giggles.

'It sounds very sexy.'

'It also sounds cold. I mean, I think it's still snowy in parts of Russia at the moment.' Antonella sighs. 'But I do love him, the darling, so I guess I will do it for him.'

Valentina looks at her friend thoughtfully. How easily she can say that she loves a man. She wonders whether Antonella really means it. Or does she say that about every man she ever sleeps with? The taxi pulls in beside a small, gated park. Valentina surveys the grand neoclassical houses that surround the park. Surely Antonella's aunt can't live in one of these buildings? They look like embassies, not domestic homes.

'Oh, here we are, Valentina,' she says squeezing Valentina's arm. 'Welcome to South Kensington.'

'My God,' she exclaims. 'Is your aunt a millionairess, or something?'

'I know; it's pretty amazing, but Aunty is property rich and cash poor. I don't quite know how she got this house, or even if she actually owns it. I think it belonged to one of her lovers once . . .'

Valentina gets out of the cab, feeling disorientated. She has only been to London once before, with her mother, when she was about eleven and her mother was doing a shoot. That time they had stayed somewhere really central, but she can't remember the name of the place. All she remembers is travelling around on the Tube, and how many people there were – so many more than Milan. And she remembers one wonderful afternoon in the British Museum, gazing at all the Egyptian mummies. She'd love to go back there.

'Hey, let's go to the British Museum while we're here,' she suggests as they drag their cases up the steps to the grand portico entrance of Antonella's aunt's house.

Antonella scrunches up her nose in distaste. 'No, thank you! I didn't come all the way to London to go to some fusty old museum . . . Oh, no . . . What I want to do is go to the Torture Garden!'

Valentina groans. 'I can guess what kind of place that is.'

'Come on, Valentina, you're the one who encouraged me to let my inner dominatrix out. We have to go there now we're in London.'

'I suppose; it's just I hate those rubber costumes. I wish we could just wear our own stuff. In fact, I think I would rather be naked, apart from a red cloak, like O.'

'Like who?'

'O in *Story of O* by Pauline Réage. It's the most famous erotic novel. Don't tell me you've never read it?'

'You know I don't like books,' Antonella tells her. 'Anyway, the whole point of going to somewhere like the Torture Garden is to wear rubber.' Antonella slaps Valentina on the backside. 'Come on! Get your submissive ass into the lift; I'm dying to sit down and have a drink with Aunt Isabella.'

* * *

Valentina opens up the *London A-Z* and looks at the street map again. She has left Antonella in the house in South Kensington with her aunt Isabella, the two of them halfway through a bottle of Soave and munching through a bowl of stuffed olives. It is quite obvious to Valentina which side of the family Antonella gets her wild side from. Despite being twice her age, Isabella still has the fiery hair and temperament that her niece shares. She is the sister of Antonella's father, Alexandro, who left the family to run off with a younger woman when Antonella was ten. Isabella, a magazine editor, took it upon herself to represent the paternal side in Antonella's life and never lost contact with her niece. She has the same sexy exuberance as Antonella – and the same brutal directness. Already she has interrogated Valentina about her erotic photography, insisting in seeing all of her work on her laptop and apparently delighted by the nude pictures of her own niece, while at the same time asking Valentina if she thought it was exploitative of women. Her final question annoyed Valentina.

'And what does your mother think of your photographs?'

Valentina made it quite clear that she has neither shown her mother her work, nor intends to. Isabella said nothing to that response, although she had arched her eyebrows in surprise. Valentina knows that Isabella was good friends with her mother when they both lived in Milan in the sixties and seventies. Isabella's enthusiastic appreciation of her pictures can't help but make Valentina wonder what her mother would make of her exhibition in London. She hasn't bothered to tell her. In fact, she hasn't even told Mattia. She has been avoiding talking to her brother since she broke up with Theo, although she was forced to tell him about that when he rang her at Christmas. She's ashamed to admit to her sibling her inability to commit, since he has been happily married for years. Although Mattia only met Theo once, she knows that he liked him. He had even hinted that he could be the 'one'. If there is such a thing, Valentina thinks, crossly.

The rain has stopped and the light is beginning to fade as Valentina walks briskly down the damp streets. So, this is Soho. It is not as she expected. She had been imagining gaudy sex shops and peep show entrances, but in fact all she can see are trendy cafés, bespoke shops, little bistros and galleries, yet there is an air of creativity and a spirit here that appeals to her. It is a tiny, warren-like area. She keeps going around in circles until she finally finds Lexington Street. The gallery is right at the end of the street. She glances at her watch: 6 p.m. Exactly on time. She rings the bell and has to wait a few minutes before the intercom buzzes.

'Valentina Rosselli to see Kirsti Shaw.'

The door clicks and Valentina pushes it open. She walks past a deserted reception area and into a large gallery space: a square white box. She can see that the exhibition is in the process of being hung. There is a ladder leaning against one empty wall, whereas the wall beside it is already hung with paintings. Two spotlights are angled to pick up the images. She walks across the space, surveying the other work. There seem to be about ten artists in the show, each of them having a total of six pieces. She can see her photographs in a stack by the far wall. There is also a long table the other side of the room, covered in pictures. She wonders where everyone is.

She bends down and starts looking through her own photographs. The gallery has chosen to exhibit what seems to Valentina to be quite a random selection of her work. There are two portraits of Valentina's new dancer friend, Celia, and her friend, Rosa, together. One shows Celia on her toes, naked, with her leg raised in an arabesque as Rosa caresses her, and the other is of the two of them together, with an antique lace scarf binding them as they touch each other. There is one of her first erotic compositions: a sepia-toned, nude self-portrait, showing her body reflected in a Venetian canal. And then there are three more recent works. One is inspired by her experience with Leonardo. It is a close-up of a bottom (Celia's), dripping with candle wax, her pussy just visible. The last two photographs are of Antonella and Mikhail. One is a black and white close-up of Antonella's face, with Mikhail's cock inside her mouth, and the second is a close-up of Mikhail holding one of Antonella's breasts and sucking the nipple. They are simple, yet striking in their explicitness.

Valentina knows that some people will call these photographs pornography yet, as far as she is concerned, there is no denying their beauty: the raw exposure of her subjects' desire, the need within them portrayed as pure aesthetics. It is not just naked bodies and sex. It is something poetic, other-worldly. Valentina believes that all those who criticise what she and her fellow photographers are doing are really just afraid. Everyone has a shadow self. Everyone has dark desires. She is sure of it.

She leafs through the pictures again. She has the feeling that there is something not quite right about the selection, but she can't put her finger on it.

She hears a woman's laugh and footsteps approaching. She notices now another doorway opposite the one to reception, leading out of the gallery into another space. A light flicks on and into the room walk two women. The first to speak is a tall, willowy woman with very long dark hair. She is wearing a maroon silk shift dress, and Valentina can't help noticing how very thin her arms are, how bony her shoulders.

'Valentina?' the woman says, walking over to her. 'My name is Kirsti Shaw. So lovely to meet you.' She has a soft American accent. Kirsti reaches out her hand, but Valentina is only half looking at her as she shakes it. She is completely distracted by the other woman in the room, for Kirsti's companion seems to have stepped straight out of a fifties burlesque show. The woman has lustrous blond hair, styled into high waves, similar to Marilyn Monroe but even more extreme. Her skin is perfect, paler than Valentina's, and she has deep blue eyes, framed with thick black liner and false eyelashes. Her lips are a perfect pink bow to match her outfit. She is wearing a fuchsia pink bustier with black lacings all the way down the front, and a matching skirt, hugging her hips and thighs. She has an hourglass figure, full breasts, a tiny waist and a curvaceous backside. To complete the look, she is wearing long pink gloves up to her elbows, fishnet tights and pink stiletto court shoes. On her elbow hangs a little pink purse on a chain. The whole look is completely over the top: a sugary sweet femme fatale. Valentina does her best not to stare, but she just can't help it.

'Valentina,' Kirsti says, 'I'd like to introduce you to one of the other exhibitors, Anita Chappell. Anita, this is Valentina Rosselli.'

Anita totters over to her and extends her hand. 'Lovely to meet you,' she says in a perfect English accent. She certainly doesn't sound how she looks: a vision from nineteen-fifties Hollywood. 'I've heard so much about you,' she says, fluttering her false eyelashes. 'I love your pictures.'

'Thank you,' Valentina mutters, wondering what kind of pictures Anita might take.

'Anita is one of the most popular burlesque performers in London,' Kirsti explains to Valentina.

'I'm not a proper photographer, like you are,' Anita says to Valentina. 'I am just dabbling. I can't believe that my work got picked.'

'Well, you are a star in your own right, now, aren't you, Anita? Of course there will be interest in your artwork, particularly considering your heritage,' Kirsti flatters the blonde bombshell.

Valentina wonders what Kirsti Shaw could mean. What is the burlesque performer's heritage?

'I really didn't think so, but my boyfriend persuaded me I should send in the pictures – and particularly the video,' says Anita.

'Yes, it is quite remarkable footage,' Kirsti says. 'Not just historically fascinating, but incredibly erotic as well.'

Anita turns to Valentina. 'I should explain,' she tells her. 'My grandfather was an art dealer who specialised in erotica. He has these very early erotic films shot in Paris in the late forties. I've incorporated them into an artwork.'

'It is quite something,' Kirsti tells Valentina. 'We haven't got it up and running yet, but would you like to take a look at Kirsti's photos?'

'I'd be so thrilled to get your feedback,' Anita adds. 'I am a great fan of your work.'

'Sure.' Valentina nods, feeling a little overwhelmed by the two women.

Anita leads her over to the far side of the gallery, to the long work table with framed photographs spread along it.

'We were just taking a look at them,' Kirsti says, 'trying to decide where to hang them.'

Valentina looks down at Anita's pictures. All of them are self-portraits, and Valentina has to admit that they are stunning. The first shot is of Anita lying on her side, wearing a purple dress with thigh-high black lace-up boots and black, lacy stockings. Her blond hair is down and her lips are plum to match the dress. Just a corner of a bare buttock is visible in the shot. In the second picture, Anita is all in black. It is a close-up and she is looking into the mirror, holding the camera, with an oriental parasol half covering her face. Only the very tops of her breasts are visible, the hard nipples pushing through the slits of a latex S&M outfit. The third picture shows Anita's whole body reflected in a mirror as she lies against a pile of white silk cushions. Her feet, in a pair of kitten-heeled pearly mules, are together, soles pressed against a mirror, her legs are bent at the knees so that they open outwards and the rest of her naked body is reflected in the mirror: her bare breasts, her pursed lips as she closes her left eye to take the picture. Despite the fact her legs are spread, she is not completely exposed as a lilac chiffon scarf trails between them concealing her sex.

'That's my favourite,' Anita says, as Valentina picks it up to examine it. 'I think it's a little more subtle than the others.'

The last three pictures are even more graphic. One is of Anita, naked, lit up by three arc lights, spaced in a triangle around her. She is on her knees and turning the camera around to take a picture. Her hair falls over her face like a blond veil but, even so, you can see her parted lips, her closed eyes.

In another black and white composition she is on her back on swathes of black silk, looking up at a mirror, her fishnet-stockinged legs crossed; just visible are the parted lips of her labia.

'Oh, this has to be my favourite,' says Kirsti, picking up the last picture, much to Valentina's surprise. Obviously the American is not as demure as she looks. To say the shot is confrontational would be an understatement. Anita is lying on her back, her legs pointing straight up in the air, sheathed in pale oyster stockings almost the same colour as her skin, her bottom facing the mirror. Apart from the stockings she is utterly naked. Her head is tipped to the right and she is staring at the mirror, surveying the viewer, the camera balanced in her right hand, her arm outstretched so that she is able to get everything in the shot. She is on display completely.

'They're great,' Valentina says.

Anita looks genuinely pleased. 'Really? That means so much to me,' she says.

'Well, I am not an experienced erotic photographer by any means . . .'

'Yeah, but you come from such a famous family. I mean, your mother – she's an icon!'

Valentina stiffens at the mention of Tina Rosselli.

'Ladies, I think we should crack open a bottle of champagne,' says Kirsti, her cheeks flushed. 'I could do with some help deciding where to hang everything. Would you have the time, Anita?'

'Well, I am performing tonight,' Anita says, 'but not until

really late. And it's only down the road. I can ring my man to come and pick me up.'

'Great. What do you say, Valentina? Are you free for a while?' Kirsti is still holding up the naked photograph of Anita as she speaks. The burlesque dancer's bare legs glimmer in the light from the spotlight behind them.

'Sure,' Valentina finds herself saying. 'I've no plans.'

She is certain that, by now, both Antonella and Isabella are stuck into a night of drinking and reminiscing. Valentina is happy to avoid that. She doesn't want to have to sit and listen to Isabella regale them with stories of all the fun she and Valentina's mother used to have back in the sixties and seventies.

Two hours later, the gallery is nearly hung; Valentina hopes it has been done well, although she suspects that they are too inebriated at this stage to tell. Surprisingly, it is Anita who seems the most together of the three of them. They are sprawled on the floor of the gallery. Kirsti's shift dress is up at her hips and she has a lazy grin on her face as she takes a sip of her champagne – the third bottle they have opened between them.

'Well, here I am in my ultimate girly fantasy,' she says, 'drinking champagne with two of the sexiest women I have ever met.'

Anita and Valentina lock eyes. Valentina has never been attracted to the femme fatale look, and yet there is something about Anita . . . something sweet and alluring . . .

'Tell me, Valentina,' Kirsti says, 'are you wearing anything underneath that dress? It is so incredibly figure hugging . . .' She reaches forward and slips her hand through the slit on to Valentina's bare leg, trailing her fingers up her thigh.

'No,' says Valentina steadily, wondering whether it would be rude to remove Kirsti's hand. 'You can't wear anything underneath; it's too tight. It shows off everything.'

'I can see that,' says Anita grinning. 'I love it; it's so bold with those black and white stripes – very sixties and free spirited. Whereas I am trussed up in all my gear . . .' she adds. 'And what about you, Kirsti? Are you wearing any knickers?' Anita giggles.

Kirsti starts to laugh, removes her hand from Valentina's leg and, all of a sudden, pulls her dress up. Valentina can see that she is completely shaved, her flesh pale and soft. It looks incongruous along with her long dark hair. She pulls a tiny thong off with her long, elegant fingers.

'Not anymore, darling,' she drawls.

'Oh, you are naughty, aren't you?' Anita teases her.

'Will you dance for us, Anita?' Kirsti asks. 'Just a private dance for myself and Valentina?'

'I've no music.' Anita pouts.

'Can't you just imagine it? We can, can't we?' Kirsti is looking at Valentina, a suggestive smile on her face.

'I should go,' Valentina says, hesitantly.

'Oh, no, please,' Kirsti pleads. 'You have to see Anita perform.'

Anita knocks back her champagne. 'Well, all right then, but it's not the real thing without the music, you know.'

Valentina is frozen, unable to get up now. For some reason, she doesn't want to offend Anita.

Anita stands up, slips her stilettos back on and picks up a chair, placing it in front of the two other women. She walks around the gallery, switching off all the lights so that only one spotlight is left on, illuminating the chair. She steps into the pool of light, her blond hair a blaze of glory, her white skin pearly, her pink lips pursed. She begins to sway her hips and spins around on her heels, pushing her backside towards them.

Is she really going to do a striptease? Valentina thinks. It seems so ridiculous and old-fashioned and yet, sitting on the floor next to her, Valentina senses that Kirsti is enjoying the show. She looks over at the gallery owner. In the gloom of the gallery she can see she has her hand slipped between her legs, and imagines her lips parted in anticipation.

Anita slowly pulls off each glove and unzips her skirt, wiggling it off over hips. Despite herself, Valentina has to admit it is sexy. Anita continues to undress, oh-so slowly, unbuttoning her little pink jacket, pulling it off and throwing it across the room. Now she is in a tiny sequined G-string, stockings, suspenders and a corset. She unlaces the corset so that it falls away to reveal an ornate brassiere. Beneath all of the upholstery of her clothes, Anita has a beautiful body: a naturally tiny waist, neat little round bottom – not too large, like Valentina's – and pert, plump breasts. Valentina can't help but feel her insides warming in response to the vision of this beautiful woman. Anita kicks off her heels, smiling all the time at Kirsti. She lifts one of her legs and puts her foot on to the chair, peeling off her stocking and wiggling her bottom as she does so. Then she twists around and sits on the chair, raising the other leg in the air and slowly pulling that stocking off. Valentina hears Kirsti's breath quickening, she glances over at the American woman, but she can't see her clearly in the dim room. The whole experience is surreal. She wasn't expecting this when she came here this afternoon, to be witnessing the gallery owner pleasuring herself while watching a striptease show.

Inside her head she hears Theo's voice: *Welcome to London, Valentina*. She remembers how he tried to encourage her to let go of her inhibitions, have fun. She can't help but feel turned on; even though she has no desire to have sex with either woman, she feels a yearning to be touched by a man – by her man. Without thinking, she slips her own hand through the slit in her skirt and touches herself. She quivers with relief. She is so wound up, she knows. All this anticipation – the exhibition, Theo . . .

Anita pings the suspender belt off, so that she is nearly naked, then she brings her hand up behind her brassiere and lets it fall away to reveal her breasts, naked apart from two sequined tassles covering the nipples. She lifts her legs in the air and does a backward bend off the chair at the precise moment that Valentina hears Kirsti gasping as she comes.

Valentina carefully retrieves her hand. She is so close, yet she doesn't want to touch herself anymore, not now Anita has finished her dance and Kirsti has obviously found satisfaction. She waits in the darkness of the gallery for one of the other women to say something. Anita sits up and begins to put on her bra. She is all businesslike now. Valentina can still hear Kirsti breathing deeply beside her. She wonders if she is embarrassed or still drunk from the champagne. A mobile phone rings. Anita totters over to her little pink purse. She is still only half dressed, just her stockings and shoes on, and her underwear.

'Hello, darling; you're outside? OK, we'll let you in now.'

Anita switches on the light and turns to Kirsti.

'It's my boyfriend. Can you buzz him in?'

Kirsti stands up, smoothes down her shift dress and picks up her thong. She is all composure now, as if nothing out of the usual has happened at all. She walks out of the gallery space and Valentina hears the door in the reception click open and the low voice of a man.

'Well, what did you think of my show?' Anita asks Valentina earnestly, as she zips up her skirt.

'I can honestly say that you were very sexy.'

Anita looks pleased. 'Thanks.' She nods over towards the door, buttoning up her little pink jacket. 'Poor Kirsti; she's always on at me to perform for her. I keep telling her she needs to get herself a girlfriend.'

'I think it's you she fancies,' says Valentina.

Anita shakes her head. 'Well, she'll have no luck. I am afraid she's just not my type.' She gives Valentina a rather flirtatious look. 'Besides, I am a bit preoccupied at the moment. I've just met someone new.'

Anita looks expectantly past Valentina at the doorway leading into the gallery. Valentina hears Kirsti's high-heeled shoes as they clatter on the wooden floor, and senses the presence of Anita's boyfriend as Anita's gaze warms.

'Talk of the devil; here he is!' Anita exclaims, beaming with delight.

Valentina turns around, curious to see what the boyfriend of the stunning Anita might look like. Yet, as soon as she catches sight of him, her whole world falls away beneath her. The gallery tips on its side and all the champagne she has drunk makes her stumble forward, her body assaulted with shock. For standing in front of her, looking equally stunned, is none other than Theo.

$\mathscr{M}$aria

SHE HAS LOST JOAN. USUALLY THEY STICK TOGETHER.
Over the past month, it has become their habit to go out
two or three times a week to listen to the new music from
America and to dance. Maria surveys the packed club. It
is hard to see anyone, it is so dark – the air thick with cigarette smoke. All that is visible is the band. Maria watches the
trumpet player as he leans back and lifts his glittering
instrument up to the ceiling, blasting out his sound. This is a
new kind of jazz, urgent and wild. It makes her pulse race
and she can't help swaying her hips, despite her anxiety.
Even so, she has to find Joan right now. It's time to go home.
They have dance school in the morning and already it is
past midnight.

She weaves through the crowd. Men look at her, one or
two try to stop her, to speak to her.

'All right, my beauty?'

'Looking for me, are you, darling?'

But most of the men are listening to the music, their faces rapt as if they are in a trance.

With relief, Maria spies her friend at a table in the corner. Why on earth did she move without telling her? There are two men sitting with her. One is next to Joan, with his arm around her shoulder, and the other has his back to Maria. Maria's heart sinks. It has been a good night so far, dancing at the Astoria and then coming here, to this little club in Soho, to listen to music that Joan claims reminds her of her American beau, Stan. But Maria is tired now and she wants to go home to bed. She promised Jacqueline she would be back by midnight. She is already late. The last thing she feels like is fending off the unwanted attentions of a man.

She sees Joan waving to her as she approaches the table.

'There you are,' Joan says, smiling up at her sweetly. 'Where did you go?'

'You moved tables,' Maria says, sitting down in the chair next to one of the strange men.

'Oh, yes, sorry,' Joan giggles. 'Ralph and his friend here wanted us to join them. You don't mind, do you? They bought you a drink.'

Joan tilts her face to her companion. Maria has to admit he is very attractive: black hair, a sculpted moustache and perfectly arched eyebrows. He looks like some kind of Russian aristocrat. He is also very drunk, hardly acknowledging Maria's presence before whispering something into Joan's ear that makes her giggle even more. Maria sits rigidly in her seat, not daring to look at the man beside her. Eventually he coughs, forcing her to acknowledge him.

'Pleased to meet you, Maria. My name is Douglas.'

He has one of those pale English faces, with sandy hair, watery blue eyes and freckles. She shakes his limp hand before taking a sip of the drink that has been bought for her. It goes up her nose, making her splutter.

'Are you all right?' Douglas asks.

'Yes, fine,' Maria replies. 'It's just I don't know what I am drinking.'

'Gin and tonic.' Douglas takes out his cigarettes and offers her one. 'Isn't that what all girls drink nowadays?'

'I have only ever drunk wine.'

'I see; I thought you looked like a Continental. Where are you from?'

'Italy.'

Douglas looks uncomfortable for a moment. 'I wish you had said you were French or Spanish,' he says finally.

'Why?'

'I fought against the Italians in Abyssinia during the war.' Douglas shakes his head and looks at the band, which is just starting up another number.

Maria is lost for words. Now she feels even more uncomfortable than she did before. Maybe she can just leave and walk back to Jacqueline's. Would it be all right to abandon Joan? Maria looks across at her friend. She is *very* drunk. She sees Ralph slip his hand under Joan's skirt.

That's it; she has to get them out of here before something happens.

She stands up abruptly and reaches over, grabbing Joan's hand. 'Let's go. It's late.'

Joan frowns at her. 'I don't want to go,' she says, pulling her hand away. 'It's just getting fun.'

'I think we should; we have class in the morning.'

'What do you girls study?' Ralph drawls.

'We're dance students, darling,' Joan traces her finger down his cheek.

'Oh, dancers! That explains it . . .' Ralph laughs and looks across at Maria with narrowed eyes. He makes her feel like she is a common tart. How dare he?

'Joan,' she says firmly. 'I am leaving now and I think you should come with me.'

Joan waves her away. 'Don't worry, darling. I'm fine – really. I am a woman of the world.'

Maria can do no more. She stalks out of the club. She is angry with her friend for being so drunk and stupid, and with Ralph for thinking so little of them. And yet she is frustrated as well. She is powerless to stop Joan from behaving badly, and a part of her feels like an idiot – a party pooper. She steps out on to the cool street and takes in a deep breath of fresh air. God, it was smoky in that place.

'Can I take you home?'

She turns in surprise. Behind her is Douglas, her evening

purse in his hand. In her haste to get out of the club, she had forgotten to pick it up from the table.

'Oh, thank you,' she says as he hands it to her, and she tucks it under her arm. He is staring at her with those washed out blue eyes, and despite the fact it is a warm night, she shivers involuntarily.

'I can walk,' she adds.

'Nonsense; I wouldn't be happy unless I saw you safely home myself,' Douglas says. 'I have the car parked just around the corner.'

Maria clasps her hands around her purse in her lap, trying to quell her anxiety about Joan, as Douglas drives them down Pall Mall and past Buckingham Palace.

'Do you know Ralph well?' she asks Douglas.

He glances over at her, surveying her coolly. 'Oh, yes; we served together in Africa,' he says. 'I can assure you he is a gentleman.'

Maria isn't so sure. She can still see his hand slipping under Joan's skirt, and the drunken haze in her friend's eyes. She shouldn't have left her behind.

'Maybe we should go back and get Joan?' she ventures.

Douglas puts a hand on her knee, and she flinches as if branded.

'Really, I think your friend is quite able to look after herself. She is not an innocent . . .' He pauses. 'Not like you.'

Maria looks across at Douglas, but he is staring out of the

windscreen, his expression indiscernible. She turns away, shifting so that his hand falls off her knee. She wills herself back at Jacqueline's as they speed past Victoria Station through the utter blackness that is post-war London at night.

When they arrive at her little street, Douglas insists on parking. He gets out of the car, walking round and opening the passenger door for Maria. She gets out rather clumsily, unwillingly taking his hand.

'Thank you,' she says, glancing up at the top floor of the house. The curtains are drawn on Jacqueline's windows and she can see no light behind them. Her mentor must be asleep.

She waits for him to get back into the car, but he is still standing on the deserted street.

'Well, good night,' Maria says, fishing in her bag for the front door key.

'Can I invite you out for dinner?' Douglas suddenly says. 'Saturday night?'

'Oh,' she mutters. 'Sorry; I'm busy on Saturday.'

There is something about the way this young man looks at her, the glitter in his pale eyes, that unnerves her. She can't think of anything worse than going out with him on a date.

'Well, what about Sunday, then?' he asks her.

'I can't; sorry.' She shakes her head.

'Monday?'

This time she has no choice but to be direct.

'No, thank you; I'm very busy, you see, with my dancing studies.'

'Did you say, "no"?' She can hear the icy affront in his voice. He has his hand on her arm now; he restrains her, forcing her to twist around and look at his face. 'What about a good night kiss, then?' he says, his mouth grimacing at her, his lips pulled back over his teeth so that he reminds Maria of a snarling dog.

'Excuse me,' she tries to pull away, 'but, really, I have to go now. Good night,' she says firmly.

But, instead of letting her go, Douglas takes a firmer hold of her arm and pulls her towards him.

'Let me go!' She is about to cry out, but he puts his hand over her mouth. His skin tastes salty, its flesh hot against her burning lips. She struggles to pull away from him, but he pushes her back down the front path and along the side of the house, into the little alleyway that leads to the back. She is so close to Jacqueline, to help, and yet she is powerless to call out. She is here in the pitch black, trying to fight off this man, but he is so much stronger than her. He pushes her back against the brick wall. She feels the roughness of the bricks on the back of her head. He crushes her with his body. She can feel his arousal pressed against her stomach. She feels sick. She tries to prise his hand off her mouth so that she can call out but he pins her arms down with his body. Then he removes his hand and grinds his mouth into hers, forcing her lips open and pushing his tongue in. His breath is thick with the smell of alcohol and she feels like retching; she can hardly breathe.

She senses him pulling up her dress. Oh, God; not this way, please, she prays inside her head. She thinks of her mother and Pina, and what they would do to this man if they knew that he was assaulting their precious Maria. She wishes so hard for a father – someone – to protect her. She twists her head and bites his tongue as hard as she can.

Douglas springs back in shock. 'You Italian bitch,' he hisses, slapping her face hard and, with the other hand, pulling her skirt up around her waist and dragging down her knickers. 'I am going to fuck you so hard,' he says. 'I'm going to fuck you to death.' He laughs nastily.

But she has her chance now that her mouth is free, and she calls out with all her strength. 'Jacqueline! Help! Help!'

Douglas smacks his hand over her mouth to silence her. 'There's no one here to help you.' He whispers into her ear. 'I am going to make you pay, Maria, for your countrymen and what they did to me . . .'

Her knickers are around her ankles, and she watches in horror as he unbuckles his belt and drops his trousers. She sees his penis: the first penis she has ever seen in her life. He is going to hurt her with this part of his body, this erect pink instrument. She shivers at the thought of it inside her, splitting her open. She tries to clamp her legs shut, but he is pulling her thighs apart, his fingernails scratching her flesh. She closes her eyes, knowing now there is nothing she can do to stop this from happening. He is too strong for her. Better to just block it out and wait until it is over. Better to pray that he won't hurt her more afterwards.

It happens so quickly. One minute Douglas is pressing against her and she can feel his hands pulling her legs apart, his penis against her thighs, on the edge of entering her, and the next minute he is wrenched away from her. She opens her eyes, gasping in shock and relief as she sees another man punching Douglas in the face. Douglas falls down. The stranger kicks him, again and again. Douglas is groaning, pleading, but the stranger is merciless. Maria is paralysed. She sinks to the ground, shaking uncontrollably. She watches the stranger kick Douglas unconscious.

'Stop!' She croaks. 'You're going to kill him.'

She squeezes her eyes shut and licks her lips.

A hand is placed on her shoulder. She opens her eyes and the stranger is crouching front of her. 'Are you all right?' he asks in a heavily accented voice.

Despite the darkness, he is so close to her that she can make out his face. And what she sees stuns her: a man so beautiful that, despite her recent assault, she feels herself melting beneath his gaze. She nods, unable to speak.

'Let me help you.' He stands up and offers her his hand. She takes it. A warm, strong hand grips hers and pulls her up. Her clothes are all ruched around her. She pulls down her dress, and looks over at the prostrate form of Douglas.

'Is he dead?' she says in a hoarse whisper.

'No, no . . . I would like to have killed him. But scum like him are not worth the trouble. I think that, when he wakes up, he will slink off back to the sewer he came from. Don't worry about him.'

'But he knows where I live.' She raises her hand to cradle her stinging cheek, where Douglas had slapped her.

'You live here? In this house?' the man asks her.

'Yes.'

'Well, so do I,' he tells her, to her utter surprise. 'So you have nothing to fear. If he ever turns up again I'll deal with him'

She begins to walk down the alley, shakily. All she wants is to get inside the house now. Lie on her mattress in her tiny cupboard room and breathe normally again. She feels dizzy, as if she is wading in mud, as if the ground is going to give out beneath her.

'Let me help you; you're in shock,' the stranger says. He slips his arm under hers so easily.

'And, miss,' he says, taking something out of his pocket. 'These are yours.' He hands her the torn knickers.

She gives a little hiccup of distress and, before she can help it, tears begin to stream down her face.

'It's all right,' the stranger says gently, guiding her out of the alleyway and round to the front of the house. 'You're safe now.'

They climb the steps and her rescuer takes a key from his pocket and unlocks the front door. They enter the hall with the flickering light bulb.

'You're still shaking,' the stranger says to her. 'Would you like some brandy? I have some cognac in my room.'

'No, thank you; I just want to go to bed,' she whispers. 'I want to forget what happened.'

They start to climb the stairs. She hesitates on the second landing. He is still behind her. She turns to him. Now she can see him even more clearly in the electric light. He is older than she initially thought, but he is still extremely handsome: tall and powerful, black hair peppered with grey, and strong espresso eyes.

'Please don't tell anyone about this,' she says, looking down and blushing.

'Are you not going to tell Mademoiselle Mournier?'

Maria shakes her head. For some reason, she feels her own naïvety is somewhat at fault here. She doesn't want Jacqueline to have a reason not to let her out again or, worse still, tell her mother and Pina what has happened.

'OK,' the stranger says. And then he does something surprising. He takes a handkerchief from his pocket and dries her eyes with it, tenderly as if she were his child.

'I think that you might need looking after, Maria,' he says, scrunching the handkerchief up in his hand.

She looks at him in wonder. She has never met such a gallant man. 'You know my first name?'

'Of course I know your name! We are neighbours.' He smiles at her.

Maria's heart flutters when she sees his laughter lines

appearing at the corners of his eyes. How old is he? Thirty? Older, even? And yet she feels wildly attracted to him, despite her recent assault.

'I am Felix Leduc,' he says.

So this is the mysterious French man that Guido had referred to. She had forgotten about his existence, for she has neither seen nor heard him once since she arrived.

'Good night, Maria,' he says, waiting for her to climb the stairs to the top floor and Jacqueline's apartment.

'Good night; and thank you, Felix.' His name feels strange in her mouth – tactile. She walks up the staircase, aware of his eyes on her back, afraid to look back in case he sees the truth in her eyes. For Maria is quite certain that she has just met the man of her dreams.

$\mathcal{V}$alentina

VALENTINA TWISTS AND TURNS IN BED. IT'S NO GOOD; she can't sleep. She sits up and switches on the bedside lamp. She looks across the room at Antonella in the other bed and she can see that her friend is fast asleep. She wonders whether she should wake her up and tell her about Theo. But Antonella might still be drunk.

When Valentina had returned to the house in South Kensington last night, Antonella and Isabella were in the middle of a dramatic argument over Antonella's father and whether he was the big bastard Antonella claimed he was. The drink had fuelled their emotions and the women ranted and raved at each other in Italian. Finally, a neighbour banging on the wall had silenced them. Valentina encouraged the two of them to go to bed and sleep on it. The evening had ended with aunt and niece tearfully embracing and professing undying loyalty and love to each other. She is sure Antonella would not appreciate being woken up now she is in the middle of a deep sleep. Besides, Antonella has never been a fan of Theo. If she tells her that he has a new girlfriend, she is certain Antonella will advise Valentina to forget about him.

She knows she should. But she just can't.

That moment when she saw him again – after all these months, and despite the circumstances – it was like being thumped in the chest. She had been unable to speak, utterly struck dumb. She had watched in disbelief as Anita had tottered over to Theo in her high heels and embraced him, planting a kiss on his lips. The whole time, Theo had been as silent as her, unsmiling, his eyes boring into her.

'Theo,' Anita said. 'I want you to meet Valentina, my new friend.'

'Actually, we know each other,' Theo said stiffly.

'You do?' Anita looked between the two of them in surprise.

'Yes, I knew Valentina when I lived in Milan,' he said, frowning at Valentina, a questioning look on his face.

'Well, isn't that just amazing?' Anita remarked, kissing Theo again on the cheek, the sweet impulsiveness of her action making Valentina's heart constrict.

'Maybe not such a coincidence, seeing as they both lived in Milan and are involved in the art world,' Kirsti suggested. Valentina detected a certain irony in the gallery owner's tone and wondered why.

'So, you know all about Valentina, darling?' Anita turned to Theo again.

'I wouldn't say that at all,' Theo said, looking uncomfortable.

There was an awkward silence, as if both Kirsti and Anita sensed his unspoken inference.

'How are you, Valentina?' he added, his voice so soft it was almost a whisper.

She had been rooted to the spot, gazing at her lost lover, her chest tight, her throat constricted. She wanted so badly to touch him. 'Fine.' She could say no more.

'It's good to see you again,' he said, his face suddenly illuminated by one of his enigmatic smiles.

Now Valentina can't get those words out of her head: 'It's good to see you again.' Had he really meant it? She had felt the same, despite the fact he is obviously unavailable. It was *so* good to actually see Theo again after all these months, and to know that he is OK. If only he wasn't going out with Anita. She suspects, by his dumbfounded reaction to her presence in the gallery, that he still has some feelings for her at least, or was she imagining his confusion and shock? Yet, even if he does still have feelings for her, she should leave him alone now. He has a new girlfriend – Anita. She is obviously mad about Theo. One of Valentina's rules is never to interfere between a couple. She doesn't want to steal Theo from Anita, that would be wrong, and yet . . . What if he wants her as much as she wants him? What if Anita's feelings are not reciprocated? There is only one person who can help her figure out what to do, and he is back in Milan. She glances at the radio alarm clock. It is one o'clock; that means it's two in Milan. Better to call Leonardo now than in the morning, when he is sleeping. She pulls back the covers and gets out of bed, slipping on her silk kimono dressing gown before dropping her phone into its pocket and tiptoeing out of the bedroom. She pads downstairs and into Isabella's living room, a plush cream space with a view of the gated park opposite. It is a windy night and, as she dials Leonardo's number, she looks out of the window at the trees, their branches waving at her from across the road as if they are urging her on.

'Valentina? Is everything all right?'

'Oh, no, Leonardo; thank God you answered.' She wishes so much that Leonardo were curled up on the couch with her. She realises that somehow their relationship has gone on to a deeper level, a real friendship, like how it is with Marco.

'What's wrong?' He sounds genuinely concerned.

'It's Theo.'

Leonardo doesn't say anything for a few seconds. 'Did you call him up?' He sounds tired – not his usual self.

'I'm sorry; have I woken you?'

It occurs to Valentina that maybe their relationship is rather one-sided. She is always ringing Leonardo and asking for his help. When she thinks about it, he has not once phoned her and asked for her advice.

'No, I'm fine . . .' he says, hesitating. 'There's just stuff going on here . . . I'll tell you when I see you. Now, tell me about Theo.'

'Leonardo, I *saw* him today. A complete coincidence: he was at the gallery where the exhibition is on.' She hesitates, not wanting to tell him about Anita just yet. 'It was like I was struck down . . . like in one of those stupid Hollywood films . . . like I was hit by lightning, literally. I was just jolted awake; it felt so raw. Oh, Leo, I've been so stupid.'

'But it's good, isn't it? Now you know for sure how you feel. Now you can tell him – get him back, like you want to.'

'But it's not as simple as I thought.' She pauses, licking her lips. 'He has a girlfriend.'

'No, not Theo.' Leonardo sounds surprised. 'Maybe she is just a casual lover, but not a proper girlfriend. He has always wanted you, Valentina; I know that.'

'You're wrong. She really is his girlfriend. I met her,' Valentina wails down the phone. 'And she is so sweet and I know she is in love with him; I can see it.'

'So what are you going to do, Valentina?'

Valentina chews her lip. Her heart is racing, her head thick with emotions. She knows now, without a doubt, that she loves Theo, but it's too late. He is with Anita.

'I don't know,' she whispers. 'I was hoping you would tell me what to do.'

Leonardo sighs. 'I can't do that.'

'Please, Leonardo, you're so wise, and Theo confides in you. Please tell me what to do.'

'Well . . .' Leonardo says slowly, 'you say this girl is in love with Theo, but is Theo in love with her?'

'What do you mean?'

'He might be going out with her to make you jealous.'

'That just doesn't seem his style. We never did jealousy,' Valentina muses.

'He must have a plan,' Leonardo says. 'This is Theo we are talking about.'

'But she is crazy about him . . .'

'How can you be sure? I mean, you only met them together once. She might be like your friend, Antonella: all show but not much heart.'

'That's a bit of a mean thing to say,' Valentina defends her friend. 'You make her sound shallow.'

'Valentina,' Leonardo continues, 'you have to find out how Theo feels about you; more importantly, you have to let him know how you feel. Once and for all, tell him you love him.'

'Even though he is going out with someone else? Isn't that a bitchy thing to do to another woman?'

'That depends.'

'On what?'

'On whether you can live without him. If not, you have to fight for him, baby. Win him back.'

'Oh, Leonardo,' Valentina sighs. 'I'm not sure. Maybe I should just come home – just continue the way things were.'

'You were miserable, Valentina. Even all my sexual attentions couldn't cheer you up.'

She closes her eyes, reliving the moment she saw Theo and how charged she had felt afterwards. She opens her eyes again, staring out of the window at the swaying trees in the park. 'I miss you, Leonardo. I wish you were here.'

'Believe me, so do I.'

She hears desperation in his voice and she wonders what 'stuff' is going on in his life. She knows he won't tell her over the phone.

'I wish we were in bed right now and you were consoling me,' she says softly.

'I could console you over the phone.'

'Are you going to talk dirty to me, Signor Sorrentino?'

She hears the ticking of a silent line, and then Leonardo speaks again, but this time his voice has changed. This time it is Leonardo the dominator who is speaking to her. Her skin tingles with excitement as she closes her eyes and imagines his hard, dark eyes pinning her down.

'What are you wearing, Valentina?'

'My dressing gown.'

'The blue one?'

'Yes.'

'And what else?'

'Nothing.'

'Are you completely naked?'

'Yes.'

'I want you to open up your dressing gown; I want to caress your breasts with your hands; pull on your nipples, feel them hardening. Now open up your legs.'

'Yes,' she whispers. 'I'm doing it.'

'Close your eyes and put your hand between your legs; stroke yourself, Valentina.'

She pushes her hand between her legs and spreads her fingers. She can feel her warmth, her need sensitising her fingertips.

'It is me touching you, Valentina; can you feel me?'

'Oh, yes.'

And he is with her, her friend, on Isabella's couch, stroking her with his fine long fingers, soothing away her distress, her pain at seeing the love of her life with another woman.

'Push your finger right up inside yourself, V. That's me inside you, fucking you, making you feel me, right up into your tip.'

In the unlit living room of Antonella's aunt, Valentina spreads her legs before the rustling city park opposite. She doesn't care who sees her and her need, her ecstasy. She spins her fingers inside herself, increasing the pace, pushing herself further and further. One moment it is Leonardo beside her, and the next she sees Theo's face, his enchanting smile, his eyes looking deep into hers. Yes, she believes he does still love her, but she can't understand why he is with Anita. As she comes, she doubles over, spent and shivering. Anita had called herself Theo's girlfriend, so he had found a girl not afraid of commitment. Was fate punishing Valentina? Is this what she deserves after the way she has treated him in the past? Theo is too good for her, she tries to convince herself; she should leave him alone in peace with someone sweet and giving, like Anita. And yet a fire is burning deep down in the pit of Valentina's belly, and she knows it will burn all reason out of her. She wants him back.

Six hours later, Antonella and Valentina are drinking coffee. They are still sleepy-eyed, with Antonella nursing a hang-over.

'I don't know how Aunty Isa managed to get up for work this morning,' Antonella groans.

'Here.' Valentina throws over a packet of ibuprofen. 'Take a couple of those; you'll be fine.'

'So, how was it at the gallery?' Antonella asks her, as she pops two tablets out of their silver foil and into the palm of her hand.

Valentina can't face going into the details. She is sure that Antonella would be fascinated to hear about Anita's private dance, although not so thrilled to learn about Theo's reappearance in her life. 'OK,' she says. 'The show looks good. There are two pictures of you and Mikhail being exhibited.'

'Great; I can't wait to see it.' Antonella gets up, pours a glass of water and knocks back the tablets. She sits down at the table and takes another swig of her coffee. 'These pills had better work. I feel terrible.'

'You were both very drunk, and shouting at each other.' Valentina refills her coffee cup.

'That's what happens when my family get together; we're a rowdy lot.'

Valentina watches her friend; she looks tired and vulnerable. Without her make-up on, Antonella seems so much younger than her twenty-eight years. She is usually so upbeat and positive, yet today her eyes are sad and heavy.

'What exactly was the dispute over?' Valentina asks her gently.

'Aunty Isabella was trying to justify the fact that my father walked out on us when I was a child . . .'

Valentina frowns with annoyance. This is one thing that unites her and Antonella: they were both abandoned by their fathers when they were little. Although Antonella has seen her father a couple of times, his contact has been intermittent. After he left Antonella's mother, he went to live in Argentina. 'So what justification is there?' Valentina says, her voice hardening with irritation at Antonella's aunt.

'She says that he did the right thing because there was such disharmony in our home. My parents were always shouting at each other.' Antonella tugs her hand through her tangled red hair. 'She claims that it's better not to have had contact with my father than to have experienced my parents at each other's throats my whole life . . .'

'Were they really that bad?'

'I don't remember, Valentina. I was too little.' Antonella offers her hands up to heaven. 'And, you know, OK, I said that maybe she was right – they should have broken up . . . But to go off to Argentina . . . ? To walk out on us all like that . . . ? I said there was no excuse. But she claims that my mother's new husband, my stepfather, wanted him out of the picture.'

'Do you think that's true, Antonella?' Valentina leans forward, and Antonella drops her arms and looks at her forlornly.

'I don't know. I never heard that before.' She looks troubled. 'I've never got on with my stepfather, but then I don't think he would have actually stood in the way of my father seeing us.'

'Well, there are two sides to every story,' Valentina says evenly. She has met Antonella's stepfather and she dislikes him intensely. He is always ogling her.

Antonella shakes herself as if she is waking herself up. She helps herself to more coffee and nibbles on the end of a piece of cold toast. 'So, why did your father leave, Valentina? Why have you never seen him in all these years?'

'I don't know. I've no idea.' Valentina hastily brings the subject back to Antonella's father. 'At least you've visited your father in Argentina. You know him now.'

'Yeah, but he may as well be a stranger.'

Valentina leans forward again. She has a sudden urge to confide in Antonella, despite the fact she is notoriously indiscreet. 'I found something out recently,' she says, pausing before continuing. 'My father lives in London.'

Antonella's jaw drops open. '*Mamma mia*! That's very exciting. Are you going to see him?'

'I don't know . . . I mean, like you say, we're strangers. Is there any point?'

'Come on; this is you. Remember Theo used to call you "Intrepid Valentina"?'

Valentina winces at the mention of Theo's nickname for her.

'Of course you are going to go and see your father. Where does he live?'

'Near the Finchley Road. That's North London, isn't it?' She takes a breath and she can taste the bitterness of her anger. Antonella is right; why should she be bashful? She is a grown woman, nearly thirty years old. She deserves some answers now.

'You're right, Toni. I want to know why he never visited, nor wrote, nor took any interest in my life at all. I don't understand it.'

Antonella reaches forward and grips her hand. It seems that her hangover has made her more maudlin than usual, for Valentina can see tears sprouting in her friend's eyes. 'I think our fathers are men who are able to compartmentalise their lives,' Antonella says. 'And I guess we, as their daughters, were boxed up and put away on the forgotten-about shelf.'

'Do you really believe that our fathers never thought about us? At all?'

'Yes, I do. How else could they live with it? We are fatherless women, Valentina.' Antonella pulls her hand away and wipes her eyes. To Valentina's surprise, her friend's face breaks into a big smile. 'And, you know what? That's OK, because there is nothing – and I mean *nothing* – worse than a Daddy's girl.'

Valentina nods in agreement. It is one of the few things that irritate her about her old schoolfriend, Gaby: the way she demands things from her father; and her Daddy always comes running to rescue her if she is short of money, or needs something done in her flat. Valentina and Antonella are the same: they have to put up their own shelves.

Antonella's smile fades and she groans.

'Are you OK?' Valentina asks.

Her friend stands up, holding her head as if it is a delicate object. 'I'm sorry, Valentina, I'm really suffering here. I have to go back to bed. I'm just not able to go shopping today. Do you mind going out without me?' She laughs lamely. 'Besides, you can go to that fusty old museum if I'm out of action. I just know you're dying to.'

Valentina sits in the café in the old Tate Gallery. She has already spent the morning trailing around the British Museum, trying to study the mummies in the Egyptian rooms, but she has been impossibly distracted by the events of the previous evening. Several times, she took out her phone and thought about ringing Theo. But what should she say? In the end, much to her delight, she didn't need to call him, for he called her. Was she free for a quick coffee? Any chance she was near the Tate Britain, down on Millbank? She didn't even consider being coy, and immediately agreed to meet him, racing across London from Russell Square to Green Park on the Piccadilly line, and then changing to the Victoria line to take her down to Pimlico. She is only in London for a few days and she is not going to turn down any opportunity to see Theo again. Besides, she tries to convince herself that maybe they could become friends. Could she be happy with just that?

Valentina orders Earl Grey tea and scones. She slathers raspberry jam on to her scone and takes a tiny bite out of it. She is hungry and yet she is so nervous that eating is hard. She glances at her watch again. He is five minutes late. She feels guilty every time she thinks of Anita, yet she is only meeting Theo for a chat. Isn't she? It is broad daylight, after all.

'Valentina?'

She jumps up, bumping the little table and knocking her teacup over, so that her scone is covered in milky tea. How did he manage to creep up on her like that?

'Don't worry,' Theo says, smiling at her, the expression in his eyes so warming that her legs begin to buckle. 'I'll get you another one.'

When he returns with their drinks, he takes the chair opposite her at the tiny café table. She can feel his knees knocking against hers. She focuses on his forget-me-not blue shirt. She dare not trust herself to look into his eyes again. Not yet.

'So, how are you?' Theo asks.

'Good,' she mumbles, suddenly unable to find the right

words to express herself. She has to speak openly this afternoon. She can't let him walk away today thinking that she doesn't care about him, and yet the words have dried up in her throat.

'And life in Milan? I hear you're still hanging out with Leonardo; having fun?'

She looks up at him, the torture in her eyes silences his teasing.

'Valentina?' he asks gently.

'Yes?' She leans forward and she can smell his Bulgari. Its aroma fills her with nostalgia. She is glad that he hasn't changed his cologne. He might have a new woman but he still smells the same.

'Did you know about my involvement with Anita Chappell before you came to London?' He looks surprisingly serious. 'Is that why you decided to exhibit at the Lexington?' he asks her, studying her face carefully.

'I had no idea about you and her!' she tells him, feeling a little annoyed at his implication. One thing she is not is a stalker. 'I was just as shocked to see you there, in the gallery.'

He looks thoughtful for a moment, picks up his teaspoon and helps himself to sugar, slowly stirring it into his cup. 'It seems to be the most incredible coincidence,' he comments. 'Seeing you again has really thrown me.'

His words are so direct and honest. Her heart does a little leap of hope. She struggles to remain composed. After all, hadn't the idea of London been to reinvent herself? To move on from Theo? And yet, as soon as Leonardo gave it to her, she had stored Theo's number in her phone. She really can't say what her intentions had been once she got to London. She never expected to actually run into him, and so soon. All she does know is how she feels, right now in this moment.

'I've missed you, Theo,' Valentina tells him.

He looks at her and beneath his smile she can see his hurt. He rouses himself, leaning down and opening his briefcase. 'The reason I called you is because I have something you might be interested in,' he tells her, hastily steering them away from her admission.

'Oh,' she says, a little disappointed that he wasn't ringing her purely to see her and for no other reason.

'I recently came across an old dance movie from the late forties. Anita has a stack of old burlesque acts and modern dances on film.'

Valentina tenses at the mention of her rival's name.

'Your grandmother's maiden name was Maria Brzezinska, wasn't it? And she was a dancer, right?'

'Well, the name is right. But I don't think she was a dancer.'

'But she could have been?'

'I suppose, though my mother never mentioned it to me. I don't think she had any kind of creative career – just stayed at home and looked after the family.'

'Did you know your grandmother?'

'No; she died before I was born, in a plane crash.'

Theo hands Valentina a DVD. Their hands brush and she

can feel the hairs on the back of her neck tingling in reaction to his touch.

'You have to look at this, Valentina. It's amazing for its time. A contemporary ballet, choreographed by Kurt Jooss, called *Pandora*. I believe it's your maternal grandmother dancing the role of Psyche. It was filmed in London in nineteen forty-eight.'

Valentina shakes her head. 'Oh, it can't be her, Theo. She never left Italy her whole life, apart from when they got on the plane to the States . . . and never came home. Really tragic.'

Valentina wonders how losing her parents in such a dramatic way affected her mother. Tina Rosselli rarely mentions them, and never talks about their deaths.

'But it says her name on the credits at the beginning of the film,' Theo insists. 'And, Valentina, when I watched it . . . Well, I know it's in black and white and very old, but I could still see a family resemblance. I think it really could be your grandmother.'

'It just seems like too much of a coincidence: first, the two of us meeting like that yesterday, and then this film. It's as if we are connected . . .' Valentina ventures.

'Maybe fate is conspiring to bring us together?'

Hope begins to bud again within her heart at his words.

'Do you really think so?'

Theo laughs, and she can't help but feel a little crushed by his reaction.

'I don't believe in fate, Valentina.' He leans back in his chair and surveys her. 'It's not so strange about the dance film. There were hardly any modern ballets filmed at that time in London. Anita has an extensive collection of old dance movies, so, if your grandmother was a dancer and was filmed in nineteen forty-eight, it is highly likely Anita would have it in her collection.'

Valentina slips the DVD into her bag, looking away from him. She feels exposed and unsure of herself in his presence.

'Thank you for this,' she says. 'For ringing me up and giving it to me.' The formality of their conversation sounds strange to her. 'I'll check it out; maybe you're right; although I find it odd that my mother never told me her own mother was a dancer.'

'I'm glad I could give it to you in person,' Theo says, his voice softer, kinder now.

Neither of them speaks for a moment. Their teacups are empty and yet Valentina doesn't want to say goodbye – not yet.

'So what are you doing in London?' she asks him. 'Are you still chasing lost art?'

She remembers Theo's revelation to her in Venice of the promise he had made to his Dutch grandfather to fulfill the dying man's lifelong quest. With unerring dedication Theo had attempted to track down all the valuable paintings that his grandfather, en employee of Albert Goldstein's gallery in Amsterdam, had lost to the Nazis during World War Two, and return them to their rightful owners.

Theo shakes his head; a strand of dark hair falls across his forehead and she struggles not to lean forward and brush it away.

'I'm nearly done with all of that,' he explains. 'Well, just one more picture to return and that's it, thank God; Glen is driving me mad. Remember him? The rather nasty art thief you came across in Venice.'

'I don't think I could ever forget him,' she says, thinking of Theo's sinister rival.

'I'm sorry he frightened you, Valentina,' Theo says, softly.

'You should be careful of him.' Every time Valentina thinks of that awful man, Glen, she feels sick. There was something about him that terrified her. And she is not a woman who is easily scared.

'He's no real threat, just very irritating,' Theo replies confidently. 'Soon enough I'll be out of his hair and he can get on with persuading little old ladies and men to part with massive sums of money in return for bringing back their art from the stolen Nazi hoard.'

'So, what's the last painting you have to return?'

'Actually, it's in your genre: an erotic drawing by the French artist, André Masson. It's in a private collection here in London.'

'And I suppose Glen is after the same picture?'

It is easier for Valentina to talk to Theo about the missing pictures. They are on neutral territory, one that doesn't involve their emotions.

'Yes, of course he is. It originally belonged to an Italian Jew, Guilio Borghetti. He managed to survive the war, although he is dead now. It is his son who is looking for it, and Glen, of course, has promised he will return it to him for the princely sum of 450,000 euros. Not as much as the Metsu, but still a large amount of money for such a small drawing.'

'And it is definitely one of the pictures that were part of Albert Goldstein's collection? Could you not just let Glen get it back and leave it be?'

'Absolutely, it is one of those pictures. And you know I made a promise to return every single one of them,' Theo says with determination.

'I know,' she nods, impetuously reaching out for his hand. She clasps it in hers for a moment, feeling the warmth of him pass into her body, right up to her heart.

'The Masson is such an obscure work and has changed hands so many times that it has taken me years to track it down. Borghetti left the drawing with poor old Albert Goldstein for safe keeping and, subsequently, with my grandfather, in Amsterdam, when Goldstein fled the Nazis during the war. Well, of course, you know what happened next. My grandfather was persuaded to part with all that art by the Hermann Göring Division.'

'So where is it now?' Valentina asks. 'Maybe we can join forces and I can help you get it back.'

Theo looks surprised by her offer. 'I would have liked that, really . . .' He hesitates, looks uncomfortable. 'But I can't involve you now. I've already got my plan in action and I'm sort of close to getting it back. It's a rather delicate matter.'

'Right . . . Sure . . .' Valentina looks down at the table, moving her hand away from his, unable to conceal her disappointment. For a second, she had forgotten their circumstances. They are not together anymore. Theo has a new girlfriend. She has to stop thinking about him.

She traces the outline of her cup with her finger, still not looking up. 'So, how long have you and Anita been together?' she asks.

'It's not what you think, Valentina,' Theo says.

She looks up at him questioningly. 'Well, what is it then?' she asks, softly.

'I really wish I could explain.' He hesitates. 'Can I just ask you to trust me?'

'What do you mean? Trust you about what?'

'At the moment, Anita and I are seeing each other. Yes, that is true, but . . .' He stops speaking, as if he can't find the right words.

'But what?' she eggs him on.

'Well, the way things ended with us, I'm not sure what to think about you anymore, Valentina.'

Valentina thinks back to last autumn in Venice, and her devastation after Theo left. 'Why did you run away in Venice?' she suddenly confronts him. 'You were gone, just like that . . . You didn't give me a chance . . .'

Theo puts his head on one side and looks at her. 'I really tried, Valentina; you know that . . . I couldn't take any more.'

She looks into his eyes and she is sure she can see a hint of his love for her within their blue seas. 'I'm sorry,' she whispers.

Theo leans forward and puts his hand over hers. He squeezes it. And, in that simple gesture, she feels his love for her.

'Theo,' Valentina says, looking directly into his eyes, holding his gaze and fighting the terror that rages inside her heart. She can say this. She *must*. 'Theo, is there any chance that we might get back together again?'

The words are out. It is as if a weight has been lifted from her shoulders. She wants to laugh out loud and cry with relief. She watches for Theo's reaction.

'Valentina, you know that I can't go back to the way things were.'

'I know, I know,' she nods. 'It would be different, I promise . . .'

Theo sighs and puts his head in his hands. 'God; talk about bad timing,' he mutters.

She can't understand it. Why is he so reluctant to admit how he feels now, when he has always been so open with her? She is sure her instincts aren't fooling her. She can feel the natural synergy between them – how right it is to be together. Only a few more words, a few more steps and they could be back together again. And yet, what Theo says to her next is not what she wants to hear.

'Valentina, I really can't break up with Anita . . . Not right now.'

'Theo,' she beseeches, realising how corny she sounds, how her mother would mock her, but she doesn't care because she knows that if she lets Theo leave this café now, without him really knowing how much he means to her, she will fall apart. 'I need you,' she says. 'In my life, I need your non-judgemental presence. You are my sanctuary.'

'Why is it always about you?' Theo snaps.

His words hurt. She sits back, stung. The old Valentina would have walked out, pride in tact.

'I'm sorry, Valentina; that was too harsh. I didn't mean it,' Theo says, looking more hassled than she has ever seen him. 'I know this is confusing, but you have to trust me. I can't break up with Anita at the moment.'

'Do you love her?'

Anita is everything Valentina isn't: girly, demonstrative, overtly sexy. She is not afraid to call herself Theo's girlfriend.

'Valentina!' Theo exclaims in frustration. 'That is not the issue,' he continues. 'I need to know, I have always needed to know if you trust me, if you love me.'

His words confuse her. If he needs to know these things, then why is he going out with Anita?

'It's hard for me to say those words . . . but I can show you how I feel,' she says. For the first time, Valentina feels tearful. She looks away, determined not to cry. She cannot let him see her cry.

Theo's hand is on her shoulder, and it sends a volt through her body. 'Please, just wait, Valentina.'

'I can't –' her voice cracks – 'bear to see you with her.'

She stands up suddenly, pulling her bag on to her shoulder. Theo stands up as well. They are only inches away from each other. She wants to fling herself into his arms, beg him to take her back, and yet, of course, she will do no such thing. He has made it clear. She has to prove herself to him and, until she does, he will not break up with Anita.

They wind their way through the café and into the gallery. They walk through corridor after corridor, not speaking, not holding hands, until they are standing in front of a watercolour painting by William Blake called *Pity*. She looks at the painting and the image before her pierces her heart. A woman is lying on the ground, her head flung back, as if she is dying. Above her, a beautiful young man rides a grey horse in the sky; in his hands, he is lifting a newborn baby. It is *her* baby. Valentina is not sure what the artist means by this picture, but it cuts her, makes her feel that what she and Theo have been through in the past may never be healed.

She is about to walk away, but Theo grabs her arm and pulls her towards him. He hugs her tightly and she inhales deeply. Oh, the sweet torture of being held in his arms!

'I do love you, Valentina,' he whispers in her ear. 'But do you love me?'

She steps back, looking up at him. Oh, she wants him so badly. She is struggling to say those three precious words. She wants him; she needs him. He is the only person in the world who understands the depths of her loss.

'Valentina?' Theo asks her again.

'I . . . I . . .' she stutters.

He closes his eyes and breathes in deeply. 'It's OK,' he says, interrupting her. 'I know this is all a bit overwhelming . . . to see each other again, and you must be confused about Anita. Let's just leave it for the moment.'

But could they not go somewhere right now? Valentina wishes. She could prove her love for him in some anonymous bed in a hotel room, like she used to do. She knows she can do that. She is sure she will blow his mind. And yet, she says nothing. She realises her fear of commitment is still as fresh and raw as she left it back in Venice all those months ago when he walked out on her.

Theo begins to walk away, towards the entrance of the Tate. She is frozen to the spot, shocked by her inability to win him back. This meeting did not go as she had secretly hoped. No emotional reunion; no racing to a hotel and making delirious love. She wants him so badly. Just sitting across that tiny café table from him was turning her on. She is vibrating with need. She has to calm down.

She takes a deep breath. She won't follow him. He is not willing to break up with Anita until she shows him her love. For now, she has to let him go.

She wanders through the rooms of the gallery. She feels the DVD in her bag, banging against her leg as she walks. She doesn't know much about her grandmother. Her mother had described Maria Rosselli as shy and reclusive – a complete contradiction to her extrovert daughter. She had been a devoted mother and wife. Yet now it seems that there was a secret side to her grandmother. Could this really be footage of her dancing a new ballet? Something revolutionary and different, as Theo had said? She is intrigued to discover this new version of her ancestor.

Walking without thought or direction, Valentina finds herself looking at one of her favourite Pre-Raphaelite paintings, *Lilith* by Rosetti. Something about Lady Lilith reminds her of Anita: her deep gold tresses, her milky skin, full breasts and sculpted features; her dark eyebrows and rose-red lips. Yet, most of all, it is the look in her eyes as she gazes at herself in the mirror: a knowledge of her power and beauty as a woman, and a certain detachment. Valentina saw that expression on the burlesque dancer's face as she danced for her and Kirsti Shaw yesterday. She can understand why Anita is so irresistible to both men and women. It is clear that Theo is not willing to let her go, not yet. Somehow, Valentina has to show him how much she loves him. Words are obviously not enough now. She bites back her disappointment at not winning him over today and tries to have faith in her intuition, for she feels, deep down, that she will get Theo back. She just has to work out how.

$\mathcal{M}$aria

THE WEEKS PASS, YET, NO MATTER HOW MANY TIMES she lingers on the second floor landing, Maria never bumps into Felix. They must keep different hours. She rises early for class every morning and isn't home until half past five or six. It could be that he leaves the house after her and, by the time he comes home, she is in bed, wiped out from her day at dance school. She spends most of her time at weekends with Jacqueline. On a Saturday, they are up and out early, taking it in turns to stand in the tripe queue at the butchers, or trying to get hold of some other staples such as bread or tea. On Sundays they go to Mass at Westminster Cathedral, the majestic basilica still baring the scars of bomb damage. Within its walls, Maria struggles to pray. She asks God to help her put from her mind the dark Frenchman who saved her from being raped, and that He guide her back to being the girl she was before she met him – a girl dedicated to dance.

It is Jacqueline who inadvertently explains why Maria

hasn't seen Felix. They are preparing dinner one evening and Jacqueline is struggling to open a tin of spam with her tin opener.

'*Merde*; it is useless – blunt,' she says. 'Be a good girl and run down to Guido and ask him if you can borrow his tin opener.'

Rather than call on the Italian, Maria sees her chance to knock on Felix's door. 'And what if he isn't in? Should I go to Monsieur Leduc's door?'

'Oh, no,' Jacqueline says, filling a saucepan with water, her back to Maria. 'He is away making one of his films in France. Besides, he is a bad-tempered so-and-so; I wouldn't want to ask him for anything!'

Maria ignores Jacqueline's description of Felix. She *knows* how good he is. Instead, she feels a thrill of excitement. Her dream man is a film director! She can hardly think of a more glamorous profession.

'He makes films?'

'Well, yes, but I think they are not very popular. I have never seen one. Guido told me they are quite strange. "Surrealist," he said.'

'What is Monsieur Leduc like? Surely he is not so bad tempered all the time?' Maria sidles up to Jacqueline, desperate to know more about her mysterious knight in shining armour, yet not wanting Jacqueline to know why.

'Have you not met him yet?' Jacqueline glances at her, before turning her attention back to scrubbing the potatoes.

'No. He's French, yes?'

'From Paris, I believe, although he lived in Lyon during the occupation, but I don't really speak with him.' Jacqueline pauses, chewing her lips. 'Even if he were in, I wouldn't want to ask to borrow anything from him.'

'But you are both French; surely you have so much in common?'

'Not really, my dear. I think that our French heritage has caused both of us considerable suffering. It is not something we want to share together.' She begins to chop up the potatoes, tossing them into the saucepan beside her. 'Although I dare say his experience of the war was very different from mine. But really I don't want to know. I don't want to be reminded of the past.'

She slams the lid on the pot vehemently and Maria is worried that she has made Jacqueline angry. But the next moment her mentor is smiling at her, giving her a little good-humoured wink. 'I don't think a pretty young girl like you should be bothering with thinking about someone like him. Now, run along and get the tin opener from your much-more-suitable admirer.'

Maria is always reluctant to call on Guido. She finds her compatriot irritating. He has taken to coming, uninvited, for dinner several times a week, each time bearing gifts for Jacqueline, such as a treasured jar of strawberry jam or a freshly baked loaf of bread, to sweeten her up. For the entire duration of the meal, he stares, moon-faced, at Maria, hardly a word passing his lips. It embarrasses her, especially now that Jacqueline has noticed and delights in teasing her. After he has sloped off back to his room, Jacqueline tells her that she is Guido's goddess and she should put the poor boy out of his misery and go out dancing with him. But Maria is adamant that she is too busy with her studies and needs her rest. She hasn't been out since that last time with Joan.

Jacqueline nods with approval, patting her on the shoulder and praising her. 'Your mother would be proud of you,' she often says.

When Maria thinks of her mother and Pina, she feels sick, she misses them so much. She tries her best not to think of them, or of Venice. How much she misses the water! She has walked down by the river in London – all along the banks of the Thames, from bomb-ravaged Westminster to the steps of the majestic Saint Paul's. But it is not the same as walking alongside the jade canals of Venice. She stares at the brown surge of the Thames, preferring to look away from the gaping holes in the city, although she can see that London is fervent with its rebuilding work, especially with the Olympics being held here this year. But her favourite place to walk is Battersea Park, where there is now an open-air exhibition of sculpture. It is not too far from Jacqueline's house. She likes to circle the little pond, looking at the ducks splattering in the water – they seem so comic to Maria – or else, if she's feeling more studious, she will contemplate one of the impressive sculptures.

Maria's claim that she is too busy with her dance studies to go out is not, in fact, a lie. Lempert is putting them through their paces. Even Joan's social life seems to have calmed down in response. The day after her assault by the Englishman, Douglas, Maria had been terrified that Joan wouldn't turn up for class. Were Douglas and Ralph in league? Would she read of her friend's rape and murder in the newspapers? Her relief nearly made her legs buckle when she saw Joan in class – granted, with very black shadows under her eyes and stinking of drink. That morning, Lempert had worked them particularly hard – as if he knew they had been out late the night before and this was their punishment.

He was already casting for the end-of-term ballet, *Pandora*, one of Kurt Jooss's revolutionary choreographies, and, despite the fact Maria felt she was not nearly good enough to dance in public, Lempert included her in his auditions.

He made the students leap across the floor of the studio, again and again and again – for much longer than usual. Usually, Maria felt effortlessly buoyant, as light as the air around her. She knew she could leap high, but that day she was no longer unencumbered and her body was weighed down by the memory of the attack on her the night before. Joan was in an even worse state: sweat coursed down her face, causing her make-up to streak.

'I feel a hundred years old,' she whispered to Maria.

'Did you get home all right?'

'Sure I did,' Joan said. 'Why do you ask?'

Maria shook her head. 'I'll tell you later.'

Joan suddenly looked worried, and grabbed her arm. 'Nothing bad happened, did it? Are you OK?'

Maria nodded. 'I'm fine—'

Lempert cornered them. 'Ladies! This is no time to be having a conversation. I want to see you moving, please.'

'Slave driver,' Joan hissed under her breath as she took off, bounding across the studio.

It was only after class that they were able to catch up properly. Instead of taking the bus, Joan suggested they walk together, it being such a fine day. As they strode down Kennington Road, Joan opened up her bag and triumphantly brandished a can of condensed milk.

'Fancy some?' she asked Maria. 'I've come prepared.' She took a can opener out of her bag and pierced the lid of the tin, offering it to Maria first. She drank from the can. The milk was warm, but it was also sweet and gave her some energy.

As they walked, Joan told Maria all about Ralph and what fun they had had. 'I brought him back to my bedsit – snuck him in. My landlady is a dozy cow, anyway,' she said, giving Maria a cheeky grin. 'Oh, it was just wonderful, Maria. It really helped me forget about Stan.'

'Did you actually sleep with him?' Maria looked at her friend in awe.

Joan cocked her head on one side. 'Are you shocked? Do you think I'm cheap?'

'No . . . it's just you hardly knew him.'

'Oh, I knew the measure of him,' she said, looking gleeful. 'I knew he was a good-time boy, nothing serious. And that suits me fine.'

'Don't you want to meet someone special?' Maria asked her friend.

'Of course I do,' Joan said. 'But I am not going to live like a nun until I do!'

They passed Lambeth North station and turned on to Westminster Bridge Road.

'So, what about you? Douglas jumped up and ran after you when you left. He seemed very keen.'

Maria stopped walking and squeezed her eyes shut. She didn't want to remember that odious man and what he tried to do to her, and yet that was the beginning of the story of how she met Felix.

'What is it? My God, Maria, you look as white as a ghost,' Joan said, the smile wiped off her face. 'What happened?'

Maria opened her eyes, looked straight ahead and continued to walk. 'He attacked me, Joan . . .'

'What? Oh, my goodness . . . Did he hurt you?'

'No; someone rescued me before he actually . . .' Maria couldn't say it.

'Who? What happened? Oh, Maria, I'm so sorry. I should have gone home with you.' Joan wrung her hands, looking contrite. 'I didn't know him at all,' she continued. 'I don't think he is even a friend of Ralph's. He was just sitting at the table with him.'

'I'm all right; it's OK . . . He didn't hurt me.'

'If I ever see him again . . .' Joan's cheeks were red with fury, but Maria cut her short.

'Someone rescued me.'

She had felt a bubble of excitement at the memory of what had happened next: Felix Leduc turning up in the nick of time and saving her.

'What? Who?'

'This man . . . This beautiful man . . .'

Joan's pained face broke into a smile. 'A real knight in shining armour?'

'Yes. And, Joan, it is quite amazing. He lives in our house. He's my neighbour!'

'Well, who is he? Tell me! Spill the beans!'

'I don't know much about him, really, apart from the fact that he is French. His name is Felix Leduc and he lives on the second floor, in the flat right below ours.'

'How romantic,' Joan sighed. 'So he can hear you walking around above him. He can imagine you in your little white virginal nightie.'

Maria blushed. 'Oh, do stop it, Joan!' She clutched her bag to her chest. She didn't want to sully any of her ideas about Felix. 'Really, I have never seen such a man . . . I think I fell in love with him right on the spot.'

Joan looked confused. 'Are you telling me it was love at first sight?'

Maria nodded, her eyes shining.

'Well, he must be something special if he has made you forget all about that disgusting Douglas. My God, if I *ever* see him again—'

'Please, Joan, let's not ever mention it. I've told no one. Promise me?'

'All right, as long as you tell me everything about Felix.' Joan gave her a nudge.

'Well, that's it and I don't know when I will see him next . . .' Maria told her.

'You live in the same house. It's only a matter of time.'

Yet that had been over a month ago and, every day, when Joan had quizzed Maria about whether she had met Felix again, she had told her 'no'. Now her friend has lost interest, completely taken over with working on the *Pandora* ballet, since Lempert has cast her in the title role. Maria feels honoured just to be in one of the chorus groups.

Joan has taken to spending extra hours after school rehearsing a particularly challenging duet with Louis, who plays the character of the Go-Getter, so Maria has had to walk down Kennington Road on her own every day, left to her own thoughts. Her imagination is plagued with images of Felix. She tries not to, but she can't help constructing a whole catalogue of fantasies.

In her first dream, she and Felix travel to Paris together. They are sitting in one of those arty cafés alongside Sartre and Simone de Beauvoir, Juliette Gréco and Anne-Marie Cazalis, drinking wine and intellectualising. She is dressed all in tight black clothes. She is so incredibly chic and sophisticated. In another fantasy, she is one of the dancers in the Moulin Rouge and Felix is watching her, sitting in the front row and looking up adoringly at her. Other fantasies involve them drifting down the Seine on a boat, kissing underneath the flying buttresses of Notre Dame, or strolling, hand in hand, by an organ grinder in Montmartre, against the backdrop of the Sacré Cœur.

As the weeks pass, she takes her fantasies further. She constructs a family background for Felix. She decides that he is an only child, like her. He grew up in a large apartment in the centre of Paris. His family is very wealthy, but they opposed the Nazis and fled Paris at the time of the occupation. In her head, Maria sees Felix as one of the brave Resistance members, sabotaging the Nazis, risking life and limb to liberate his country. She decides that, since he is so much older than her, he must have been in love once before, yet his true love was brutally murdered by the evil invaders, and Felix joined the Resistance to enact his revenge. He is a good man, but tortured by what he has seen in his native France during the war. That is why he appears bad tempered to people now. He needs a woman, a young fresh-eyed girl, to come into his life and heal him, for that is why he hides from the world in his flat in their house in London: he is waiting for a girl like her. That is why he makes his strange, surreal movies – to express all the horror that he has witnessed. But now they have met. And, just as he saved her from being raped, she will save him from his dark solitude. Maria becomes so wrapped up in her fantasies of Felix that, as the weeks pass, she begins – almost – to not want to meet him again. What if he is different from her dream man? Yet, what if he is the same? What then? In the real world, can she live her dream love?

Maria doesn't understand Joan and her casual attitude to the sexual act. But she doesn't judge her, either. She is truly fond of her friend and her open, warm manner – so different from most of the other girls in the dance school, who are stand-offish and competitive. Yet she can't help wishing that Joan respected herself a little more. She has read it in magazines: if you are too easy, no man will ever want to marry you. And isn't that what Joan wants, at the end of the day? To be a wife, have babies, settle down? Isn't that what every single girl wants?

Maria has been raised amongst women. All men, including her father, have been figments of her imagination. Despite her liberal upbringing, the daughter of two women in love, Maria secretly wants to be one man's princess. She wants a summer wedding; she wants the happy ever after.

It is mid-summer. London is warming up. It is nowhere near as hot as it can get in Venice, but, even so, Maria makes two summer dresses out of fabric her mother has sent over from

Italy. Jacqueline and she have pored over pictures of Christian Dior's 'New Look' in *Harper's Bazaar*. Clothes rationing still restricts them in London, so her mother's package of materials made both of them cry, as if they had been sent the crown jewels. How on earth had Belle found such beautiful textiles in Italy?

Maria is a talented seamstress, taught by Pina to sew when she was a little girl. She promises Jacqueline that they will both be 'New Look' girls before the summer is out. How well Belle knows her colouring! With her dark, curly hair, pale skin and blue eyes, Maria looks best in jewel colours. And so Maria makes two dresses for herself, but, instead of the pastels favoured by other girls, she makes one in ruby red, with the Dior fuller skirt, and one – a little more girly – in sapphire blue with tiny pink buds, a pleat and tuck on the back of the skirt to accentuate her bottom, and a bolero jacket to emphasise her waist.

Wearing her new summer dresses, Maria feels a spring in her step, and knows by the admiring glances of the Londoners that she looks good. Her English has improved immensely and she is really beginning to feel like she fits in here. Now that the Olympics are almost upon them, there is a festive feeling in the city: an excitement and pride.

In dance school they have been rehearsing *Pandora* relentlessly. Today in class, Joan collapsed, sobbing on the floor of the studio after Lempert had made her repeat the same phrase what seemed to be a hundred times. Maria is glad she is only part of the chorus. She wouldn't be able to cope with such pressure at the moment. Yet, although Lempert is a hard taskmaster, there is something about him that makes you want to do your best for him. You want to work hard. You want to shine and do this provocative ballet justice.

It has now been two months since Felix rescued her and, for Maria, he has become a fictional character. She has lost hope that she will ever see him again.

It is a Friday, and the girls are packing up their dance things after life drawing class. Joan grabs Maria's sketchbook and flicks through it. 'Oh, these are great, Maria; you really are good at picking up each pose.'

'To be honest, Joan, I don't understand why we have to do life drawing when we are dancers.'

'It's about looking at the body, studying another dancer in a pose and seeing the line through them,' Joan says. 'Were you not listening to Lempert when he explained?'

'Yes, of course. I would just rather be dancing . . .'

The changing room has cleared and it is just the two of them left. Maria notices her friend is still in her black leotard and tights. 'Are you not coming with me?'

Joan sighs. 'No. I have to rehearse some more, with Louis.'

In these final few weeks before the show, Louis and Joan have been doing even more extra work on their duet in the evenings.

'OK. Well, don't overdo it.' Maria checks her face in her compact. 'See you on Monday.'

She is several streets away and in a shop buying cigarettes when she realises she has left her purse behind on the bench in the girls' changing rooms. She supposes that, since Joan and Louis are still at the studio rehearsing, the door will be open. She needs to get her money. She had all of her allowance for this month inside the purse, as well as her ration cards.

Maria walks briskly back up the street. She is in her blue dress with the pink flowers. She feels delicate in it, like an oriental bloom.

Sure enough, the front door of the dance school is still unlocked. She pushes it open and walks as quietly as she can down the corridor. She doesn't want to bump into Lempert, or disturb Joan and Louis. All the girls adore Louis. He is from the Caribbean, with such beautiful skin that Maria is constantly tempted to reach out and stroke him. He is built like a pure powerhouse. It is hard not to be bewitched by him when he is dancing. His synergy can be blinding. Joan had been nervous about her duet with him. He seems to be one of the few men that she has ever been tongue-tied around. Yet it appears to Maria that their partnership is going well. When they dance together, they look so good.

Maria rushes down the corridor, glancing at her watch. She has promised Jacqueline she will go to the butcher and get into the tripe queue before it is too late. She is hoping that her dress might inspire the butcher to give them something other than tripe – maybe a paltry chop or two. As she approaches the studio, she is surprised not to hear the pianist. Maybe he has gone home already. Passing the door, she hears a strange noise. She is not sure what it is but, without thinking, she pushes open the door. The studio is deserted, yet she can still hear the same sound: a cry, or something more like a mew. It is coming from the gallery above the piano. She slips off her shoes and tiptoes across the wooden floor. She is not really thinking about what she has heard; she is just curious. Maybe a cat is trapped inside the studio and needs to be let out? She climbs up the stairs and peers around the corner. What she sees makes her jaw drop.

Her friend, Joan, is lying on the table that, less than one hour ago, they were all sitting around and drawing at. She is lying on her back, facing Maria, but she cannot see her because tied around Joan's eyes are a pair of black dance stockings. Her bare legs are up in the air, so that she is an L shape, and, pressing against her, with his back to Maria, is Louis. Both of them are naked. Joan's skin is cream to Louis's rich colour. Maria cannot take her eyes off his buttocks. She has seen his body every day in his leotard, and yet, to see those buttocks naked and moving, thrusting forwards . . . Louis has Joan's little feet balanced on his shoulders and he has pulled her right to the edge of the table. He is pushing in and out of her, and the mewing is Joan herself, as he goes further and further.

Maria brings her hand to her mouth in shock. So this is it:

146

the sexual act. She has seen pictures of it, of course. She has imagined it, but never like this – never as primal, urgent and raw. She looks up at the back of Louis's head and hears him panting as he bangs his body harder and harder into her friend. What should she do? Should she stop them? Run away? Maria does neither. She crouches down at the top of the stairs and she watches. She cannot help it. She is an eighteen-year-old virgin in love with a fantasy man and she wants to see what this act is that Joan refers to all the time. She wants to see what pleasure is. She feels a mixture of emotions: shock, wonder, disgust and yet stronger than all of these is a throbbing between her legs, the way her limbs feel liquid and the strange palpitations deep within her.

Louis speeds up and their lovemaking becomes more ferocious. It is a dance – the first dance of all, Maria thinks, as she watches him cry out with one final thrust and then collapse on to the bare chest of her friend. Maria quickly ducks and slides down the stairs. Joan must never know she saw this. She slips out of the studio and runs to the changing room, quickly retrieving her purse from where it has fallen beneath the bench. It would be a disaster if she bumped into Joan – especially after she has seen her so exposed.

Back outside, she hurries down Kennington Road. All looks normal. It is just another sunny afternoon in London. The sunlight streaks her face as she rushes away, but she feels damp beneath her clothes and her breath is short. She realises there is a whole world that she is not part of. Do husbands

and wives make love like that? she wonders. Or is it just for
lovers – illicit love?

Afterwards, Maria always felt that what she witnessed that
day cracked the perfect mirage of her princess dream. It
changed her fate. She believed it was no coincidence that,
when she turned the corner of her street, carrying her parcel
of tripe in one hand, the powerful aroma of raw meat filling
her nostrils, its bloody smell mixing with the June roses in the
gardens she passed by, *he* would be walking towards her in
the other direction.

At exactly the same time, they reach the gate to number
eighteen. When he turns to look at her, he is just as he is in her
dreams: a tall, dark stranger, with brooding eyes and full lips
– a man straight out of one of the gothic novels Pina reads; a
man you cannot refuse. And so, before Felix even speaks,
Maria is his.

Valentina

AS SHE TURNS OFF THE FINCHLEY ROAD, INTO THE LEAFY street in Hampstead, the sun comes out, streaking the oily road with rainbows. Yet inside Valentina is feeling blacker and blacker. Her anger is gone. All she feels now is fear. What if he slams the door in her face? Can she really handle the cold reality of her father rejecting her? What with everything else going on in her life right now, why on earth is she putting herself through this?

Yet it is precisely her torment over Theo that has led her to find her father. After another restless night trying to figure out how she could prove her love to Theo, she has come to the conclusion that she still cannot completely trust him. He has asked her to trust him. He told her he loved her. Yet she can't work out why he is going to continue to see Anita. As the hours ticked by, and she listened to the soft snores of Antonella in the bed beside hers, Valentina realised that another twist of fate could not be ignored: the fact that she went to see Garelli

149

the very day she was leaving for London, only to discover that her long-lost father lived in London. Maybe here is the key to the puzzle of her own heart? If she can face her father, and her fear of him rejecting her, she might begin to trust Theo and ultimately win him back by showing him this. But she is still wavering. She wants Theo back, but she is afraid of exposing herself. She wishes Anita was off the scene and she had no competitor.

As the grey dawn began to seep through the gap in the curtains, Valentina got out of bed listless and on edge. She decided to distract herself by watching the old film footage of Maria Brzezinska dancing in the Ballets Jooss's *Pandora*. Despite the name of the dancer and fact that she did bear a striking resemblance to herself, Valentina just couldn't believe that she was her grandmother. This ethereal, creative spirit was at odds with the shy wife and mother she had heard of. In any pictures of her grandmother that she had seen, Valentina remembered a small, plump woman. There was nothing about her that suggested she was once this waiflike creature, flitting about the stage. Moreover, if it really was her grandmother, why did she never tell her daughter that she was a dancer? Why did she keep that part of her past secret? Valentina tried to follow the dance, but the footage was disjointed and then, all of sudden, stopped when the character that looked to be her grandmother was lifted into the air by one of the other dancers.

Valentina turned off the film footage and put aside her

laptop. She lay on her back on the couch. She wanted to wake Antonella and confide in her. She wanted to tell her about seeing Theo. Yet she knew that her friend would instruct her to forget about him, especially since he was going out with someone else. She may be promiscuous and adventurous, but Antonella is not into stealing men off other women, just as Valentina had thought she wasn't, either. And yet she can't quite believe that Theo is serious about Anita. Something has reached beyond her concern for the other woman's feelings. She knows it isn't a nice thing to want to break them up, but she can't help it.

Valentina's pace slows to crawl. She pulls the address Garelli wrote down for her out of her coat pocket and reads it again. She is only a few houses away. A man is walking towards her. Her stomach clenches and her palms feel sweaty. He looks to be in his sixties, tall, with thick grey hair and spectacles. It could be him. She is not certain how much he has changed since she was six. She walks towards him mechanically, her throat tight with fear. Just as he approaches her, she looks into his face. He has very dark skin and thick, bushy eyebrows. Close up he looks nothing like the old photographs she has of her father. She quickly glances away, embarrassed, her heart rate slowing with relief.

Now she is outside her father's house. It is a narrow, terraced house with sash windows and a small front garden. It is a miniature house, but looks well maintained – cared for. This handsome little house doesn't fit with the new image of her father, the wandering investigative journalist, the man who doesn't care about his own children . . . So how does he find it in his heart to care about a mere house?

She takes a deep breath and is just about to walk up the steps to the front door when something catches her eye. She sees a figure in the periphery of her vision; someone lurking behind her. She spins around and, to her utter shock, standing on the other side of the road and staring at her quite blatantly is none other than Theo's art thief rival, Glen. She takes in his height and his blond hair, shining like a gold crown in the sunlight. He looks like some kind of futuristic avenging angel. Despite it being a warm day, he is wearing a heavy long black coat. His hands are shoved in the pockets. He doesn't move, or walk away. She realises that he is standing there waiting for her. She wonders how long he has been following her. Could he have trailed her all the way here, to a place that is so personal?

Her emotions flip and now her terror at meeting her father turns to rage at this man for intruding in her life yet again. She marches across the road until she is right in front of him, yet he doesn't move to accommodate her and her heels are tipping off the edge of the kerb. He is so tall that she is forced to look up at him. She is glad she is wearing sunglasses so that the sun doesn't glare into her eyes, and she can look at him with the loathing she feels without him actually seeing it so blatantly.

'What are *you* doing here?'

'Hello, Valentina; how nice to see you again,' Glen says smoothly, in a crisp English accent. 'You are most welcome to my home city.'

'How dare you follow me? You stay away from me.' She is so angry that she points her finger in his face.

'My, my! You are in a bit of a temper, my dear,' he replies. In a flash, his hand springs out and he grabs her pointing finger, squeezing it tight.

Pain shoots down Valentina's hand and arm. 'Let go of me,' she hisses.

His eyes glitter. 'I must say,' he says evenly, still gripping her hand tightly so that she feels like her finger might snap off, 'I am so glad we have run into each other like this. It is so convenient.'

'What do you want?' she asks, twisting to get away from him. 'If you don't let go, I'm going to scream.'

He smiles and then drops her hand. 'I do apologise. I didn't mean to hurt you,' he says, in a way that makes Valentina feel that his intention was just that.

'Stay away from me,' she hisses. 'Otherwise I'll report you to the police.'

He crosses his arms. 'Well, now, we know, Valentina, that you and your boyfriend don't want to get the police involved in our affairs.'

'He's not my boyfriend.' She laughs, suddenly glad to have the upper hand. 'Theo and I are over – have been for months.'

Yet Glen shakes his head, looks down at her, all knowing.

'Oh, no. Anyone can see that you two belong together. You are one of the great love stories, my dear. I have every confidence that one day you will be wearing Theo's wedding band on that little finger there.'

He prods her sore hand and she thrusts it into her pocket defensively.

'You're wrong. He has a new girlfriend. Why don't you go and harass her?' She turns on her heel and starts to walk back down the street. She can't go and visit her father now – not with Glen stalking her. She can hear his footsteps behind her and, no matter how fast she walks, he keeps up. She feels anger coursing through her and she stops, spinning around. 'What do you want? What?'

He saunters up to her, so that his lips brush the tip of her head. She feels his breath on her forehead and she can smell him: that overwhelming male musky scent that had been so suffocating the first time she met him at Marco's party in Milan.

'You can give Theo a message from me,' he says, smiling at her, sweetly.

'Why don't you tell him yourself?'

'Because he won't listen to me, Valentina, but I am confident he will listen to you.'

She shrugs, trying to appear as if she doesn't care. 'Well, OK; what's the message?'

'Tell him he owes me one million dollars.'

She snorts derisively but Glen looks serious.

'Tell him that's what Gertrude Kinder had agreed to pay

me for retrieving the Metsu painting,' he says, referring to the Dutch Master Theo had found before Glen could, and had returned to its rightful owner free of charge. 'That's my livelihood.'

Valentina crosses her arms. 'Don't you think it's immoral to demand such a huge sum of money from a little old lady for giving her back something she owned in the first place?'

Glen laughs nastily. 'Don't get all moral with me. I see the way you live, the things you do, Valentina . . .' he sneers. 'You are a very naughty girl.'

She feels disgusted by his innuendo. 'That's completely different.'

He cocks his head to one side. 'Well, we all have our moral codes. And I don't see what is wrong with being paid for doing a dangerous job. My very liberty is at stake. Besides, do you know how rich Gertrude Kinder is? Why shouldn't she pay me?'

'I don't think there's much point in me telling Theo that he owes you all this money . . . even if I actually see him while I am here in London,' she adds.

'But I have an offer for him,' he says. 'I know why he is here. I know what he is after.'

Valentina casts her mind back to the conversation she had with Theo yesterday. He had of course told her that he and Glen were after the same picture.

'You can tell him that, if he lets me have the Masson . . . well, then I will let bygones be bygones. Otherwise—'

'Otherwise what?' she interrupts, hotly.

'I will have to take you.'

Valentina widens her eyes at the man's audacity. 'What makes you think I will let you "take" me? I don't belong to any man; I never have and I never will.'

'Believe me, you will have no choice in the matter.'

There is something in the way Glen says this that frightens Valentina, although she is determined not to let him see her unease.

She puts her hands on her hips and gives him her coldest stare. 'I have a piece of advice for you,' she says. 'Stay away from me. If you have messages for my *ex*-lover, deliver them yourself. It's nothing to do with me.'

Before he has a chance to respond, Valentina jumps on to the back of a double decker bus that has just pulled in at a stop on the Finchley Road. She climbs up the tiny stairwell, her heart pounding, wondering if he has got on behind her. Yet, when she sits down and looks out of the window, she sees Glen still standing on the street looking up at her. His eyes are black with menace. Despite Theo's assurances that the man is harmless, Valentina's skin is prickling with apprehension.

She is still spooked later that evening, reluctant to go out with Antonella. However, after a two-day hangover that had her bedbound most of the time, Antonella is determined to make up for lost time.

'We're only here another few days, Valentina; we have to

go out. Besides, Aunt Isabella has got us tickets for The Crazy Horse's "Forever Crazy" tonight.'

'Isn't that a Parisian burlesque show?'

'Yes, but it is in London for the first time, on the South Bank. I've always wanted to go.'

Valentina remembers now she saw a poster for the show as she was travelling back by Tube this afternoon. It was a close-up of the women's faces and they all had the same wig on: Louise Brooks-style black bobs, just like her.

'Isn't that the sort of thing you go to with your boyfriend? Not two women on their own.'

'Three,' says Antonella, kneeling down and unzipping her suitcase.

'Are you telling me that your aunt is coming with us, as well?' Valentina asks, astonished that the older woman would be interested in the burlesque show.

'Of course; she bought us the tickets.' Antonella starts pulling clothes out of her suitcase. 'Now, what to wear? We have to look stunning, of course . . .'

'I don't think there's much point trying to compete with those beauties,' says Valentina, remembering the poster.

Antonella twists around and smirks at her. 'Quite the contrary; Aunty says that there will probably be groups of young men there, so we should be prepared to do a little flirting during the interval.'

'Your Aunt Isabella said this?'

'Yes; she is on the hunt.' Antonella giggles.

Valentina rolls her eyes. 'Why doesn't she do something a little more demure, like internet dating?'

'She's tried that – said she only met a load of perverts that way. She says it's better to actually size someone up in the flesh first, before you send any signals.'

Now Valentina feels even less like going out. The last thing she wants to be part of is a girls' pick-up night with Antonella and her flamboyant aunt.

She flops down on the bed and considers telling Antonella about Glen . . . Theo . . . her disastrous non-meeting with her father, but she doesn't quite know where to begin.

'Where were you all day?' Antonella suddenly asks her, as if reading her mind. 'I went over to the gallery in Soho, but you weren't there.'

Valentina fiddles with the eiderdown. 'I was just walking around, thinking.'

Antonella stops pulling clothes out of her suitcase, and looks over at Valentina. 'Have you decided?'

For a moment Valentina thinks Antonella is talking about Theo, but then she realises she hasn't told her friend about meeting him. 'Decided?' she says.

'Are you going to go and see your father?'

She looks down, unwilling to tell Antonella the truth: that she went to see him earlier that day and ran away. 'Maybe.'

'You've nothing to lose, Valentina.'

But that is where her friend is wrong. She has everything to lose, starting with her composure, which has taken her so many years to construct, which Theo has already begun to unsettle. 'Don't you think it's too late?' she says, quietly.

Antonella pulls out a scarlet minidress and holds it up to her busty frame, looking at herself in the mirror. 'It's never too late, Valentina.'

Valentina has to admit she has actually been looking forward to the Crazy Horse's show. She remembers her mother telling her about seeing the burlesque dancers perform in Paris, years ago. She told her that the cabaret harks back to the original shows in the early fifties, when Paris was a cultural hotbed. Valentina wishes she could go back in time and see the real thing.

The first number opens, revealing nine almost-nude girls in Coldstream Guard get-ups, complete with bearskin hats, strutting and saluting in regimented time. To Valentina, they seem like mannequins not real women: tall, long legged, with perfect bottoms, neat breasts and deadpan faces. It is all a little surprising and not quite what Valentina expected. Despite Isabella and Antonella's obvious enthusiasm, Valentina is not finding the dances as erotic as she expected. What makes something sexy? Valentina wonders. She would like to see diversity: a shorter woman, a softer belly, a pair of broader thighs or a bigger chest. The Crazy Horse girls are just too alike. But one dance she does really enjoy: a naked girl sweeps her arms in a circle in the air and an arched light follows her hand, like a sudden rainbow, yet white – filled with the black silhouettes of flowers. The dance is slow, melodic and poignant, its gentle simplicity making it far sexier than the more explicit dances.

Despite the fact she enjoyed the show so much, Isabella is disappointed by her fellow audience members.

'Oh dear,' she says as the lights come up. 'There isn't a single man in sight.'

Indeed, nearly all of the audience is made up of couples or groups of women like them.

'Come on, girls,' Isabella walks between Valentina and Antonella, linking arms. 'Are you hungry?'

They leave The Crazy Horse Spiegel tent and make their way along the South Bank towards Westminster. There is a wind blowing off the Thames and it cuts into Valentina. She shivers just as she feels the first few drops of rain on her head.

'Oh, this dreadful English weather,' Isabella groans, pulling them into a brisker pace.

They eat in a Brazilian restaurant, discussing the Crazy Horse show over caipirinhas.

'It's strange, isn't it, how most women enjoy looking at other women's naked bodies and yet they are not necessarily gay?' Antonella says as she pulls apart their plate of nachos. 'I mean, they find it sexy. I'm straight, but I still think looking at a woman's body can be sexy – how she uses it.'

'As if you are looking at an image of yourself?' Isabella suggests.

'Yes; but tonight, those naked bodies just left me cold,' Valentina comments.

'Really?' Isabella says as she and Antonella both look at her in surprise.

'I loved it!'Antonella exclaims.

'You know,' Isabella says, pausing to take a sip of her drink, 'you are the image of your mother, Valentina. I feel like I have gone back in time and it's me and Tina again, out on a night prowl.'

Valentina scowls, hunching over the table as she helps herself to Nachos.

'Aunty, Valentina *hates* being compared to her mother,' Antonella tells Isabella.

'Why? She is an incredible lady . . . Although I haven't seen her for years. Where is she now, Valentina?'

'America,' Valentina says, sullenly.

'I know that . . . But where?' Isabella persists.

'New Mexico was the last place I heard. I haven't seen her in a while.'

'Eight years,' Antonella says, tactlessly.

Isabella turns on Valentina, looking aghast. 'But why? Did you have an argument?'

'No . . .' Valentina trails off. She wishes Isabella would drop the subject.

The last conversation she had in the flesh with her mother was so long ago that it is hazy now. It had been over her mother interfering in her love life and Valentina had lost her temper. She had probably overreacted, yet she didn't deserve to be abandoned. She was only nineteen, after all. And yet, by leaving Milan and moving to America without Valentina, that's what her mother had done, wasn't it?

Valentina waves over the waiter to order more drinks. 'She can come and see me in Milan any time she wants,' she says, defensively.

Isabella puts her hand on her arm. 'It is not good to hold grudges for so long within a family. I should know that. Go and see your mother.'

Valentina shakes her head. Isabella is making her angry.

Luckily, Antonella intercedes. 'Aunty, let's not get so serious, please. Valentina doesn't want to talk about it.'

'OK, OK. I just wish Valentina had known her mother the way I knew her. She had such spirit.'

Valentina stands and picks up her purse. She is sick of hearing about how great her mother was. Can she not even escape her here, in London?

'I'm just going to the bathroom,' she tells the others. She doesn't need the toilet but she wants to get away from Isabella's prying. Antonella's aunt is a strange woman. Despite the fact that she is nearly thirty years older than Antonella and Valentina, she appears to be more open-minded than either of them. What would she think of Valentina's confusion over Theo and Anita? Like her mother, she probably wouldn't bat an eye – she'd tell her to get on with it, steal him off the other woman if she wants him back so badly.

162

It is on her way back from the toilets that she thinks she hears a voice calling her name. The voice is familiar and yet strange to her at the same time.

'Valentina?'

The second time she hears it, she turns around. Right behind her is a grey-haired man, staring at her intently. The hair is different and yet she has never forgotten that face.

'Valentina? Is it you?'

Years fall away from her. All her poise is undone and she is nineteen again, looking at the first man she ever loved.

'Francesco?' she whispers, in shock.

'It is you!'

Without prompting, the man leans forward and kisses her on both cheeks. She stands back, coldly surveying him, unnerved by the rapid beating of her heart. She had never thought she would see him again.

'It's so wonderful to see you. I have thought of you so many times over the years.'

'Really?' she says, sarcastically. She can't help it. There is still a blade of hurt lodged deep inside her heart. He was the one who first broke her heart. He is the reason she couldn't trust Theo.

He puts his hand on her arm. 'Valentina,' he says softly. 'Are you still angry with me?'

'No, of course not,' she laughs shortly. 'Why, it was years ago . . .' She coughs, trying to appear cool. 'So, how are your wife and child?'

EVIE BLAKE

'Lucia is seven now.' His eyes shine and it hurts to see his fatherly pride. 'She is gorgeous – such a live wire. And so English . . . It's funny to see!'

She nods politely, beginning to move towards the others, but Francesco squeezes her arm. 'And my wife and I got divorced,' he blurts out.

'Oh.' She looks him in the eye. 'I am sorry about that.'

'I never could get over you, Valentina,' he whispers.

She feels a blaze of annoyance. How dare he tell her this now, when so much time has passed? 'Then why didn't you come back to me?'

'Your mother . . . she made it impossible,' he says. 'And Lucia . . . I had to try for my little girl.'

She pushes his hand off her arm. 'OK. Well, whatever,' she says, beginning to walk away. 'Nice seeing you.'

'Who's that man you were talking to?' Antonella asks her as soon as she sits down again. Valentina glances behind her. She sees that Francesco has joined two other men, both of whom are younger than him and more casually dressed. He is still looking at her, his interest in her undisguised.

'Yes, Valentina –' Isabella ogles the men – 'who are they? I like that guy in the blue shirt. He's cute.'

'And way too young for you, Aunty,' Antonella chides her. 'Who says—?'

'*That* man,' Valentina interrupts, rimming her glass with her finger, 'was my first love.'

'Francesco?' Antonella hisses. 'The married guy?'

164

'Yes, but he is not married anymore.'

'Interesting,' Isabella says, crossing her legs and smiling slyly. 'So is he the man who took your virginity?'

Valentina looks across the crowded restaurant at Francesco and his friends. Her first lover stares back at her. 'Yes,' she says, slowly realising that now she can have her answers at long last. Had Francesco ever loved her like she had loved him?

She watches Francesco lean over and talk to the two young men opposite him, both of whom look across at the three women at exactly the same time. She sees the appreciation in their glance, and senses both Antonella and Isabella sitting up, as if to attention.

'I think, my young ladies,' Isabella rolls each word over her tongue in glee, 'that our night is only just beginning.'

Maria

MARIA THINKS ABOUT PANDORA: THE BEAUTIFUL WOMAN without a soul, sent by the jealous gods with a gift of a box to mankind. Deceived by her beauty, men strive to possess and open the box but, when they succeed, instead of happiness, all the evils and miseries are let loose. Lempert tells them that their dance of *Pandora* is about the conflict between good and evil within man. Here is Pandora, Joan, in her snake headpiece and crimson veil and skirt, in opposition to Psyche, danced by the redhead, Alicia, all in white, Joan's compact, sensuous body contrasting with the height and slenderness of Alicia. Maria sees it as a struggle between the material and the spiritual, what is instinctive and what is rational. Now that she has met Felix, she understands this conflict. It seems to scream out at her from every corner of her life.

When they go to see the film *Black Narcissus* in the cinema, it is not Deborah Kerr's Sister Clodagh with whom Maria identifies, but rather the sexually frustrated Sister Ruth. The final images of Sister Ruth, now no longer a nun, as she throws open the doors of the fortress convent on top of the windswept mountain in the Himalayas, stay with Maria. The Sister is standing on that wild mountain in a scarlet dress, her eyes dark, her lips pale, her hair loose, and beads of sexual need perspiring upon her forehead. She is possessed, not by something evil – but by her own desires. Maria feels sorry for Ruth and dislikes the prudish Sister Clodagh. And worse even than her is the general's agent, Mr Dean, who rejects Sister Ruth. Maria wants something to happen. She wants there to be passion and yet the film ends in death. It seems the message is that a woman who puts her instincts first is doomed.

Her mother's favourite film is *Pandora* with Louise Brooks. It is different from their dance in its approach to the myth. Louise Brooks's Pandora is a loveable, almost unwitting, temptress. She just can't help it. And yet her desire for intimacy, her potent sexuality, is what destroys her in the end. Maria thinks that, if there were a male version of Pandora, it would be Felix when he was younger. There is something so dangerously tempting about him. She knows he is no good for her, and yet she wants him. Her reason tells her that he is too old for her and he will not be satisfied with a timid good-night kiss for long. He is certainly not obvious husband material. No stable job, and seemingly no property or wealth. And yet she cannot resist his company. She sees the way other women look at him when they go out together. It makes her flare inside, so that she wants to scratch their eyes out and scream at them, *He is mine! He is mine!*

He is far from hers. Their meetings appear random but are always orchestrated by him. She might be on her way home from dance school and suddenly he will appear behind her. He will say nothing, just fall in step beside her. Her heart will be fluttering, her cheeks flushed with pleasure at his appearance but she will do her best to maintain her composure. They might walk the length of Kennington Road, even across Westminster Bridge, before he speaks to her. He will slip his hand in hers, squeeze it tight and lead her in a different direction from home: along the Embankment, up the Strand and into the warren that is Covent Garden, all the way to Charing Cross Road.

Having led her astray, far away from their home territory, he will cock his head on one side. 'Tea, Signorina Brzezinska?'

In a smoky, dingy tea room across from Foyles Bookshop, they will add to the smoke, puffing away on cigarettes, letting their tea go cold, staring into each other's eyes. In Felix's eyes, Maria sees the promise of what she witnessed Joan and Louis doing. It makes her grip her hands and dig her nails into her palms at the thought of this man, naked and in control of her. She is not sure if she is frightened or thrilled by the thought. He is a real man – not a boy, like Guido, whose advances she can easily bat away. She knows that she is caught in Felix's web. When he so chooses, she will be unable to refuse him. Is this what she wants?

She is still not sure. All she knows is she wants him to take care of her. She is certain her mother and Pina would be shocked at this craving. She was brought up to need no man; Belle had been adamant that her daughter would never have to go through the imprisonment of a marriage like hers. Signor Brzezinski had been a brute, beating his wife – and Pina, Belle's former maid. It was because of her miserable and abusive marriage that Belle had sought a double life as a prostitute and, through that, she had met the love of her life: Santos Devine, Maria's father. It had, in fact, been fortuitous that Signor Brzezinski lost all their money in the Wall Street Crash, for it had led to his suicide and her freedom – too late for her and Santos, for he had already disappeared into the mists of Venice Lagoon, but Belle had still grabbed her liberation in both hands and set up home with Pina. Maria's mother had never let another man possess her. Yet Maria's secret wish is to be the sole object of a man's attention, to be what he treasures most.

Felix may live in a modest flat in their building, yet Maria has the feeling he is important in his world. He disappears for days on end, and alludes to films he is making. He tells her he goes to Paris and meets with other artists and writers. She longs for him to invite her to go with him.

'Why do you live in London?' she asks him. It mystifies her why Felix would choose not to live among his compatriots.

He sits back, eyes narrowed, inhaling his cigarette, before

speaking slowly. 'I like to keep some distance,' he says. She is not sure what he means.

Before they reach the house off Ebury Bridge Road, they separate. It has never actually been spoken about that, despite the fact they live in the same house, neither of them is willing to reveal their 'relationship' to the other tenants. Even if she were brave enough to tell Jacqueline, and Maria is sure her guardian would not approve of her fledgling relationship with the Frenchman, she is unsure of how she would describe what is going on between herself and Felix. He has not even kissed her properly yet. They have been seeing each other often over the past two weeks, and he has done no more than kiss her on the cheek. And yet she knows something is brewing. The more she thinks about it, the thirstier she is. A tiny voice at the back of her head, her instinct, calls to her, warns her that, despite his initial reserve, this man is insatiable. She knows he is circling her, closing in until she has no way out. But stronger than her fear is her longing. She wants him to trap her.

Two weeks before *Pandora* is due to open, Alicia sprains her ankle in rehearsal and Lempert has to recast Psyche. To her utter surprise, Maria is selected. Apart from Joan, the other dancers respond coldly, appraising Maria for the first time properly, arching eyebrows, almost hissing with hostility. Maria is terrified. She knows she cannot refuse Lempert and yet she is not sure she is ready for this exposure.

After school, when the others have gone, Maria looks for

her dance teacher. She can think of at least three of the other dancers who would be better suited to dance the part of Psyche than herself.

As she is knocking on Lempert's office door, it occurs to her that she has never actually seen behind it. She wonders what it will reveal of the man. He is almost as mysterious as her Felix: a foreigner in London; a refugee since before the war. She knows he is Jewish and from Germany, but she has no idea if he is married or has children. She has never seen him with a family.

He calls her in. In fact, his office tells her little about him. It is sparsely decorated, the walls bare, painted an institutional pale green, and the tiny room dominated by a big desk, stacked with newspapers. The man himself is sitting in a wing-backed chair at the desk. He is reading *The Times* and, when he lowers it to look at her, she is surprised to see a pair of glasses perched on the end of his nose. It is unnerving to observe this man, usually always moving, so still, considering her.

'Well,' he says, as if he is in the middle of a conversation with her. 'What do you think, Signorina Brzezinska? Are we on the eve of another war?'

Maria remembers Guido ranting on about the likelihood of a third world war: Russia versus America, the rest of Europe caught in the middle.

'I don't know, really,' she says, vaguely.

'You are Italian,' he says, 'yet your name is not . . . Brzezinska. Polish? Jewish?'

'I grew up in Venice,' she says. 'My mother is Polish but she never speaks about her homeland. I don't know where she came from.'

Lempert nods sagely. 'I imagine that not many of your people are left, if they stayed in Poland.' He sighs shaking his head. 'I left Germany long before the war, but still I feel the loss of my homeland, of what it used to be before . . .'

The last thing Maria wants to do is talk about the war with her dance teacher, and yet how can she change the subject? 'Were you in London during the war?'

'Devon,' he tells her. 'We started our dance theatre in Devon, after we left Germany. I came to London in nineteen forty-six. This school is new – not the building, of course – but we have only been open two years. But, of course, your dear Jacqueline must have told you all about that . . .'

'Yes, she did.' Maria licks her lips nervously.

'Well, my dear, why are you visiting me?'

'It's . . . It's . . . Well . . . I don't understand why you have cast me as Psyche . . .'

Lempert arches his eyebrows, looking annoyed. 'What do you mean?'

'I just don't think I am good enough . . . ready . . .' She stumbles over her words.

'I think I will be the judge of that,' Lempert says.

'But I have only been here three months.'

'Let me explain.' Lempert leans forward. 'You must remember that, important as technique is, it is not the only thing I am looking at when I cast my dancers. For Psyche, I need a certain lightness – an otherworldliness. Alicia has this quality. The only dancer in the company who is close to her is you.' He coughs and begins to fold up the newspaper. 'I agree it is not ideal but, Maria, if you work hard, I believe you can do it.' He gets up and brushes his trousers down.

She knows she is being dismissed, yet panic fills her. She knows she isn't ready to dance a solo. How could he not see it?

'Sir . . . I just don't think you should risk casting me as Psyche. I am not ready—'

He interrupts her. 'When in life are we ready for anything, my dear Maria?' and he leans down suddenly and catches her chin in his hand, raising it so she is looking directly into his eyes. The intimacy of his movement shocks her. She has the feeling that he is talking about something other than dancing. 'You have to jump off the edge of the cliff. Be brave. You may fail, but there is no shame in that, if you get up again . . .'

Maria is almost in tears as she walks down the street. She doesn't want to have to be brave. She doesn't want to open herself up to ridicule. She can already see the derision of her fellow dancers – her humiliation. She is so preoccupied that, for just one second, she doesn't notice Felix is beside her, not until she feels his hand upon her shoulder. She stops dead and looks up at him.

'Why, Maria,' he asks her, 'what is the matter?'

'The girl playing Psyche in *Pandora* has sprained her ankle, and Lempert has cast me in the role,' she gabbles tearfully.

He looks confused. 'Isn't that a good thing?'

'Not if I am not good enough for the part – which I am not.'

'Of course you are. He wouldn't cast you otherwise.'

'I don't know why he chose me,' she says desperately. 'He said something about lightness . . .'

'Ah, he sees the ethereal Maria.'

Despite her upset, Felix's compliment sends a warmth into her heart. He tucks his hand into her pocket and she can feel his fingers spreading, pinning the material of her skirt to her legs, his fingertips pushing through the fine material, into her flesh.

'He sees the angel that you are. He wants something seraphic.' Felix nods knowingly. 'I doubt any of the other dancers are as pure as you.'

She blushes deeply, for she knows that Felix can tell how untouched she is.

'You must dance this part, Maria,' he says. 'Do not be afraid. I will come to see you. In fact, I will film you.'

'That makes me even more nervous,' she mumbles, yet secretly she is thrilled. Felix wants to film her dancing!

This evening, they walk in Battersea Park, admiring the sculptures together, hand in hand, like any other young couple in love, despite the fact that Felix is old enough to be her father. She looks up at the strands of grey in his hair and she loves every single one of them. He is blinking in the sunlight, silent and thoughtful. She wonders what he really thinks of her. She cannot imagine why he wants to be in her company when he must know so many other women, far more interesting than her.

Felix leads her down a path, through a cluster of rhododendron bushes, to sit on the grass by a small, murky pond. He spreads his jacket for her to sit upon. Here they are shielded from weary, grey post-war London, struggling to get back on its feet. Here they are in a little oasis of green. Maria pulls off her shoes, wiggling her stockinged toes through the blades of grass.

'Such tiny ankles,' Felix says, leaning forward and picking up one of her feet, cradling it in his hand.

'But my feet are awful,' Maria protests. 'All dancers have terrible feet.'

'Not awful; just hard-working.'

Felix strokes the underside of her foot; the nylon slides against the flesh. She giggles, feeling stupid and self-conscious. She tries to pull her foot away, but he grips it tighter.

'Let me?' he asks.

She looks at him under her lashes, curious as to what he might do. She leans back on her elbows. Why not let him stroke her foot? It is an innocent enough occupation. Besides, they are concealed from the rest of the park, their only witnesses a few ducks. She feels the sun on her brow and closes her eyes, letting the tension, the fear from the news that she is to dance Psyche, fade away. Felix is kneading the soles of her feet, working his fingers around her ankles, and suddenly gripping them tight. She can feel his fingers digging into her ankle bone through her stocking, yet – although it hurts a little – this sensation is pleasurable. She likes this sense of restriction.

'Am I hurting you?' he asks.

She opens her eyes and looks at him. 'A little . . . but I like it.'

He smiles slowly. 'I thought you might.'

He puts her foot back down. She feels her breath deepen, the release after the pressure of his fingers on her flesh. He picks up her other foot and massages it, circling his fingers upon its sole. 'I wish you weren't wearing stockings,' he says. 'Then I could really feel you.'

He squeezes his fingers tightly around the ankle of her left foot, and again Maria is constrained by him. She tests him, tries to raise her leg, but it is impossible. He is holding her foot down, impeding all movement. She is trapped by him, and she likes this feeling. His strength; what he could do to her.

'I have to feel you,' he whispers, and, before she can stop him, he has snagged her stockings with one of his fingernails, which he pushes through the nylon to feel her bare leg.

'Felix!' She is a little annoyed. 'It's not easy to get stockings, you know—'

'Shush . . .' He warns her with his eyes. 'I will bring you plenty of stockings, I promise.'

He takes his finger and suddenly pulls down with force, so that the stocking ladders down to her foot. He rips it sideways, unwrapping her foot, and resting it in his palms.

'So much better,' Felix sighs, dancing his fingers over her skin.

She has to agree. Now the layer of nylon is removed, his touch is even more electrifying.

He lifts her foot and pulls her towards him so that she is sliding on his jacket. He raises it higher and she does nothing to stop him. She knows he can see her underwear, beneath her skirt. She doesn't care. She likes him looking at her. He lowers her leg and rests her bare foot on his lap. She can feel him, beneath the cloth of his trousers. She imagines it growing, and for a second she remembers Louis's naked body.

'Point your toes,' Felix tells her. 'Arch your foot.'

She does as he asks and he cups her foot around himself. She feels him growing into her arch, unfurling the essence of him. The sun is beating down upon her, and she can feel herself glowing. She has never felt so hot in her life. Her body is yearning to be released from the restriction of her dress.

'Can you feel what you do to me, pretty lady?' Felix asks her.

She nods, unable to think of anything to say back. She tries to lean forward, feeling him in the curve of her foot as she does so, wanting so badly to see what lies beneath the cloth of his trousers.

'No,' Felix says, gently pushing her back. 'Not today. This is enough touching for today.'

She lies back, disappointed, her eyes glistening with need. He lifts her foot off his lap and then suddenly, light and quick, he takes his finger at the torn end of her stocking and rips it all the way up her leg. He pauses just below the hem of her skirt, and then, locking eyes with her, he rips the stocking higher and higher, his hand going beneath her skirt. Maria feels a fluster of panic. What if someone were to come walking down the path and see them? Yet she doesn't want him to stop. His finger has now reached the top of her thigh, right where the suspender is clipped to her stocking. He expertly unclips it, his fingers lingering at the top of her legs.

'What do you want me to do now, sweet Maria?' he whispers.

She squirms beneath his magnetism. She cannot say. That deep pulse she felt when she watched Louis and Joan is back: an ache that is all consuming. 'I want you to touch me more,' she eventually whispers, her cheeks blooming with self-consciousness.

He smiles victoriously and sits back on his heels, looking at her. 'Not yet,' he says. 'I would not be a gentleman if I did such a thing.'

She realises he is teasing her. She should be annoyed, and yet she can't be. She likes this game of his empowerment over her. Besides, maybe she will manage to come to her senses and resist him next time. She knows what she is doing is not the sort of thing a good girl does, and yet who are these good girls? Not Joan, or any of the other dancers she knows; not her mother nor Pina. These 'good girls' are just dreamt up by men, impossible images of perfection so that the same men can pull them down and women end up feeling ashamed. She may be innocent – shy, even – but she is also a free spirit, just like her mother. She refuses to feel as if she is a sinner.

For a while, they sit on the grass in silence, watching clouds forming in the sky. Maria has removed both her stockings and stuffed them into her bag. Her body is still tingling with sensation but her heartbeat has slowed.

'We should have brought some bread for the ducks,' she comments.

'I think that it's hard enough to get bread ourselves, without worrying about the ducks,' Felix says.

'Do you think this austerity will last forever?' Maria asks. 'Jacqueline says that they won't be rationing bread soon.'

'Have you ever been hungry, Maria?' Felix asks her, ignoring her question. 'I mean close to starving . . .'

The way he asks her this question, she knows that he has.

'No, not really hungry,' she says. 'There were shortages . . . I mean, we certainly didn't live like kings, especially at the end of the war, but my mother and Pina were resourceful. We always had just enough.'

Felix plucks a daisy from the grass and pulls its petals off one by one.

'When did you come to England, Felix?' Maria asks him. 'Your English is very good.'

Felix says nothing for a moment. His face is guarded and for a while she thinks he isn't going to reply.

'Nineteen forty-six, but my grandmother was English. I learnt to speak it as a child.'

'So you came to London just after the war, then?'

'Yes.'

'And where were you during the war?'

'Lyon,' he says, brusquely, standing up. He reaches out his hand to help her and dusts the grass from her skirt, like a father might.

'But Felix, why did you leave France after the war? Why would you come to London?'

He stops what he is doing. He steps back and looks at her coldly. 'That, young lady, is none of your business.'

His voice has changed so dramatically that it gives her a fright and she steps back in shock. 'I'm sorry; I didn't mean to pry.'

'Well, stop asking me questions, then.' His voice softens. 'You should know better; you're an intelligent woman. What people want now is to move on. They don't want to go over the past . . . I don't want to talk about it – not with anyone.'

He picks up her hand in his, but she feels rigid, cold, with a sense of something uncertain. Who is this man she desires so much?

'Come on; I had better get you home. Your Jacqueline will be wondering where you are.'

It is just as they are about to separate, at the gates of Battersea Park, that she sees Guido. He is coming towards them, at speed, on his bicycle. His thick, curly hair is blown into a big bush on top of his head. She glances behind her, wondering if she can dash away into the trees, but it is too late, for she can see that Guido has stopped cycling and is staring, blatantly, at both of them, from across the road.

'It's Guido,' she whispers to Felix.

Felix shrugs his shoulders as if not to care, but she can feel his body stiffen. They cross the road together, pointedly not holding hands.

'Good afternoon, Signor Rosselli,' Felix tips his hat.

Maria cannot look Guido in the face. She feels the eyes of the Italian on her, and a flush creeping up her neck, burning her cheeks. Why does she have to feel so guilty? All that happened was that Felix stroked her feet. Besides, it is none of Guido's business who she spends her time with. And yet, when she does finally look up to acknowledge Guido, she is unsettled by the expression on his face. For once, he is not transfixed by her. He is looking instead at Felix, the unguarded hostility in his eyes visceral. Why does he hate the Frenchman so much?

$\mathcal{V}$alentina

THEY ARE IN ONE OF THE MEN'S APARTMENTS. SHE ISN'T sure if it is Francesco's place, or that of one of his companions. Wherever they are, it is obviously a bachelor pad: minimalist designer furniture, mammoth white leather couch, state of the art speakers to go with the iPod, giant flat-screen TV overshadowing the sparse art work on the walls, and non-child friendly glass dining table with cream leather chairs. She reckons it has to be one of the younger men's places. There is no sign of anything belonging to a seven-year-old girl. If it were Francesco's flat, then surely there would be something of Lucia's here? They are drinking tequila – always a risk, where Valentina is concerned, but especially after the caipirinhas they have already consumed in the Brazilian restaurant.

She can't believe she is sitting next Francesco on the couch – not after her initial hostility towards him in the restaurant. It seems that alcohol is a great healer of grudges, for now she is happy to be with him. She is drawn to his presence yet again. He is flirting with her and it feels good to be wanted. The thought of Theo flickers in her mind. She should forget about him. Leave him and Anita to it.

They are playing a game. One of the Englishmen, Peter, has told them they have to relate three things about themselves, but only one is true. The others have to guess which it is. It is Isabella's turn. She is sitting on the lap of the blue-shirted fellow, Rupert, her skirt hitched up to her thighs, her eyes squiffy with drink. Yet, despite the fact she is nearly twice as old as her, Valentina thinks she looks gorgeous: confident in her sexuality, free from the self-consciousness of being young.

'OK,' Isabella says, holding up three fingers. 'Here are my three: one summer, when I was a student, I worked as a call girl in Milan.'

'Oh! Oh – it has to be that!' screeches Antonella.

'The best sex I ever had was with another woman,' Isabella continues, winking at Valentina mischievously.

'Oh, no, I don't think so.' Antonella grimaces.

'And, finally: I had sex with my ex-husband's divorce lawyer, on top of my ex's car bonnet in the car park of his offices.'

'What kind of car was it?' Francesco asks, refilling their glasses.

'A Ferrari, baby; what else?'

'It's the call girl. It has to be,' Antonella chants excitedly. 'I always knew you had a dark secret, Aunty.'

'I think it's the sex with another woman,' Peter says.

Rupert is too busy nibbling Isabella's ears to have any idea at all.

'It's the car-bonnet sex . . .' Valentina says, because she knows that this is the sort of thing her mother would have done.

'Correct!' Isabella cries out.

'Really? Oh my God, Aunty, you are very bad.'

Isabella winks at her niece. 'I guess that must be where you inherit those genes, then.'

Antonella gets up from her seat, rather unsteadily. 'I've had enough of this game; let's dance.'

'Your friend is a little hyperactive, isn't she?' Francesco whispers into Valentina's ear.

Peter puts on some music and Antonella dances around him, yet Valentina can see that his attention is on Isabella and Rupert, kissing on the couch.

Valentina stands up shakily. She should go. She should gather up Antonella, at least. She has a feeling Isabella is here for the night. They have the keys to Isabella's, so they could call a taxi. They really should go.

She turns to Francesco. 'Where's the bathroom?'

She leans on the edge of the sink and stares at herself in the mirror. Her expression is impassive: no emotion. She feels a little sick and unsteady. She shouldn't have drunk that tequila. She knows what happens when she drinks tequila. She smiles at herself in the mirror as she remembers the way Francesco has been looking at her. He has been hanging on her every word all evening: in the club they went to, drinking; in the taxi; here, in this apartment. Suddenly, it is clear that she is not going home. She knows exactly what is about to happen. And she is glad. It will take her away from Theo.

There is a knock on the bathroom door.

'Valentina? Are you OK?'

She opens the door and Francesco is leaning against its frame. He is not much taller than her, yet he is still fit and lean for his age. She sees the wrinkles that line his cheeks now, the laughter lines at the edge of his eyes, and they just add to his allure. She pinches herself. For so long she had pined to be with this man, and now he is right in front of her, offering himself to her. Of course, it's way too late, for her heart is another's, but maybe he can help her tonight to let go. Of her past? Of her attachment to Theo? She is not sure.

He pulls her out of the bathroom and kisses her in the dark corridor. She opens up her lips to his. She and Leonardo never kiss properly. That is their rule. She realises that it has been months since she let a man kiss her in this way. Not since Theo left her. Francesco pulls away and takes her hand, leading her down the corridor. The door to the sitting room is open. What she sees astonishes Valentina, for things have changed since she went to the bathroom.

Aunty Isabella is on her hands and knees in her stockings, stripped of her dress and her underwear. Her head is pushed into the belly of Peter as she sucks him. Peter's eyes are closed in bliss, his lips parted, his head raised to heaven. Meanwhile, Rupert is behind Isabella, stroking her backside, pushing it into his stomach and pulling her down so that his cock is brushing against her pussy.

'Where's Antonella?' Valentina hisses in alarm. Her friend is nowhere to be seen. Did she run away into the night, all on her own?

'I'm afraid she had a little too much to drink,' Francesco whispers, his eyes glittering in the dark. 'I put her to bed. Don't worry; she is all tucked in, fast asleep. Safe as houses . . .'

Francesco pulls her close to his chest. She feels him harden against her pelvis. She imagines how it might feel to have him inside her once again, after all this time.

'Do you want to watch, Valentina?' he whispers into her ear, swivelling her head, holding her between his two hands so that she sees the moment Rupert pushes deep into Isabella. 'Or do you want to join in?'

She pulls her head from his hands, steps away, and shuts the door behind her.

'No, I don't want to watch and I don't want to join in,' she says.

He looks at her quizzically. 'What do you want, then?'

'I want you to show me that you remember . . . us.'

'Of course I remember . . . I told you, I have thought of you so many, many times over the past years.' He sighs. 'Valentina, it was my obsession with you that ruined my marriage.'

'I don't want you to tell me that . . . Just show me.'

'How?'

'I want you to do exactly what you did the first time we made love. I want you to show me how you took my virginity, all over again.'

He takes a breath, says nothing for a moment.

'Have you forgotten?' she whispers.

'Of course not.' His words are barely louder than his breath. 'I am just thinking of how I can do this.'

He takes her hand and she follows him down the corridor and into the kitchen. It is all stainless steel and modern appliances, so different from the scene in their past. Francesco drops her hand and opens the ice compartment of the freezer.

'How fortunate it is that I happen to have what we need right here,' he says, pulling out a container of ice cream.

'So this is your apartment?'

'Of course,' he says, opening the lid of the ice-cream tub. 'But you know, Valentina, we are going to have to improvise. I don't possess a car anymore.'

'That's OK; we'll imagine it.'

She closes her eyes and remembers back to the summer she was nineteen. Francesco had driven them out of the city in his Fiat Bambino. They had headed towards the lakes, but never made it that far. On the way, he had pulled into a garage and bought them ice creams, making her hold them, one in each hand, while he drove on, pulling off down a bumpy track and on to the parched verge. The roof of the car had been open,

187

but that had just made them hotter. He had fed her ice cream, kissing her creamy lips between each bite. He had covered his tongue in thick, ice-cold vanilla ice cream and gone down on her. And she had melted into him. 'Oh, you are so sweet,' he had said. Those hot leather car seats sticking to their bare skin and ice cream running over their bellies – all this sensation had been her undoing.

She had not told him she was a virgin, but he could tell. As soon as he pushed into her, he felt her tightness, heard her gasp – the tiny twist of pain, and then the release of her sexuality, pouring into him, her heart cascading afterwards.

The memory of the innocence of her love for this man makes Valentina want him once again. She lets him feed her vanilla ice cream in his modernist kitchen and, when she can take no more sweet cream inside her mouth, no more its scent of heat and honey, he lifts her up on to the kitchen table, and kneels before her. He takes a scoop of vanilla out of the tub, fills his mouth with it, and parting her legs with his hands he pushes his full mouth, his ice cold lips against her hot pussy. She remembers now how he had licked her, adored her. And when she is so close to losing herself completely he pulls back, wipes his mouth upon his arm, a smear of cream upon his dark skin. He stands up, and they observe each other. Together they look deep into their past hearts, and honour the passion they had once felt for one another. His lovemaking is more measured, less urgent than that time, long ago, and yet it goes on forever and ever, taking her deeper and deeper inside herself. She doesn't want Francesco to make her orgasm and yet he does. She cannot help it. His seed mixes with the melted ice cream, smearing down her thighs. All this softness is too much for her and, afterwards, instead of lying in each other's arms, stroking each other tenderly, she reaches down and commands his cock with her touch.

'Fuck me now,' she whispers through gritted teeth, 'like you never have before.'

He answers by rolling her over on to her front. She grabs him and pushes him inside her. He is panting, out of breath, but she gives him no respite, demanding more and more, pushing back against him so they are writhing like a torn beast, like the broken, conflicted part of her heart. For Valentina is looking for herself: the girl who loved Francesco. Would it not be better to be her than who she is now?

ℳaria

SHE AND JOAN DANCE TOGETHER: PANDORA AND Psyche, locked in the eternal struggle between the material and the spiritual.

'You are the universal soul,' Lempert had told her, 'battling against all of man's weaknesses.'

Pandora is the darkness; she is the light. It is easier, Maria thinks, for Joan to show her shadow side. There is freedom within the confines of the dance for her to slide and slither like a snake. When she sees Joan moving – her cat-like grace, the threat of her malevolence – she is reminded of the primal part of herself, the part that enjoyed watching Joan and Louis together, her titillation at their coupling, her temptation to watch them again, all fuelling her desire to have sex with Felix. And yet all her dance teacher wants is for her to be pure. She is supposed to contrast with Joan's passion, to cool her down.

'Show me the unselfish devotion that is Psyche,' Lempert

screams at her as she sobs at his feet, worn out, desperate at her failure to articulate with her body what he needs.

Devotion. She raises her head and stares up at him, all of a sudden comprehending. Of course, she has been focusing on what her body demands, but she should just listen to her heart. She is in love with Felix. Of that she is sure. She loves him so much, she would do anything for him. She is *devoted* to him. And, when she thinks of this, she is able to get up and dance again. Let this be a private dance for her would-be lover, to show him that she is his to take.

'At last,' Lempert says, clicking his fingers in time with the pianist. 'At last, you see.'

To her relief, Maria feels the glow of her teacher's approval, but is it too late? Tomorrow is opening night. She knows she isn't ready, despite the hours spent rehearsing late every day. Her body is so tight and sore, her feet covered in blisters. Yet, no matter how much she strains her body, she knows she is not the dancer that Joan is. She remembers Jacqueline's surprise when she told her that she had been cast in one of the main roles in *Pandora*. Although she said encouraging things to her, Maria can tell that she doesn't believe she is ready.

'I wonder why,' she commented, not three nights before, as they laboured over some stringy grey veal.

'Why, what?'

'Why Lempert cast you as Psyche.'

'He said that I was the only dancer who had the same lightness as Alicia.'

She nodded. 'Yes, but Alicia has been dancing with him for two years. She was at Dartington, like Joan, and before that she trained in ballet.'

Maria valiantly chewed the tough meat, forcing it down her throat with a swig of water.

'Would you like me to talk to him for you? Ask him to cast someone more experienced?' Jacqueline asked Maria. 'I mean, if the worst comes to the worst, I could even do it.'

To her surprise, Maria felt annoyed. Having not wanted to dance the part, she now felt affronted by Jacqueline's lack of faith and her suggestion that she take over. 'I think I should do it . . . Don't you? Besides, it's too late now.' She challenged her with a glare.

Jacqueline looked down at her plate and began sawing away at another piece of meat. 'Of course, my dear. Your mother will be very proud. Did you write and tell her?'

Maria nodded. Her letter had been shamefully short, for she had been unable to write to her mother about Felix. She can't work out why. Her mother and Pina are not narrow-minded. And yet she remembers Pina's last words as she left Venice: 'Be careful.' And her mother's explanation that she meant to be careful of men. It was as if her mammas were saying there was some hidden evil in the gender, which Maria had no clue about.

Even more surprising had been the fact that Guido had said nothing to Jacqueline about Felix, not even after he had confronted Maria. She had been avoiding him ever since he saw them leaving Battersea Park together. Yet, last Saturday, she came across him in the stairwell. She is certain Guido had been lying in wait for her.

'Good morning,' she said brightly, trying to slip by him.

'Maria, wait,' Guido had said, behind her.

'I can't. I have to get into the tripe queue. I don't want to be stuck all day waiting.'

'I'll come with you.' He followed her outside.

It was raining and she had forgotten her umbrella, but she didn't want to go back inside and give Guido a reason for delaying her further or, worse still, risk the two of them bumping into Felix.

Guido fell into stride beside her. She couldn't help noticing how skinny he was. His trousers hung off his hips and his face had a beaky quality to it – pointed, with his thick moustache and long, fine nose, his glasses perched on its end. He looked like Groucho Marx. A comedian. Yet she had never met anyone with so little sense of humour before.

'Should we not go back for an umbrella?' Guido asked her, wiping his spectacles with a handkerchief before putting them back on, only to get wet all over again.

'No; I don't mind the rain at all,' she lied, bustling along, head bowed down.

'You are used to water, I suppose,' he commented, 'being from Venice.'

They had walked for several minutes in tense silence,

Maria skirting around the larger puddles, while Guido splashed through them.

'Do you like London?' Guido suddenly asked her.

'Yes, I do,' Maria said, realising all of a sudden that she had developed a fondness for the city. 'There are all sorts of people in London. I like that,' she added.

'That is true.' Guido paused. 'But that is why you need to be careful, because not everyone is who they seem to be.'

'In what way?'

'Well, for instance, you might be prejudiced against all these German prisoners of war who are living here now, but in fact they could be viewed as victims as well. If you actually talk to them, they are young men who had to follow orders. They had no choice.'

'Do you know any German prisoners of war?' She looked at him with interest for once.

'I do, indeed. In fact, the porter at my college is assisted by one such fellow. He is called Hemmel and he is very, very sad. He told me that he has lost everything – all the people he loved.'

Maria pursed her lips. 'So many nationalities suffered during the war—'

'I know,' Guido interrupted her. 'The Italians no less than anyone else. That is not my point.'

'What is your point?' she asked him, suddenly irritated. 'I am in a hurry, you know.'

'To get into a queue at the butchers and listen to all the

English housewives gossip?' He gave her a mocking glance.

'Yes,' she said, defensively. 'It can be very interesting, actually. We are not just chit-chatting about rubbish; in fact, at the moment, everyone is talking about the fact there will be a third world war. It seems the Russians are coming.'

Guido narrowed his eyes. 'I do not understand why the working men and women are so afraid of communism. It is all about liberating them.'

'Are you a communist?' Maria whispered, shocked at the possibility.

He shook his head and took a step back, but there was something in his denial that made Maria think he might be.

'Maria,' he said, 'I am not accompanying you so that we can talk about our political beliefs.'

'Well, why are you following me, then?'

'I saw you with Felix the other day, coming out of the park.'

He turned his rain-streaked face towards her, but his glasses were so wet she couldn't read the expression in his eyes.

'I know, but what business exactly is that of yours?' she replied, speeding up. If only he would just go away.

'I didn't know you were friends.'

'Well, we are,' she spat at him. 'If you bothered to talk to him, you'd find he is a very nice man.' She sounded ridiculous, she knew. The last word she would use to describe Felix was 'nice'. 'Interesting'; 'complicated'; 'intriguing' – but never 'nice'.

'You should be careful,' Guido said. 'He is not what he seems.'

'What do you mean exactly?' She stopped walking and turned to face him, not caring that both of them were getting soaked. She was so annoyed with Guido. How dare he judge Felix when he didn't know him? She felt protective of the Frenchman.

'Let me explain,' Guido said, hastily, obviously picking up her hostility. 'If we were in Paris now, rather than London, it would be quite a different story.'

'How so?' she said, coldly.

'The English were united. The French were not. Have you not heard of the purges?'

She shook her head, feeling stupid. 'I know a little,' she said. 'But those men who were purged were collaborationists and traitors to France.'

'Of course; but during the war many of them were, in fact, the government. It is thought that there were as many collaborating French as there were non-collaborators.'

'Are you accusing Felix of being a collaborator?' Maria had said, hotly. How dare this snooping little Italian make such an accusation! 'You told me he was in the Resistance.'

'I am not accusing him of being a collaborator. Far from it.' Guido sounded exasperated. 'Look, I can't say any more. I am just warning you. He is not the *nice* man you say he is.'

He put his wet hand on her arm. She could feel it imprinting her damp coat, pressing down against her clammy skin. 'Please, Maria, stay away from him. I don't want anything bad to happen to you.'

'Guido, I am not a child,' she said, haughtily, before knocking his hand off her arm, and marching down the street away from him. She had been furious. How dare he imply that Felix was a collaborator? How on earth could he know such a thing? Guido is a physics student at the University of London; he is half the age of Felix. Yet, despite her resolute denial that there could be any truth in what he had said, she can't help feeling unsettled, for Felix is still refusing to tell her any details about his past. She has told him plenty about Venice, about growing up without a father and with two mothers instead. She has revealed all to him, and yet he holds back, evading her questions when she asks him about France. She resolves that, next time she sees him, she will force him to tell her something, just to reassure herself.

She has her opportunity the day of *Pandora*'s opening. Lempert has given them the day off, telling the company to rest before the evening's performance. She wakes to untroubled summer skies, the week of rain having steamed off into an invisible vapour. Already it is hot. The flat ticks in silence; Jacqueline left early. Maria remembers that today is her mentor's full teaching day, when she travels around schools in North London, teaching ballet to the daughters of the wealthy. Maria is on her own and free, for once. She has the whole day to herself.

She starts by trying to write a letter to her mother and Pina. She sits at the table, the coffee brewing, filling her with the smells of their kitchen at home. She untwists the lid of her pen and smoothes down the paper in front of her.

Dear Mammas,
    I have met a man. He is French. His name is Felix and he makes films.

What else? She can't say he is the same age as Pina, but she knows he must be – if not older. She scrunches up the paper and throws it in the waste-paper basket. She knows that Jacqueline will scold her; paper is scarce. The coffee begins to bubble. She gets up from the table and takes it off the hob, pouring the treacle-black liquid into a teacup. Her stomach groans, but all there is to eat is porridge – not even a slice of bread this morning.

She takes their ration books out of the kitchen drawer. One of the first things Jacqueline made her do when she arrived in London was to get a National Registration number and her allowance of ration coupons. Maria is mystified by the extreme austerity in Britain. She has heard some of the girls at dance school talk about trips to Holland, Denmark and Belgium, where they could eat sweets and chocolates freely. Maria groans at the thought. How she would like to eat a brioche, pumped with rich chocolate! She knows that, even if she goes down to the bakery with her coupons, there will be no such fancy delight available. She sighs and opens one of the cupboard doors, pulling out a saucepan. She supposes she should make some porridge. Maybe she could sweeten it with some cinnamon.

There is a knock on the door. She frowns. She hopes it's not that pest, Guido. She braces herself to tell him to go away. Yet, when she opens the door, Felix is standing on her threshold, clutching a brown paper bag. She is so taken aback that she says nothing for a moment.

'Have you had breakfast?' he asks her.

She shakes her head.

'Good,' he says, wagging the bag in front of her face. 'Chelsea buns, freshly baked – they even have sugar on top. Not exactly croissants, but still, better than nothing.'

'Where did you get them?' she says, grabbing the bag out of his hand in excitement and opening it up, inhaling the spicy scent of brown sugar and cinnamon. He taps his nose, sauntering into Jacqueline's flat.

'Now that would be telling.' He winks at her. 'Do I smell coffee?'

She is all aflutter. How did Felix know she would be here all day on her own? She hands him her cup of coffee and prepares to brew another for herself. Her mouth waters involuntarily at the thought of the sugary bun, but she wants to have it with her coffee, so she holds back. Felix sits languidly at the table, looking around the flat.

'This apartment is much nicer than mine,' he comments. 'More light.'

'So you have never been in here before?' she asks him, carrying her coffee over to the table.

'No. Not in the two years I have lived in this house.'

She sits down opposite him and begins to unwind her Chelsea bun. 'Can I ask you why you and Jacqueline never speak?'

'But we do speak . . .'

She pops some soft sugary dough into her mouth. It is delicious. She feels like swooning with delight. 'You don't really talk. I mean, you are both French; why do you avoid each other?'

Felix says nothing for a moment. Then he looks at her, his gaze unflinching. 'You want to know the truth?'

'Yes, of course.'

'It is to do with your friend, Guido. He is obsessed with me – and not in a good way – and Jacqueline considers her loyalty to him as a fellow Jew more important than the fact we are both French.'

Maria leans forward. It is all sounding rather strange. 'What do mean, "obsessed"? I don't understand.'

'He thinks I am someone else. He thinks I left Paris to escape the purges of collaborators, because he believes I am one.'

'And are you?'

Felix looks at her with stern eyes, his mouth tight with disapproval at her question. 'No. Not at all. He could not be more wrong.'

She fidgets with her teacup of coffee, waiting for it to cool.

She has to be brave and ask him this question. She needs to hear the answer. 'So why did you leave France?'

'It's complicated. Let's just say, I got sick of the vengeance of young communists – young men and women, just like Guido.' He gets up and turns his back to her. His voice is a growl and she realises that this is how he sounds when he is angry. 'Why should I justify myself to that young idiot?' He turns and looks at her, his expression clouded, by what, she isn't sure: memories too dark, too terrible to articulate, perhaps.

'I'm sorry,' she says. 'I don't mean to stir things up.'

His face softens. 'So you are a curious cat?' he whispers, coming over to her and leaning down, licking the sugar off her lips.

His sudden intimacy causes her cheeks to flush pink, her heart to race.

'So precious this sugar, we must taste every last granule of it, must we not?' He holds her chin with his hand and tips her face up so that she is blinded by his gaze. 'So, do you wish to be mine, Signorina Maria Brzezinska?'

She nods, entranced by his magnetism.

'Well,' he says, pulling his hand away, letting her head drop down again. 'Would you like to go boating?'

He lifts the oars out of the river and carefully places them either side of him in the boat. She watches droplets of muddy water spattering her stockinged legs and pale blue skirt, like a dirty squall of rain. He says nothing. The boat drifts downstream and, for a moment, it is as if there are no other people in the world, just the two of them, unmoored upon the Thames, beneath the limitless blue sky.

They look into each other's eyes. His are gentle brown, appealing to her. She believes she can see his love for her in them. This, then, is her moment. She will give herself to him, for the first time. She wants to. It is wrong, she knows. They are not married – not even engaged. She knows so little about him, and yet she trusts him.

She looks around her. The bank is empty. It is the middle of the week, after all. The only living creatures are they two and the river birds: moor hens cooing, families of ducks and a lone heron, silently surveying them as they eddy downriver.

A giant dragonfly spins by, its transparent wings brushing her cheek, its energy wild and abandoned. She takes it as her cue and begins to undo the tiny, mother-of-pearl buttons of her blouse, one by one. She remembers her mamma sewing each one on, and now she is undoing herself – what her mother made. He watches her, his expression pensive, and she opens up her blouse and shows him her breasts. The moist damp air caresses her nipples and she senses them harden with expectation.

And, within a second, all that was hazy and in slow motion is suddenly fast. He springs forward and pins her to the bottom of the boat. Her blouse falls from her shoulders as he begins to kiss her, hungrily. What he is doing transforms her. She is delicate, yet as charged with energy as that dragonfly.

She is softening, unable to stop herself pushing against him, although she is afraid as well. She is on the edge of her maidenhood, the thread of it can be broken so quickly.

He pulls back, cradles her face in his hands and looks deep into her eyes.

'My darling,' he whispers. 'Tell me to stop.'

She shakes her head. She wants him to continue.

He sits back on his heels as she lies before him on the bottom of the boat, her breasts naked and exposed. He picks up her blouse and makes to cover her, but she pushes it away with her hand and begs him, with her eyes, to come to her again.

'I am too old for you,' he protests. 'You are too good for me.'

She reaches out with her arms. 'I love you,' she murmurs.

He can no longer resist and falls upon her again. He kisses her and she tastes the sweetness of his lips on hers, inhales him as if he is the very breath of her life. She wriggles beneath him, tentatively reaching forward with her hand and touching him. Some wildness takes over her. She did not imagine that it would be she who took the initiative, and yet it is Maria who unbuttons Felix's trousers, and Maria who slips her underwear off and opens up to him. He pushes up inside her with such force she gasps. Her insides are opening to him as he fills her.

'Maria, I love you,' he whispers, as he begins to push against her body. His words ignite her further and she is in unison with him. The boat rocks beneath them in accompanying rhythm. It feels right to be doing this on the river. She was born in a city upon a lagoon, the daughter of a sailor, and thus her virginity belongs to a watery world. She closes her eyes, letting his passion wash over her as he picks up momentum. She feels his breath quicken and she arches against him, letting his pleasure seep into her heart. There is no going back now, for she loves this man. And he loves her.

And now the day is nearly spent and yet Maria feels her life has only just begun. Within that tiny fracture of time when he was inside her, she believes that her soul merged with his. She *is* his. He *is* hers. As he took her virginity on the rocking boat, the river lapping in applause, so began her need. Now all she wants is to be with him, and yet tonight she has to dance the most demanding role of her life. Her body is vibrating from his touch, trembling with desire and she has to stifle all of this and become Psyche, a creature as light as air, without material substance.

They are performing, not in their school, but in a hall nearby. It is not the premiere of *Pandora*, although the work hasn't been performed for four years. Lempert claims that now, after the war, it is even easier to see its relevance: the eternal conflict between good and evil within man.

Joan is already in full costume by the time Maria arrives. She is attired in her robe of crimson, white and purple, with a headdress of snakes. Her face is painted white, her eyes wide and dark, and a black pencil line arches above her eyebrows.

She is sitting at the mirror, smoking a cigarette, staring at herself while all the other girls bustle around her, getting ready.

'There you are!' She locks eyes with Maria in the mirror. 'Where have you been?'

Maria sits down beside her, picks up the container of face powder and blows on it gently to create a tiny puff of white.

'I went boating –' she pauses for effect – 'with Felix.'

'Ah, the mysterious Frenchman to whom you refuse to introduce me.' Joan pouts.

'That's not true. He nearly always meets me from school, but you've been staying late with Louis.'

Joan sighs. 'Well, that's not going to happen anymore.'

Maria ignores Joan's long face. She is too happy to worry about her friend's love life.

'Hey,' says Joan, noticing. 'What are you so smug about?'

'Oh, nothing,' Maria says, lightly. 'Except, I'm in love.'

Joan stubs out her cigarette with gusto. 'What exactly happened on your little boating trip with Felix?'

Maria blushes and looks away from her.

'Oh, I see,' Joan says. 'Well, good for you.' She gets up and smoothes down her costume. 'You had better hurry up and get ready. We shall have to discuss *all* the details later.' She winks at Maria.

She is waiting in the wings, alongside Joan and Christopher, who plays the part of the Youth. She watches the first group of dancers, the common men and women of the earth, as they articulate, through movement, mankind's search for something to worship. Do we all need someone to guide us? she wonders. Will she let Felix be her guide?

Now Joan is on stage as Pandora, entrancing the group, followed by Christopher, as the innocent Youth. It is her turn soon. She must appear as a vision for the Youth, an apparition of goodness. She thinks of Felix watching her out in the cavern of the dark theatre. He spoke to Lempert about filming the dance, and she knows that he will be shielded by his camera now, documenting her movements. She cannot escape his eye.

She is out now, the stage lights blinding her and yet filling her with energy so that she does, for a second, forget she is Maria, the girl who just lost her virginity, and becomes the spirit, Psyche – the triumph of intellect over instinct. Yet the common people reject her and she is forced to retreat as they vie for Pandora's box. Louis, as the Go-Getter, and Stephen, as the Strong Man, dance a fight for it, Louis winning out. The second chorus group rushes upon the stage, monsters of evil, gathering Pandora up, thwarting the Strong Man. Maria is in the shadows now, watching them crown Pandora with a grinning death mask with white crystalline spikes on its top.

There is a short interval. They rush into the dressing room, a bubble of first-night excitement. Lempert comes in. Maria can tell he is pleased with them. He pats her shoulder with his hand while talking to Christopher about the final dance between the Youth and Psyche, the point at which they have to bring the world out of darkness and back to the light. She suddenly feels weighed down by the responsibility. Her body is so tired, not just from dancing, but from the new sensations it experienced today. She needs some air.

She glances at the clock on the wall. She has ten minutes for a quick cigarette. She slips out of the dressing room and out the back of the building, where she stands in the alleyway, shaking a cigarette out of the packet.

'I am sure Psyche is far too pure to smoke.'

She jumps. There, in front of her, is Felix.

'Where did you spring from?' she asks him.

'I was here all along, smoking. I saw you come out. You look like a phantom in your white robe.'

She leans forward and lets him light her cigarette. 'What do you think?' she asks, nervous for his approval.

'You are superb, my darling.'

Maria beams from within. It means so much to her that he thinks she is good.

'I am really very interested to see how it will turn out on film,' he says. 'I have never filmed a dance before.'

'And what do you think of the others?'

'Well, some of the other dancers need a little more experience, but the girl who plays Pandora is expert.'

'That's Joan, my friend,' Maria tells him, but he is not really listening to her. His eyes flash and his hands sweep in an arc around him as he talks about the meaning of *Pandora*. She imagines him on set: Felix the film director. She pinches herself. She has to keep reminding herself that this talented man actually loves her.

'I think the choreography is quite fascinating. This dance has a political subtext . . .' He pauses before taking another drag on his cigarette. 'Yesterday's good can become today's evil . . .'

His words trail off into the dark alley and she cannot see the look in his eyes, but she knows he is not just thinking of the dance now. He is thinking of his mysterious past: a part of himself he refuses to share with her. The stage door opens, light spilling out on to the street, illuminating the two of them.

'There you are!' Joan says. 'Come on; curtain's up in five minutes.'

She suddenly notices Felix.

'Oh, hello . . . Are you the famous Monsieur Leduc?'

Maria blushes to her roots; how could Joan be so tactless?

'I think I must be.' He puts his head on one side and gives her a penetrating look. His expression is far from friendly and, for a second, Maria can see what Jacqueline is talking about when she says that Felix is difficult – yet, not with her. With Maria, he is so tender, so soft and kind.

Joan ignores Felix's snub and instead turns to Maria, giving her an inquiring look, before disappearing back inside. She knows what Joan is thinking. She can even hear her voice inside her head: *He's a bit old for you, darling, isn't he? A little bit grumpy looking . . .*

She drops her cigarette butt on the ground, its red tip still burning in the dark. 'I had better go back in,' she says. 'See you afterwards?'

Felix suddenly takes a hold of her arm. 'Actually, darling, that's just it . . . I am going to have to dash off.'

'Oh,' she says, disappointed. She had been looking forward to showing off her intellectual film-maker boyfriend to the rest of the dance company. 'Will I see you later tonight?'

'Maria, my love,' he says, spinning her around so that she is trapped by the beseeching look in his eyes. 'Before we came out tonight, I got a telegram. I have to go to France . . . tonight. It's rather urgent . . .'

She looks at him in shock. What can he be saying to her? Their relationship has only just begun; how can he be leaving now?

He kisses her quickly on the lips. 'You have to go back in, darling,' he says, pushing her towards the stage door.

'But for how long?' she manages to get out.

'Not long . . .' He pauses. 'I promise I will be back in a couple of weeks. You can wait for me, can you not?'

As she dances, she cannot get Felix's announcement out of her mind: he is going away, tonight – just when she had fallen so completely in love with him. How can she bear to be apart from him, even if it's for two weeks? And at the back of her mind is another voice, the doubt that still resides in her heart: will he ever come back? Has he tricked her into giving him her virginity, and now wants no more to do with her? Surely not?

She saw how he looked at her just now, told her she was superb. After all, he is filming her. All these things tell her that he is not lying to her when he says he will come back. She just has to be patient and she has to trust him. Yet anxiety bites through her composure as she tries her best to focus. She senses Christopher's consternation; she hears his whispered instructions. Psyche and the Youth are engaged in their final dance, where her power as Psyche outweighs Pandora, and they banish her from the world.

I will not let Felix discard me, Maria vows, as she spins around Christopher, her mind in a tumult. It is in this moment of distraction that she makes a mistake. It is a tiny one, yet it unbalances them both. She is too far away for him to lift her up, and she takes a clumsy step forward. Now she is too close. Christopher lifts her anyway, but he is forced to grab her from above her waist. She is bottom heavy, and she can feel him straining to maintain their balance. She looks out desperately into the audience, imagining Felix out there, the camera rolling, and knowing she is about to fall, knowing that her humiliation will be irredeemable.

Valentina

SHE WAKES ANTONELLA AS SOON AS IT IS LIGHT.

Her friend is confused at first, her head still groggy with alcohol. 'Where are we?' she asks.

'Shush . . .' Valentina puts her finger to her lips. 'I'll tell you on the way back. I've called a taxi.'

'But where is Aunty Isabella?'

'I don't know,' Valentina says, truthfully. 'Back at her house?'

She doesn't go into the bedroom to say goodbye to Francesco. All she wants to do is get out of his flat. As soon as she woke, she had wanted to leave. Francesco was still fast asleep, his breath deep and melodic, his back to her in the bed. She looked at his figure, innocent in slumber, and honestly wondered how she could have been in love with him before. Despite their lovemaking last night, in the cold light of a sober morning, she feels nothing for him. All that has happened is that she feels even more distraught about Theo. She wants him back even more now. She knows she is a hypocrite. She has just fallen back into the arms of an old lover, and not with much persuasion. There had been a little part of her that needed to do this, she knows. It was unfinished business; now it is over. She feels it deep down inside herself. She has no idea how Francesco feels, but she has no intention of seeing him again.

They ride in the taxi through the deserted streets of London, enveloped within a thick mist. This muffled white world makes her feel outside of her body, as if she is in one of her psychedelic dreams.

Antonella cuddles next to her on the back seat. 'Mio dio, what happened last night? I can't remember anything,' she says, yawning.

'That's what tequila does to you,' Valentina says, dryly.

'What happened to Aunty Isabella? And, more to the point, what about Francesco? Did you sleep with him?' She gives Valentina an inquiring look.

Valentina nods and Antonella looks puzzled.

'So what are you doing racing home in a taxi with me, rather than staying in bed for a day of sex with Francesco?'

Valentina looks out the car window at the impenetrable mist, a completely white world with no beginning or end to it. She feels as if they are driving towards oblivion.

'Maybe he is the one, Valentina? He was, after all, your first love,' Antonella says.

But Valentina shakes her head. 'No. It's too late to go back. He broke my heart once. I won't give it to him again.' She dare not tell Antonella her feelings about Theo.

Her friend pats her hand. 'OK,' she says, knowing when not to push her. 'So, what happened to my aunty?'

Valentina doesn't speak for a moment. She knows how scandalised Antonella will be to hear all about Isabella's antics with Peter and Rupert, but something stops her from telling her. That is between Isabella and Antonella, especially since Antonella seemed to have her eye on Peter, before she passed out.

'I don't know,' she tells Antonella. 'Isabella must have gone home earlier.'

The thick London fog chills her right down to the bones, making her shiver as they walk away from the taxi. Valentina glances at her watch. It is six thirty, and few are venturing on to the streets of South Kensington quite yet. Antonella is ahead of her, opening the ironwork gate and trailing up the path to the front door of her aunt's grand house. Valentina feels her back prickling. Instinctively, she knows someone is watching them. She turns, hoping to see Theo behind her, but knows deep down that it isn't him. She only has one stalker. Sure enough, there, on the other side of the street, is Glen, standing out in all the white in his long black coat and dark glasses. She is too tired to bother with him now, and she doesn't want to worry Antonella, so she just ignores him and walks with determination up to the front door, slamming it hard behind her.

Isabella is already up, looking immaculate in a tailored skirt-suit, her long hair pulled into a tight, shiny bun, her face fresh, not a dark shadow in sight. She is sitting at the breakfast bar, sipping a small cup of black coffee and going through her iPhone.

'Good morning, ladies,' she says, smiling sweetly. 'I wasn't expecting you home so early.'

'Where did you go, Aunty?' Antonella flops on to the couch. 'You just disappeared.'

'It was you who disappeared, darling. I believe you went to bed . . . on your own!'

Antonella begins to bite her nails, looking out of the window. 'It is a funny thing,' she says. 'I thought something was going to happen with that guy, Peter, when we were dancing, but then I started to think about Mikhail.'

'Your Russian lover?' Isabella asks.

'Yes. I think I miss him.'

Isabella smiles knowingly. 'Darling, I think you more than miss him. What is your theory, Valentina?'

Valentina takes a mug out of the cupboard and pours herself a coffee. She wants to take a shower; underneath her dress, her skin is sticky with caked-on ice cream. She wonders if either of the women can smell the vanilla on her.

'I think Antonella is a romantic, although she tries her best to suppress it,' Valentina says.

'What do you mean?' Antonella asks, sitting up, defensively crossing her arms over her chest.

'It's nothing to be ashamed of, darling,' Isabella says. 'It is very sweet, really.'

'I think that, underneath your very adventurous exterior, deep down, you believe in the fairy tale . . .' Valentina says, sitting down next to her friend on the couch and offering her a sip of her coffee.

'What fairy tale?' Antonella says, taking the mug.

'That one day your prince will come,' Isabella says.

'Oh, that's not true . . . I think that is crap.'

'Do you really? You know most women, secretly, deep down, dream about it . . .' Isabella taps her fingers on the counter top. 'It is nothing to be ashamed of. It shows great optimism. I'm afraid, my dear, I am a realist, as I suspect is Valentina.'

Isabella raises her eyebrows in a question and Valentina looks into her eyes. She wonders if Isabella knows that she saw her with those two young men. This woman obviously lives a secret double life.

'Well, my darlings,' Isabella says, gathering up her handbag and keys, 'I have to get to work. I will see you tonight at Valentina's opening. Ciao!'

The friends agree to sleep for a few hours. Antonella disappears into her aunty's bedroom, leaving the other room to Valentina.

Before she gets into bed, Valentina showers. She turns the temperature of the water up as high as she can stand. Steam billows around her and the water pressure is so strong, its jet stings her skin. She is washing away the ice cream, Francesco's scent and the memory of last night. She is washing away her past. She closes her eyes and pushes her face under the shower head. It is gone, the loss of Francesco – that first heartache she had nursed for years. Yet, frustratingly, she never realised she was free of it until she had lost Theo.

Can she and Theo ever manage a proper relationship together? It would never be normal. Not like the Hollywood-movie perfect couples the world pretends to believe in. The truth is that most couples are imperfect. And perhaps the happiest are those who are honest with each other, and have open relationships, like Leonardo and Raquel. Maybe Theo might like that kind of relationship, as well. She thinks back to last autumn and the erotic adventures she experienced in Leonardo's club. All of those experiences, and her seemingly promiscuous behaviour, had actually been devised by Theo himself. He had no issue with her sleeping with other people . . . In fact, he had been a part of it himself. In Venice, when she had asked him why he had done it, he claimed that he wanted to show her that he loved her so much that he didn't want to change who she was. He understood she was a free spirit. What Theo was trying to say was that it is possible to be liberated and in a relationship, as long as you trust each other. Trust: it all hangs on this one word. That's what Theo had demanded of her the day before yesterday. If she can show him that she trusts him she will have proven her love for him. But how can she do that?

Valentina slips under the cool sheets, her naked body still hot and silky from the shower. She is exhausted, her whole being sinking into the mattress, and yet, once she tries to, she can't sleep. She knows she must. It will be a long night and she needs to be at her best. It is the opening of the show, and Theo and Anita will be there. She will have to be strong to face them together.

She turns on her side and clutches the sheets. She feels raw panic. The idea of Theo and Anita together torments her. She sits up in bed, the sheets falling from her naked breasts. She needs to talk to someone. There is no point waking Antonella up, she is prejudiced against Theo. Who loves them equally? Who will be unbiased?

As soon as she hears Leonardo's voice, she feels better. As if she has drunk a mug of rich hot chocolate, his voice comforts her.

'Hello, darling; how is London?'

'Confusing.'

She tells Leonardo everything; things she would tell no other soul. She tells him she can't stand the idea of seeing Theo with his new, beautiful girlfriend at the opening tonight. She tells him about going to see her dad yesterday, and her expedition being aborted by the appearance of Glen.

Leonardo seems rather perturbed by Glen's threats. 'Did you tell Theo?' he keeps repeating.

'No; I haven't seen him. I didn't want to call him because I don't want him to think I am chasing him.'

'Valentina, you need to tell Theo about Glen. Maybe you should even call the police.'

'He is just a bully; don't worry. What use am I to him, if I am not with Theo?' she says bravely.

'OK,' her friend says, reluctantly. 'Just promise me, if you see him again, you'll do something about it.'

'OK, but, Leonardo, I haven't told you what happened last night. This is more important than creepy Glen hanging around.'

Valentina tells him about meeting Francesco and their re-enactment of her first time. When she has finished, he says nothing for a few seconds. She hears the empty line buzzing. She wonders if he has hung up, although why would he? Leonardo would never ever judge her.

'Leo, am I bad? Tell me, why did I sleep with Francesco?'

'I think you were saying goodbye to a part of yourself,' Leonardo says, softly. 'Or maybe you were trying to retrieve the girl you once were.'

'But *why* did I do it?'

'Because you are frightened of your feelings; you're trying to convince yourself that you don't want Theo, so you plunged headlong into bed with the nearest available male,' her friend says, matter-of-factly.

It strikes Valentina that Leonardo sounds subdued – not his usual buoyant self.

'Is everything OK, Leo? You sound different.'

'Everything is fine,' he says, tightly.

'I can tell that something is wrong. What is it? Leonardo, answer me,' she commands him.

'If you must know, Raquel and I broke up.'

Valentina can't hide the astonishment in her voice. 'But you had the perfect relationship. What happened?'

'It's complicated. I'm sorry, Valentina. I don't want to talk to you about it over the phone.'

She feels a little hurt. Here she is opening up completely to Leonardo and yet he doesn't want to confide in her. Still, she has to respect his wishes. 'OK; well, I'll be back in a couple of days. We'll talk then.'

'Maybe you won't come back to Milan, Valentina.'

'What do you mean?'

'Theo.'

There is a strange tone in his voice and Valentina wonders what it is.

'But he has a new girlfriend. I don't think I will win him back now. She is so sexy – a real femme fatale.' She sighs.

'Come on, Valentina,' Leonardo encourages her. 'I told you that you might have to fight for him. You can't give up.'

'But what should I do, Leo? How do I show him that I love him so much, I would do anything for him?'

'Well, you must find that "anything" and do it,' Leonardo says simply.

'If I could just be near him again . . . touch him,' Valentina says. 'He would know how I felt if we slept together . . .'

'So seduce him!'

'I can't . . . It would be a really terrible thing to do to Anita. I don't want to be that kind of bitch.'

'You could never be a bitch, Valentina.'

The faith of her friend touches her. 'Leonardo, I'm really sorry about you and Raquel,' Valentina says. 'I wish you were here and I could give you a hug.'

Valentina is not the hugging type, and yet she means what she says.

At last, she sleeps. She dreams she is sitting on an empty Tube train, hurtling through the dark tunnels. She is naked and alone. The train pulls into a station. She looks out of the window, but the name of the station is flashing by too fast. Is it Gloucester Road? It looks like it, with its ochre brick walls and modern art panels. The doors slide open and a woman gets on at the other end of the carriage, carrying a suitcase. She has short, blond bobbed hair, in a similar style to Valentina's own hair, and is wearing an old-fashioned silk skirt and top, with a long scarf wrapped around her neck. Valentina gets up. Maybe the woman has some clothes in her case that she can borrow. Yet, as she approaches her, the woman spins around, pinning her with eyes like her mother's.

Valentina realises that the woman looks just like Tina Rosselli, apart from the blond hair. She says nothing, just offers Valentina the suitcase. Valentina clicks it open, but the case is empty. She has nothing to cover herself with.

Valentina wakes. She is lying on her side, her knees up to her chest, her arms wrapped around her waist. She wonders why she is so compressed. She tries to stretch out her legs and realises that she is restrained from doing so by the edges of something hard. She unravels her arms and has the same experience. She feels the edges of what she is constrained in with her hands. It's a hard box, lined with red silky material, and there are straps with little clips on them. It dawns on her that she is inside the very case the woman gave her in her dream. She is still asleep. And now she sees herself from above: a woman trapped in a suitcase. Why can she not climb out? She hears footsteps approaching, and next she sees a pair of shoes standing right beside the case: they are black leather, expensive, yet a little scuffed, the laces slightly lose. Whose shoes are these? She looks up, but all she can make out are a pair of legs in pinstriped trousers, and then they disappear into that London mist. Who is it? Theo? Francesco? She knows what will happen next and her throat is tight with anticipation. She cannot call out. Suddenly, the lid is slammed down on top of her and now she is in complete darkness. She is this man's possession. It is her greatest fear.

She wakes standing. The empty case is discarded by

her side and she is back inside the Tube train, trying to keep her balance as the train shuttles through the tunnels. She is still alone. Or is she? She feels that familiar prickle down her spine – the sense that someone is watching her. She holds her breath, afraid to turn and see who it might be. She can feel his breath now on her neck as he stands behind her, puts his arms around her waist and bends his head down to kiss her neck. His lips upon her tender skin make her shiver. He kisses her slowly; he keeps kissing her. She feels the skin on her neck puckering, and then a little stab of pain, something sharp cutting her. She struggles now, but he holds her even tighter in his arms; he is clamped on to her neck, sucking the love right out of her. The lights flicker inside the train and, for a moment, she sees herself and her assailant reflected in the windows. He finally lifts his head and stares back at her. Terror courses through her. It is Glen, his lips soft and red with her blood, his eyes gleaming.

'I will take you from him,' she hears him whisper, softly.

'Valentina! Wake up, Valentina!'

She sits up with a gasp. The bedroom is almost dark, full of dusky shadows. Antonella is leaning over her, shaking her. 'Valentina, are you OK?'

She comes to slowly, nodding mutely, looking around the room wide-eyed. It was only a dream. She is safe.

'You were screaming,' Antonella says. 'You must have been having a really bad nightmare.'

Valentina nods, still feeling a shiver of fear when she remembers the vampire, Glen. 'I was.'

'What was it about?'

'I can't remember now,' she lies. 'It was just scary.' She doesn't want to start explaining about Glen to Antonella. She knows how easily spooked her friend can get. She pulls herself back against the headboard and looks out of the bedroom window. The curtains are still open. It is a bluey dusk outside, the street lights already on. 'What time is it?'

'Five to six. Can you believe it? We slept all day.'

It is an hour and a half before the opening – just enough time to get ready.

'I'll grab the bathroom first. You make some tea,' Antonella orders, charging out of the bedroom.

Valentina sits for a few moments longer, letting her heart-beat slow. She is still shaken by those strange images in her dream. Tonight she will have to face Theo and Anita together. It could be her last chance to win her love back. She realises that it is more important to her than anything, even her debut as an erotic photographer in one of the hippest galleries in London. If she lets Theo go home with Anita tonight, she believes she will have lost him forever.

Maria

HE HAS BROUGHT HER TO PARIS WITH HIM. IT IS BEYOND anything she could have dreamt of. It is the shimmering silver lining to the very black cloud of her failure as a dancer.

After the disaster of her fall during *Pandora*, Maria had made matters so much worse by not continuing the duet. She had run off stage in a flood of tears, leaving poor Christopher stranded to continue the final act on his own. She had not only humiliated herself but shamed the whole company. She had let everyone down. She will never forget Joan's shocked face. She dare not imagine how furious Lempert must be with her – not for the fact that she had fallen, but for running away. A real dancer would just get up again and continue. They were students, after all. It was the premiere. It was not a complete disaster if someone slipped up. And yet, to Maria, it was. She felt like she was falling apart. It was not just the dance but also the tumult of emotion she was feeling: the elation at her love for Felix, the desolation at his impending departure to France. She could not bear to face anyone, not even her beloved Jacqueline, who must have been sitting in the audience, horrified. So, before the final curtain had even dropped, she had fled the theatre, running alongside the Thames, wanting to hurl herself into its murky depths. It was at Waterloo Station that Felix caught up with her. He set the case with his camera down as she fell into his arms, sobbing desperately.

'Shush,' he said again and again, as he stroked her hair.

Eventually she calmed down and he loosened his hold on her, handing her a handkerchief. She wiped her eyes but, as soon as she remembered that dreadful moment again, as she felt herself falling, as she landed with a thump on to the stage, she buried her face in her hands.

'Come, now,' Felix said, gently, pulling her hands away from her face. 'It's not the end of the world.'

She shook her head mournfully.

'Why did I run away?' she wailed. 'I can never go back now.'

'Of course you can,' Felix said. 'You are an exquisite dancer. You must.'

'I can't face them,' she said. 'I have failed.'

'My darling, we are meant to fail sometimes in life,' Felix tried to explain, 'so that we fight on, so that we can finally win . . .'

Yet his words did not console her. All she was thinking was that soon he would be gone to France and she would be all alone in London. She couldn't face Jacqueline again . . . at least not for a few days. She couldn't bear her mentor's disappointment. Maria believed that if she really did have ambition, a burning passion to dance, then she would go back and face her failure and she would work hard to redeem herself. But she didn't want to. She clutched Felix's handkerchief, damp with her tears. It dawned upon her that she was not here in London fulfilling her own dream of being a dancer, but her mother's dream that she might become a dancer. She wished she had never left Venice. And yet, if she had not, she would never have found Felix.

'Bring me to France with you,' she whispered.

Felix looked taken aback. 'Darling, I'm sorry, that's just not possible.'

She grabbed hold of his arm and pulled on his sleeve. 'Please bring me with you.'

'I can't,' he said awkwardly. 'I have business there.'

'I know,' she said, 'and I won't interfere, I promise. I just want to be in another place for a week or two with you. I can't bear to be without you.'

'But what about your dance?'

'Felix, I *can't* go back.'

He shook his head. 'Maria, darling, if you came with me, I would have to abandon you in Paris overnight . . . I don't want to do that.'

'I don't mind. I'll just sleep and rest and wait for you.' She shivered in her scant Psyche costume and he pulled her to him.

Neither of them noticed the curious stares of passers-by, for they were a small spectacle in Waterloo Station, Maria still dressed as Psyche, a white waif, in the arms of the stern, dark-haired man.

'I love you, Felix,' she whispered, and she felt him quivering in response to her words and, despite his age and his experience, she knew they meant so much to him.

'All right,' he said hoarsely, and her heart leapt with joy. 'If you really are sure you don't mind that I may have to disappear to sort out my business.'

She showered his cheeks with kisses. 'Oh, yes . . . yes . . . I don't mind.'

He pulled away from her and held her at arm's length. 'And no questions, Maria,' he said, looking serious. 'You must promise me that you never ask me anything about my affairs in France.'

She frowned, a little perturbed by what he had said. 'But why not? You can trust me.'

His voice softened. 'I know that, darling, but I just don't want you to be concerned with things that have no meaning for us . . .'

'Us?'

He nodded. 'Yes, us. For are you not mine now?'

'Oh, I am, Felix,' she held him to her again.

All the way from Victoria to Folkestone, she sleeps in his arms. They stay the night in a dingy little bed and breakfast in

227

Folkestone; she is so exhausted that she falls asleep immediately and he does not disturb her. They wake early the next morning, breakfasting on whale meat sandwiches provided by the landlady. Maria has never eaten anything quite so disgusting in her life, but she is hungry, so she forces it down. As they board the boat, she holds Felix's hand tightly, her heart jittering with nerves. She is following this man back into his world, into the unknown. She is trusting him with all her heart. In her other hand, she grips her one small case – not even full. She had packed in haste, afraid Jacqueline would turn up and change her mind for her. She left her ration books on the kitchen table, with enough money to cover her lodging for the next month. Lastly, she had scrawled a note to Jacqueline – inadequate she knew.

Dear Jacqueline,

Tonight I understand I will never be the dancer you and my mother hope I might be. I am sorry to disappoint you but I do not want to continue my studies at the Lempert School. I am so grateful for all your help, but I need to go away for a little while. I am travelling with a friend who will take good care of me. I promise I will write and let you know where I am and I will write to my mother too. Please do not worry.

With all my love and affection,
Maria

She had not mentioned Felix by name, for she knew that it would make Jacqueline angry and worried to think she has fled with the Frenchman. In fact, she would not have been surprised if Jacqueline had followed her to Paris if she had known he was her companion.

On the boat, they eat lunch in silence. Maria is so shocked at her own actions that she is unable to speak, and Felix seems preoccupied, every now and again patting her knee or refilling her glass with water.

It is a calm enough crossing. Most of the five hours they sit on deck, holding hands, watching the English horizon disappear, searching for France to begin.

The scars of the war appear even deeper in Boulogne. The quays and all the neighbouring buildings are destroyed. She feels a twinge of fear in her heart. She is now in Felix's country. She is now completely in his hands. After a wait of several hours, they board the train for Paris, squeezing into a compartment that they are forced to share with a couple and their five children. This experience seems to make Felix even more stern and taciturn, although Maria finds it a relief to chat with the mother, who is Italian – from Turin. She has spent the war years in England, her husband being English, but now her father is dying and they are returning to Italy to be with him in his final days, and hopefully to bring her mother back with them to their house in Surrey. Maria plays snap with the two eldest children as the others sleep, all apart from Felix, who is watching her with lowered lids as the train trundles through the night.

At Gare du Nord they say their goodbyes to the Italian family. The mother hugs her tightly, inviting her to their home in Surrey whenever she pleases. They disappear into the night, the mother's Italian echoing after her, pulling on Maria's nostalgia for home.

Felix leads her across the city of Paris. Unlike London, there are neon signs in the shop windows and young men and women bustling along the dark pavements. She feels a sense that the night has only just begun – so different from the dour evenings of post-war London. These people have just woken up; they are coming alive: intense-looking men with glasses and little beards, and gamine young women with loose dark hair, blunt fringes and heavily made up eyes. They are lost in their own dramas and hardly give her and Felix a second glance. She cannot help looking at them. They look so different from London folk.

Felix takes her south of the River Seine, into a district he calls Saint-Germain-des-Prés. They walk past cafés he tells her he likes to frequent. He names them, one by one: Café Flore, where Sartre and Simone de Beauvoir used to go before they became too well known; Deux Magots; Rhumerie Martiniquaise; and the Bar Vert. She wants to stop, eat something, have a glass of wine, but he hurries her along, telling her he wants to check into the hotel first.

She follows Felix down narrow cobbled streets, gently dipping between tall houses that lean this way and that. Everything is dark grey: the roofs, the walls, the cobbles, the shutters, the paintwork. Finally, he approaches a dilapidated-looking hotel.

Her stomach knots with excitement. It has been barely two days since he took her virginity on the river, since her disastrous performance as Psyche, and only twenty-four hours since they eloped. During all that time he has not touched her, apart from to hold her hand. Not on the train from Victoria to Folkestone, or in the bed and breakfast, not on the boat across the Channel, or the train from Boulogne to Paris. At the sight of the hotel, all thoughts of food are gone. What will happen now? Should she insist on her own bedroom? She knows, even before they walk through the door, she will not.

They enter a dimly lit lobby, thick with the odour of tobacco and cheap cologne. Maria takes in the peeling paint on the walls and the worn carpet. It is hardly the Ritz. She trails behind Felix as he approaches the concierge, a large woman with red hair piled on top of her head, and lips painted scarlet to match. She is smoking a cigarette and reading a newspaper. As soon as she looks up and sees Felix, her eyes light up.

'Monsieur Leduc! So long it has been since we saw you last. Welcome, welcome.' She gushes in French, leaning across her desk, kissing Felix on both cheeks.

'Good evening, Madame Paget. I would like to introduce you to my companion, Signorina Maria Brzezinska.'

In his native tongue Felix's voice seems to have dropped an octave, and he appears even more refined a gentleman than he was in London.

Madame Paget looks at her with steely eyes, and Maria feels herself wilting under her gaze.

'Good evening,' Maria says, shyly in French. Despite the fact that the French Jacqueline taught her is nearly as good as her English, Maria and Felix always speak in English. Is it because they met in London, or is it the language of their love?

Madame Paget brusquely kisses her on either cheek. 'Welcome,' she says, immediately turning her attention back to Felix. 'So is it your usual room you require?' she asks Felix.

'Yes, thank you.'

She takes down a key as he signs the register. 'Things have changed, you know, since you were last here.'

'How so?' Felix asks her.

'So many more foreigners in Paris now. Americans everywhere,' she says, disdainfully, looking Maria up and down again, as she twists the key in her hand. 'Everyone wants to come to Paris and, in particular, to our little district. They call themselves existentialists, but they have no idea what it means. All they really want is to dance all night and get drunk.' Madame Paget sniffs, staring at Maria, her gaze arctic with disapproval. 'And they closed down Le Tabou, did you hear?'

'So where does everyone go now?'

'There is a new club, just opened. All the great jazz will be there. It's Vian's place: Club Saint-Germain.' She hands the key to Felix. 'Enjoy your stay,' Madame Paget says to Maria.

Maria heads towards the old cage lift, waiting dutifully at the gate for Felix as he gathers up their bags.

'She is different,' she hears Madame Paget say to him.

Her words unsettle her. Different from what or whom? Has Felix brought other women here? Of course he has, and what is wrong with that? He is so much older than her. How can she be so naïve as to think not? She should be glad to hear Madame Paget call her different. Doesn't that mean she could be the *one*?

The room is tiny, the walls in as bad a condition as the lobby. It is completely dominated by a large brass bed. Maria notices that at least it is made up with clean crisp sheets. The room might be tatty but it is spotless. There is a sink in the corner, and a small window under the eaves of the sloping ceiling. She walks over to the window and opens it, leaning outside. Her chest constricts with excitement as she looks out across the skyline of Paris. It is a dream to be here, and with the man she loves – the man she hopes will marry her one day . . . maybe here in Paris?

'Darling . . .' Felix murmurs behind her. 'Welcome to my Paris.'

She turns around and he is standing with his back to the closed door, looking at her, his eyes pensive.

She walks towards him, hypnotised, yearning to be kissed.

He surprises her by taking her hat off and laying it carefully on top of the bed. He kisses her forehead gently.

'So, can I trust you?' he asks her, softly.

She looks up at him, nodding earnestly. 'Of course you can.'

'And, most importantly, do you trust me?'

She looks into his eyes. They are a brown of a hundred shades, flecked with green, amber, chocolate and charcoal. She picks up his hands, holding them tightly. 'Yes, I trust you,' she says with all her heart.

He doesn't smile. In fact, he looks even more serious. 'Good,' he says. 'That is important, otherwise I made a mistake.'

'Mistake?' she asks, shuddering involuntarily.

'Bringing you here.'

'But you haven't made a mistake. I would do anything for you.'

'You really mean it, don't you?'

'Yes.'

'How could I wish for any more?' It is a rhetorical question as he gathers Maria up in his arms and buries his face in her neck. 'Promise me that you will always love me?' He sounds so needy and desperate that it shocks her.

'Of course, darling, of course.' She kisses the top of his bowed head. He raises his face to her and presses his lips against hers.

She wants him to make love to her again, as he did in the boat when he took her virginity. She can feel that tightening of her stomach, softening between her legs.

He pulls apart from her, and now he looks different: no longer vulnerable and wounded. Now his eyes are gleaming and he looks at her with pride. 'There is something about you,' he says. 'You have this effervescence, this incredible spirit.'

He pulls her summer coat off her shoulders and begins to unbutton her blouse – one button by one. Her nipples stand to attention. His admiration makes her stand tall. She is no longer shy. He unlatches her brassiere, and now her top half is completely naked. She wriggles out of her skirt, letting it drop around her ankles. She takes off her shoes and stands in front of him in her stockings. She wants to offer her heart and body to him.

'Maria,' he says softly. 'Would you like to be *my* student now?'

He steps even closer to her. He is still fully clothed; he doesn't take anything off – not even his tie. He unclips her stockings one by one, so that now all she has on is her knickers, nothing else. She is scared, yet excited. She has done this already with him in the boat, but that was spontaneous, instinctive, whereas this feels choreographed, like a dance she must learn.

'Sit on the bed.' His voice is commanding, yet his eyes are pools of yearning.

She walks over and sits on the end of the bed. It sinks beneath her, the springs obviously ancient and worn.

'Take off your underwear.'

She wiggles out of her knickers, feeling self-conscious yet, at the same time, a little excited by his gaze upon her naked breasts. Her nipples are still erect, begging to be touched.

'Now,' he whispers. 'Slowly, very slowly, open your legs. Show me yourself.'

She hesitates and, watching his lips, the way his tongue flicks over them, she slowly opens her legs.

'Oh, my darling,' he whispers, walking over towards her and kneeling down in front of her. 'I am going to play you now, and you are going to sing for me.'

He leans forward, trailing his finger down the inside of her thigh and bringing it right up between her legs. She gasps as he pushes his finger inside her.

'You like this, don't you?' he asks her.

'Yes,' she whispers. 'Oh, yes.'

He pulls his finger out and licks it. 'You taste so sweet – still virgin fresh.' He puts his hands on either one of her knees and pushes her legs open wider still.

Maria lies on her back on the bed and closes her eyes. His head is between her legs as she feels his tongue begin to explore her, touching her in places so sensitive she never knew they existed. At the same time, he brings his hands up, cupping one of them under her bottom while, with his other hand and middle finger, he pushes deep inside her again. She wants to feel more than his finger inside her. She wants him to make love to her, to feel that unity with him like she did on the little rowing boat. Yet Felix remains on his knees, caressing her with his mouth and his hands, working her up into an ecstasy of sensation. She is lost in the wilderness of his attention – completely at his mercy. He is on his knees, lapping at her, and she has an image of him as if he is a big black panther and she is somehow his prey. And yet he is adoring her, is he not? He does not stop, not for a moment; steadily, precisely, he brings her closer and closer to a place of pleasure she has never entered before. He pulls away his head, taking breath.

'Come on, my little one,' he purrs. 'Open up to me. Be mine.'

He bends down and, once his tongue touches her again, the tip of it circling her relentlessly, she feels herself sliding on to the thin ice of her abandon.

'Felix!' she cries out, and with his fingers he presses down on her in unison with his tongue. The pressure is so intense, so fine. She lets go, her body flying into rapturous spasms, her entire being begging for him to enter her, and yet he doesn't.

She is unable to move for a few minutes. Her whole body is in shock and her mind is reeling from what he has just done to her. She opens her eyes and is surprised to see that Felix is sitting on the bed, staring down at her. He is still fully dressed. She blushes, aware of her nakedness and her exposure.

'Darling Maria, will you be mine?' Felix asks her.

She is not sure if he means metaphorically or if he is actually proposing to her. She doesn't care, for her response is immediate. 'Yes, oh yes,' she gushes, for this man has initiated a craving deep inside her. She wants to be one with him for all eternity. She is his.

Valentina

THE CROWD FROM THE GALLERY IS SPILLING OUT ON TO the streets of Soho. Valentina feels a clench of nerves inside her stomach. She and Antonella follow in the wake of Aunty Isabella, the essence of Milano chic in her Armani dress. For once, Valentina is wearing a designer dress, as well: Balenciaga, lent by Isabella. At first, Valentina was wary of wearing so much colour but, having looked at herself in the mirror before they left Isabella's house, she was surprised to see how well it suited her. She considers that it might be to her advantage to look a little different from usual, to draw Theo's attention.

The dress is a vibrant floral print – blue, yellow and pink – made up of a series of panels, with a cinched-in waist, cup sleeves and a very, very short skirt. Normally it is Antonella who is showing off her legs, not Valentina, but, as Isabella instructs the two girls, Valentina's best asset is her legs, whereas Antonella's is her chest. Thus, she has dressed her niece in a scarlet wool-mix dress from Dior, which gives her hourglass figure even more emphasis.

Tonight, Valentina has departed from her normally sleek bob, backcombing her hair and using gel to create a jagged, bed-head look. She totters into the Lexington Gallery, feeling slightly as if she is a spectacle – especially as her ankle boots are far higher than she would normally wear. Yet she needn't have worried, compared to the rest of the gathering, she looks almost understated.

Valentina admires the peacock crowd, so different from Milan where there is an unspoken uniform of classic style. In Soho, it seems, anything goes. She supposes it must be because of the nature of the exhibition itself, since most people look as if they are attending a fetish club, not an art opening. Tattooed men and women, some with shaved heads, others with thick lustrous locks, or red, blue, purple hair, wearing body-clinging and revealing clothes in black, scarlet and white, mingle with tweed-jacketed art critics and combat-wearing photographers. She pushes through the throng, scanning the crowd for Theo, but she cannot see him anywhere. In the meantime, Isabella secures them three glasses of champagne from a passing waiter.

'Salute!'

The three women chink their glasses.

'So, let's take a look at this famous photography of yours, which so eloquently portrays my niece,' Isabella says.

'It's this way.' Valentina begins to weave through the

crowd. At least it's not like a Milan opening, she thinks, with people recognising her and tugging at her the whole time. At least in London she is just like everyone else. She likes this feeling of anonymity.

There are her prints, hung in a perfect sextant in the left-hand corner of the space.

'Oh, I can see them! Look, Aunty!' Antonella cries out, leading the way in her scarlet dress, her breasts bouncing proudly before her and causing more than a few admiring glances. Antonella seems completely unselfconscious about the fact that she is standing in front of extremely explicit, naked images of herself.

'Do you mind?' Valentina whispers to her, suddenly considering her friend's modesty.

'Mind what?' Antonella asks her.

'Being displayed, naked, in front of all these strangers?'

'Of course not, do you?' She indicates the watery reflections of the naked Valentina in Venice – the first erotic pictures she ever took.

'No. I don't, actually,' Valentina says, surprised that she is not embarrassed by them; but so much of the content in the show is explicit, and many are self-portraits, like Anita's pictures, that any kind of modesty seems irrelevant.

She feels a sharp nudge in her rib cage and looks at Antonella questioningly. Her friend is looking right behind her, at someone they obviously both know, her eyes wide open in warning. Theo? Valentina whips around and, to her horror, it is not Theo but Francesco who is in front of her.

'Good evening, Valentina.'

She says nothing. She doesn't know what to say. She has no memory of telling him about her exhibition but she was so drunk last night she could have mentioned it.

'How are you?' he asks, looking at her with expectant eyes.

'Fine. Tired,' she says, listlessly.

He moves in closer, putting his hand on her bottom. 'Me, too. I wonder why that might be.' He winks at her.

She steps back. She can't believe he actually winked and patted her bottom. In the atmosphere of this gallery – full of the new, the exciting, pulsing art scene of London – Francesco looks even older than he is. In his tired blue shirt and navy blazer, he is from another world. She sees him for who he is: he wants to hang on to her coat-tails. A part of her feels guilty about sleeping with him last night and leading him on, but stronger than that is her urge to get away from him.

'Excuse me,' she says, trying to move away. Both Antonella and Isabella seem to have dematerialised and she doesn't recognise anyone around her.

'I like your pictures,' Francesco says.

'Thank you.' She doesn't say any more.

He is waiting for her to speak, to explain herself, but she just wants to get away from him.

'I just have to speak with someone,' she lies, and turns to walk away. But Francesco has his hand on her elbow.

'Valentina, wait,' he says.

She turns to face him, reluctantly.

His eyes are doleful. 'Why did you walk out this morning? What happened? Did I do something to upset you?'

'No; you did nothing wrong,' she says.

He begins to look more hopeful.

'I'm sorry, I was drunk . . .' she tries to explain. 'I shouldn't have—'

But he interrupts, his face charged with excitement. 'Don't you think it's incredible the way we just bumped into each other again, after all these years? Doesn't that tell you something?'

'Yes, it is quite incredible,' she agrees. 'But I always felt I would get the opportunity of seeing you again one day.'

She recalls her frustration when her mother had banished Francesco before she had had the chance to tell him what she really thought of him for cheating on his wife, and for taking her innocence, her trusting heart and breaking it. It is nearly ten years ago now, and yet she still feels angry with her mother about it.

'Yes,' Francesco continues to speak enthusiastically. 'I always believed we would see each other again, too.' He smiles, looking triumphant. 'Valentina,' he says, taking her hand in his, 'we are meant to be together.'

'No,' she says, the word coming out more harshly than she expects. She pulls her hand away. 'I don't mean it the same way as you do.'

'What do you mean, then?' He looks confused for a

moment. 'Do you want to talk about it somewhere else?' He winks again. 'At my place. You like it there, don't you?'

The man she first loved is a loser, she thinks to herself. His flat is swanky, yes, but it's soulless. And also rather puzzling . . . It occurs to her what it was that made her surprised to discover that the sleek, minimalist bachelor pad was his.

'When do you see your daughter?' she asks him.

'What?' Francesco looks even more perplexed. 'What has that got to do with anything?'

'Well, when do you see her?' she persists.

'Do we have to talk about Lucia *now*?'

'I just wondered because, when I first met you in the restaurant, you talked about her but I didn't see anything that belonged to her in your apartment.'

'You wouldn't,' he mumbles, squirming under her glare. 'The truth is, I don't really see my daughter much. She lives with her mother and her stepfather . . . and . . . well . . . I think she is better off without me.'

'You mean you can't be bothered to see her?'

Francesco starts to look cross. 'Can you stop interrogating me, here of all places? You never used to be so judgemental, Valentina.' His tone softens again. 'Come on, let's get out of here; you can question me all you want in bed.' He leans forward and takes her hand in his.

She pulls it away again. 'No, I said.' Her eyes are like flint. 'You don't understand. The reason I knew we would see each other again is because I wanted to hurt you, like you hurt me.'

He looks startled.

'But I realise it is a pointless exercise,' she continues. She knows she is being cruel, that it is unfair of her to judge him, yet she is fuelled by this passion, this anger on behalf of little Lucia. 'The kind of man who doesn't care about his own daughter can't have much of a heart to hurt.'

'Hey, that's not fair.' Francesco looks wounded. 'You don't know the whole story.'

'I know enough,' she says, turning on her heel and strutting away, her heart pounding inside her chest. She is astonished at herself. Why is she so furious? She has never judged anyone the way she has just judged Francesco. He is right. She doesn't know the whole story. Yet she can't help it. She could never let him touch her again, even if she wanted to, because she cannot respect him.

She charges through the crowd. She is pretty certain he won't pursue her now, but, to be on the safe side, she goes into the small gallery that adjoins the main one. It is a small box-like space, unlit; film is being projected on the far wall. She sits down on a seat, relieved to be on her own now, with just a few other people around her in the dark, silently watching the installation. She focuses on the images in front of her. It is a black and white film and is in the style of an old movie – thirties or forties. In fact, she wonders if the artist is actually using original footage. There is a flickering shot of a window under the sloping eaves of a ceiling and the camera zooms in to reveal a vista of Paris. She can see now that it is probably just after the war. She can see some bomb damage and a few old cars travelling up and down the broad boulevards. The screen goes to black and titles appear in white.

Quite fortuitously, it appears she has sat down right at the moment of the beginning of the video installation.

Projected on the black, in white, are the words:

Beginning of O, an erotic fairy tale by Anita Chappell

Based on the film, *The Fall of Psyche*, by Felix Leduc, 1948

So this is Anita's video installation that Kirsti Shaw was so excited about. A woman's voice speaks in a crisp English accent and, as she listens to it, the grainy black and white film rolls before her. She sees a young woman sitting on the bed in the room with the window, her face slightly out of focus, hands in her lap, naked and staring into the camera. There is something about this young woman's stare, her demanding eyes, that entrances Valentina. The voice speaks:

'Another version of the same beginning is more complicated, less direct. Before the young woman was taken off by her lover and the second man, an unknown friend of his, and before her lover prepared her by tying her hands behind her back, unfastening her stockings and rolling them down, removing her garter belt, her panties, her brassiere and blindfolding her, and before they drove her to the château where she would receive her instructions, before all of this, was the beginning of O. She arrived in Paris uninitiated in pleasure, afraid of pain.'

The image of the girl sitting on the bed disappears and is replaced by a close-up of her lips. The camera slowly moves out and we see her face, still out of focus and hazy. Yet her eyes are huge, as if shining in adoration, as she looks into the camera. She says something to the camera but, of course, it is impossible to hear what she is saying, for the film is silent.

'What is she saying?' the narrator asks. 'Is she asking for him to touch her?'

The camera pans out and now Valentina can see the girl is on her knees, almost as if in prayer, and naked. She reaches up to the cameraman, again asking him something.

'He teaches her to pleasure herself,' the voice says.

The next image is of the same girl sitting on the bed, leaning back against the headboard, with her knees pulled up and her legs open. She is touching herself; her eyes are closed but she is speaking – the same words again and again and again. The footage is remarkable. It is obviously an early pornographic film, and yet it does not appear vulgar to Valentina.

'He watches her, taking herself all the way to the edge.'

Valentina is astonished to see the woman actually having an orgasm on screen; something about it is incredibly erotic. She feels a tightening between her legs and wonders if the other people watching are feeling the same way.

In the next image from the film, the camera is again close up. We see the back of the girl's head, her dark curly hair tumbling down her naked back. She turns around for a second and smiles at the camera. There is something familiar about her face. Now the girl is on her knees, her back to the camera, her arms splayed, her wrists tied to the bedstead. The camera focuses on her bottom. It appears pearly white and smooth in the black and white images, like a beautiful marble sculpture – not a real body. The camera pulls back even further. Suddenly, the girl pushes her backside up higher, as if she has been instructed to do so, and spreads her legs wider.

'He begins his possession of her.'

Now Valentina sees another figure in the room. It is a man, but his back is to the camera. He is fully clothed and stands in front of the bare bottom of the girl. He unties his belt and lets his trousers slip down so that his firm buttocks now replace the girl's soft curves. Valentina sees his hands grip the girl's waist and then he pushes into her. She finds herself not looking at the man fucking the woman, but at the back of the woman's head as it rocks back and forwards, and she wonders what expression she has on her face. Is she smiling with pleasure? Is she twisting her mouth in pain? Is she indifferent – her eyes shut, her mind elsewhere? Is it just another pornography film? Or is she really a young woman at the beginning of her sexual life, like this video artist's O?

'The beginning of O was when her body became a messenger for her heart. Is her love for man so great that she can sacrifice herself or does man love her so much she is adored? Is she divine or diabolical?'

The old black and white movie ends abruptly and the audience is bombarded by fast cutting: image after image of women in bondage, and the monotone of the narrator repeating again and again, 'Do you like it? Like it? Is it your fairy tale too?'

Despite the fact it is Anita's creation, Valentina had been enjoying the video installation and the use of the old porno film by the Frenchman, but all of the modern-day images irritate her. She stands up and walks out of the space. She has been in here ages, anyway. Just as she is stepping back into the light, she feels a light touch on her arm.

'Valentina?'

Her heart is skewered by the sound of his voice. She only saw him the day before yesterday and yet it feels like so much has happened since then.

'Theo,' she says, turning around to face him.

They say nothing for a moment, only gaze into each other's eyes. She is so close to kissing him. She doesn't care that they are in a crowded art gallery. She can see his feelings in his eyes. She knows Theo loves her, she just does.

'So, what did you think of Anita's video installation?' he asks her.

'I liked it at first, but I didn't like the end.'

'The girl,' he says, 'in the old movie. She reminds me of you.'

'She does . . . ?' Her voice trails off. All she wants to do is embrace him. 'Theo . . .' She takes a step forward.

'Valentina!'

She hears her before she sees her: Theo's beautiful burlesque lover, her rival, Anita. She tries to cool down her heart, prepare herself for what she is about to say, but, as soon as she actually sees Anita, the breath is knocked out of her. She blinks. The last time she saw this woman, she had curled blond hair and was wearing a busty pink burlesque outfit, but tonight she is dressed completely differently. She is wearing a sixties black and white mini dress, very similar to the Bridget Riley one that belonged to Valentina's mother. She has black thigh boots on and, worst of all, she is wearing a wig of a perfectly geometrical, shiny black bob. In short, the woman is an exact image of how Valentina usually looks. Anita has not only taken her man away from her, but also her very identity.

$\mathscr{M}$aria

WHEN SHE WAKES, HE IS GONE. ON THE LITTLE TABLE BY the window are some coins and a letter.

> My darling, I will be away tonight, as I told you, but I shall return tomorrow. Here is some money. Explore Paris. Felix. x

His name ends with a kiss, she thinks. She climbs back on top of the bed, places his letter on her naked chest and closes her eyes. She returns to last night – those sublime sensations she experienced within her body when he adored her with his tongue. And then afterwards they had made love again, and it was even more incredible than the experience on the boat. She feels as if she is weightless, floating on the elation of her love for Felix.

That day and night she waits for Felix to return feel like the longest hours of her life. After drifting in and out of sleep, dreaming of him inside her, and waking alone in the bed, she determines to follow his advice and take a look at Paris.

She washes in the little cracked sink in the corner of the room and dresses carefully. She is wearing her jewel-blue dress with the pink blooms and her little bolero jacket that she made with the material her mother sent her. She thinks of her mammas. What would they say about her and Felix in Paris? She knows that Pina would disapprove – say she was too young, reckless. But Belle? She has a feeling that her mother might understand her actions. For she, too, threw all caution to the wind when she fell in love with Santos Devine.

Maria walks down the cobbled streets of Saint-Germain-des-Prés, smooth and slippery from all those who have walked before her: the young and idealistic in love in Paris. She feels like a flower fed by rays of sunlight. Felix has made her beautiful and she cannot help but notice men look at her as she continues on her way. She has no idea where she is going, apart from that she is heading towards the river. She passes a *boulangerie*, and then turns around and walks back in. She is hungry. For a few centimes, she purchases a baguette of fresh bread. She devours it, sitting on a wall, looking across the Seine at the startling vision of Notre Dame. The bread melts in her mouth; the soft dough tastes sweet, like cake, after weeks of having to eat grey, coarse ration loaves in London. She cannot understand how it is that the French seem to be eating better than the English, when they were the ones who were occupied.

Her mind strays and she wonders what business it is that Felix is doing here in Paris. Against her will, she recalls Guido warning her about Felix. The Italian had said he was not nice. Well, of course not; Felix fought as part of the Resistance during the Second World War, it is only natural he would have had to do things he would rather forget about. But why does it have to be so secretive? Maybe Felix is hunting collaborators and bringing them to justice? It doesn't seem to fit with his role as a film director, but anything, of course, is possible. The war made heroes out of the most unlikely candidates.

She is tired – weary from the drama of the past couple of days. She turns her back on the river and the view of the Île de la Cité. Another day, she will sightsee – with Felix. He can show her his city and where he grew up. Maybe she will meet some of his family? Surely he will tell her something of his past, now they are in France. And last night, was he actually proposing to her? She has a vision of herself and Felix walking down the lopsided street in Saint-Germain-des-Prés and ahead of them runs a little girl with black, unruly hair. She turns and she calls to her daddy, and Maria sees Felix scooping her up and swinging her in the air. And he is happy because of her, Maria, and what she has given him.

During the night, he comes back to her. She stirs as he slides under the sheet next to her. He holds her in his arms. She is still asleep, but in her dreams she thinks she can hear him crying. He sobs as a child might, inconsolable.

After a while, the crying stops and he is kissing her, stroking her limbs.

'Felix,' she murmurs, waking up and putting her legs around his waist, instinctively guiding him into her.

He rolls her on to her back and he presses down upon her. She bears all his weight and she can feel his sorrow. It cuts her. Her poor darling; what has happened to him?

'Never leave me,' he whispers, urgently.

'Never,' she promises.

He moves with fervour now. In the dark, she cannot see the expression on his face, but she can feel his wet cheeks and she knows that she did not imagine that he was crying. This mature, powerful man cried in their bed while holding her. He needs *her*. He pushes himself deeper and deeper inside her and she gathers him into her. She holds him tight as he rocks within her and allows himself to escape into the safety of her loving body.

How many days do they spend in the little hotel bedroom in Paris? She loses track. The heat rises from the pulsing city, pouring through the open window, the sounds of life outside trickling in through the cracks in the ancient paint-work, yet Maria has no desire to leave the room. She has all that she needs behind the closed door, under the single sheet of their bed.

She is intoxicated by sex, enthralled by Felix and what he does to her. At the back of her head is a tiny voice, pleading with her to get out of the bed. Telling her to run away from her heart and its exposure, just to get up and out of the room, to walk the baking streets of Paris and calm down. Yet she can't. She is trapped by her own volition. She is held captive by her own desire. Not even hunger forces her to leave the room. While she sleeps intermittently between their love-making, Felix goes and gets them food, for, when she wakes up, he has provisions: fresh baguettes, ripe creamy cheeses, and red wine to drink. France is most certainly not living under the same austerity as England. She demolishes the food, instantly hungry, and allows him to trickle red wine between her thighs before licking it off her skin, damp with heat and longing.

'It's hot out there,' Felix tells her, the hairs on his bare chest glistening with sweat. 'They say it's a drought; the harvest will fail.'

She is not interested in the weather, or the disastrous harvest and its consequences for the people of France. She doesn't care about anyone else apart from herself and Felix. When he enters her, she wants to slip inside his skin and become part of him. She grips him tightly with her legs around his waist and bathes in the glory of their union. She sucks him deep down inside herself. He climbs higher and higher, scaling the pinnacle of her desire. Together they peel back the layers, turn inside out, sensations swarming around them, making her dizzy. Always, they climax together. And when he finally pulls out of her, she often finds herself crying.

'What's wrong?' Felix asks. 'Why are you crying?'

She shakes her head, unable to say why. It's not tears of joy, but nor is she unhappy – far from it. It is an instinctive reaction to his withdrawal, as if her body has died a little death to feel him come from inside her.

They lie for hours on top of the damp sheets: she, propped up on his shoulder, he with his arm around her, his hand playing distractedly with her nipple. They are bathed in heat, inside and out.

One morning, she wakes to the sound of marching. She hears footsteps above her head and wonders if they have travelled back in time to the occupation. When she opens her eyes, she realises that it is not marching feet she hears, but rain falling on the roof. The window of the room is still open and it is as warm as ever. She watches a torrent of rain as it cascades out of the sky; there is a flash of lightning. Suddenly she feels an urge to dance in the rain. She wants to go outside of their room and get soaked through. Felix is sleeping beside her. She shakes him awake.

'It's raining,' she says.

He sits up in bed and looks at her with sleepy eyes. 'Thank God.'

'Let's go out.'

'In that?' He points at the lashing rain. 'Are you crazy?'

'Yes.' She laughs, feeling not herself but another Maria – a wild, free-spirited creature.

She jumps out of bed and starts to pull on her dress, still

abandoned on the chair where she had left it, how many days ago, now? She has no idea. She doesn't bother with underwear or stockings, just slips on her shoes.

He is watching her, a smile spreading on his face. 'You're serious, aren't you?'

They run through the slippery streets of Saint-Germain-des-Prés, holding hands. The rain pelts their bodies as they splash through puddles. Maria can feel her flimsy dress sticking to her body, but she is beyond caring what people think of her. There are few out, anyway; most have taken shelter in the smoky cafés and bistros. They run across the square, past Deux Magots and behind the old abbey. Felix pulls her into the doorway of the abbey and she clings to him, feeling his muscled flesh through his wet shirt and trousers. The rain is so heavy it is like night. She imagines they are hidden from the real world, and maybe that is why she lets him do what he does. He lifts up the skirt of her dress and touches her. She pulls him back with her, against the old stone of the abbey, and raises her right leg, wrapping it about his waist. In the matter of just a week, she has become as expert as any experienced lover. It is second nature to her. Felix needs no encouragement. He pushes into her with a small grunt. The rain continues to beat down against them as they make frenzied love. A bolt of lightning cracks just metres from them, but they do not stop – they cannot stop. She could die right in the here and now and it would not matter. For making love with Felix is her life. If she dies in this storm, she doesn't care, as long as they are together.

Walking back to the hotel, her body still tingling with sensations, the rain stops quite suddenly. They are splashed by sunlight, the heat of its rays immediately prickling her skin. The wet pavements dry up almost instantly as the rainwater evaporates in the heat. Paris has been washed clean by the storm. The city smells almost sweet to Maria. They walk back arm in arm, their damp clothes crinkling as they dry, her bare legs enjoying the freedom of being stockingless. She doesn't care how she looks. None of those who live in this distract care either. They have seen far stranger things than a woman with no stockings on. Down the narrow cobbled street, they pass a large door of a porte chochère that is open. Maria glimpses a small courtyard with tubs of red geraniums, a flash of colour in all the grey. To her delight, Felix pulls her through the open door and over towards the flowers. He looks around him furtively and then he bends down, picks three geraniums and hands them to her.

'Oh, they're beautiful,' she whispers.

'Come on, before we're caught,' he says, catching up her hand again and leading her out of the courtyard.

When they get back to the hotel room, she fills an empty wine bottle with water and squeezes the stems of the red geraniums into it, proudly displaying the arrangement on the windowsill.

Felix watches her, bemused. 'They are nothing special,' he says to her.

'Oh, but they are,' she contradicts him. 'No one has ever given me flowers before.'

He comes over to her, kisses her on the forehead, takes her hand and places it on his heart. 'You make me feel young again,' Felix says.

She blushes with pleasure, smiling shyly at him. He is right. He does look younger – or is it less worried? In London he had seemed so serious, but here in their den in Paris he is all boyish charm. His distress from the other night is gone like a puff of smoke. She wonders if she dreamt that he was crying, although she remembers the sensation of his wet cheeks against hers. But she had not asked him about it the next morning, and now the last thing she wants to do is remind him of something that will make him sad.

'Let's go out tonight,' he says, out of the blue. 'Let's eat at Le Petit Saint Benoit.'

'Do we have to?' she says reluctantly. 'I would rather stay here.'

'We have to eat more than bread and cheese at some stage, my dear, otherwise we will get scurvy. Besides, I'd like you to meet some of my friends.'

She stiffens at the thought of other people. She wants it to be just her and Felix, completely exclusive. 'Maybe I should stay here . . .' she says, hestitantly.

'Not at all; why would you do that?'

She convinces herself that this is a good thing. If Felix wants to take her and introduce her to people then this is the first step towards their engagement, isn't it? She is on the road to being part of his life forever. She wonders who they will meet and how much of Felix they know. For, even though they have been inseparable this past week, she knows no more about his past than she did the day she stepped off the boat at Boulogne.

She stands by the open window, watching the sun sinking behind the rooftops of Paris, fiddling with one of the red geraniums, its petal velvet against her fingertip. There is no trace now of the earlier downpour; the city is as parched and cracked as it was the day before, the heat slapping her face and making her hands clammy with sweat. She doesn't want to go out, not just because it is uncomfortably hot, but also because something tells her that, as soon as they break the spell of their love nest, it will be hard to recreate. The honeymoon will be over.

Valentina

OF COURSE, THE MORE SHE EXAMINES ANITA AS HERSELF, the less like her she looks. In fact, in the Bridget Riley-style dress, she looks more like her mother than anyone else. The angular perfection of her black wig and her heavily made-up eyes make her look like a graphic novel character more than a real woman. Even so, it is disconcerting.

'What do you think?' Anita says, grinning at her. 'I wanted to pay homage to your mother.' She does a quick spin in the black and white dress. 'I am a great admirer of her work as a fashion photographer in the sixties,' she says. 'In my opinion, she is up there with David Bailey and the rest of the greats.'

Anita is now hanging on to Theo's arm. Valentina wants to push her away from him.

'What do you think of the exhibition?' Anita asks her.

'Well, it's certainly popular,' Valentina says, indicating the packed gallery.

'Oh, these sorts of things are always busy,' Anita says. 'Especially given the content. And there're some big names in the show. We are hanging alongside real erotica virtuosos, Valentina.'

'Your work looks good,' Theo says to her.

'Thanks.' She cannot look him in the eyes. He will see the nakedness of her want. And that is humiliating.

'What did you think of my video installation, *Beginning of O*?' Anita asks.

'I loved the old film footage,' she says, avoiding commenting on the rest of the piece.

'That is footage by a man who made some of the most explicit erotic films of the late forties,' she tells her, enthusiastically. 'His name was Felix Leduc – a Frenchman; he also made more abstract surrealist stuff.'

'I've never heard of him before.'

'He was part of that whole existentialist scene in Paris with Sartre, de Beauvoir and Boris Vian. Later on, Pauline Réage also knew him,' Theo tells her.

'Pauline Réage, who wrote *Story of O*?'

'Yes; that book is my inspiration,' Anita tells her. 'You see, my grandfather was a dealer in erotic art and literature in London in the fifties and sixties. Somehow, he got hold of Leduc's footage. After he died, I inherited all of his collection. I found this in a shoebox. I couldn't believe the content.'

'It is quite remarkable, isn't it?' Theo asks her.

But Valentina is remembering some of the narration from

the film: 'The beginning of O was when her body became a messenger for her heart.' Valentina can make her body speak for her, but it seems that that is not enough. It is clear now that the voice and words from the film are Anita's. So is that how Anita feels about Theo?

'Have you read *Story of O*?' Anita asks Valentina.

'Of course she has,' Theo says, before Valentina has a chance to reply. He looks directly at her and she knows he remembers the two of them reading *Story of O* in bed together, how parts of it had excited her and parts of it had disturbed her. No woman should submit to that degree.

'What's the story again, about the author?' Valentina asks, trying to ignore Anita still holding onto Theo's arm.

'It was written by a French academic who has several noms de plume: Anne Desclos, Dominque Aury, Pauline Réage. She never revealed her identity until she was an old woman,' Theo says.

Valentina loves that look on his face: the academic imparting knowledge.

'When *Story of O* was first published, people believed that it was written by a man,' he continues to say.

'But Pauline Réage wrote it as a challenge to her lover, didn't she?' Valentina adds, remembering the full story behind the book. 'He told her that women could not write erotica. So she wanted to prove him wrong.'

'And what did you think of it?' Anita asks her, looking genuinely interested.

'It's a strange book.' Valentina pauses. 'The way it starts . . . I mean, the content is very disturbing, abusive even, and yet there is something about it that is incredibly erotic. I can't explain it.'

'Maybe she felt totally free because she thought it was something private between her and her lover,' Theo suggests.

'But she allowed it to be published and read by the masses,' Anita points out. 'On some level she must have been trying to provoke.'

The three of them are standing in a triangle, herself at the apex, facing the couple: Theo and Anita. Yet, to Valentina, the connection between herself and Theo feels as if it could be visible – as if it is a rope that binds them. They are staring at each other, unable to unlock their eyes. As if sensing this chemistry, Anita lets go of Theo's arm and takes a step towards Valentina, almost blocking Theo from her view.

'So, did you come with anyone?' she asks her, her expression a warning.

'I came with Antonella and her aunt Isabella, but I seem to have lost them in the crowd.'

Just as she is saying this, she sees Antonella on the far side of the gallery and, to her surprise, she is arm in arm with her Russian lover, Mikhail, who Valentina thought was back in Milan. Antonella sees her and gives her a little wave, dragging Mikhail through the throng to meet them.

'Hello, Mikhail,' Valentina says, kissing the suave Russian on both cheeks. 'What are you doing here?'

'He claims he came to see himself on show in your pictures, but I know he's really here to see me,' Antonella says, looking pleased as punch. When she notices Theo, she stiffens. 'Hello, Theo,' she says, coldly. 'What are you doing here?'

'Evening, Antonella.' Theo pecks her politely on the cheek. 'I am here with Anita Chappell. She is one of the exhibitors, as well.'

'And his girlfriend,' Anita adds, emphatically.

Girlfriend. The word cuts through Valentina like a knife. Theo lets Anita call herself his girlfriend. She wonders now whether she has met his parents, too.

Meanwhile, Antonella is looking Anita up and down, taking in the Bridget Riley dress and black bob wig. She turns to Theo. 'Well, it seems that, since you can't have the real thing, you've gone for a copy.'

Valentina cringes with embarrassment. Sometimes Antonella's outspokenness is downright rude. Yet, for some reason, Anita is completely unabashed. Either she is stupid or she has thick skin.

'Yes, I know of course I don't look as good as Valentina, especially in that amazing dress,' she gushes. 'In fact, I am emulating her mother, Tina Rosselli. She has inspired one of my new routines.'

Valentina shivers in shock.

'Anita is a burlesque performer,' Theo tells Antonella.

'Oh, cool,' Antonella begins to thaw towards Anita. Valentina knows her secret dream is to perform burlesque.

Valentina looks away, feeling a little sick. She can't think of anything worse than a burlesque performance based on her mother. She stares down at the white floor of the gallery, swallowing her disappointment. This night has been a disaster. First of all, there was Francesco cornering her, and her unexpected anger and cruelty towards him. Is it karma that she now has to witness Anita and Theo as a couple? It looks to her that Anita is all over Theo. The whole thing has completely distracted her from actually focusing on making contacts and selling any work. Isn't that why she came to London? But she can't help it. She just can't take her eyes off Theo. And, despite the fact that Anita is draped all over him, she can't help noticing that he only has eyes for her. So why is he with the other woman? She can't understand it at all.

She wishes she could escape. What she needs is a saviour to whisk her away, yet the man she wants to save her is the very person it seems she can't have. She shuts out the chatter of the others and lets her gaze drift over the crowd. She sees a Leonardo lookalike in the crowd: olive skin and brown eyes, with thick black hair, not quite as long as her friend's. The man looks up; he is obviously searching for someone. To her astonishment, she realises it really is Leonardo with his hair cut short. She blinks; looks again. It can't be possible. They were only talking on the phone this morning. How could he be here? Yet it is her friend. She feels a well of joy at seeing him.

'Leonardo!' she calls out and waves.

'I meant to tell you,' Antonella pipes up, 'Leonardo and Mikhail came together. We split up looking for you.'

'Leonardo!'

He sees and hears her, his face breaking into a wide grin. He makes his way over to them, looking dashing as always in a maroon shirt, his black hair as shiny as crow's feathers.

Valentina gives him a huge hug. It is unlike her to be so demonstrative but she is so happy to see him. 'I can't believe you're here!'

'It was a spontaneous decision. I really wanted to see the show,' Leonardo says, smiling at her.

'It's really good to see you,' Theo says, slapping him on the back. 'How are you?'

'I'm well. Things are changing in my life but I think that's a positive thing.'

'Leonardo, I'd like you to meet Anita,' Theo says.

Valentina watches Leonardo's reaction to Anita. He politely shakes her hand, giving nothing away. She wonders what he thinks of her adversary. Does he think she is as sexy as Valentina?

'Lovely to meet you, Leonardo,' Anita says.

Valentina feels better to have Leonardo beside her. He is a different kind of friend from Antonella. Something about him makes her feel safe, and more confident. He reminds her of her power, of why she is in London in the first place: to showcase her erotic art.

Their group begins to break up again as they explore

different aspects of the show. Antonella and Mikhail go to look at Anita's *Beginning of O* video installation, while Kirsti Shaw appears to whisk Anita away to introduce her to a buyer. It is just Theo, Leonardo and Valentina now. They stand in a strangely awkward silence for a few seconds.

'Where are your pictures, Valentina?' Leonardo asks.

'Over there.' She waves over to the far side of the gallery.

'I'll go take a look. See you in a minute.' He tactfully disappears into the crowd. At last, she and Theo are alone.

'Do you want another glass of champagne?' Theo asks her.

'No,' she shakes her head, suddenly nervous that Francesco will reappear and reveal what she has been up to since she arrived in London. Why does she constantly sabotage herself? And yet she has no reason to feel guilty. After all, Theo is with Anita, right in front of her.

'Theo,' she whispers, gripping her empty champagne glass. 'I've been thinking about what you said.'

He looks anxious. 'I don't think we should talk about it here,' he says.

'But I'm afraid I won't see you again after tonight,' she says.

'Of course you'll see me again.'

She is unable to say anything for a moment. It is taking all of her self-restraint not to touch Theo. He is so close to her. She smells his Bulgari, and his own unique musky manliness – a scent that turns her to liquid and makes her want to fall into his arms. She looks at the fuzz of golden hairs on his

267

forearms; his crisp white shirt is pushed up to the elbows and she wants to reach out and stroke his arms. She wants to raise her hand to his cheek, put her finger on his lips and push it into his mouth. She wants to feel his tongue on her fingertip, his teeth clenching, to see his eyes, brittle with desire just for her. She remembers how he felt inside her, how full he made her feel and how wanting when he wasn't inside her. She wants him now. She wishes she could find a small cupboard somewhere in this gallery and fuck him senseless. She is sure she could win him back then, once he remembered being inside her, once he remembered how much he had loved her.

'I really will see you again?' she asks. She can't believe she is being so needy, so insecure.

Theo puts his hand on her arm and she almost drops her empty champagne glass as her body charges in response to his touch.

'Remember, I told you to trust me . . .'

She nods. 'I know; I think I do. I mean, I do.'

'Things are complicated at the moment,' Theo says.

'About Anita?'

He nods. 'I told you the other day that I love you. All I need to know is that you love me and trust me back. It's simple, Valentina.'

'But I don't understand why you can't just break up with her.' Valentina's voice cracks. 'It's not fair to lead her on . . .'

'I can't explain right now—' Theo suddenly stops talking. He is looking over the top of her head, his eyes narrowing, his expression becoming distant. 'I don't believe it,' he hisses.

Valentina spins round to see the source of Theo's discomfort. She is not surprised to see their old adversary, Glen, dressed impeccably in a dark suit, milling through the crowd.

'I'm sorry, Valentina; I have to go and head him off.' He turns back to her, all of sudden reaching out and ruffling her hair playfully. 'By the way, I love your new hairdo,' he says, before rushing off into the crowd without another word.

She is stunned, winded, as if he has punched her in the stomach. Why couldn't they have just ignored Glen? Or faced him together? Why has he run off and left her stranded, gaping after him in front of everyone? She tries to compose herself but, to her shame, tears begin to sting the corners of her eyes. She feels rejected to her core. She thought that Theo still loved her. He said he did, but his actions speak volumes and, to an outsider, it would seem that he had moved on. Maybe he is just leading her on, ruffling her hair like that. He could be playing some game with her – some sort of revenge for breaking his heart. She can't believe it. She would never have thought that Theo was the vengeful type. And yet, when she considers her treatment of Francesco, she has to admit that a broken heart can make you mean. She had never forgotten how her first lover had hurt her and now, nearly ten years later, she had been motivated to hurt him back.

'Are you all right?' Leonardo has appeared by her side, tucking his arm under her elbow. 'You look a bit pale.'

'Glen is here,' Valentina says.

'Where?' Leonardo says angrily. 'I wouldn't mind having a word or two with him.'

'He seems to have disappeared,' Valentina says, looking through the crowd, which has multiplied in size since Leonardo's arrival. 'Theo just ran off on me in mid conversation to talk to him.'

'Well, it must be important.' Leonardo tries to console her. 'Did you tell Theo that Glen has been following you?'

'Not yet,' she sighs. 'I guess you're right. Maybe Theo is trying to work out some kind of deal with him.'

'Look, do you want to get out of here?' Leo suggests. 'I'm starving.'

'Sure; I just need to go to the ladies' first.'

Valentina squirts some fancy soap into her hands and turns on the tap. She looks at herself in the mirror above the sink. With her new hairstyle she does look different from usual. Theo had said he liked it. Despite her hurt at his abandonment in the gallery, it gives her a tiny buzz of pleasure to think he has noticed the way she looks tonight. The door of the ladies' opens and the last person she wants to see comes strutting in: Anita, still dressed as Valentina's mother in the Bridget Riley dress and black wig.

'Valentina, there you are!' Anita exclaims. Her wig has gone a little wonky and her face looks flushed, her eyes slightly unfocused. She appears to have drunk too much champagne.

Valentina takes out her lipstick and repaints her lips, coolly surveying Anita in the mirror. Her rival rips off the wig and tugs at her blond hair, so that it comes lose and falls around her shoulders.

'Thank God,' she says. 'The wig was making me itchy.' She grins at Valentina, revealing a slightly crooked mouth of teeth. Not such a perfect face, after all. Yet her expression is so open and friendly that it makes Valentina feel guilty that she wants to steal Theo away from her.

'Are you enoying yourself?' Anita asks her.

'Sure, although I'm not so keen on big crowds,' Valentina admits.

'Me, neither,' Anita says. 'I'd love to get out of here but I can't find Theo. Have you seen him?'

Valentina suspects it is better not to let on about Glen. It is just too complicated to explain and, besides, she is pretty certain that Anita doesn't know about Theo's alter career as an art thief.

'No, I haven't seen him in a while . . .' she says, putting away her lipstick and tucking her clutch purse under her arm.

'Can I ask you something personal?' Anita says, swaying on her heels.

'I'd rather you didn't,' Valentina says, tightly, but it is as if Anita hasn't heard her.

'You and Theo knew each other in Milan and I am guessing you went out together, right?'

'It was just something casual,' Valentina mutters.

'I have seen the way he looks at you,' Anita says, hiccupping softly before she continues. 'I don't think it was too casual for him.'

Valentina walks past Anita towards the exit. She is suddenly annoyed. How dare this woman interrogate her about her private life? 'Well, it's long over, so it shouldn't concern you now,' she snaps.

Anita catches her arm with her hand. She can feel her fingers digging into her flesh, and it forces her to look into Anita's face at her big doll eyes and plush pink lips.

'I am sorry; I didn't mean to offend you,' she says. 'It's just, I have a question for you because . . . well . . . maybe you can shed some light on something that is bothering me about Theo.'

Valentina shakes the other woman's hand off her. She should leave right now and not continue this conversation but, of course, curiosity gets the better of her. 'What would that be?' she says, primly.

'Well, when you and Theo were dating . . . or together, or whatever it was . . . did you sleep together?'

Valentina glares at Anita, incredulous at her impertinence. She has no intention of answering her question.

'You see,' Anita continues, her words slurring slightly, 'I've never been in this situation before, dating a man for a couple of months who neither wants to break up with me nor take it to the next stage . . .'

'What stage?'

'Sex.'

The word drops in front of them, its openness forcing Valentina to look directly into this pretty girl's face. She can hardly believe her ears. Is Anita Chappell telling her that she and Theo have never slept together – despite the fact they have been dating for several months?

'I don't know what to do,' Anita continues. 'I mean, he tells me I am beautiful and we kiss but, you know, when I start making moves, he just backs off.' She sighs. 'It's getting very frustrating.'

'I really don't think I should talk about this with you, Anita,' Valentina says. 'It's a very personal matter.'

'Yes, but you know Theo and I wondered, how long was it before you two slept together?'

Valentina cannot stop the words from slipping out. 'The first night.'

'Do you mean that the first night you met, you had sex together?'

Valentina nods. She feels like a bitch as she sees the other woman's face fall.

'But that doesn't mean it was a good thing,' Valentina adds, for some reason wanting to make Anita feel better. 'I mean, look, we broke up, didn't we? Maybe he doesn't want to sleep with you yet because he respects you . . .'

Anita doesn't look convinced, and nor is Valentina.

Leonardo and Valentina find a little wine bar around the corner from the gallery. They order a bottle of ripasso and a plate of Manchego cheeses, olives and bread. Valentina begins to feel better as soon as she is sitting in a quiet corner with Leonardo. Her friend leans forward, tips her chin with his elegant finger, and looks deep into her eyes.

'So, Signorina Rosselli, what's up?'

She takes a sip of her wine and thinks for a moment. 'What did you think of Theo's new girlfriend, Anita?'

'She is a very attractive young lady,' Leonardo says, grinning mischievously. 'And not only that, she seems to be talented and intelligent too, as well as wealthy. What more could you ask for in a girlfriend?'

Valentina gives Leonardo's arm a gentle slap. 'Oh, stop teasing me! You know what I mean.'

'Well, I did think she was a nice girl . . . but too nice, too easy a woman for my dear friend, I believe.' Leonardo feeds her an olive.

'She told me that they haven't slept together yet,' she tells him.

Leonardo looks as shocked as she was to discover this fact. 'She must have been lying. I can't believe that!' he exclaims.

'Really . . . I think it could be true. She said he would neither break up with her nor sleep with her.'

'How very queer,' Leonardo says, taking a sip of his wine.

'It gives me hope,' Valentina admits, 'that he really does mean it when he tells me he still loves me, and yet I don't understand why he can't just drop Anita.'

'You just need to trust him, Valentina.'

'Do you think she was telling the truth, Leonardo? Do you really think that they haven't slept together?'

'It is rather surprising,' Leonardo agrees. 'But then, I can sort of understand Theo's decision.'

'In what way?'

Leonardo smiles at her wistfully. 'What I am about to say is going to shock you a little.'

She takes a sip of her wine, waiting for him to continue.

'I have decided to take a break from sex for a while.'

Valentina splutters on her wine. 'Are you joking? You, of all people? Why?'

'It's to do with the break-up with Raquel. I feel a little derailed. I need to get back on track. I don't want to sleep with anyone when I am feeling so vulnerable emotionally.'

'But surely having sex is going to make you feel better?' Valentina argues.

'Always so direct, my dearest Valentina.' He pauses, taking a slice of bread and dipping it in the olive oil. 'I don't agree with you, though. It might, in the short term, but I want to sort myself out first.'

'But you and Raquel had an open relationship. I don't understand why you are so upset by it,' Valentina persists.

'Because she broke my trust . . .' Leonardo looks irritated all of sudden. 'I really don't want to talk about it, Valentina. Let's just focus on you and Theo, shall we?'

'But does that mean you won't even sleep with me?' Valentina asks, realising that it is not only Leonardo's shorter hair that makes him look different. There is something else – a stillness about him tonight.

'Yes, Valentina. It especially means I shouldn't sleep with you.'

Later, as she tries to fall asleep, she mulls over Leonardo's words: 'It especially means I shouldn't sleep with you.'

She doesn't understand why he wouldn't want her to comfort him. They have always been able to do that thing – sex with no strings. Why now has he refused? She is feeling so insecure about Theo. Leonardo always has the effect of making her feel more confident.

She tosses and turns, trying to get to sleep. She wishes Antonella were here so that they could share a cup of tea and a chat, but she is on her own in the apartment. Antonella went back to Mikhail's hotel with him, and Isabella never returned. Goodness knows what she is up to. Something about Antonella's aunt annoys Valentina. Is it her refusal to act her age? Surely Valentina should think it is cool that Isabella is so liberated and unapologetic about the fact she is in her mid-fifties and still having fun. Valentina suspects her irritation with the woman is because, deep down, she equates Isabella with her mother. She behaves in a way she imagines her mother would. After all, they were part of the same scene in Milan in the sixties and seventies, a time which Valentina suspects was way more experimental and promiscuous than now. It is weeks since Valentina last spoke to her mother. In fact, it was New Year's Day, nearly four months ago. She had phoned her because her mother hadn't been in touch over Christmas. As usual, she had cracked first.

Her mother, the eternal narcissist, had spoken about herself most of the time. She was ranting on about working as a healer in New Mexico. The idea, of course, was ridiculous to Valentina. How could her mother be a healer when she couldn't even fix her relationship with her own daughter? Eventually, her mother had shown an interest in Valentina's life, asking her about recent photographic assignments. Valentina was careful not to tell her about any of her erotic photography. She knew her mother would love the idea of it, but somehow, somewhere along the line, she knew she would take credit for it or tell her that she had done that already. The conversation came to an uneasy pause and Valentina built up to saying goodbye but, before she got her chance, her mother spoke.

'So, Mattia told me that it didn't work out with that American guy.'

Could she not even remember his name? 'His name was Theo, Mamma.'

'Yes, Theo . . . what is it? Steele? No, no – Steen, that's it. A Dutch surname, just like your father's name: Rembrandt.'

Valentina took her opportunity to change the subject. She didn't want her mother asking about what happened with Theo. She didn't need to hear the 'I told you so' and the 'Remember, Valentina, we are free spirits' speeches. Besides, it was rare that her mother mentioned her father. Valentina had thought then about what Garelli had said in Venice: 'Your father would be proud of you.' She had put it to the back of her mind since she'd returned to Milan, and not re-examined it. Now she might get some answers.

'Why am I called Valentina Rosselli and not Valentina Rembrandt, after my father?' she asked.

'Because I think it sounds better,' her mother said.

'But Mattia's second name is Rembrandt.'

'Yes, because I thought that sounded better, too. Mattia Rembrandt: very strong. Masculine. Valentina Rosselli flows better; it's more feminine – better for a girl.'

'Mamma, why did our father leave?'

Her mother didn't answer for a moment. 'That is a very big question, Valentina,' she said finally. 'I would rather not talk about it on the phone.'

'So, if I came to America, you would talk about it?'

'Of course,' she said. 'You should know the truth, now you are grown up.'

'Can you not just tell me on the phone? America is a long way and I am not coming to see you any time soon.'

'Please, Valentina. It is a complicated story. I will tell you when you come. Just give me a date and I will buy you a ticket.'

'Mamma, I don't want to go to America. Besides, shouldn't you come back here, to Milan? This is, after all, your home.'

'Not any longer.' She could hear her mother's voice had hardened. 'I have to go; I have an appointment.'

And that had been it: unsatisfactory, as usual. Valentina clenches her fists and grips the sheets tightly, her eyes squeezed shut with rage. Her mother has always made her feel a poor second to everything else in her life. Valentina owes it to herself to confront her father, no matter how frightening the prospect is. She was so close the other day, until Glen came along. She must go back to Hampstead and do it before she leaves. Yet, as she finally drifts off to an uneasy sleep, she is still not sure she will find the courage to do so.

Maria

AS THE SUN SINKS, LEECHING BLOOD SHADOWS ACROSS the grey roofs of Paris, Maria lets Felix wash her. He fills the sink with hot water and then, taking a tiny bottle from his waistcoat pocket, he sprinkles a few drops into the water. Immediately, the aroma floats through the steam into the room. It is spicy sweet – a mysterious combination of freshness and warmth.

'Oh, what is it?' she asks him.

'L'Heure Bleu. It is a perfume by Guerlain.'

'The Blue Hour,' she whispers, trying to banish the thought of where Felix got the perfume and who the original owner might have been.

'It is the smell of dusk,' Felix says. 'It is the anticipation of night, before the stars come out.'

He gently washes her, encasing her body in the scent, so that she feels velvety and seductive before they have even left the room.

* * *

She dresses while Felix goes out to buy some cigarettes. She is glad now that she brought her ruby-red dress – the one she modelled on Dior's 'New Look'. She hopes she is stylish enough for Paris. It is, after all, a home-made dress. When Felix returns, he is lugging a large brown suitcase into their bedroom.

'Where did that come from?' Maria asks him.

'Madame Paget has been looking after it for me,' he says, before casting his eyes over her. 'Darling, you look stunning.'

She blushes with delight at his comment, while still regarding the case. It is huge and leather bound, the size of a trunk. She wonders what on earth could be inside it. 'Why have you waited to collect it until now?' she asks him.

'Because I forgot it was here, and I was thinking you might need it.'

Maria frowns in confusion. 'I only have two dresses with me, Felix. I think my own case is adequate.'

He comes over to her, puts his arm around her waist and draws her to him. 'And so pretty you look in your dress, too,' he says, giving her a quick kiss on the lips. 'But I would like to buy you a few more clothes, if you'll allow me.'

'Won't that be expensive?'

'Don't worry about money. I have plenty.'

She is astonished by his comment. In London, Felix had behaved as if he was living like all of them in the house, on a restricted budget. So how can he afford to buy her a new wardrobe to go inside this huge trunk?

'Whose case was it?' she asks him, feeling a prickle of concern.

'It was mine,' Felix says emphatically. 'And now it is yours.' He kneels down and clicks it open.

The case is empty. It is lined with red silk and has an array of little pockets and compartments within it. It is the most luxurious trunk she has ever seen in her life. It looks big enough to sleep in.

'Goodness! It's very grand,' she says.

'Well, my dear, I was once quite grand myself.' He stands up again, strokes her hair, and plants a kiss on her lips as if to reassure her. She wants to ask him, *In what way were you grand? Who are you?* But he is so happy at his gift to her, so excited by the thought of buying her clothes, that she doesn't want to break their harmony.

Felix sneaks his hand under her dress and touches her. His physical presence is clouding her judgement. Something about the trunk bothers her. She doesn't want to accept it, but it seems rude not too. Felix begins to stroke her back and forth, and she gives a tiny gasp of desire.

'You look luminous tonight,' he whispers. 'I want to show you off to my friends.'

She looks at him with such longing, not caring anymore about the case. She just wants him now, the ache between her legs blossoms, so that she leans into his mouth and begins kissing him.

He backs her across the room until she is up against the wall, right by the little window. She can hear the sounds of Paris: the odd truck trundling by, the squeak of a bicycle that needs oiling and the heels of Parisian women as they walk along the cobbled streets. He pulls back from kissing her.

'So, sweet Maria, will you play a little game with me?'

She nods, her longing making her speechless. He unbuttons her dress and she slips out of it. He takes it from her, carefully spreading it out upon the bed, before turning back to her and admiring her in her bare skin. He stands in his shirt sleeves, his hands on his hips, and she can see his desire for her pushing against the material of his trousers. He is waiting for her, she can see it in his eyes, and his look makes her feel wanton and reckless. She steps away from the wall, and reaches forward, grabbing his belt with both hands and pulling him to her. His clothes feel rough against her silky perfumed skin. She tugs at his shirt, while he loosens his belt and lowers his trousers. Now he is in charge again. He lifts her up and she opens her legs, instinctively wrapping them around his waist. He pushes up into her, groaning with satisfaction.

'You fit me so perfectly, my darling, I believe we are made for each other.'

He carries her back to the edges of their room. Maria is slammed up so hard against the wall, she can hardly move. She clings on to him, letting him pound into her. She wants it to go on and on. She never wants this feeling to stop. They are like two rare birds, let out of a cage, spiralling in the sunshine, united and elated in their abandon. She is climbing with him, up and up into the oneness of that millisecond when all her life feels worthwhile, just for this precious moment of completion.

Afterwards, they slither down the wall and she sits on his lap, his power curled beneath her, brushing against her nakedness.

He breathes into her neck. 'Do not doubt that I love you, Maria,' Felix says.

She tries to twist her neck around to look him in the face, but he holds her tightly and all she can do is feel his lips on her neck as he speaks.

'Never doubt it,' Felix repeats.

'I don't,' she says, her voice trembling with joy to hear him say he loves her. 'I love you, Felix. You are the man of my dreams.'

'Or maybe your nightmares,' he whispers, and his words make her shiver.

'Don't say such a thing,' she begs him.

'But, Maria, I worry that I will stain your perfection. I am not good enough for you.'

'Hush, don't say such things.' She pushes aside his dark words and changes the subject. 'What game is it that you want me to play with you?'

'Would you do something courageous for me, Maria?' he says. 'Will you forego wearing any knickers tonight?'

She wriggles off his lap and turns to look at him, expecting him to laugh, yet Felix looks deadly serious, his eyes challenging her.

'You want me to wear nothing under my dress?' she asks him, incredulously.

He nods. 'Just your stockings and brassiere, and this.' He pulls out what looks like a piece of jewellery from his trouser pocket. It is a very thin strip of velvet with a clip at either end, like those on her suspender belt. Part way down and embedded in the velvet is a small golden ball, about the size of a marble.

'What is that?' she asks him.

'Let me show you.' He grins, looking boyish again.

He makes her stand and then crouches on to his knees. He kisses her pussy. 'Oh, you smell so sweet, darling,' he says, before taking the velvet, one end in each hand, and bringing it under and between her legs. He lifts it up and she feels the cold golden ball knock against her flesh. He then attaches one of the clips to the back of her suspender belt and brings around the other end of the velvet to clip it to the front. She doesn't understand the purpose of this garment. The gold ball is against her bottom. It feels stupid.

'I don't understand—'

'I have not finished,' he interrupts, putting his hand underneath her and pulling the ball along the velvet. His fingers pass over the most private part of herself with the ball and it makes her jolt involuntarily. He moves on so that the ball is positioned just in front, against a part of her body that Felix has led her to discover this week – a part of herself that

285

is constantly craving more attention from him. She feels him fingering her, opening her up. Her knees are buckling as she weakens. Now she feels him positioning the little gold ball inside her warm, tender flesh. He pulls back, looking pleased with his work.

'Now,' he says, 'I can imagine that little ball is me, touching you all night long. Keeping you primed.'

She moves, feels the ball rolling against her flesh. The sensation is an exquisite combination of pleasure and intrusion. 'I think you should undo it,' she whispers. 'It is too much.'

He looks amused. 'Are you on the edge, Maria?'

She nods.

He kisses her on the lips. 'Do you think you are brave enough to see how far you can go?'

'I'm not sure,' she says, uncertainly.

'You can take it off any time.' He pauses. 'You can take it off now. This is for you, Maria. It is about *your* enjoyment.'

She is not sure what to say. Part of her is scared of what will happen to her body when they go out. She is not in control. And yet another part of her is excited. What *will* happen if she lets her body run wild? She is reminded of Lempert talking about dance, of the challenge of balancing tension and release, of its parallels with life. Isn't this little game of Felix's all about that? She is a trained dancer. She should be able to handle the pressure of a little gold ball nudging her sex as she walks around a room. And yet there is a Maria inside her screaming to be released.

'All right,' she whispers, much to her own surprise. 'I'll try it.'

Felix strokes her face tenderly with his finger, kissing her again on the lips.

'I find this very erotic, my darling. I like to imagine your nakedness so exposed and yet untouchable in company. I like to imagine you on the edge, desperate for satisfaction.'

She sits on a chair in front of the mirror, looking at her parted red lips, her eyes dark with desire, her ripe body in the red dress. She sees a reflection of Felix standing behind her. Her knight, but not so shining now: he is a tall, shadowed figure with glittering eyes. She senses his secret self and she wonders if he is right, if maybe he is too dark, too broken for her. Yet her love binds her to him. She believes it lights the way for both of them, so that he will let her heal him.

Valentina

IT FEELS LIKE THE FIRST PROPER DAY OF SPRING. AFTER all the rain and cold, the temperature has risen and Valentina has taken the risk of coming out without her coat. Everyone appears to be stepping as lightly as she, lifted up by the bright skies and warm breeze. This is a London she could live in – learn to love. She wonders if that might happen, if Theo comes back to her.

After popping into the Lexington Gallery to see how she did last night, she has taken the Tube back to South Kensington to meet Leonardo for coffee, before he flies home to Milan.

'So, are you pleased?' her friend asks her, once they have settled down on high stools, two cappuccinos steaming on a counter in front of them. They are facing the street outside, looking out of the window of the café at the pedestrians as they pace by.

'I sold them all!' she says, brimming with pride. 'I can't believe it . . . I mean, even those really explicit ones of

Antonella and Mikhail. God knows who bought them!'

'That's great Valentina,' Leonardo says. Yet his voice is quieter than usual.

Her friend looks tired this morning, as if he hasn't slept at all. She spots a grey hair in all the black and, although she had always assumed they were the same age, she wonders now what his real age is. She thinks he must be very heartbroken over Raquel.

'So, are you going to tell me what happened with you and Raquel?' She stirs her cappuccino, watching the creamy heart sink in the middle.

Leonardo says nothing for a moment, taking a sip of his coffee and avoiding her eye. 'There is not so much to actually tell,' he says, eventually. 'She met someone else.'

Valentina turns to look at him, but Leonardo avoids her eyes, staring down at his coffee cup intently.

'But I thought you guys had an open relationship. Shouldn't that sort of thing not matter?' She asks him softly, sensing that she needs to step carefully here for her friend to confide in her.

'Well, it matters when she wants to end our "open" relationship and have a closed one with someone else.'

He looks up at her, and Valentina is astonished by the blaze of anger in Leonardo's eyes. She has never seen her friend look even remotely cross, let alone angry and hurt.

'So, is it because she wanted you all to herself? Do you think you could have done that?' she asks tentatively.

Leonardo scowls even more. 'Of course I could have, but that's not what she wanted.' He pauses, sweeping his hair back from his forehead with his hand.

'That wasn't it, Valentina,' he sighs, no longer angry now, but sounding sad. 'We broke up because she didn't want me in her life anymore.'

'She's crazy,' Valentina says without hesitation, putting her hand over his on the counter top.

'When it came down to it,' Leonardo says, 'she was thinking of the future.'

'You mean children? But you had agreed to have a baby together, to shut down the club. You were going to change your life for her.'

'Yes, but it wasn't enough. I am too much of a risk, Valentina.' Leonardo stares straight ahead out of the window, as if hypnotised by the moving people passing by.

Valentina squeezes his hand. 'How can that be?'

He pulls his attention away from the pedestrians outside and back to her in the café. He looks crushed. Valentina feels like giving Raquel a good shake. How could she let such a good man go? 'Raquel wants a decent, stable environment for her children, with a man who has a secure job and a good income. She wants to make a proper family.'

Valentina shrugs dismissively, making her opinion quite clear: Raquel is a complete disappointment as a woman. And yet her friend loved her. She has to be careful not to be too harsh on her. 'There's no such thing as a proper family,' she says carefully. 'It is better for a child to have love rather than material stability. It is love that makes a child feel secure.'

'I agree,' says Leonardo. 'But that isn't Raquel's opinion.'

'I'm sorry, Leo . . . You know, I don't think she was right for you, anyway,' she ventures.

Leonardo smiles a little. 'Really? And who might be right for me?'

Valentina thinks hard. Of all her friends, there is not one of them she can see with Leonardo, apart from Celia, possibly.

'What about Celia?'

'Maybe, but we are friends, really – like you and me, Valentina. She is also on the other side of the world at the moment.' He pauses, taking another sip of his coffee. 'Besides, I think I should be on my own for a while.'

Valentina can't help feeling a little glad that Leonardo is not on the hunt for a new woman. It worries her that he might meet someone who will take him over and not understand their friendship, or be jealous of the time they spend together.

'So, that's enough about me,' Leonardo says, glancing at his watch. 'I have to go for my flight in about twenty minutes. I don't want to waste our last moments moaning about my sorry private life.'

Valentina leans over and kisses her friend on the lips. He tastes as buttery as her croissant.

'What was that for?' Leonardo says, looking pleased.

'I do love you, Leonardo,' Valentina says. 'You are the best friend in the world.'

'But what about your other friends?'

'Yes, but you know me inside out. It's a funny thing, since I have been friends with them all for far longer than you. Yet I feel like I have *always* known you.'

'Like we were meant to meet?' His brown eyes gaze at her warmly and she can see that her words have cheered him up.

'Yes. It's our fate to be friends.' She takes a sip of her cappuccino. 'Leonardo, I have been thinking about Theo and how strange it was that we ran into each other, right out of the blue, and then something occurred to me.' She pauses, finishing off her crossiant and licking her fingertips. 'Two of the pictures that were exhibited in the Lexington were very recent. I don't remember sending them in my original submission, although they requested prints of them for the show. So how did Kirsti Shaw get to see them?'

Leonardo shifts in his seat, looking a little uncomfortable.

'I knew it!' she exclaims, pointing her finger at him. 'Did you send the images to Theo? And then he showed them to Kirsti Shaw and pushed her to include me in the show?'

Leonardo says nothing for a moment, but he is blushing with guilt.

Valentina can see that she is on the right track. 'And, if that is the case, Theo actually conspired for me to see him here in London. I think the whole Anita thing is to make me jealous like you said, so he can really see that I love him. He wants me to react.'

Leonardo reaches out and puts his hand on her arm. 'Valentina, I have to stop you there,' he says.

'I can see that you are hiding something from me, Leo,' she says triumphantly. 'You did send him the pictures, didn't you? He is trying to make me jealous, don't you think?'

Leonardo shakes his head, looking quite sorrowful. 'I don't think Theo has any intention of making you jealous, Valentina, not since I saw him last night. Besides, he knows you are not the possessive type.'

'Well, the funny thing is, Leo, I am a bit jealous. It's never happened to me before. Usually, if I can't have a man, I just shrug my shoulders and walk away, but I just can't bear to lose Theo to Anita . . . I can't understand it.'

'You're in love, my dear – really in love.' Leonardo pats her hand, looking sad again.

'But I don't believe it is just a coincidence that Anita and I are in the same show. It can't be.'

'You're right on that score,' Leonardo says, not looking her in the eye. 'But I am afraid it was me, not Theo, who sent your recent work to Kirsti. As far as Theo is concerned, he had no idea you were in the show with Anita.'

'*You* sent the images directly to the gallery?' she asks him, shocked that he would do such a thing without telling her.

'Theo had told me about the exhibition. On the one hand, I thought it would be a great opportunity for you. I knew you had already submitted to the gallery, so I just reminded Kirsti Shaw of your existence and showed her some new work.'

'I can't believe you would go to so much trouble for me.'

'Well, I also had an ulterior motive. You and Theo were driving me mad. He would email me asking how you were, and you would be asking me how he was, but, whenever I suggested to either of you to break the deadlock, you were both too stubborn, or hurt, or proud to do something. I just thought it was a terrible shame.'

He pauses, pinning her with a piercing stare. 'You should be together. So that's why I thought, if you were in the show, it would be a chance for you to bump into each other naturally.'

'But, Anita?'

'I had *no* idea about Anita. I was as shocked as you were to discover he had a girlfriend,' Leonardo says, shaking his head and looking genuinely sorry.

She stands up from her stool and, uncharacteristically, she leans over and gives Leo a massive hug. She steps back and he looks completely mystified.

'What's that for?'

'For caring so much about my happiness.' She really is touched that Leonardo believes in her and Theo.

'Valentina,' her friend advises her, 'don't give up. The fact that Theo and Anita aren't sleeping together speaks volumes. I still think you two could get back together.'

'But to do that I have to break them up.' Valentina struggles with the idea. 'I actually rather like Anita. I don't know if I could do such a nasty thing to her.'

Leonardo smiles benignly. 'You may appear a cool customer, but you are just a big softie deep down, aren't you, V?'

She sits back down on her stool, feeling a little self-conscious. 'I don't know; my mother tells me I am hard hearted . . .'

'What does your mother know?' He picks up her hand and squeezes it. She likes the feeling of her little hand tucked inside his.

'Of course,' Leonardo says, his voice dropping to avoid being overheard, 'there are other ways around this conundrum.'

'What do you mean?'

'Well, you said that Theo needs you to prove your love to him . . .'

'Yes, but how do I do that?'

'A man will always feel his woman's love through sex, so, by enacting his ultimate sexual fantasy, you could show him your love.'

'Yes, but I just told you, I don't want to make Theo cheat on Anita . . . or break them up.'

'Indeed, I am not suggesting you do so, for what do you think might be the common fantasy for most men?'

Valentina doesn't even need to think about it. 'Two women together, with him.'

'Exactly,' Leonardo says, his spirits obviously lifted again as he gives her a cheeky grin.

'Are you suggesting that I win Theo back by taking part in a threesome with him and Anita?' Valentina is appalled.

Leonardo can't be serious. 'Apart from the emotional mess that could entail, isn't it immoral?' she continues.

'Of course not. Look, I have thought about this whole question a lot. Not just threesomes, but orgies as well.' Leonardo looks at her earnestly. 'I mean, I was raised a Catholic, after all. And a lot of people who come to my club are motivated by a sort of twisted relationship with sex and religion. They crave to be sinners so that they can then cleanse themselves.'

Valentina shudders. 'I have never felt like that, Leonardo,' she says. 'I never felt I was doing something bad, not if no one was being lied to or hurt.'

'You see, the difference between the sex lives of humans and animals is erotic pleasure.' Leonardo is becoming himself again: sexual guide and guru. His earlier distress about Raquel seems to be fading away now that he is talking about his favourite subject. 'We don't have sex seasonally and we don't have sex just to procreate. We also have sex to experience sensual raptures . . . Is that not so?'

Valentina nods. She loves listening to Leonardo talk about sex and eroticism. She always feels she can learn so much from him.

'I think, as soon as man became aware that he was mortal, then that's when eroticism came into existence. Both sex and death represent a kind of violence that interrupts the regular order of things. When you climax, it has been called the "little death", and thus eroticism can actually be a celebration of life within the knowledge of our mortality.'

'You make it sound so lofty,' Valentina says. 'But other people would say we are depraved, unable to commit, lascivious . . .'

'That is the problem for us all.' Leonardo looks solemn. 'When we begin to bring morality into the equation, it corrupts sex. Eroticism should have nothing to do with morality.'

It occurs to Valentina that her mother has said such things to her in the past, that, possibly, these are the principles by which her mother lives her life, and this may be why Valentina has found it natural to adopt them herself.

She looks outside the window of the café, watching the rhythm of passers-by, and considers Leonardo's suggestion. Could this be a way to show Theo her love? Could she seduce both Anita and Theo, in which case she wouldn't actually be stealing him away from the other woman, would she? It seems like a completely crazy idea, and yet it does appeal to her libertine heart. She found Anita attractive from the moment she met her. She didn't like to see her dressed like her mother, but when she was blonde and coquettish . . . well, she did rather like that. Of course, really, it is just Theo that she wants to be with, but this could be a way forward, if Anita is open to it. It would be such a powerful message to Theo. Last year, the way he had shown her how much he trusted and loved her was by setting up different scenarios in Leonardo's club. The three of them – Leonardo, Theo and Valentina – had been together inside the Dark Room, the room of her ultimate sexual fantasies. Theo had done all this to show Valentina that he loved her for who she is, and did not want to change her. Can she not do the same for him? She knows that Leonardo is right, for Theo has told her it is a particular fantasy of his – himself, Valentina and another girl – and, when they were together, she had been very open to the idea. Her heart rate begins to speed up. Could she somehow orchestrate this threesome? The idea of it is at once exhilarating and terrifying.

'Hey,' Leonardo says, gently tapping her hand. 'I have to go.'

She pouts. 'It feels like you just got here.'

'I could only get away for the night.'

Valentina squeezes his hand tightly before releasing it. 'Thank you so much for coming, my dear friend.'

Valentina is alone again. She walks down Old Brompton Road, past all the museums, sunlight speckling her skin, her mind in turmoil. Now she has got into the rhythm of her walk, she doesn't want to stop. Could Leonardo be right about the idea of a threesome? And, even if he is, how on earth is she going to make it happen? She has not heard from Theo since he disappeared last night. She is loath to ring him after he dumped her at the exhibition. Valentina keeps walking as if, at the end of her march, she will find her answer. She walks all the way into Knightsbridge and past Hyde Park. Tomorrow she is supposed to return to Milan, which means that tonight is her last chance. Of course, there is also the issue of her father . . .

She comes to a halt and looks around her. Where is she now? She has no idea. Behind her is Hyde Park and ahead stretches another park. The road is thick with cars as they race past her. She can see a Tube station sign ahead of her and she goes towards it: Green Park. She takes out her *London A to Z* and looks at the back cover. Green Park is on the jubilee line – the same line as Finchley Road station, near where her father lives. It seems quite providential that she should be standing outside this particular Tube station. Maybe the first step to working out what to do about Theo is to work out who she really is? To do that, she has to face her fear and see her father. She knows she will regret it if she doesn't. She has the rest of the day to herself. Antonella and Mikhail are busy sightseeing, and Isabella is at work. There is no need for her to go into the gallery now that she has sold all her work.

Her phone buzzes. She takes it out of her pocket, praying that it is from Theo, but instead it is a message from an unknown number:

> Hi Valentina. Sorry about last night. I was drunk
> ;) Want to come to a party at my place tonight?
> Theo tells me it's your last night in London. Please
> come! Let me know and I will text you my address.
> Anita xx

Despite the fact the message is from Anita and not Theo, she feels that, indirectly, it is him who is communicating with her. Anita had texted that Theo told her it was Valentina's last night in London. How did he know? He must want to see her again. If she goes back to Milan without Theo's love, when will she ever see him again? She cannot suffer the indignity of begging him to come back, and so she has to win him back, even if it means hurting Anita.

It is at that very moment, as Valentina struts into Green Park Tube station, her mind made up to face her father once and for all, that she also knows she is not going to let Anita take her man. It is her time of reckoning.

$\mathcal{M}$aria

THE RAPTURES OF HER NIGHT BEGIN IN A LITTLE restaurant in Saint-Germain-des-Prés. Such a meal they eat, the like of which she has not tasted in years – not since before the war, when she was a girl. A plate of endives and huge giant prawns, creamy mushroom soup, followed by garlicky snails and freshly baked baguette, all accompanied by a plummy red wine. She wonders how the French are able to source all this food when the diet in England is still limited. Felix tells her it is because of the Americans and the Marshall Aid Plan. He says that, less than a year ago, the residents of Paris were starving, their only source of meat, rabbits.

As they eat, Maria begins to understand just how clever her lover is. He tells her all about the politics of the day in France: how, since the Berlin Blockade had begun earlier that summer, the Americans had been panicking that France would be overtaken by communists. And so, not only had they started pumping money and American goods into the country, but also the Americans themselves had been coming in their droves.

'To experience the sophistication of Parisian life,' Felix says, disdainfully, as he removes a buttery snail from its shell and pops it in his mouth. 'But their politicians want us to learn their American ways – what it is to be a good worker.'

'Do you think that there will be another war?' Maria asks Felix. 'The women in the tripe queue think so. So does Guido, although he says we shouldn't be so afraid of the Russians.'

'Are you and Guido close friends?'

'Not at all.' She blushes, wondering why she is thinking of the Italian. She has almost managed to banish all thoughts of London – and even Venice – for the past two weeks, so completely entranced has she been by Felix and their lovemaking. 'But he seems to know a lot,' she explains.

'He is just a young boy,' Felix says, his voice scathing. 'He knows nothing about what is really happening in the world.' He pauses, mopping up the garlicky butter from the snails with a piece of bread. 'There won't be a war. Neither the Russians nor the Americans can risk it.'

'But Berlin is blockaded by Stalin. Isn't that just the beginning?'

'If Stalin wanted a war, it would have started by now.' Felix pours some more red wine into both their glasses.

'Let's not talk about war anymore,' he says. 'It is war that corrupts all that is beautiful. And I want tonight to be sublime.'

She sips the wine, and its sweet berry tang heartens her, makes her feel more comfortable in her erotic undergarment.

'There are two good things about the Americans being here,' Felix says, as he feeds her one of his snails. 'One is their jazz music, and the second is their interest in movies – a fact that is most beneficial for me.'

'What kind of film are you making at the moment?' Maria asks him, shyly.

'Since my life is full of love at the moment, it is, of course, a love story, Maria,' he says, grinning at her.

After dinner, they go to a bar close to their hotel. Felix leads her through the smoky throng; all the while the little golden ball spins around inside her. She feels as if she is tiptoeing on eggshells, her breath caught in her mouth. There is a powerful odour of strong tobacco, cheap wine and unwashed bodies in the bar, and yet there is something cosy about the place. Felix finds a tiny table in the corner, orders a bottle of wine and they squeeze in. Maria notices that most of the crowd are radiating from the other corner of the bar. There is a great deal of talking and it is hard for them to hear each other over the babble of voices.

'So,' Felix says, indicating the crowd, 'do you know who is holding court with all those young men and women?'

Maria shakes her head.

'None other than the great existentialist writer, Jean-Paul Sartre,' Felix tells her.

Maria has no idea what existentialism is but she is too embarrassed to admit it. 'Do you know him?' she asks, craning to see over the mass of heads, but it is impossible to do so unless she stands up and makes a show of herself.

'Yes, actually, I do,' Felix says, filling up her glass. 'But I do not like the man. He is a womaniser, of the worst sort.'

'What is the worst sort?' she asks, curious.

'He has no humility. It is grating.'

Before they can continue their conversation, their table is surrounded by a group of people, all greeting Felix at once, as if they have not seen him for a decade. And maybe they haven't, thinks Maria, although – according to Jacqueline – he often visited Paris during the two years he's been in London. She squirms in her seat, embarrassed by the fact they are ignoring her, and equally embarrassed Felix doesn't introduce her immediately.

Finally, a woman of about thirty, with burnished copper hair cut in a short crop, turns to her. 'Hello,' she says. 'Who are you?'

'Maria.'

'Nice to meet you. I'm Vivienne. Are you Felix's new girl?'

The way she says it makes Maria feel awkward. She wonders how many 'new girls' Felix has presented to his friends, yet, at the same time, the wine is beginning to work its magic and she is starting to relax. She can hardly believe it. Here she is, right in the thick of it, in the most chic and edgy place in Europe . . . and with such a clever, sexy and talented man – a man who knows Jean-Paul Sartre; a film-maker, no less.

Conversation flies around the table at breakneck speed. Maria's French is good but, nevertheless, she is finding it hard to keep up. She gathers that most of the people at the table are fellow film-makers, writers, musicians, artists and playwrights. She is particularly intrigued by one man, who says practically nothing, constantly making little pencil drawings in a tiny notebook, which he keeps bringing out of his coat pocket and putting back in again. Most of those at their table are busy chatting among themselves and, apart from Vivienne, only one other person talks to her: a small, plump man with round spectacles, called René, who tells her he is a poet. After a couple of hours in the bar, Vivienne suggests they go dancing.

'Le Tabou has closed down, but there is Club Saint-Germain. Let's go there,' she suggests. 'Boris Vian is playing his trumpet tonight.'

'I prefer his writing,' Felix comments.

As Felix speaks, his eyes roam over the bar, as if he is searching for someone, until they come to rest on her. He stares straight at her, as if he is seeing her for the first time. There is a hunger in his gaze that pierces her, makes her a little frightened, but also arouses her as well. She is suddenly more aware than ever of the little gold ball lodged within the soft folds of her flesh. She shifts in her seat and it rolls in a tiny circle within her, grazing her, minutely stimulating her. She holds her breath. How is she supposed to endure the night with this attire on? She knows she is free to go to the toilet and take it off, and yet she doesn't want to disappoint her lover. She wants to show him she is adventurous, like he wants her to be. And, despite the slight discomfort, it is also a little exciting to be wearing it with no other underwear, and to be sitting with this group of strangers and not one of them know what she and Felix are up to.

It is only when she stands up that Maria realises just how intoxicated she is. She looks across at Felix, wondering if she could suggest they go back to the hotel now, but he is wrapped up in conversation with René and one other man.

Vivienne links arms with her. 'Do you like dancing, Maria?' she asks her. She has clear green eyes, the colour of sea glass.

Maria is about to tell her that she is, in fact, a dancer, when something stops her. She can't say that now, can she? She has turned her back on dancing, for good. At one time, dancing was like life for her, and yet she doesn't have what it takes to be a great dancer. She failed. Maybe a woman has to choose between love and life. If that is the case, she chooses love.

'No,' she replies to Vivienne. 'I don't dance.'

'Oh, but you must,' Vivienne trills. 'It is not your usual dancing. It's jazz. It's really energising . . . fun . . .'

'No, really, I don't think I can.'

Maria considers what the little gold ball would do to her if she actually started to dance. She is certain that she would completely lose all control.

* * *

Club Saint-Germain is smokier, darker and more packed than the bar. She tries to stay close to Felix but it is impossible. She wants him to take her home. Walking through the cobbled streets of Paris in her high heels with the little golden ball swirling around inside her has stimulated her even further. Deep inside her pelvis, her muscles are in spasm. It is all she can do not to collapse and cry out, hysteria bubbling out of her in laughter and tears. Has he no mercy? Surely he must know what this is doing to her. But every time she catches his eye, gives him a begging look, he smiles with delight before turning away and talking to René.

Eventually she has her chance when their group take to the dance floor; even the stout René jives away with abandon, while Vian and his fellow musicians blast out the latest sounds from New York.

Felix remains standing, leaning against the wall of the club, smoking a cigarette and watching the dancing crowd, as if surveying it from afar. Maria slips in next to him, nuzzling into his side. He puts his free arm around her waist and draws her closer to him. He hands her the cigarette and she takes a puff.

'I thought you'd be out dancing with the others . . .'

'I can't dance, Felix,' she whispers, handing him back the cigarette. 'And certainly not with that thing inside me.'

He turns his head and whispers in her ear, 'Are you on the edge yet, Signorina Brzezinska?'

He puts out the cigarette and brings his free hand over and rests it on her stomach, slowly spreading his fingers across her belly so that the very tip of his middle finger touches the outline of the velvet strip beneath her red dress.

Her breath quickens; she cannot speak for a second, she is so aroused. 'Please,' she whispers, 'can we go back to the hotel?'

'Not yet,' he says. 'I need to meet someone first.'

'Who?' she asks, impatiently.

'I'm sorry, darling; I can't tell you that,' he says. He turns and looks at her. 'I can see your nipples through your dress,' he comments, grinning cheekily.

She blushes, her cheeks as crimson as the dress. 'Oh, no.'

'Don't worry; it is so dark in here, no one will notice. Only me. I can see how turned on you are, my darling. I love you for this . . .'

His words are like a balm to her frustration. She can do this. She can hold on for a little longer. If she stays quite still and can just stop that ball from rolling around and around her, taking her further and further away from their surroundings and into her own rapture . . .

Felix is staring at her as if he is looking at her for the first time. Despite the fact they are in company, he leans forward and kisses her on the lips. The effect is devastating; just the touch of his lips on hers is causing a ripple effect within her body. She pulls away.

'What is it?' he asks.

'You can't kiss me,' she whispers.

'Oh, I see.' His smile spreads. 'OK, darling . . . I understand. Let me just find this person and deal with him. I'll be back as soon as I can, and we'll leave.' Felix pulls his arm away from her waist and disappears into the dancing crowd.

She stands awkwardly on her own, trying to keep as still as possible. She feels self-conscious – aware of men looking at her. To her relief, she spies Vivienne weaving through the crowd towards her.

'I just love jazz,' Vivienne says, breathlessly, her cheeks flushed from dancing. 'Isn't Vian amazing?'

Maria nods, taking a swig of her drink.

'So, how long have you and Felix been together?' Vivienne asks her.

'Two weeks,' Maria says. 'But I knew him in London before we came to Paris.'

'I thought you were Italian?'

'Yes, but I have been living in London. I met Felix there.' She doesn't want to expand. The last thing she wants Vivienne to find out is that she was a dancer. 'Are you from Paris?' Maria asks Vivienne, changing the subject.

Vivienne shakes her head. 'No, I'm from Lyon. I met Felix through the Resistance.'

Maria is stunned by this information. 'You were *both* in the Resistance during the war?'

Vivienne looks surprised. 'Has Felix not spoken to you about his time in the Resistance?'

Maria is embarrassed that she knows so little about her

lover, and yet her curiosity overcomes her pride. 'To be honest, he has told me very little about himself.'

'Oh my goodness! So you don't know the whole story?' Vivienne asks her, her green eyes flashing.

'No,' Maria whispers, ashamed.

Vivienne picks up her hand and squeezes it, looks at her warmly. 'I'm sorry,' she says, looking genuinely concerned by Maria's embarrassment. 'I just assumed you knew all about Felix, but I guess he doesn't shout it from the rooftops.'

'Shout what?'

'Your lover is one of the bravest members of the Resistance. He's a hero, darling.'

'Oh.' Maria swells with relief. So Guido really had been so wrong. Felix wasn't a collaborator. He was, in fact, the opposite – just as she had always believed.

'But,' Vivienne continues, 'it came at a price for him.'

'What do you mean?'

'Well, I don't know all the details, but his wife—'

'He's married?' Maria interrupts, in panic.

'*Was* married,' Vivienne corrects, looking a little nervous as she licks her lips. 'Maybe I shouldn't tell you all about this. You should ask him yourself. It's pretty grim.'

'Please, tell me . . . I won't let on you did,' Maria asks her, urgently. She is certain she won't be able to get Felix to talk to her about it.

Vivienne shakes her head. 'No. It's not right. He'll tell you about what happened when he's ready. It's just . . . Well . . . You do look rather like her.'

Maria feels her heart plummet. Is she just an illusion to this man? What if he only says he loves her because he thinks she looks like his wife? And where is his wife? Vivienne referred to the wife in the past tense. So is she dead? Are the circumstances of her death his dark secret?

'I'm sorry; you seem upset,' Vivienne says. 'Look, I have never seen him so happy; obviously you are doing something wonderful for my old friend. I promise you, his wife is long gone and she is never coming back – that is for sure.' Vivienne squeezes her hand reassuringly.

So the wife is not dead, but gone? Where?

'He is with *you* now. Just focus on that,' Vivienne continues.

Maria shifts her legs; the ball spins inside her and she feels a jolt of arousal. 'Yes,' she says, huskily.

'Well, then – stop worrying about it. You are very pretty. In fact, I would say far more attractive than she ever was . . .' Before Vivienne has time to finish her sentence, Felix has suddenly materialised again. 'I'm off to dance some more; do you want to join me?' Vivienne asks Maria.

'No; she can't,' Felix interjects. 'We're leaving.'

Maria almost collapses with relief. At last, they can go back to the hotel room; at last, she will be able to let go.

'Did you find who you were looking for?' she asks Felix, as they make their way through the crowd towards the exit.

'Yes,' he tells her. 'Thank you for being so patient, darling.'

He squeezes her hand. 'I will make it up to you.'

Despite his words, she feels a tension in his body as they walk out of the club, hand in hand. His light mood has darkened. She wonders who it was that he had to meet. She wonders about his wife. Vivienne had said she was long gone. But to where? She is still not sure if she means that she is dead.

As they approach the exit of the club, Maria sees a tall, white-haired man leaning by the door. He has his hands in his pockets and she can feel his eyes upon her, watching her as she walks out with Felix. She knows instinctively that he is the person her lover met.

'Who was that man?' she asks Felix, once they are out on the street.

'What man?'

'The one by the door, with white hair?'

'You saw him? Olivier?' He pauses, saying no more and, for some reason, she senses she shouldn't ask again.

They speed up. She can feel the hard outline of his hip as it presses into her waist, his chest against the side of her breasts. He hurries her along the street. Has he forgotten that she is wearing the ball? Surely he must guess what this is doing to her? She senses it swivelling around inside her, forwards and then backwards against the outside tip of her most tender self, so that she is gritting her teeth in an effort not to cry out. His physical proximity to her is beginning to turn her on further. It is a hot night as it is, and now she feels like she is on fire, her body breaking out in a sweat. All the time, as they walk, as

Felix pushes into her, touches her, she is getting more and more aroused.

'Felix!' she cries out, coming to a sudden standstill in the street.

He seems to come to his senses, remembering her situation. 'Sweetheart, I'm sorry . . .'

She grips her sides, panting, trying to cool down.

'Come, my darling; I think I need to get you back inside. I cannot let you suffer further.' He suddenly scoops her up in his arms.

'Felix! Put me down!' she giggles.

'You are as light as a feather,' he says, carrying her through the dark streets. It is some relief to lie, like a dying swan, in his arms. Yet the ball has done its work. She is teetering on the edge.

In the hotel foyer, Madame Paget is nowhere to be seen. Felix sets her down in front of the lift and pulls back the cage door.

'Do you know what I would like to do to you in here?' he says to her, as they ride up to their floor.

She shakes her head; her eyes wide open with desire.

'I would like to tie you up, to these bars, right here,' he says, stroking the metal bars behind her, 'and I would like to take you from behind . . .' He strokes her bottom lip with his finger, and she opens her mouth, sucking its tip. She finds herself wanting him to do just what he describes. She wants him to take her in the lift. She cares not who sees them. Yet now they have arrived at their floor. Felix pulls back the gates and she follows him down the corridor into their hotel room. Just one more step, she promises herself, the sensation of the ball keeping her balanced on the precipice.

And now the door has closed behind her, and her lover is looking into her eyes. It is a look of adoration and longing, and yet, behind that, there is darkness and a secret she craves to know. She closes her eyes for a second. If she were another woman, she would tear off the little gold ball attire and storm out of the dingy hotel room forever. But it seems Maria, like her mother, Belle, before her, is a risk-taker. She opens her eyes.

'How beautiful you are,' Felix says, as he slowly unbuttons Maria's red dress.

She clenches her legs, feels that evil ball stimulate her further.

Her dress cascades in a flurry of scarlet, a flood of red on the bare boards, and she stands before Felix, naked apart from her brassiere, her stockings and the velvet ribbon attire.

She sways against him as Felix unties the velvet strip and, with his fingers, retrieves the ball from within her flesh. She gives a little shiver and a gasp when he removes it, and leans into him even more. She wants him so badly now.

What is happening here in this little room in Paris? Is this a dream she is in? Is it real? All she knows is she wants Felix inside her.

As her gaze travels around their love nest, her eyes come to rest upon Felix's movie camera, sitting on the chest of drawers. 'Does it work?' she whispers to her lover.

'Does what work?'

'The camera.'

'Of course,' he says.

She presses up against him and, on her tiptoes, puts her arms around his neck. 'Film us?' she asks.

He leans back and looks into her face. 'Are you serious?' he asks her, his expression deepening into one of awe.

'Yes,' she says, for she wants their passion documented. She wants him to watch it, to know that she is the one for him. Just her.

'Are you sure?' he says again, releasing her before picking up the camera, turning it over in his hands.

'Yes.' The word hisses out of her mouth, so loaded with her desire that Felix has no need to ask her again.

'We will need more light, and I will need to set up the tripod, get it rolling . . .'

They become performers within the motion picture of their love, he leads her to the bed, pulling her on to it, so that she is on her hands and knees on the soft mattress.

Felix produces a silk scarf of black from beneath the pillow. She has never seen it before. He puts it around her eyes. All light is gone; she is in the heart of darkness. All she can do is smell him, and all she can hear is the whirr of the camera.

'I love you, Maria,' he whispers. His words feed her courage. She wore the golden ball, and now he will reward her with his love. The idea of the camera recording their love-making turns her on further.

He traces his finger down her spine so that she shivers. She can feel beads of sweat falling between her breasts, her mouth watering with desire. She follows the sensation of his finger down her back, over her bottom and underneath, as he caresses her, bringing her back to the point of desperation the gold ball had her in, just a few moments before. He pulls his finger away and she waits to feel him in her but, for a moment, nothing happens. She pushes her bottom up, offering herself to him. And then, suddenly, he enters her. His thrust is so powerful she is pushed all the way forward, her head grazing the wall. He pulls out slowly, so very, very slowly, so that the tip of him is rubbing against the very edge of her, teasing her tender skin.

He is in her again, pushing hard and deep. As he begins to pull back again, she feels her womb suck back, her insides quiver, and something takes over her. Maybe it is because she has drunk too much wine tonight, or maybe it is the after-effects of wearing the little gold ball, or maybe, even, it is the idea that she is being filmed that connects her to the violent, most instinctive part of herself – just like Pandora. Whatever it is, Maria abandons all sense of normality. She lets Felix penetrate her, deeper and deeper, right to her core. She loves him so much that she is no longer afraid, not of her heart nor of her body. There is a part of her that craves him to be bound to her more than he ever was to his wife, whether she is dead or alive. As he releases within her, she climaxes as well, convulsing in ecstasy, crying and laughing all at the same time.

Hours later, in the pearly hour before dawn, it is just her and Felix. The camera lens is blinkered as it lies harmlessly within its case. She wakes to feel his lips upon her skin. She opens her eyes and sees the shadow of his head on her belly as he caresses her with his tongue. She closes her eyes, her body so exulted that it feels apart from her mind, melting into his mouth. She opens herself so completely to him and, as he adores her, she comes again, imagining her love raining down upon him, healing him. For she knows her lover bears a burden from the past, and only she can save him.

Valentina

VALENTINA SITS IN A CROWDED TUBE CARRIAGE AND
remembers that, last night, she had the same dream as she had
the day before. There she was, sitting naked in the Tube train,
careering past stations without stopping, looking at an image
of herself, the giant, empty suitcase at her feet. But this time
there was no vampire Glen sucking the life out of her. Instead,
she encountered all sorts of creatures: a rhinoceros, a large
mastiff dog, even dinosaurs. She has no idea what it all means.

Are all these creatures a part of her psyche? Do they represent
her animalistic side, or her instinctual nature? Is there a
diabolical part of her that emerges through her free spirit? She
thinks again of her conversation with Leonardo this morning
and her question about whether they were bad people. He had
talked about the fact that morals should not apply to the
world of erotica.

She looks across at the people sitting opposite her. They

are all studiously avoiding each other, reading the newspaper, or a book, or listening to music on headphones, or staring into space, just like her. We are all together and yet utterly disconnected, she thinks. What a miracle it was that she and Theo had fallen in love in such an environment as this, and yet they had. She will never forget their magical connection on the metro in Milan. She remembers how their eyes had locked through the hubbub of other passengers. So much had been said just by looking at each other on that journey through the underground tunnels of Milan. Not one word was spoken between them. They had exited the metro at exactly the same time, and all Theo had done was reach for her hand. She had led him, silently, all the way from the metro back to her apartment, where they had made passionate love all night long. It was only the following morning that they exchanged names. She had thought it was going to be the best one-night stand of her life. Instead, that stranger on the metro had become the love of her life.

The train pulls into Finchley Road station. This is where she needs to get off. She gets up, suddenly feeling very reluctant. Why is she putting herself through this? Does she really need to meet her father now? But it seems that her body is propelling her forwards and she knows that she will only regret it if she doesn't follow through and be brave. Before, she had the excuse of not knowing where he lived. Now she has this information, she feels impelled to act upon it, even if she ends up hurt, or disappointed.

Outside the Tube station, the blue skies have disappeared to be replaced by dark, loaded clouds. She shivers, regretting not bringing her coat. As she turns off Finchley Road and up the warren of streets leading towards Hampstead village, it begins to rain heavily. She breaks into a jog, trying her best to protect herself with her bag on her head as she turns into her father's street. It occurs to her that it is most likely that he won't be home. After all, it is the middle of the day; most people are out at work.

And now she stands before the house again, like she did just two days ago, when her plan had been disrupted by Glen. She looks to her right and left. To her relief, she sees no sign of her would-be stalker. She wonders if Theo sorted him out last night – warned him off. Or maybe he has given up, she thinks, hopefully, while knowing in her heart that she has not seen the last of Glen. She pushes her concerns about the unpleasant art thief out of her mind. She can't think of that now. Finally, she has reached the point she had been hoping to get to all these months, ever since Garelli spoke of her father to her.

'He would be proud of you, Valentina.' That's what the policeman had said, and she takes a strange comfort in those words.

She approaches the door slowly, despite the rain soaking her dress, penetrating through to her underwear. Hesitantly, she rings the doorbell, hearing it echo down the hall. She waits. For a moment, she thinks she is saved. In fact, she is just about to walk out of the gate and back down the road when the door suddenly swings open. For a second, she is speechless. They are face to face, and what is most startling of all is that he looks exactly like her brother, Mattia, just with grey hair. Her father says nothing, either, for he looks just as shocked as she is. His face is as white as the wall behind him and his mouth has dropped open.

'Tina?' he croaks, looking confused and frail.

She realises now – he must think she is her mother. 'No,' she says, finding her voice. 'No; I'm Valentina.'

He knows who she is. Of course he does. He seems to collect himself, and colour comes back into his face. 'Valentina! Of course! Well, I . . . This is a surprise,' he splutters.

'Yes. I suppose it must be,' she says, not knowing what to say next.

'Come in,' he offers. 'You are getting drenched.'

She enters his hall. It smells of sandalwood and is opulently decorated: a plush red carpet and silky white walls hung with painting after painting in all manner of styles, from early-looking Dutch prints to modern abstract paintings. She can't help thinking how much Theo would like this hall and all the art.

'Can I offer you a cup of tea?' he asks.

He doesn't confront her, or ask her why she is here. In fact, after his initial shock, he seems quite relaxed in her presence. It surprises her – makes her feel cross already. Shouldn't he have the decency to look a little shamefaced?

She follows him into a spacious kitchen with a large wooden table in its centre. Again, the walls are hung with a myriad of art.

'Please,' he says, 'sit down while I put the kettle on.'

They say nothing as she watches him fill the kettle with water and put it on to boil. He opens a cupboard and takes out a teapot covered in a delicate rose pattern, and two cups and saucers with the same design. He lays the table with the crockery and fills a jug with milk. He opens another cupboard and produces a cake tin, which he opens. She is quite fascinated by his fastidiousness, so different from her mother.

'Would you like some carrot cake?' he asks her. 'I made it myself.'

She shakes her head, surprised that her mother's ex-lover would know how to bake a cake. 'No, thank you; just tea is fine.'

'Are you sure?' He looks a little anxious. 'You must be hungry; it's lunchtime.'

'No, really. I don't want anything.'

He looks crestfallen and closes the cake tin, putting it back in the cupboard.

Her father brings the brewed teapot over to the table and fills their cups, before sitting opposite her and waiting expectantly for her to speak. She is at a loss. It all seems so surreal. After all these years, here she is drinking tea with her father – *her father* – the man who is half of her. And yet he may as well be a stranger.

'Well,' her father eventually says, 'how are you?'

'Fine, thank you,' she replies, stiffly.

'And how is your brother?' he says. 'I hope all is well with him and Debbie, and the kids.'

She drops her mouth open in surprise. How does he know all about Mattia's family? Did her mother tell him?

'And Tina?' he says, tightly, and she notices a slight twitch in the corner of his eye as he says her name.

'They're all fine,' she replies. 'In America.'

'Yes, I know. And you are living in Milan now?'

'I never left. I stayed.' She cannot help but emphasis the last word.

He nods. 'I haven't been back to Milan in all these years, you know,' he says, wistfully. 'I am based here in London now.'

She cannot believe he is so tactless. It is astounding.

'So, what brings you to London?' he asks her.

'I'm in a photography exhibition in the Lexington Gallery in Soho. I was over for the opening.' She leaves out the fact that it is erotica. Somehow it's not something she wants to explain to her new-found father.

'That's fantastic. Your mother must be so proud of you.'

'She doesn't know about it,' Valentina blurts out. 'I haven't told her.'

'Oh?' her father looks confused. 'Why not?'

'We don't really get on that well.'

'I'm sorry to hear that,' he says, giving her a kind smile of the sort you might give an acquaintance, not your own flesh and blood.

She suddenly feels incensed. How dare her father sit in front of her, as cool as a cucumber, and act as if he has done nothing wrong? She wants to make him feel as uncomfortable as her, as awkward and as hurt. 'Why did you walk out on us all?' she spits out, aggressively.

There. She has said it. Finally, she is asking him why he rejected her.

Yet she can't look him in the eye while she waits for him to reply. She stares down at the kitchen table, counts the whorls in the grain of the wood. She dare not look at his face.

He says nothing for a moment. 'I am sorry about that, but things were getting very complicated. I was very fond of you, Valentina. You were such a lovely little thing.'

'Excuse me . . .' she hisses, glaring up at him with loathing. 'How can you talk about your daughter as if she is a puppy or a doll that can be discarded?'

The colour drains from her father's face and he looks genuinely shocked, speechless.

'How could you just walk out on me and Mattia?' she continues to rant. 'How could you let *her* drive you away from your own children?'

She is building up to a huge indignant outburst, yet her father reaches out and puts a hand on her arm. His touch is cool; to her surprise, it calms her down.

'Valentina,' he says, his voice hoarse with concern, 'I had no idea . . .'

'What do you mean?' she says, confused.

'That you don't know.'

'What don't I know?' Her voice rises in panic as she looks into the gentle blue eyes of her father and begins to suspect something, even before he says it.

'Valentina,' Philip Rembrandt says to her. 'I am not your father.'

Maria

SHE CHANGES HIM. BEFORE MARIA, FELIX'S FILMS WERE
surreal, fantastical fairy tales, much admired by the new
young Parisian intellectuals. Now she is his muse. She has
inspired him to take the dark matter out of these fairy tales
and translate them into erotic adventures. This is their
clandestine film-making. It is not decadent, not pornography,
for this is the art of their love. It is just for them.

In this new, liberated world she inhabits, she can believe
that what they are doing is not immoral. Everything challenges
her preconceptions. She sees plays that seem to have no drama
but are just pure ideas – anti-theatre, Felix calls it – where the
most outrageous language can be expressed, she listens to jazz
music that ignites her sexual essence, and she goes to art
exhibitions of erotic drawings – one so explicit that it is shut
down by the gendarme. Felix tells her that the erotic drawings,
by the artist, André Masson, are a direct response to his
traumatic experiences in the First World War.

'I understand now that I am the same, my love,' Felix tells her. 'My films are a consequence of the war. They are a free expression of that love of life . . . That is what eroticism is.'

Maria examines Masson's erotic drawings, looks at the swirling mass of naked bodies. All seem to be women – full breasted, heavy limbed – spiralling skyward, like an exploding volcano, in a combined ecstasy. She thinks of the films that she and Felix are making and she wants to ask him . . . It is on the tip of her tongue . . . *What traumatic wartime experiences did you experience? Reveal to me the mystery of your disappeared wife.* The woman Felix never mentions, yet who, since the day Maria knew about her, has never left their hotel room. She is always there, an imaginary observer behind the rolling camera. Yet she dare not ask him. She is too afraid that he will not want her anymore if she pushes him for answers. She thinks she would die if that were to happen.

Their days in Paris take on a natural rhythm. The mornings are for just the two of them. They stay in bed late, until the summer sun is high in the sky and the room stifling with heat. Yet it doesn't bother Maria, for these, to her, are the best hours of the day. Felix is all hers. No camera is running, as has usually been the case the night before. It would make sense to film in daylight, yet it never feels right to do such a thing in the morning. They need the build-up of the evening, the play of wine and food upon their senses, the nocturnal flavour of Paris, stirring the blood in their veins, making them both brazen and abandoned once Felix turns on the camera. She trusts that he will never show these films to anyone else. She imagines them both old together, after the children are grown, the grandchildren . . . She imagines finding these ancient movies and watching them. They will have been together all those years and still be in love, filled with nostalgia at watching their love enacted in front of them in black and white.

On these Parisian mornings in their little sweaty hotel room, she lets Felix choose what they do. Sometimes he wishes just to pleasure her alone and sometimes he wants to make love to her. All of her sense of reason, her rational mind, has abandoned her. She imagines it is a little bluebird, flying out of their attic window and away across Paris. She cares not if it comes back to her.

By early afternoon, they are hungry. They dress quickly; usually, he insists she puts on another new dress he has bought for her. She wonders where his money is coming from, but then she decides not to think about it. They go for lunch in a local bistro. Usually, they will be joined by other thespian friends of Felix and, after the first bottle of wine is shared, the conversation will become more and more animated. A decision will be made then about what to do with the rest of the day. They will go to an exhibition, or shop for new clothes. Felix not only transforms her wardrobe, but his own, as well. Gone are the tweed suits from London; now he wears tailored suits and polished shoes. He gets his hair cut shorter, and it makes him look younger. Every day, he goes to the barber and never again does she feel the roughness of a day's growth of stubble against her skin. Now his cheeks are baby soft.

In the early evening, they might see a play or a film – maybe a new American film noir or a French film. This Maria loves – to take sanctuary in the darkened cinema, lost in a parallel world. Felix takes her to see *La Belle et la Bête*, directed by his friend, Jean Cocteau. She falls in love with the fairy-tale movie. Is this a parallel for her and Felix, she wonders? Is he the beast she must learn to trust? Will her love save him and turn him back into a prince? To Maria, he is already a prince, yet she does notice that, to others, he is less tender.

She remembers Jacqueline's comments on her countryman, and she has seen how strangers, even some of his friends, react to Felix's brusque manner sometimes, and his rather caustic tone. It embarrasses her and she wonders if he is aware of how it makes him sound to outsiders: rude and difficult. Often she gets a sympathetic glance. The only person who seems not to mind Felix's rudeness is Madame Paget at their hotel, and she suspects that is because she is rather in love with him. It would explain her hostility towards Maria.

After the theatre or the cinema, it is time to go to a bar for drinks with friends, then maybe they will eat again and the night truly has begun. They go to a club to listen to the new jazz stars of America: powerful black men that stir her passions when they play their music. Sometimes they stay out so late that they have coffee and croissants in Le Tabou to herald a new morning, and then it is time to sleep. Upon these mornings, they will not be filming. However, most nights they go back to their little den, set up the camera and create a new scene. Usually, they film themselves together – this is something Maria finds most erotic – but sometimes Felix says he wants to film her on her own. She sits on the bed, facing him, looking straight into the lens of the camera, as if they are the eyes of her lover, and she speaks to him.

'I love you,' she says, again and again, 'I love you,' as she touches herself, takes herself further and further into her rapture. She resists closing her eyes, and continues to stare into the camera, imagining Felix playing this film again, sometime he may be alone, and remembering how much she loved him. This footage of her climaxing in front of her lover's camera, showing him that even the idea of his love is enough to bring her such pleasure, is evidence, she hopes, of how much she trusts him. She does not want to hide her feelings for him.

They become addicted to the rush of their passion. They are drawn to doing what is forbidden. One night, after they have been clubbing, Maria asks Felix to make love to her in the cage lift at their little hotel. This time they forget about the camera, for they need to be stealthy. Although Madame Paget appears to have retired for the evening, she is a rather nocturnal creature herself. Maria wonders how she would react if she saw them making love in the lift.

She presses the button to call the old cage lift and they can hear it clanking all the way down to the ground floor. Her heartbeat begins to quicken and she looks over at Felix. He smiles back at her, conspiratorially. The lift jolts to a stop. Felix pulls back the cage doors and ushers her inside. He takes the black silk scarf from his pocket.

'Would you like me to blindfold you?' His voice is cooler now, as if he has taken on another persona.

'Yes,' she breathes.

She turns to face the back of the lift. She examines the iron bars, the network of metal netting. She is literally in a cage. She is, of course, free to stop their game at any stage, but the sense of entrapment excites her. It is a surprise, since she has never liked confined spaces. Maybe it is because she feels so safe with Felix. He is with her in their cage. She is not a prisoner on her own. Felix places the scarf over her eyes, and now all is black. He ties it tightly at the back of her head, kissing the back of her neck and causing a thrill to shoot down her spine.

He spins her around, pushes his cheek against hers, putting his hand between her legs and touching her gently with his fingertip. 'Do you trust me?'

'Yes,' she says, fiercely, with all her heart.

He catches her affirmation in his mouth, kisses her deeply with his lips. He pauses and she senses him step away. She hears the door beginning to slide over, the latch shut, and the lift clanks into action, slowly travelling upwards.

Felix comes back to her and kisses her again, placing one hand on her waist and, slowly, steadily raising the hem of her dress with his other hand. He now places both hands underneath the dress, on either side of her waist. She is wearing no underwear tonight, something she often does to excite him when they dance and he can sense her nakedness beneath her dress. He presses his fingers into her, peeling back the lips of her labia, massaging her. Maria's knees begin to weaken, and again she feels she is stepping into her other self – the dark, desirous part of her, where all reason, all logic, is completely defied. Society would say they are depraved to have sex in public, and yet it no longer feels wrong to be in a lift with Felix pleasuring her. He is the giver and Maria is the receiver, and both roles can be sacred.

The lift has come to a halt. She senses Felix leaning over and pressing one of the buttons, and then it starts moving again, on its journey back down to the ground floor. What if there is someone in the hotel reception, waiting for the lift? What if they are discovered? The thought turns her on even more. Felix pushes her against the side of the lift, so that the hard bars are pressed into her back. She raises her arms, gripping on to the bars on either side of her as he lifts her legs and she wraps them around his waist. Still pulsing from Felix's fingertips, she feels her nipples harden, while down below she is soft and pliant. Felix is inside her, slamming her against the side of the lift. They are riding down still, and he is pushing up into her. She knows she can stop it. She can pull off her blindfold and make the lift stop whenever she wants. Yet she doesn't want this journey in their lift of seduction ever to stop.

They shudder to a halt, and Felix pauses. She holds her breath, waiting to hear voices . . . yet all is silent. The next thing she hears is the lift starting up again and they begin to rise. Felix pushes up deep inside her again, and they are rocking back and forth now, urgent to fulfill their desire before the lift lands on their floor.

Up and down she rides in the lift with Felix. The most primal part of her is exposed. She is a wild maenad, a woman beyond all sense of herself. She is a receptacle and yet spinning within her own sensations. She pulls off the blindfold so that she can see her love. The expression in his eyes blazes into her. She feels the heat of his love as, together, they climax, tumbling on to the floor of the lift as it shudders to stop, their bodies vibrating around each other.

They fall into bed and sleep the exhausted slumber of those fully sated. The morning brings fresh hope into her heart. She wakes before him and looks at his untroubled face on the pillow. She prays that their love can sustain them forever, yet, deep down, Maria knows all of this is, in essence, transient. She knows, one day, the rhythm of their little world will flounder and she prays that they can keep on going, even if it must change, even if reality finally does intrude. She has not forgotten the fact of Felix's wife and she has not forgotten the white-haired man. She is just making them wait their turn. For now, Felix is all hers.

This morning, she wakes him with her lips. She hears the little gasps of her lover as she thrills him with her tongue, bends down further to lick his balls and trails her tongue around their circumference and up to the base of his cock. All the way she licks, up to its helmet and the slit at its tip. She opens her mouth wide and sucks him right down to the back of her throat, for she adores him so much, she wants to abandon all self.

That very night, they start to play a new game. In fact, it is she who begins it. It is hard to believe that, just one month ago, she was an innocent, untouched by any man. Now Felix has opened her up. She believes that she is a better lover than she ever was a dancer.

They are in one of their favourite clubs, surrounded by a new crowd, many of whom are young Americans – ex-GIs, studying in Paris, or those brought over as part of the Marshall Aid Plan, working for the new Economic Cooperation Administration.

These young American men have been well fed most of their lives. They are bigger and broader than the French. Of course, she is devoted Felix – he is the man of her heart – and yet she cannot help letting her eyes trail over the bodies of these energetic young men. What might it be like to feel one of them inside her? She is immediately shocked at the thought, yet somehow Felix manages to read her mind.

'I see you watching them,' he says. 'Would you like me to invite one of our new companions home with us, my dear?' He smirks at her.

'No, not at all,' she says, blushing and lowering her eyes.

Felix puts his hand on her waist and leans towards her ear. 'I like the idea of it,' he whispers. 'You and me and someone else . . . Do you?'

'Not a woman,' she says, immediately. She could not share her love with any other woman, but maybe a man . . . No; what is she thinking! She has had too much to drink. Yet now it seems that the thought has entered Felix's head; he has turned to chat to a tall James Stewart lookalike to their right. She starts to panic. She didn't mean it – not really. She only wants to make love to Felix. She manages to drag him away from the American and on to the dance floor.

'You look worried,' he says, smiling mischievously.

'What were you saying to that man?' she asks.

'He is called Richard, and he is a very interesting young man. He works at the embassy. I have invited him back to our hotel for drinks.'

'Felix!'

'My dear, it was your idea that we play this game . . .'

'But I don't want to, now,' she says, almost tearful.

He kisses her on the lips – no more teasing, all tender concern. 'OK, my darling,' he says. 'Don't worry. I shall cancel my invitation. To be honest, I am not sure I could have stood it . . .'

Later, back at the hotel, he films her again.

'Think of me,' Felix coaxes her. 'And think of Richard.'

Her fingertips soften, moisten, and she can almost imagine

they are Felix's tongue and that it is morning now and he is in the bed with her, caressing her. She begins to put pressure on herself, circle her finger around and around. Instinctively, her legs fall out to the side, so that she is on view. She hears the camera starting up. She continues to rub herself, bringing her out of her rational thoughts and to a place of instinct. She opens her eyes now and she does not only see Felix and the camera; to her surprise, she imagines that the American, Richard, is here, sitting on the chair and staring at her, wide-eyed. She licks her lips to show him what she would do to his cock if she could, and continues to stroke herself. Her eyes travel down the length of his face. She imagines the stubble on the American's chin brushing against her soft pussy, those lips kissing her. Her eyes trail down his chest, the shirt tight against his lean frame, and down to his lap. She can see he is hard, his cock straining to be released from the cloth of his trousers. She sighs, pushes her head back against the bedstead and closes her eyes again. She is getting closer and closer, yet she doesn't want to climax, not on her own.

'Oh,' she moans, widening her legs further.

Felix cannot hold back any longer. The mattress springs as he climbs on to the bed, and instantly he is above her. She opens her eyes to look into his. Her love has returned. In her deepest fantasy, she is here with Felix and Richard. Maria and two men, adoring her. She wonders if one day they will ever actually act upon this fantasy. Felix unbuttons his trousers. She stops touching herself and reaches down for his cock. She trails her finger up and down it, feels a bud of his seed at the tip and brings her finger up to her mouth to lick it off. The taste of him, so salty sweet, makes her stomach contract with desire. She grips him again. She is throbbing at the thought of it deep inside her. He is holding her down by the shoulders and, still with his cock in both hands, she pushes him up inside her.

She no longer hears the camera. All she is now is a part of Felix, thoughts of another man gone. She wraps her legs around his waist, her arms around his chest, as they move in unity together. Their bodies comprehend each other perfectly. She closes her eyes again, losing herself in an ether of passion. She and Felix are all sensation. Together, they climb higher and higher, their lovemaking more and more frantic. She cannot stop herself now. She wants his seed to spill forth inside her. His cloudburst brings forth her shower of ecstasy. She cries out, vibrating around his cock, soaking in his essence. She imagines his seed lining the insides of her with gold, sliding down her thighs like priceless syrup. This oneness, this tiny moment when the egg and sperm connect – this is what she has been searching for in all her weeks with Felix. And yet she will continue to search for it for the rest of her life. For Maria is not to know that this will be the last time she is at one with her love, that this is their last precious millisecond of passion.

Valentina

SHE IS A BLUE FLAME OF RAGE AS SHE MARCHES DOWN
Finchley Road towards the Tube station. Hours later, and still
she hasn't managed to calm down. She knows she is not in the
best state of mind to go to Anita's party. She is so angry, she
is not sure how she might behave, but she is in no mood for
staying in, especially with Aunt Isabella, a woman who
reminds her of her mother, and thus of how she has been
deceived her whole life. Antonella had texted Valentina an
hour ago to tell her that she and Mikhail were going to a fetish
club night at the Torture Garden in the Ministry of Sound,
and did she want to join them? Valentina had turned her
down. Her mission is to get Theo back. Even the revelation of
today, the fury it has put her in, is not going to destroy her one
chance. How is it that her mother manages to sabotage her
love life, even if she is hundreds of miles away?

Valentina spent the whole afternoon with Philip
Rembrandt. She had let him feed her tea and cake. In fact,

between the two of them, they had eaten a whole carrot cake while he tried to explain to her just who she was.

'My whole life, I thought you were my father,' she said to him, as he looked at her with his steady blue eyes. 'I was so angry with you for leaving . . . and with my mother for letting you go.'

'It wasn't like that, Valentina,' Phil said. 'It was complicated.' He cut her another slice of cake and slid it on to her plate. 'I didn't want to leave Tina at all, but I was working on a really hot Mafia case as an investigative journalist. I had received a couple of death threats, so I didn't want to endanger my family. That was why I left, initially.'

'But why didn't you come back when it was safe again?' Valentina bit into the moist sweet sponge.

'Your mother told me not to. She was going to move to Berlin with you, she said, since Mattia had already left home for the States.'

'So, if I am not your daughter, is Mattia still your son?' she questioned him.

'Yes, he is,' Phil said, looking shamefaced.

To know that she and her brother do not have the same parents hurt even more.

'So, have you spoken to him over the years?' Valentina remembered Phil's comment about Mattia's wife and children earlier, as if he knew them.

'Yes,' he said, looking embarrassed. 'I visit them once, sometimes twice a year.'

Valentina felt wounded. She had been deceived, not just by her mother, but by her brother, as well. She expected it of Tina, but Mattia? She had thought he really cared for her.

'Please don't blame Mattia,' Phil said. 'I am sure he wanted to tell you but obviously your mother insisted you shouldn't know.'

'Why the hell not?'

'I can't really understand why. It was a very messy situation. As I told you before I assumed you did know, Valentina.'

They sat in awkward silence for a moment.

'How messy can it have been to make you walk out on me and never ever contact me again? OK, I was not your real daughter, but I thought I was. How could you do it?'

Phil looked genuinely upset. 'I did it to protect you. I missed you terribly, Valentina,' he said, softly.

He shifted in his chair, got up and walked around the kitchen. 'I thought I was doing the best thing for us all. And, besides, since I was not your real father, I had no rights because your mother and I were never married.' He turned to her, clutching his hands, looking almost as if he might beg her forgiveness at any moment. 'I was so fond of you, Valentina. It was very hard to walk away, but I really feared for your welfare. The people I was exposing were very, very nasty.'

'Why? Who were they?'

'I was writing a piece on a Mafia head in New York, called Caruthers, and his family, who were based just south of Naples. During my research on the article, I found out some crucial evidence concerning three rather gruesome murders in the area around Naples that implicated members of Caruthers' family. This information I passed on to the police.'

Valentina thought back to her conversation with Garelli the day she left Milan for London. He had said that Philip Rembrandt had saved his life.

'Unfortunately, my contact in the Mafia would only communicate with me. I eventually persuaded him to talk to a friend of mine in the police force, called Garelli.'

Valentina didn't interrupt. She could tell him later about her connection with Garelli.

'But it was a set-up . . . There was a shoot-out. I took a bullet and spent several weeks in hospital. Your mother was furious when she discovered the danger I had put us all in.'

'Where were you shot?'

Phil tapped his left shoulder. 'Just a shoulder wound, but it gave Garelli the chance to call for back-up.'

'So what happened in the end?'

'We took Caruthers down, uncovered a whole viper's nest of drug deals, but in the process we made lots of enemies. It was too dangerous to stay in Italy. Mattia was already in America, so I suggested to Tina that we join him or go to London together, but she had other ideas.'

'So you wanted us to come with you?' Valentina checked.

'Yes, I did, but your mother insisted she was going to relocate to Berlin. She said I could come as well, if I wanted.'

'But we didn't go to Berlin. I mean, I vaguely remember we

went away for a week or so when you left . . . It could have been Berlin . . . but, in the end, we came back to Milan.' Valentina pushed her memory back to when she was a little girl. There was a city she went to with her mother when she was about six. Could it have been Berlin? Her mother had never mentioned the trip to her, ever.

'I didn't realise that you hadn't moved away for good, because I left Milan first. I didn't know that you were still there for years, not until Mattia contacted me again . . . and then it really was too late to go back. You were nearly an adult and I didn't want to upset you.'

'You already had!' she spat at him. She turned away. She could not bear to see the regret on his face. She looked out of the window of his kitchen. It was in the basement of his house and she watched the feet of people walking by on the pavement above them. She could see that it was still raining, despite the number of pedestrians wearing sandals and flimsy trainers. Were they optimistic or just fools like her? she wondered, looking down at her own footwear – wedge sandals from MaxMara, their pale suede now stained from the rain.

'I am so sorry, Valentina; you have to believe I felt I had no choice but to leave at the time. Besides I thought you knew I wasn't your real father. Mattia never told me otherwise.'

'Why didn't we all go to Berlin?' she asked him, sullenly.

'I didn't go because I couldn't do it anymore.'

'Do what?' She stared at him, examining his face. Again, she was struck by how like Mattia he looked. Finally, the man in the photographs was a real man sitting across the table from her.

'Be the ideal of what Tina thought her partner should be: a man who loves her, no matter who else she sleeps with; a man who will always be there to support her, despite her promiscuity.' He sighed and cut himself another slice of cake. 'I thought I could be that man. I loved your mother so much, but one day I just couldn't do it anymore, Valentina.'

His words pierced her. She couldn't help but think of herself and Theo – all that Theo had been through last year to try to show her that he loved her, no matter what she did . . .

'Why didn't you take me with you?' she said in small voice.

'You were not my child. Besides, Tina told me she was taking you to Berlin to live with your real father. She wanted me to come, too. She wanted us all to live together. One big, happy family,' he said, with vinegar in his tone.

'My real father is German?' Valentina asked him, her heart beginning to thump.

'No; he was from Prague, but he lived in Berlin.'

Valentina felt as if she was shrinking in her chair. She looked over at Phil Rembrandt and, despite the fact she had not seen him since she was six, she realised she had not forgotten him. She would have recognised him anywhere. He had been a part of her life for the first six years. As an adult, she was beginning to understand why he left, but, as a child, she was not sure she would ever forgive him.

'More tea?' Phil asked, hovering by the kettle, looking at her anxiously.

She nodded.

'I am so sorry, Valentina,' he said again. 'I should have come back, no matter what Tina said.' He poured fresh water into the teapot and dropped in another two bags. 'But I am glad you found me. It's best that there are no more secrets.' He gave her a tentative smile as he poured her tea and offered her milk.

She nursed her cup of tea between her hands, trying to process all this new information. 'So, tell me,' she said finally. 'Who is my real father?'

'I never met him, but he was a Czech musician she met in Berlin – a cellist. His first name was Karel. I don't know his second name.' He paused, running his hand through his grey hair. 'I have no idea where he is now. You should talk to your mother.'

Phil Rembrandt's words echo inside her head: 'You should talk to your mother.' But how does she have this conversation on the telephone? She is certain her mother will just hang up on her. She is so angry with her, and with Mattia. And she feels ashamed, as well, in a strange way. She is the accident – the mistake her mother could never erase. Maybe that is why she does not love her as much as she loves Mattia, because she is a reminder of an affair gone wrong – for it must have done, if they never relocated to Berlin. Her mother lost Phil

Rembrandt for no reason. Despite her indignation that he abandoned her, Valentina cannot help but begin to like him. He is all that her mother isn't: rational, caring and honest. He spent the whole afternoon talking to her, and feeding her cake. Spontaneously and without hesitation, he put his life on hold for her for this one day. All of these things she feels her mother has never done.

As she travels on the district line towards Anita's party, Valentina's anger, her thoughts on her family, finally begin to subside. She can't let herself get into a state right now, when tonight is about winning back Theo. She tries to analyse every word he has said to her since she arrived in London, to work out if he wants them to get back together. She remembers their meeting in the Tate, and how sure she had been that he still loved her. Yet he refuses to give up Anita, despite the fact he hasn't even slept with her. Valentina has to convince Theo of her love for him. She has to be ruthless and not think of Anita's feelings. This is her quest tonight. Afterwards, if he still rejects her, she can face the rest of her life knowing she did everything in her power not to let him go. She shivers, despite the fact the Tube carriage is hot and stuffy. The idea of spending the rest of her life without Theo is a chilling one.

Valentina walks along the South Bank, all the way down, past London Bridge and then past Tower Bridge. She studiously follows Anita's directions, coming into a residential area of riverside apartments, connected by walkways. She walks across a little bridge over the water and enters a narrow street on her right, lined with old warehouses that have been converted into state-of-the-art apartments. She is buzzed in via a videophone. Gripped by a bunch of nerves in the lift on the way up, she wishes Antonella were with her – despite her friend's disapproval of Theo. Or, better still, Leonardo. It would be good to have some support. In her Mary Quant miniskirt, inherited from her mother, and her miniature black biker's jacket, she may look the height of cool, but inside she is still the jilted lover: insecure, and desperate to get her man back.

Anita's apartment is a dream place. Valentina is let in by a young woman with short, spiky red hair and kohl-rimmed cat's eyes, wearing an electric-blue sequined dress.

'Hi, I'm Anita's cousin, Chloe,' the girl says, her plummy accent crystal clear, despite the background noise of music and chat.

'Valentina.'

'Oh, I've heard all about you; do come in,' Chloe says, offering her a glass of champagne.

Valentina tries not to gawp at the splendour of Anita's apartment. It is a huge, open-plan loft apartment, packed with the young and the beautiful, against the backdrop of the Thames and the city skyline. She can see Tower Bridge spanning the dark river, and the lights and energy of the city of London blazing on the other side. All the walls of the apartment are dripping with expensive-looking art. Interestingly, most of them are nudes. She remembers Anita telling her that her grandfather was a dealer in erotic art and literature, so, obviously, this must all be work she has inherited from his collection. She spies the charming Anita herself in a backless magenta silk dress, mingling among her guests. Her blond hair is loose tonight, and falls in luxurious locks down her bare back. She cannot see Theo anywhere, though. Her stomach is clenched tight in anticipation. Anita sees her and waves, sashaying through her friends to join her.

'I am so glad you came,' she gushes, kissing Valentina on both cheeks. She smells as luxurious as her apartment.

'Your place is amazing,' Valentina says, stepping back slightly. Already she is feeling guilty about her plan to steal Theo away from this sweet-faced woman.

'I'm very lucky,' Anita admits. 'But, of course, as I told you before, all of this amazing art was inherited from my grandfather.'

'It is quite an astonishing collection,' Valentina comments.

'Yes, it is and I am so, so glad you came, because I discovered something today that I think would really fascinate you.'

Valentina looks at her with interest.

'Remember my *Story of O* installation?'

'Of course,' Valentina says.

'Well, I believe that the actress in the film is none other than a young Italian woman called Maria Brzezinska. It makes sense, because the film is made by Felix Leduc and she is in the old dance film Theo gave you, remember?' Anita says, smiling with delight at her revelation. 'Isn't that just amazing? Her name is not on the credits, but I read about it in this biography on Felix Leduc, and the writer, a man called René Mauriac, actually knew Leduc and his associates. He mentions her by name, and says that Leduc and Maria were lovers and these were initially their own private movies. Goodness knows how they managed to survive or how they got into the public arena. Isn't that so wonderfully exciting?'

Valentina feels as if the wind has been knocked out of her. Did Anita just tell her that her maternal grandmother was a forties porn star?

'There must be some kind of mistake,' she protests, remembering all the stories of how devout a Catholic her grandmother had been. 'My grandmother may possibly have been a dancer but, I can promise you, there is no way she would have been in Paris in the late forties, acting in erotic films and, as for being Leduc's lover, well, that just sounds completely unlikely.'

'But it is her, Valentina,' Anita insists. 'I have done my research, you know. René Mauriac is quite clear that she left the Lempert Dance School and came with Felix Leduc to Paris in July, nineteen forty-eight.'

Valentina frowns, she still can't quite believe her. She remembers again her mother's descriptions of her grandmother: not just religious, but also shy, quiet and demure. And yet it is true that, despite the face being slightly out of focus, when she watched that footage yesterday, she had felt the woman looked familiar. Could it really be possible?

'Mauriac writes that Leduc met her in London when she was training to be a dancer.'

'Theo told me she was a dancer but that was the first I'd heard of it.'

Anita looks at her curiously. 'I had no idea that you didn't know she was a dancer or lived in Paris.'

'My grandmother died before I was born. I never met her.'

'Oh, I'm sorry,' Anita says. 'I really did assume you would know all about her . . . apart from these films, of course.'

If both Theo and Anita are right, her grandmother was a dancer and a participant in erotic films. It could be possible her mother kept this information from her. After all, she has just found out she has lied about who her father is her whole life. But why would she do that? She would imagine her mother would be proud of this libertine heritage.

'So, what else does this René Mauriac write in his book?'

'He writes about how much Leduc loved Maria. Then the chapter sort of ends abruptly and, in the next one, the book jumps about three years. I have no idea what happened to Maria in the end, or why things never worked out between them. Leduc ended up being married to someone else.'

Valentina knocks back her champagne. So how did her grandmother Maria transform from free-spirited Parisian to conservative Milanese? This information is astounding. First the revelations about her father, and now she is finding out that her devoted homemaker of a grandmother was in fact an erotic movie star, of sorts.

'Gosh,' says Anita. 'Are you all right? You look a bit shaken.'

'Well, it's a shock to find something like that out.'

'Yes, it changes who we are to learn the secrets of our ancestors, doesn't it?' Anita looks quite pensive for a moment.

'You see these erotic drawings and paintings on the walls?' she says, sweeping her arm in an arc around the living room. 'They all belonged to my grandfather. He was an art dealer in London in the fifties. He bequeathed half the collection to me and half to my cousin, Chloe.'

'It's an incredible collection of paintings,' Valentina says, politely.

'It is thanks to my grandfather that I have a passion for art. And it is also thanks to him that I have been able to create my artwork without any financial worries. Every so often, I just sell a painting.'

Valentina feels a tiny stab of envy. What would her life be like if she could give up the day job, and just focus on her art photography? Yet, even as she has this thought, it occurs to her that she likes to make her own money, to know that it is by her own merit that she has achieved what she has.

'Would you like to see my favourite piece?' Anita asks her, and, without waiting for a reply, she takes Valentina by the hand and leads her away from the living room, thronged with guests, and down a long corridor to the back of the apartment.

They enter what must be Anita's bedroom, a boudoir befitting a burlesque dancer, with flock wallpaper on three of the walls and a velvet chaise longue in the middle of the room. The fourth wall, facing the bed, is painted white, and hanging on it is a large painting in the style of the Impressionists. It is of two women lying on a bed, one is on her back with one of her arms raised and resting on her forehead, while a second woman is leaning over her, looking down at her. The first woman's gaze is not directed at the other woman's face, but dropped to some space between the two of them. They are very close to each other, scantily clad in petticoats. The painting is full of suggestion. What is the first woman looking at? And what is the second woman doing to her?

'What do you think?' Anita asks her, standing right behind her, so that she can feel her breath upon her neck.

'It's really beautiful; it reminds me a little of Toulouse-Lautrec.'

'It *is* Toulouse-Lautrec!'

'My God! It must be worth a fortune.'

'Which is why my apartment is alarmed up to the hilt. It's called *Abandon*. I just love the subtext.'

'It's incredibly erotic.' Valentina turns around and looks at Anita curiously. What is this woman playing at? And *where* is Theo?

Anita leans forward and tucks Valentina's hair behind her ears. 'Have you ever slept with a woman, Valentina?' she asks her, giving her a sweet, almost goofy, smile.

Rather than shaking her off, or changing the subject, Valentina actually finds herself drawn to her. 'Yes, I have,' she says.

The two women look at each other and Valentina knows that something could happen between them. Yet it is Theo she wants. She considers the idea again of a threesome, a way to show Theo she trusts him, but is she brave enough to go through with it? Could she share him with another woman?

The silence hangs between them for a loaded moment; finally, Anita shrugs her shoulders. 'Will we rejoin the party, then?'

It is at least an hour later and there is still no sign of Theo. Valentina is determined not to text him to see where he is, and she doesn't want to have to ask Anita, who is now surrounded by all her glamorous friends on the other side of the room. Valentina is sitting on a huge sofa among a group of art-world strangers. She looks out of Anita's extensive French windows at a view of the river and Tower Bridge and listens to her music. It doesn't surprise her that the burlesque dancer favours music from the past. They have been listening to Billie Holiday, Frank Sinatra, Marlene Dietrich and now Valentina recognises a more modern homage to the singing diva: Paloma Faith's latest album. She is singing one of Valentina's favourite songs, as well. Every word that Faith sings in her song 'Just Be' seems to be about her and Theo: the idea that they could grow old together and, no matter what, be linked for the rest of their lives. Could it be possible? Is this just a hitch in the story of their love? As she lets Faith's powerful voice lift her spirits, she spies several people from the opening, the night before. She is not so out on a limb, then. There's Kirsti Shaw on the far side of the room, wearing an all-in-one black silk jumpsuit and stilettos. She could go and chat with her. Yet Valentina is loath to move. She is waiting for Theo. She wants him to see her as soon as he enters the room. She crosses her legs and continues to stare at the view.

A thought occurs to her: maybe Theo isn't going to turn up. Indeed, Anita never mentioned his arrival when they were talking earlier. Could they have broken up? Is she wasting her last night in London at this boring party? Yet she senses he will come; tension lodges in her belly like a heavy stone. Now and again, some random man tries to strike up a conversation with her. She responds but she is not there, and soon he gives up.

She looks out of the wall of glass in front of her, at the dark, swirling river, the humming city, the night sky stained sepia by the city lights. She is drinking in the view and thinking about Maria, her grandmother, as a young dance student in post-war London and then as a participant in erotic films in the heart of liberated Paris. She was more adventurous than Valentina and her mother put together. And yet, Valentina's mother had always criticised Maria. She said her mother had never understood her. Well, Valentina knows just how that feels. If she ever has a daughter, will she be just the same as her mother and forget how it feels to be the child of a narcissist?

She senses someone sitting down next to her on the sofa; a polite, male cough, but she is too distracted to respond. Another cough, and then the voice speaks.

'Did you pass on my message?'

She is jolted out of her reverie by a crisp English accent. She starts with fright, her heart sinking. She recognises that voice. The last thing she needs is that creep, Glen, ruining the night. She can smell him – she doesn't even need to look at him. She shifts away from him on the couch but there is not much room, so many others are piled on it. She turns to glare at him. He is so close to her; she notes how pale his eyebrows are, his eyelashes so fair that they are almost invisible.

'I told you,' she says, with ice in her voice. 'Theo and I are not together anymore. I have nothing to do with him.'

Glen's eyes narrow as he snarls at her. 'Now, that just isn't true, is it, Valentina? I saw you together only last night, at the exhibition opening.'

She gives him a stony stare.

'By the way, your work is very interesting,' Glen continues to speak, his voice laced with sarcasm. 'Although I told Theo I thought it rather vulgar for my tastes. He was quite defensive about you . . .'

She turns her head away from him and stares out of the window; her heart is thundering at the mention of Theo. What had those two spoken about last night? 'If you don't stop harassing me,' she hisses. 'I *will* go to the police.'

He says nothing in return.

'Do you hear me? I really mean it!' She turns to confront him again. Yet, to her astonishment, he is gone and the seat beside her is empty. She looks around the room but she can't see him anywhere. Did she just imagine Glen was here? Yet his scent lingers.

Valentina hears laughter behind her. She recognises Theo's rich melodious laughter instantly. She turns on the couch, clasping her glass of champagne, emotion rising in her chest. She only saw him yesterday and yet his presence in the room transfixes her. She cannot believe that, this time last year, she had this man in the palm of her hand, and she let him go. How could she have been so stupid? Now here he is, in front of her, but not available. For, hanging on to his arm, is the delectable Anita in her silk magenta dress, which skims her perfect body and seems to scream out passion. How can Valentina possibly compare with this luscious woman, all sexy curves, cascading blond hair, plush lips and big, come-to-bed-with-me eyes? She is the kind of woman every man craves. Anita looks in her direction and their eyes lock instantly; Valentina's rival smiles at her. Valentina knows that Anita can see her longing; her smile widens and her eyes darken as she drinks Valentina in. It is obvious what she is thinking; there is such suggestion in her look. She looks like the cat that got the cream.

Maria

SHE AWAKES AND IS IMMEDIATELY AWARE THAT FELIX IS gone and she is alone in the bed. She sits up at once, alert. Something feels different. A faint breeze rustles the leaves in the trees outside the window, bringing the scent of summer into their room. The sound reminds her of the wind rippling the lagoon in Venice, and she feels a sudden pang of nostalgia. Could she persuade Felix to come with her to Venice and meet her mother and Pina? She would like them to be married first. To be able to do that, she needs to know if his wife is still alive.

It must still be early, for there is little sound from the streets below. She wonders where Felix has gone. He must have been hungry, and went to get them some croissants from the *boulangerie*. Yet something feels different in their room. She is unreasonably disturbed by his absence. She swings her legs out of the bed, sits on the edge and dangles them. She thinks about their lovemaking last night, and what had happened in the club beforehand. Had Felix seriously meant to proposition that young American? She admits that the thought of the two men with her had aroused her, and yet she is devoted to Felix. How could she want another man to make love to her, if she loves only him?

It is when she stands up, breathing in deeply, that she realises what is different. Normally, Felix stores the camera in a case in the corner of the room, but it is gone. She frowns and hesitantly walks over to the wardrobe. It is full of her new dresses, resplendent in all their jewel shades, but Felix's spare suit is gone, as is his case. A scream of panic struggles in her throat, and she chokes it back down. Where has he gone? She pulls one of the dresses off a hanger and hurriedly gets dressed, not caring to put on make-up or fix her hair. She dashes down the stairs, not quite knowing where she is going to go to look for him. She guesses she will start at one of the cafés they frequent.

'Mademosielle! Stop!' Madame Paget calls to her, as she flies through the lobby of the hotel.

'Mademosielle, Monsieur Leduc has left a letter for you,' Madame Paget says, waving an envelope in her hand.

Maria colours with embarrassment. Why did Felix leave her a letter with the concierge, when he could have left her a note upstairs, or even woken her up?

She takes the letter and thanks the woman, who scrutinises her curiously over the rim of glasses, her hair even brighter and redder than Maria remembers it.

'You know, the rent is due tomorrow,' Madame Paget says to her, her lips pursed in a thick red gluey line.

'Yes, thank you,' Maria says, getting away from her as fast as she can.

It is a long time since she has been up this early in the morning. If she were not so anxious about the letter in her hand, she might have enjoyed a morning stroll through Saint-Germain-des-Prés. She scurries down the cobbled streets, looking for a park or somewhere to sit. Eventually, she finds a little café that they have never been to before, orders a coffee and croissant and sits down, tearing the envelope open as fast as she can.

My dear Maria,

I need to go away for just a couple of days, my darling, to work on a film. Here is the money for the rent and for food. Enjoy your freedom. I will be back soon.

Your Felix. x

She pulls out a bunch of francs, gripping them in her fist, her alarm abating. All is fine. He is just away for a couple of days. He has even left her money.

She traces his handwriting with her finger. He has called himself 'Your Felix'. So he is hers. Oh, why hadn't he woken her and made love to her this morning before he left? She misses him so much already.

* * *

She spends the day listlessly walking around Paris. She leaves their district and walks across the Seine into the Ile de la Cité. The people are different this side of the river. There seem to be greater inequalities. On the one hand she sees poorer people huddled in doorways, refugees, lost and hungry people, and on the other hand there are smarter people – brisk businessmen, bristling with purpose, well-fed Americans and fashionable ladies-about-town. She even sees one woman wearing Dior's 'New Look'. She cannot help but stop and stare in admiration. How inadequate her home-made version is! The dresses that Felix bought her are pretty, but none are quite as fashionable as this woman's dress. The silhouette of the woman reminds her of a ballerina: tiny cinched waist and full skirt, her little feet and slender ankles like a doll's.

Maria stands outside Notre Dame, pondering its majestic façade, meditating on whether she is worthy to step inside. Her mother had not raised her any religion, but she had gone to a convent for her education. Some of it has rubbed off on her. What would the nuns call her now? Whore. Sinner. Fallen. And what about Felix? Is he the devil himself? And yet, when they are enacting one of his scenes, there is a feeling within it that is sacred: the communion between her and Felix. They have chosen to articulate some kind of exultation, to explore the religious depths to which eroticism can go. She should not feel ashamed. Even so, when she steps into the cathedral, she cannot help but bow her head. The scent of church incense overwhelms her, making her feel dizzy, insubstantial. For a second, she remembers how she felt when she was dancing Psyche: ephemeral, light as air, fluid. Since she lost her virginity, it is as if she is filled with rich earth: heavy limbed and loaded with the weight of her blood, her passion. It is as if she is never sated.

She makes her way to one of the side chapels and looks up at the statue of the Virgin Mary before her. Her benign smile and the pure contours of her drapery, her hand raised in forgiveness, make Maria want to reach out and touch her. She lights a candle and drops a few centimes into the box, falling on her knees, closing her eyes and clasping her hands together. And yet she does not know what to pray for. She summons to mind her mother and Pina, and prays for them to be safe and happy. She prays for Jacqueline in London, that she will forgive her for running away, and she prays for Joan, hoping that she has found the right man to love her at last. She even prays for Guido. Finally, she prays for Felix. Her man. She prays for his safety, that he will return to her again. She squeezes her eyes tight and prays for his soul, that he will be healed and that soon they can have a normal life.

She is on her way back to the hotel when she runs into Vivienne.

'Maria, my darling, where are you off to?' the foxy redhead asks her.

'Hotel Montana,' she tells her.

'And where is Felix?'

'He had to go away to work.'

'So you are on your own?' Vivienne's eyes light up. 'Well, darling, you must come out with me. When the cat's away, the mice must play!' And, refusing to take no for an answer, she links arms with Maria and joins her step for step. 'Let's get dressed up first. You should wear that ivory evening gown and that amazing red cape I saw you in one night. We shall go for some dinner first, where we will drink lots of wine, and then we will go to the best new jazz club in town. Do you have money?'

As their heels clatter in accompaniment on the cobbled streets, Maria's heart lifts. All of a sudden she is glad to be rescued from the loneliness of their hotel bedroom by the vivacious Vivienne. 'Yes, I have some money,' she says.

'Excellent,' Vivienne says.

It is another long, hot night in Paris. Vivienne and Maria are jammed into yet one more new jazz club, listening to the effervescent Boris Vian. They are surrounded by Americans. Maria is a little nervous she will run into Richard again, and he will ask her why she and Felix abandoned him last night. Vivienne's English is excellent and she keeps the company entertained with stories of the Resistance and their heroic actions during the war.

'Why is it that every Frenchman I meet insists he was a member of the Resistance, or a Gaullist during the war? I mean, lots of your guys collaborated with the Germans, so where are all those bastards now?' one of the Americans asks.

Vivienne shrugs. 'Did you never hear of the *épuration sauvage*?'

'Nope.'

'You think the Terror was bad after the Revolution – well, this was just as harsh. We purged our traitors.'

Vivienne speaks matter-of-factly, her green eyes glinting almost snake-like in the gloom of the club.

'Surely not all of them? I mean, your government collaborated with the Nazis; there must be some of them still in the system . . .'

Vivienne sighs as if impatient. 'We got most of them.'

'I heard about it,' says another American. 'Pretty nasty stuff, all right. Didn't you shave the heads of women who slept with Nazis?'

'Sure we did. They deserved it,' Vivienne says, severely. 'They were collaborators, too.'

'Of the horizontal kind.' One of the Americans laughs.

'It's not funny,' says Vivienne, suddenly serious, and, for some strange reason, looking directly into Maria's eyes, as if she is telling her something more. 'I mean, our men were risking their lives in the Resistance – in hiding, or prisoners of war for years. How do you think they felt when they returned and found out their own wives had slept with Nazis, even had one of their children? Isn't that a double betrayal?'

'Yeah, but what if her kids were hungry and a woman thought she had no choice?' said one of the Americans. 'She knows that, if she sleeps with some bigwig Nazi, he'll get food for her kids.'

'*I* was hungry – *my children* were hungry – but I still didn't sleep with the enemy for a slice of bread,' Vivienne says, passionately, knocking back her drink in one go, her eyes blazing.

'OK; cool it lady, remember France is liberated now. How about you come dance with me?'

Vivienne takes off across the dance floor with one of the young Americans, dancing with more fervour than Maria has ever seen. Maria remains stunned by her friend's admission. So Vivienne had been, or even still was, married? And she had children? It made sense, of course. She is at least thirty, if not older. It's just she is out every night with their group, partying. She had told Maria she had been a singer before the war, but Maria had never heard her sing. And she had never heard her mention children.

One of the Americans asks her to dance, but she shakes her head. She is tired now, wants to go home and sleep, hoping that, in the morning, her lover will have returned. Now he is away, she begins to doubt her life here in Paris. Is he really making a film? For he never mentioned it to her before. She remembers her first day alone in Paris, all those weeks ago. He had never explained to her where he had disappeared to.

'So, where's Felix?'

She turns to see René, the small, bespectacled writer she had met the first night she and Felix had gone out in Paris.

'He is away, filming,' she tells him, as she takes the proffered glass of wine he is offering her.

'I didn't know he was making a film at the moment.' René looks at her curiously.

'Well, he is,' she says, feeling a little irritated by his question. She sips the red wine, wondering why Felix could not have taken her with him on his film shoot.

'I suppose he may have gone to see Matilde,' the little man says, watching her closely as she freezes in horror at his words.

She has to ask him, although, in her heart, she already knows the answer. 'Who is Matilde?'

René hesitates, looking troubled. 'Oh dear; I thought you knew . . . Matilde is Felix's wife.'

She feels the blood drain from her face; her hands are gripping her glass of wine so tightly that it feels like the glass will shatter.

'I am so sorry,' says René. 'I assumed you knew, that you were in on the secret.'

'I thought Felix's wife was dead,' she says, her voice barely above a whisper. 'Vivienne said she was long gone . . .'

'And so she is, metaphorically speaking, but Vivienne doesn't know the whole story. We can't tell her, you see, because of what happened to her . . .' René sighs, looking troubled. 'I really am so sorry to stir all this up. I just thought you knew.'

Maria looks at him and she is wondering if he is telling the truth, for he does look very concerned. 'But . . . but . . . if you knew about Felix's wife, who did you think I was? A whore?' Her voice is shaking as anger begins to contaminate the love inside her heart.

'Of course not! My goodness, no. I assumed you knew everything – how impossible things are for Matilde and Felix . . . I thought you were part of it.'

Maria fixes the quaking René with an icy glare. 'And what part of it did you think I was?'

'Why, his mistress, of course,' the little man gushes. 'The woman that Felix loves now – that much is quite obvious.'

Maria looks away from him in distress. She can feel the tears pricking her eyes, and she bites her lips in an effort to stop herself from crying. She needs to get out of here. She scans the crowd for Vivienne, but she has disappeared. Instead, she sees someone else, a figure she had put right to the back of her mind and tried to forget about: the white-haired man from that first night she and Felix had gone out in Paris. He is looking right at her, and is walking directly towards her.

'Do you know who that man is? The tall one with the white hair?' she hisses at René.

'Why, of course I do!' René exclaims. 'That is Olivier, Felix's brother.'

Felix has a brother! He has a secret wife and a secret brother. Who and what else is he hiding from her? It hurts so much that he hasn't told her anything, that he cannot trust her.

And now Olivier is standing before her, shaking René's

hand, his face wearing a haughty expression. Of course, she can see now that he is Felix's brother. They have the same deep-set eyes and brooding air.

'I believe you haven't yet met Maria,' René is gabbling nervously.

'Have you been spouting off again, René?' Olivier says to the little man.

'Well . . . I . . . I thought she knew . . .' René wilts under the other man's glare.

Olivier turns to give Maria his full attention. He is obviously the elder brother, yet he still maintains the same commanding air as Felix. 'Mademosielle,' he says, formally taking her hand. 'I am pleased to meet you, although I think my brother would have preferred to be here to make the introductions.'

And yet Felix could have introduced them before, Maria can't help thinking – that night a few weeks ago, in the club.

She is beginning to recover from the shock of discovering that Felix's wife is still alive. Not only that, but, according to René, Felix is with her right now, as she stands here in this club with his brother. 'Where is Felix?' she asks Olivier, coming directly to the point.

'Why, he is at the château,' he says. 'He will be back tomorrow. You will see him then. He can explain everything when he comes back to Paris.'

'No,' she says, emphatically. 'I want you to take me there now.'

He frowns, looking quite bewildered by her request. 'But it is the middle of the night . . . My dear, it is a long drive from here.'

'Do you have a car?'

'No, so it is quite impossible—'

'I have a car,' René pipes up. Olivier shoots him a furious look.

'I insist you bring me to this château,' she says, turning on René. 'Otherwise, I shall leave Paris tonight and Felix will never see me again. And it will be your fault, René.'

'But I don't know the way,' René protests.

'Then you must come too, and show him,' she says, boldly, to Olivier.

Felix's brother reaches out and puts a cold hand on her bare arm; he shakes his head mournfully. 'But, Maria, Felix has told me so much about you,' he says gently. 'He loves you very much. Don't you think you can wait for him to come back to Paris?'

'No, I can't,' she says, surprised by her own anger. 'I need to see him now. I have to know the truth.'

'The truth,' says Olivier, darkly, 'is a very, very complicated matter.'

Valentina

THERE ARE FOUR OF THEM LEFT, SPREAD ABOUT THE couch and chair, listening to the Irish singer, Clara Rose, and her song, 'Girl'.

> I once knew a girl, she had no head for circumstance
> She went to a party, got burnt
> I stayed at home, drinkin' alone
> But I was happier in the end

She is the girl in the song. She should have stayed away. Watching Theo all night with Anita at his side has made her miserable, and yet she can't quite give up. She can't walk away forever – not yet. Valentina watches dawn begin to push the night sky away, as if a blind is being drawn up to the heavens. The river now looks like a sheet of polished metal, so still, as if its current has stopped to take breath.

'I think I'll be off,' says Chloe, Anita's cousin, as she gets up out of the armchair and smoothes down her spiky red hair.

'Are you sure, darling?' Anita drawls. 'You're welcome to stay; there's plenty of room.'

Does Chloe sense the sexual tension between the three of them that has steadily been brewing all night long? Or does she just want to go home to her own bed? In any case, Anita's cousin makes her adieus and, a few minutes later, the three of them are left together, sitting in a row on that huge white couch, sipping a tumbler of whisky each and looking out of the window at London. Valentina knows that she is no longer being subtle. Yet now, at the moment when she is about to give up, she begins to sense some game being played by her rival. Instead of seeming disturbed by Valentina's continued presence, Anita has almost encouraged her to outstay all the other guests. But what about Theo?

When he first saw her, she had seen him flinch. There was surprise in his eyes (it had not even occurred to her that Anita hadn't told him she was going to be here), and he looked unhappy that she was at the party. She had nearly left right then, she was so hurt by his reaction. But then, as the night wore on, she noticed him looking at her – all the time. She saw his eyes watching her, regarding her as she took off her jacket to reveal a skintight, sleeveless rib top, looking at her when she was talking to any other man in the room. Yet, when she tried to approach him on her own, Anita was suddenly by his side. She had even determined to ask him about Glen and what was going on with the Masson picture, but again there was always someone within earshot. So she had started to drink some more champagne and now, with the addition of the whisky, all this drink really has gone to her head. She doesn't care anymore about exposing her feelings.

She is sitting on a couch with her ex-lover and his new girlfriend. Anita is sandwiched between them, her silk-clad body wedged beside Valentina, who can feel their hip bones touching and the softness of Anita's thighs, and smell that scent of wealth off her. She is all glossy, luxurious sexuality and, on the other side of her, sits the man who melts Valentina to the very core.

Valentina is beyond all reason, all rationale, when – without any kind of premeditation – she turns, instinctively, to Anita (and does the other woman turn to her at exactly the same time?) and kisses her on the lips. The kiss deepens, as sweet and soft as vanilla sugar. The two women twist around to embrace each other, and Valentina feels the ample breasts of Anita pressed against her own. The image of the Lautrec painting, *Abandon*, comes into her head. This, then, is her abandonment. She opens her eyes and, over Anita's shoulder, she sees Theo staring at her. His blue eyes have turned indigo with desire and he passes his tongue over his lips. She senses him holding back, watching the two women as they caress each other before slowly pulling away.

* * *

'So . . .' Anita places her hand on Valentina's shoulder, fluttering her false eyelashes at her. 'Shall we three play?'

Valentina looks across her at Theo. 'Would you like to?' she asks him, directly.

For the first time since she has known him, Theo looks thrown, beyond words. 'Do you really want to do this, Valentina?' he finally says, his voice hoarse.

She nods as Anita takes her by the hand and pulls her up off the couch.

'I have done this before,' Anita tells them. 'Three is *always* better than two. Besides,' she smiles mischievously, 'I believe the only way I will get Mr Steen to actually sleep with me is if Valentina is there as well. In the light of what we agreed earlier, tonight will be my last chance.'

Valentina is not sure whether she is referring to her discussion with her, or something she and Theo have spoken about. She doesn't really care.

'Come,' Anita says, leading Valentina out of the sitting room so that Theo stands up to follow her. Valentina twists around and reaches out her hand to Theo and he takes it. They are together, now, within this erotic adventure and she is not sure whether it is her or his fantasy they are about to enact.

Anita instructs Valentina to go into the bathroom and fill the jacuzzi up while, in the meantime, she brings Theo into the bedroom.

Valentina hesitates.

'Don't worry, darling, we are not going to do anything until you get back. I just want to build up the anticipation,' Anita tells her.

The bathroom is in a similar style to the bedroom. There is a large iron claw bath in the centre of the room, but Valentina ignores this and turns on the sunken jacuzzi in the corner. She is in a hurry, anxious to get back to the others before anything happens, or before she might sober up and change her mind.

When she walks into Anita's bedroom, Theo is sitting on the bed, while Anita stands in front of him. It is as if they are frozen in tableau. Theo seems more relaxed now, and pats the bed next to him. Valentina slips off her high-heeled ankle boots and slides on to the bed. She feels the warmth of his body up against hers and inhales him. It is all she can do to stop herself from throwing herself on top of him. Music begins to fill the room, gathering them into a sensuous mood. It is classical – a woman's voice scaling a delicate aria – but Valentina is not sure what it is. She doesn't care. She is transfixed by Anita, who begins to sway her hips in front of both of them. She is dancing for them. There is not much for her to take off. She unties the halter neck of her magenta dress and lets it slither and slide down her body. She is wearing no underwear whatsoever. Her body is perfectly balanced: her full, pert breasts, her tiny waist, and the gentle curve of her hips. Valentina's eyes trail down to the tiny little square of Anita's pubic hair and the delicate V between her legs.

Anita reaches out her hand to her. Valentina looks across

at Theo and he is looking at her intensely. She wonders if he is turned on by the naked Anita. He must be. And yet his eyes are on her.

'Do you want to, Valentina?' he asks her.

'Shush,' she says, bringing her finger to her lips. 'No words.'

She stands up and lets Anita begin to undress her, as if she is her servant. Anita unzips her little Mary Quant skirt and lets it fall around her feet. Valentina steps out of it. She pulls her little rib top up, over her head, so that now she is just in her bra, G-string, stockings and suspenders.

'Au naturel,' Anita whispers, pushing her fingers around the edge of Valentina's G-string and stroking her, pressing her finger in further, so that it tips the lips of her labia. Valentina steps back, a little shaken. Anita has felt how turned on she is. Anita looks up at her with glee, and then removes her hand. She walks around her and unclips her bra. Now Valentina is naked apart from her G-string, stockings and suspender belt. She doesn't take her eyes off Theo. Is he comparing her imperfect body with the perfect Anita? Yet Theo is holding her gaze, looking only at her. He speaks with his eyes, and what they say warms her, gives her strength.

Anita unclips Valentina's suspender belt and her stockings roll down her legs. She lifts Valentina's feet, one at a time, and pulls the stockings off. Then she stands up again and turns Valentina to face her. The two women are about the same height, yet their bodies are completely different. Anita's breasts are so much plumper, her nipples look like lily pads, their stems hard buttons of arousal. She has narrower hips than Valentina, a smaller bottom, yet her legs are just as long. Anita surveys Valentina as if she is a prize she has just won. She turns her around, puts her hands on Valentina's waist and drags both her hands down the sides of her bottom.

'What a heavenly behind,' she comments.

'It is a bottom that deserves to be spanked,' Theo says, his voice laced with humour.

'Indeed,' Anita murmurs, turning Valentina around again and leading her to the bed where Theo sits, still dressed.

He stands up suddenly and takes Valentina by the hand. 'Would you like me to spank you, Valentina?' he asks her. 'I will only do it if you want me to.'

She looks into her love's eyes. 'Yes,' she whispers. 'I really want you to do that.'

She feels a thrill within the pit of her stomach. Theo sits back down and Anita positions her so that she is bent over his lap. Theo caresses her bottom, stroking it with his hands, massaging her cheeks.

She closes her eyes, preparing herself for the slap of his hand upon her tender behind. Down it comes. A quick, playful slap – not too hard – the slight pain of it soon replaced by a quickening in her blood, a deep vibration within her body, echoing, calling to her essence.

'Again?' Theo asks.

'Yes,' she whispers.

He smacks her a little harder this time. She cries out.

'Did I hurt you?'

She hears the concern in his voice. She twists around to look up at him. 'No, I liked it.'

It is true. She can't say why she likes it. Is she a sham of a feminist to want her lover to give her a little spank? Yet it is always a game – always has been with her and Theo – and she likes all his attention, the way she knows he is admiring her bottom. It makes her want him inside her so very much.

'That's enough,' Anita says. She seems to be in charge of both of them tonight.

Theo gathers Valentina up in his arms.

'Let's get into the jacuzzi,' Anita says. 'Let's make you feel better, Valentina.'

Theo carries her into the bathroom and Anita follows. The room is filled with fragrant steam. He places Valentina back down on her feet. She wants so much for him to keep holding her in his arms. Yet Anita has her by the hand now, and is dragging her away from him. 'Come on,' she says, stepping into the bubbling water.

Valentina follows her in and the two women bob either end of the jacuzzi as they watch Theo undress. Every article of clothing he takes off makes her loins soften further. The white shirt is discarded and she looks with longing at his chest, remembering how it felt to have his strong arms around her. He drops his trousers to reveal his long, muscled legs. He takes off his pants and the two women admire his powerful erection. Valentina sighs inwardly as she watches him get into the jacuzzi, the water sloshing over her as he sits down. She thought she would never see Theo up this close again. She thought she would never have him inside her again. She is so close now. She just wishes Anita were not here.

And yet it is Anita who moves across the water to her first. 'Sit between my legs,' she tells Valentina.

Valentina slides back between Anita's legs. She feels the other woman's pussy pressed against the top of her bottom, her breasts against her back. It is erotic, there is no doubt. The other woman slowly begins to stroke her shoulders, reaching around her and massaging her belly. Jets of water shoot up around them and through them.

'Massage me?' Theo asks Valentina.

She opens up her legs in answer and he slips between them, just as she slotted into Anita. She pushes up against him and reaches round his middle. She wants to savour this moment of touching Theo so intimately again, after all these weeks. Slowly, she works her hands over his chest, through the tuft of hair at the base of his belly and down.

Gradually Anita releases her from between her legs while Theo reaches around Valentina and gently removes her hands from his cock.

As if choreographed like a dance they all change places. Theo turns and grabs Valentina by the waist, pulling her towards him as he now slots her between his legs. Valentina can feel his cock pressed up against her back, his breath upon her neck. He brings his hands around her waist and tiptoes them down her stomach, across her pelvis, to between her legs, gently circling his finger around her clitoris. Meanwhile, Anita has repositioned herself, this time in front of Valentina. The women face each other and now, with raised knees, Anita puts her legs either side of Valentina and slides towards her through the water. Valentina looks at the other woman, her eyes brimming with desire. She knows what she wants. Instinctively, she reaches forward and touches Anita with her fingertips. She begins to do to Anita exactly what Theo is doing to her.

The three of them are locked within a sacred ring of sensual pleasure. Theo is pleasuring Valentina, and she is pleasuring Anita, as the power of Theo's sexuality passes through her into Anita. Theo is still circling her clitoris with his fingertips, while with his other hand he makes strong vertical strokes between her legs making her vibrate deep down within. The sensation of his caressing yet forceful touch upon her – combined with her compression against Anita's body, her soft contours, his musky scent, the feel of soft tender flesh against her fingers – brings her closer and closer to a place of utter abandon. She closes her eyes and now she imagines the three of them no longer in Anita's bathroom in her flat in London, but in a tropical rock pool somewhere far out on a South Pacific island. They are in a humid, fertile place, pulsing with giant luscious flowers, the water as hot as a sauna, the steam rising, tropical rain falling upon them, all mixing with their perspiration so their naked bodies begin to melt into each other and unify like lava. Valentina is aware of Theo's arm grazing against her as he spins his fingers within her, faster and faster. She continues to stimulate Anita in rhythm with her own body. And thus it is that both Anita and Valentina climax within the same second, as if they are erotic twins bound by their desire for one man.

Valentina's head drops on to her chest as she pulls her hands away from Anita. Theo gently releases her and Anita drifts back, a lazy grin on her face as she floats in the water. 'Shall we all go into the bedroom?' she asks Theo.

Valentina raises her head to look at Theo as he stands up, steps out of the jacuzzi and shakes himself, spraying water upon her. He looks magnificent. She can't take her eyes off his erection. She wants him so badly. It is as if all of her insides are aching with a deep pulse at the base of her soul. He turns to look at the two women, his eyes gleaming like shards of blue topaz. The door to the bedroom is open behind him, the giant bed beckoning.

'Shall we three go to bed?' Anita asks Theo again.

Despite what has just happened between them in the jacuzzi, and the fact she desires Theo so much, Valentina suddenly feels cold with realisation. She knows with certainty that she cannot go any further with Anita. She could never watch Theo make love to another woman, even if she was a part of the threesome. She cannot do it. Is it because she loves him too much, or not enough?

This, then, is the moment when she will know whether she has won him back. Whatever Theo says now, in reply to Anita's question, will seal the fate of their love forever.

Maria

THE NIGHT COOLS AS THEY DRIVE OUT OF THE CITY, YET Maria is bathed in sweat. Even so, she doesn't take off her red cape. She wraps herself up in it as if it is a red sheath around her heart, protecting it, and she lifts the hood to hide her face from the two men. René is driving, and Olivier sits in the passenger seat beside him. She is in the back.

Maria is beginning to doubt the wisdom of her insistence that they take her to this mysterious château where Felix and his wife are hiding away. What does she hope to achieve by doing this? How can she stand to see him with her? She will lose him for good now. And yet she needs to know everything about the man she loves. She needs to see the extent of his betrayal.

Maybe her love for Felix is not of the healthy kind. Is it a kind of sickness, whereby she is powerless to her own sexual needs and desires? Has he enchanted her? And, if so, maybe if she sees him outside of Paris, with his wife, she will wake up and be strong again. She will be able to keep her dignity and walk away.

'Mistress.' That's what René had called her. Could she accept that position in Felix's life? He had also said that Felix loved her. Could that be enough for her?

As they drive out of the city, her thoughts drift back to Vivienne. Maria had been unable to find her to say goodbye at the club. She wants to know why Vivienne had told her Matilde Leduc was long gone.

'Why does Vivienne not know about Felix's wife?' She directs her question to the back of Olivier's head, but he neither speaks nor turns to her.

'It is because of what happened to her during the war,' René speaks up. 'It is better that she doesn't know.'

'Why? What happened?'

Olivier remains silent, but René continues to chat. 'Vivienne was married once, but her husband died during the war.'

'That's terrible,' she murmurs, finding it hard to picture the vivacious redhead as a grieving widow.

'He was in the Resistance; a key figure, getting intelligence out to the English. He worked in Lyon, like Felix and Vivienne herself, but they caught her husband. He was tortured to death.'

Maria shivers. She realises that, in Venice, despite the fact they were occupied by the Germans during the war, their time had been relatively easy. Yes, they had risked dangers by hiding Jacqueline and the others, but still it hadn't felt dangerous at the time.

'And where are her children?' she whispers, fearful of what she will hear him say.

'They died too. After the father was caught, they sent the family to a camp,' Olivier tells her, his voice devoid of emotion.

'Vivienne was the only one to survive. She had two little girls,' René adds.

'That's terrible,' Maria says, her eyes filling with tears for her new friend.

'They say that she used to sing to her girls and the other children in the camp, but one day the German commander in charge heard her sing. He thought her voice so special that he decided to spare her, but it was too late for her children. They were too sick. So he separated them,' René continues.

'She told me that she was a singer,' Maria says.

'She was – a fine one. But she cannot bring herself to sing for an audience . . . not since she lost the little girls,' René tells her.

'She blames her talent for the fact they died alone, without their mother to comfort them,' Olivier adds.

'It's such an awful story,' Maria says, trying to imagine how it might have been for Vivienne. 'But what does it have to do with Felix's wife?'

'I will let Felix explain, when you see him,' Olivier tells her.

She says no more. She lets his words hang in the air like a loaded gun.

* * *

They drive through the deepest hours of the night, moonlight slashed across the road, illuminating forests on either side. She feels like she is in one of those American film noir movies. How well does she actually know these two men who are driving her into the unknown? Is there really a château? Yet she certainly cannot take René as a threat. There is something rather comical about his appearance. Olivier is a different matter. And yet, he is Felix's brother; surely he would protect her for Felix's sake?

Eventually, they pull off the main road into a drive, bumpy with potholes and overgrown. Shrubbery scrapes at the window by her side as she peers out the front. They drive around a corner, and now she can see something in the distance: the blinking of lights. As they get closer and closer, she can see the outline of a grand building, illuminated against the night sky. The full moon shimmers in front of them and the sky is clear, packed with stars. There is something quite fairy-tale about the place. It has battlements on its roof and a tower attached to one of its wings. She imagines Felix filming one of his fantasy films – a surrealist retelling of Sleeping Beauty, maybe, or Snow White – within the walls of the château. If only that were what he was doing, rather than hiding from her, with his wife.

René pulls up outside the château and turns off the car. The three of them sit in silence in the vehicle, listening to the ticking as the engine cools down. Now that they are actually here, she is terrified. All of her earlier anger, and the courage it brought with it, has dissipated. She wants to run away. But she can't. She has to see it through. She can't look weak in front of these men. Eventually, René gets out of the car, followed by Olivier, who opens her door for her. She clambers out and stands uncertainly in her red cloak, with the hood still up, clasping her hands. She looks up at the sky and catches sight of a shooting star. Is this a sign of hope? she wonders. Olivier had said that Felix needed to explain things to her. Maybe his wife is a lunatic or an invalid and they are only man and wife in name? She could possibly live with that.

Maria turns her back on the dim forests, the openness of the country night, and faces the château, bathed in shadows and moonlight. 'Whose house is this?' she asks the men.

'Why, it is my brother's,' Olivier says.

Maria's jaw drops. Felix *owns* this huge castle? She feels a stab of anger. Why had he pretended to be so poor in London? Why were they living in a grotty little hotel in Paris, when he owned this? He had bought her some expensive clothes, but still . . . they were insignificant compared to the kind of money he must have. Was he some kind of baron or count, even?

She picks up the skirt of her red cape with one hand and climbs the stone steps to the front door, René and Olivier on either side of her.

'I think I should go and tell him you are here first,' Olivier says.

'All right,' she agrees. She realises she doesn't want a big dramatic scene – just the truth. She knows that, as soon as she sees Felix, she will know if he loves her. Can she even bear to meet the wife?

There is no bell, but there is a large knocker in the shape of a ram's head with curling horns. Olivier picks it up and drops it against the door. She hears it echoing through the castle, imagines the sound of her arrival reverberating through the inner rooms. She is trembling with fear, her reason trying to calm her down. She is the innocent party, so why is she worried now that she is intruding? She steps away, suddenly besieged with a bad feeling. She wants to go back to Paris. She can't face Felix and his wife. But, just as she decides to do this, the door is opened and, as the light from the hall illuminates her, she realises it is too late.

She and René wait while Olivier disappears down a long corridor, led by the old man who let them in. He is obviously a servant. She wonders if there are maids and a cook in this huge house, too. Inside the château it is surprisingly sparse. There are no paintings on the walls, and there is the bare minimum of furniture. They are standing in a large hall with heavy beams and stone walls. A huge wooden chandelier hangs in the centre, filled with candles, casting shadows upon the blank walls.

'A German general lived here during the war,' René says, as if reading her thoughts. 'Stripped all the walls of the Leducs' heirlooms and packed them off, back to Germany. The château has been in their family for generations. They lost a lot.'

'So why is this château Felix's and not Olivier's, if he is the eldest?'

René scratches his head and thinks for a moment. 'I suppose because Olivier has the house in Paris.'

'There's a house in Paris?'

René nods, looking at her curiously. 'I didn't know that you knew so little about the Leducs,' he says.

She feels her cheeks burning with shame. She is a fool. That is how she looks in René's eyes. 'You must think I am very stupid,' she murmurs.

René smiles at her kindly, his grey eyes like the points of a lead pencil behind his thick glasses. 'Not at all, my dear . . .' He pats her arm. 'I think, once you have listened to what Felix has to say, you will realise you have made rather a fuss unnecessarily . . .'

Her back arches. 'I don't think discovering the man you love has lied to you – has a *wife* – constitutes an unnecessary fuss.'

'Just let Felix explain . . .'

That is what René and Olivier keep saying: 'Let Felix explain.' Well, she is fed up of waiting in this draughty hall. Why should she give him time to make up more lies? She wants to see him face to face now. All of a sudden, she doesn't care if the wife finds out about her, because surely it's better for her if she knows, anyway. It occurs to Maria that everything about Felix is a fabrication, like one of his films. She will not be made to wait in the hall. She will not suffer it any longer.

'Maria, wait! Where are you going?' René calls after her as she storms down the corridor the same way that Oliver went. 'We have to wait here!'

She shakes her head, her hood falling down, her dark curls tumbling free upon her shoulders. Her anger from earlier has returned to her, it propels her down the corridor. She passes silent door after silent door until, at last, she sees one with a line of light at its base and she can hear voices behind it. Without hesitating, she turns the handle and walks in.

Her lover faces her. She has never seen him so smartly attired. He is wearing dress trousers, a starched white shirt with a black silk bow tie, gold cuff links and a black waistcoat. His unruly grey and black hair has been tamed and is a glossy sheen, combed back, revealing the whole of his face: his broad, clean-shaven cheeks, his mouth a deeper red than she remembers.

'Maria!' He looks horrified. The expression on his face fans her anger further. He doesn't want her here. She stares right into his eyes, afraid to look elsewhere, afraid of the figure she can discern out of the corner of her eye, sitting on the sofa behind him. 'My God, Maria, what are you doing, bursting in here . . . ? Olivier told me you were waiting in the hall.'

Without thinking, she steps forward and slaps him roundly on the cheek. The sound of her hand on his flesh echoes in the vast room. There is a shocked silence, broken by René tumbling into the sitting room. He has the sense not to speak, and instead helps himself to a glass of wine and a seat at the edge of the room.

Felix stands, staring at her, his hand to his cheek. The look of horror has now been replaced by an unreadable mask of indifference. It hurts even more to see his lack of reaction to her slap. She focuses on the red mark of her hand upon his cheek and then she lets her vision widen, as she takes in the room. Here, at least, some paintings have been replaced. A fire crackles in a grand fireplace, despite the warm night, and all the windows are closed, crimson velvet curtains drawn. The room is oppressively hot. She sees Olivier sitting on a chair by the fire, surveying her coolly, and on the sofa beside him, facing her, is a woman. It can be no other woman than the wife. She turns her gaze to Maria and the two of them look at each other. Maria is expecting hostility and yet the woman is gazing at her in awe. She can see that she was attractive once, but she must be at least twenty years older than Maria, and her face looks pinched and tired, her eyes sad.

'Oh, Felix,' the woman says. 'This must be her.'

Maria jolts in surprise. The woman speaks as if she knows who she is. Indeed, she is certainly no madwoman or invalid. She turns to Felix, her heart on fire. 'Why did you lie to me?' she hurls at him.

'But, Maria, I didn't lie to you,' he answers, truthfully. 'I just never spoke to you about my wife.'

My wife. The words cut into her. He will never call her those words. 'How could you be with me when you are married?' she demands.

'Please, calm down,' he almost snaps at her. 'Sit down and have a drink, then I can explain to you.'

She remains where she is, standing in her red cape.

Felix turns to René. 'My instructions were that you were to wait in the hall.'

'She just ran away; I couldn't stop her.'

'And why the hell did you agree to drive her down here in the middle of the night in the first place? Why couldn't you stop him, Olivier?' Felix turns to his brother.

'It was her,' Olivier says. 'She was determined to see you.'

Felix turns his attention back to her. 'For God's sake, sit!' he commands her, and, to her surprise, she flops down on a chair the other side of the fire.

Felix goes over to the sideboard and pours a large glass of red wine from the decanter. He hands it to her, skillfully avoiding looking at her. She wants to touch his hand, feel the warmth, the intimacy of his flesh on hers, but she holds back.

No one speaks. The only sound is the hiss and flare of the fire. The tension is almost unbearable but, after her outburst, Maria feels drained, like a shadow of herself. The whole scene doesn't seem real. Is she really here in this castle, confronting her lover and his wife? Even more confusing is the calmness of the other woman – the fact that she seems to know of Maria's existence and it doesn't bother her.

'Felix,' she now hears the wife speak. 'I think you need to tell this girl everything.'

'But, Matilde, we are supposed to limit the number of people who know to the essentials.'

'This is essential, I believe, Felix.'

Maria notes the coolness with which they speak to each other, and the fact that Felix doesn't sit down next to her but remains standing.

'Why couldn't you trust me?' He now turns to Maria, and she hears the emotion in his voice. His façade of indifference to her is cracking. She knows she is not imagining it.

'I did . . . but then I found out you're married.' Her voice breaks against her will. 'Felix, how *could* you?'

She is self-conscious in front these strangers and yet no one steps out of the room. Maybe it is just as well. Maybe she would weaken and fall into his arms if they were alone.

'Because I thought you would understand . . . I hope you still will . . .' He pauses, licks his lips.

'Is this lady,' she can hardly look at the woman sitting on the couch, 'your wife?' she whispers.

'Yes, this is Matilde Leduc,' Felix says, avoiding her gaze again. 'She is my wife, but only in name. We have no relationship anymore.'

'If that is the case, why are you living together, in this house—'

'We are not living together. I live in London, remember?'

'But she is in your house,' Maria persists. 'If you have no relationship, why are you not divorced?'

'Because she needs protection.' Felix sighs. 'It is a long story, Maria.'

'*Mon dieu!*' Matilde interrupts, impatiently. 'I assure you that my husband and I are not together anymore. In fact, he quite hates me. I am hated by most people in these parts.' She turns to Maria with a sorrowful expression and, if she were not Felix's wife, Maria would almost feel pity for her.

'Why?' she whispers.

'I am considered a traitor. During the purges at the end of the war, those good communists took me out into the village square. They shaved my head and stripped me naked, they—'

'Enough Matilde,' Felix interrupts her.

But Matilde ignores him. She stares at Maria, her expression pale and haunted. 'I was what was called a "horizontal collaborator". Have you heard of the term?'

Maria remembers what the American had said to Vivienne earlier on tonight, in the club. 'Yes; I know what that is.'

Matilde looks so ordinary, and yet she betrayed her husband; she slept with a German while Felix was fighting in the Resistance. How can he tolerate her, let alone protect her? Maria turns to him now, looking at him in confusion.

'When I found out what Matilde had done, I felt like the villagers, too,' he explains. 'I wished my wife were dead . . .'

Felix looks away from her now, into the flames of the fire. 'But then I found out why she did it.'

No one speaks for a moment. Maria summons her courage. She needs to understand everything. 'Why did you do it?' she asks Matilde.

The woman looks over at her; her expression now is defensive, wounded.

'Was it for love, with a German?' Maria asks her.

Matilde laughs bitterly. 'Oh, yes – for love, but not love for the man I was sleeping with.'

'What do you mean?' Maria persists, but Matilde shakes her head, refuses to expand.

'When all this was happening, Felix was in Lyon,' Olivier suddenly speaks up. 'Like Vivienne's husband, he had been caught and he was being tortured in the same prison.'

Maria turns her gaze to Felix, but he is facing the fire with his back to her and it is impossible to know what he is feeling. She can't imagine what horrors he must have gone through in that prison in Lyon. Vivienne's husband died, but Felix survived.

'Matilde travelled down to Lyon, where she met up with Vivienne. She offered to try to persuade their husbands' captor of their innocence,' Olivier continues.

'I speak German,' Matilde adds. 'My mother was German. It was a great advantage to have this skill during the war.'

Maria can guess what happened in Lyon, how it was that Felix was freed and Vivienne's husband was not.

'I slept with him,' Matilde says, quietly. 'It was the only way.'

'So you see, Maria, Matilde saved Felix's life,' Olivier says. 'But, unfortunately, Felix's German captor wanted Matilde to be his mistress. To sleep with her once was not enough. She did it to keep her husband safe from further arrest.'

Maria looks across at the plain little woman on the couch. It is hard to imagine her as the desired lover of a German Gestapo head, but maybe the attraction was precisely that she was Felix's wife.

'Matilde's life has recently been threatened by communist purgers.' René speaks up from the edges of the room. She had almost forgotten he was there. 'That's why she is here, for the moment. No one would dare to harm Matilde if Felix Leduc is still married to her, but if he casts her off . . . Well, then she is very vulnerable.'

So this woman loves Felix too. She has to. How can Maria compete with that? With a devotion that would sell its soul to the very devil to save the man she loved? Matilde looks back at her with unblinking blue eyes, swimming in sorrow. Maria turns to Felix and, to her surprise, he is now looking at his wife with something close to repulsion.

'I owe it to Matilde to protect her, yes, that much is true, but I cannot forgive what she did.'

His words seem to pierce Matilde; she drops her gaze and stares at the floor, her pale cheeks suddenly flaring red.

'Felix, she saved your life,' Olivier protests.

'I wish she had not,' her husband says, levelly. 'She knew what kind of man I was. I would rather have died than know my wife had slept with the enemy.'

The clock suddenly strikes as if underscoring his statement.

'How could I not try to save you?' Maria hears Matilde whisper.

Maria is speechless. Torn. She loves Felix precisely because he is the man he is: strong, courageous and capricious, and yet here he is so unforgiving. She considers what Matilde did, and she knows, if she could have saved Felix's life by sleeping with a German, she would have done exactly the same thing.

'You see,' Olivier says to her. 'I told you the truth is very complicated.'

She leans back in the chair. She suddenly feels so tired; now the anger is gone, she has no energy.

'Darling,' Felix says, directing the endearment to her, in front of his wife, who sits quite still, as if she is not flesh and blood, as if she has been turned to stone. 'You look very tired. Why don't you go to bed? We'll talk more in the morning . . .'

He hasn't begged my forgiveness, she thinks.

She gets up wearily, her body heavy, her mind dizzy.

Felix takes her up the stairs. He puts his arm around her waist and guides her to a bedroom. She doesn't stop him. She is drawn to him. She can feel her body gravitate towards him, begging her to let him touch her. Yet he is not the man she thought he was.

He leads her into a dark bedroom and switches on a lamp by the bed. The room is quite luxurious. It is decorated with pale primrose damask wallpaper, with a pattern of pink roses. There is a four-poster bed, covered in a counterpane of primrose, embroidered with white silk roses. Despite its grandeur, the room smells fusty, as if it hasn't been aired in months. Felix walks across the room and opens the window. It is such a still, hot night that it makes little difference, but she is glad for the open curtains, that she can see the moon and stars from inside the room. She sits on the bed and lets her red cape fall from her shoulders.

Felix comes over to her. He kneels before her and takes her hands in his. 'I love you, Maria,' he says, gazing up into her eyes.

She pulls her hands away and brings one of them up to touch the mark upon his cheek where she slapped him. 'I am sorry I hit you,' she says.

He smiles at her, his face now relaxed in a way it was not downstairs. 'That's OK,' he says, taking her hand in his and bringing it down to his lap, putting it over him so that she can feel his cock beneath his trousers, growing into her palm.

'I want you so much,' he says. 'You look like a piece of moonlight, sitting on the bed in your silver dress.'

He slips his hand under her dress and begins to stroke her legs. She wants him, and yet she knows it is only her body that is responding to him. Her heart is cluttered by confused emotions: her love for him in conflict with her sense of betrayal. And something else . . . She cannot put her finger on it, but all of a sudden she knows she needs to be alone this night. She pulls away from him and he stops what he is doing, looking questioningly into her eyes. 'What is it, darling?'

'What will happen, Felix?'

He sighs, sitting back on his haunches. 'You see, this is why I came to London – to get away from all of this.' He shrugs. 'I knew I should not have brought you to France . . .'

'What about us, Felix? What are we to do?'

'I love you, Maria. Is my love not enough for you?' He pauses. 'In a few years' time, I should be able to divorce Matilde and she can disappear from our lives. It's just, at the moment, she needs me to protect her, and I owe her.'

'So you want me to be your mistress?'

'Yes,' he says. 'But you are my wife, really, my darling . . .' His voice trails off.

'Why can you not forgive her?' Maria whispers.

'I don't want to talk about it anymore,' he snaps, standing up, a haughty expression replacing his look of adoration.

She dreams she is dancing. The walls of the bedroom have become a golden meadow, and she is dancing upon it. The grass is as soft and plush as a carpet, the aroma of summer roses seeping into the pores of her skin, making her as sweet and yielding as their falling petals. She dances on her own, in this open and free space. How good it feels to let her spirit fly again! Her body obeys her thoughts and she is able to leap high across the field. There is nothing to make her sad in this place where she dances. Her joy is her liberation. Yet now she dances on the edge of the field, and here there is a dark wood. It draws nearer and nearer to her, as if the trees themselves are creeping towards her. Their shadows fall across the golden lawn, and she pauses in her dance. She looks between the trees and sees a face: a pale orb, like a disc of moon, that is Matilde Leduc's face. Her eyes speak of her love for a man who despises her. It is too painful to look at her face. Maria turns away, but not before she hears the other woman speak: 'Love and hatred are bedfellows.'

Maria sits up in the bed, her heart pounding. She looks out of the open window and she can see that it is still night; dawn a far way off. She can only have been asleep a short while. She pulls the sheet up to her chin and she wishes now she had not turned Felix away earlier. She wishes he were with her, holding her, reassuring her. Why can they not continue as they are? He said that, in a few years, he would be able to divorce Matilde. He said that he loved her – Maria.

She pulls back the covers and gets out of bed. She is still wearing her evening gown from the night before. She will go to him now. She needs him; that is all she knows. Her body craves her lover's touch.

She opens the door of the room and looks up and down the corridor. She has no idea which room could be Felix's. She tiptoes along the landing, opening each door as she goes along.

Most of the rooms are empty. She opens one and sees René's glasses on the bedside table, hears a soft snore from the mound beneath the bedcovers. She pulls it shut. She has to find Felix. She wants to be held within his arms, melt into her lover, feel him inside her again. She is empty without him. It is the only thing that will make her feel better.

She pushes open the last door on the landing. The first thing she sees is an open window and moonlight spilling into the room. The room is bathed in silvery blue shadows. A large four-poster bed faces her. She has found him, and yet what she sees freezes her into speechless horror. For it is not only Felix she sees, but Matilde as well, the wife she thought he hated. The two of them are fast asleep, entwined around each other in the bed. They look so innocent, so perfect together. It tears her heart apart. She hears Matilde's words again from the dream: 'Love and hatred are bedfellows.'

Maria turns and runs out of the room, back down the corridor. She cannot stay. She cannot bear it. Her heart is breaking and she will die if she has to spend another minute in this nightmare château. Maria bursts into René's bedroom and shakes the little man awake.

'René! You have to take me back to Paris, *now*.' She is sobbing, almost hysterical, her mind seared with the image of the man she loves at peace in the arms of his wife.

*V*alentina

THEO IS A SPACEMAN, A VISITOR FROM ANOTHER galaxy. He is dressed entirely in his silver space suit, his head protected from her kisses by his helmet; Valentina cannot even see his eyes, only her reflection upon its visor. He takes her by the hand and points up at the night sky as they stand together on the balcony of the apartment. She knows she has to jump and not be afraid that she will fall and smash on to the street below. She has to trust him. It is easier than she thought it would be. All she has to do is suspend her mind and listen to her heart. And so, together, they leap forward into the London night sky. They drop for a second, the tips of their toes brushing the tops of one of the old towers on Tower Bridge, yet she keeps her faith in him and, sure enough, a rush of warm air pushes them skyward and they begin to rise again, drifting to the left and above the large, cigar-shaped Swiss Re building. They are floating, weightless, drifting far, far away from life's reality, into another universe. She is stargazing, looking at constellations of their love, of how it is mapped so clearly for her to read within the astronomical messages of the sky. She and Theo are just one tiny speck of perfection within the infinite whole. All this love she feels cannot just belong to her and him.

She wakes within his arms. The joy she feels brings tears to her eyes. It is not a dream. She is here in bed with her spaceman. She looks at Theo's sleeping face. To her, he is more beautiful than any celestial being, more irresistible than any other man she has ever been with. She knows that they could never just be friends – not the way she is with Leonardo. With Theo, it has to be all or nothing. She wants to reach out and touch him, and yet she doesn't want to wake him, to crack the perfection of her fantasy that they are back together. She is not sure what he is going to say to her once he wakes up.

He had turned Anita down. She spins the memory of that definitive moment around as if it is a small crystal ball in the palms of her hands. She and Anita were still in the jacuzzi, gazing up at Theo in his resplendent nakedness, and she had just realised that she couldn't go through with the threesome, that maybe she had lost him forever, when Theo had said the magic word.

'No.'

'Are you sure?' Anita had said, pouting – although, strangely, Valentina didn't think she looked too upset. 'Such a shame,' she continued, flicking water out of the jacuzzi, as if displeased, although her eyes were still smiling.

'Sorry, Anita. I told you before, I'm now a one-woman man.'

Anita crossed her arms over her ample breasts, flesh spilling out on either side of them. 'To a certain extent,' she said. 'But I think we can all agree that we enjoyed our little bath together. Didn't you, Valentina?'

'Yes,' she whispered, barely able to speak, her chest was so tight with suspense. What could Theo have meant when he said that he was a one-woman man?

Yet her answer was immediate when Theo turned to her and reached out his hand for her. 'Well, Valentina, are you coming home?'

She stood up in a rush, water spraying off her.

'I think she wants to!' Anita commented, sarcastically. 'Go on then, you two lovebirds – clear off.'

Valentina turned to look at the other woman, momentarily concerned that they were being cruel.

Yet Anita smiled back at her. 'Don't look so worried, darling. I'm fine. I knew I couldn't win him off you the first time I saw you . . . but a girl can try, hey? And, in any case, I kind of fancied you just as much, to be honest.'

'I'm sorry,' Valentina said.

'Don't be,' said Anita. 'I've plenty of friends who will play with me.'

She had sunk down under the water and Valentina took

her cue. She grasped Theo's outstretched hand and stepped out of the water.

Still damp from the jacuzzi, the two of them had run into the morning together. The sky was a delicate blue, tipped with hues from the heart: rose, fuchsia and honeysuckle spread out before them, making the urban skyline look like the outer reaches of a magical city. They ran down the cobbled streets, past the old warehouse buildings and away from the river. Valentina had no idea to where they were running. It was enough to be holding Theo's hand, to be with him again.

They crossed a road, ran down a street lined with houses and across another road, until they were at the entrance of an estate of run-down-looking flats.

'I'm renting an old council flat,' Theo explained as he led her into the second block of flats and up the stairs.

He fumbled with his keys as he opened the door. She almost felt as if he was going to kick it down in his fury to get her inside, away from the outer world and back within his arms again. They charged through the flat and straight into his bedroom. He fell back on to the bed, pulling her with him, their bodies still damp, their skin still opened up from the steam of the jacuzzi and tingling from their exposure to the morning chill. She didn't even notice what kind of room it was. There was a bed and that was all she needed. She sat astride him and he offered his cock to her. They looked into each other's eyes, searching for an answer to their union. The emotion blazed between them like a fire trail. She tucked him up inside her and squeezed him tight, hugging his cock within the lips of her pussy. Instantly, she was back again where they left off in Venice the morning she had lost him. This was what she had been craving since he walked out of her life. It was such deep soul sex, working its way right into her inner core. They were in perfect synchronicity. One swaying entity, they were rooted together, sucking each other in further and further. There was no rush. It felt as if they had all the time in the world. In the vastness of the bed, they were in their own country and everything outside of it, even Anita, back in her apartment, was forgotten about.

'Oh, Valentina.'

She heard the anguish in the way he said her name, and it fuelled her love for him. She bent down and kissed him on the lips. He opened his mouth to her, hungry for her love, something he thought he could never have.

She had never given so much in her lovemaking. Her rapture derived from his. All her years of self-preservation shed, exposing her fluttering heart and her erotic need for her lover to fill her again and again. Every divinely measured movement between them, every deep thrust that Theo made, each time she locked her pelvis and sucked him towards her womb, each time he tipped her, left her teetering on the edge of her abandon. It was bliss. She actually spoke while making love: 'I love you.'

Her words rocked him, she could feel it. He held her

tighter, pushed even higher inside her and, entranced by the power of their own love, the two of them climaxed together, their cries and gasps mingling.

That first time had not been the end for them. So hungry they had been for each other that they had made love two more times before they both fell into an exhausted sleep. Not for one moment did Valentina think of Anita . . . until now. The whole threesome thing was just so bizarre. And yet she had enjoyed it when they were all in the jacuzzi together ...

She gets out of bed, glancing at Theo, who is still fast asleep. She wanders out into the flat. Earlier this morning, it had looked very rough from the outside. An old council flat, Theo had said, but inside it is quite lovely: simple but tasteful – so Theo. The sitting room has an antique leather couch, and is lined with bookshelves. On the walls are some modernist prints. He has a walnut bureau in the corner, the lid opened, with his laptop on it and, much to her surprise, there is a framed photograph of the two of them. She picks it up and stares at it, nostalgia for the past moving her. The picture was taken when they went on holiday to Sardinia. She remembers that Theo had asked another tourist to take the picture. They are standing on the beach, she in her none-too-flattering bikini, arms linked, squinting in the sunlight and smiling goofily into the camera. She looks at this girl and it is plain to see she is happy, and in love. Why had she denied it for so long? And why did Theo have this photograph on his desk? Does this mean he never gave up on them?

She finds the bathroom and wraps herself up in Theo's white towelling robe before going into the kitchen and filling the kettle. A little window faces out on to a drab balcony and a rather ordinary view of the estate of flats, with a scruffy green in front of it, a broken swing and a forlorn-looking see-saw. Yet it is a sunny, bright day and Valentina thinks it an endearing view. She imagines living here in London with Theo: a new life and a new beginning for both of them. She glances at the kitchen clock; it is just after midday. Her flight is at six. If she is going to go home today, she has very little time to get back to Aunt Isabella's and pack. She has no idea where in London they are or how near it is to Isabella's. She makes two mugs of tea, pondering her options. She doesn't want to go back to Milan – not yet, not now she has been with Theo. She would only want to go back if he came with her.

Valentina wanders back into the sitting room with two mugs of tea and puts them down on the coffee table. There is her bag, abandoned on the couch from earlier this morning. She opens it up and takes out her phone. There are two messages from Antonella.

Where r u?

Going to Moscow with Mikhail! Call me.

Maybe Antonella has finally found 'the one'. She must be very keen on Mikhail if she is going to Russia with him. She really hopes that it works out for them – that Antonella doesn't lose interest in him. There is something about the taciturn Russian that Valentina really likes and thinks is good for her boisterous friend.

'There you are.'

She turns to see Theo standing in the doorway, bare-chested and in a pair of silk pyjama bottoms that hang off his hips seductively.

'I was worried you had run out on me.'

Now, in the cold light of day, can she respond as she feels?

'I could never run out on you; not now.'

Theo smiles in delight at her words. This is not the unexpressive Valentina he once knew. 'Do you mean that?'

She nods, suddenly nervous that last night was a delusion and that he is now going to tell her it was just a one-off.

'What's the story with Anita?' she says, immediately cursing herself for bringing up the name of her rival.

'Like I told you in the Tate, it's complicated.'

Valentina frowns. He comes up close to her, tucks her hair behind her ears. 'Don't look so worried; we never had anything romantic or sexual going on . . . Not until you were involved, actually!'

'So why did she call herself your girlfriend?'

Theo goes over and picks up one of the mugs of tea, sits

down on the couch and beckons for her to join him. 'It was all a front,' he explains. 'I guess you could say we "dated" for a while, but I eventually explained just why I wanted to get to know her.'

'And why was that?' Valentina asks, still not understanding.

'I thought you might have worked it out by now,' Theo says, prodding her tummy through the dressing gown. 'Anita owned the André Masson drawing I was after. Remember I told you about it, that day in the Tate Gallery?'

'Of course,' Valentina reflects. All that art was on the walls of Anita's apartment . . . Suddenly something occurs to her. She brings her hand to her mouth. 'Glen was there,' she says. 'Last night.'

She sees a spot of anger on each of Theo's cheeks.

'God, that man is unbelievable,' he says. 'When I saw him at the exhibition, I warned him to stay away from you. Well, it's too late for him to steal the drawing, anyway. I got it last night. I have it here.'

He gets up from the couch, walks across the room and picks up an attaché case, leaning beside the bureau. He opens a little drawer in the bureau, takes out a key and unlocks the case. He pulls out a small, framed drawing and hands it to Valentina, sitting back down next to her again. 'It's called *Damned Women* – dated to around nineteen twenty-two.'

Valentina examines the drawing. It is a frenzy of naked women, and she finds it hard to distinguish the bodies. Their breasts and pubic hair are more articulated than their faces. They seem to be a writhing mass of sex.

'How did Anita end up with it?' she asks Theo.

'Despite the fact her grandfather fought in the war against the Nazis, he seemed to have no misgivings about acquiring this picture from a known dealer in hoarded work in nineteen fifty-three.'

'So, did you steal it from Anita's apartment last night? Is that why you were pretending to be her boyfriend?' Valentina asks, intrigued that Theo would have been able to steal the picture right under the noses of everyone at the party.

'That was the original plan,' he says, taking the picture from her and locking it back into the case. 'That's why I told you to trust me, just to wait. I was never interested in Anita as a girlfriend. I know it was heartless of me, but I had to get that picture back.'

Valentina remembers something Anita said last night, just before they had all been together. Something like, it was going to be her last chance with Theo, as if she knew she wouldn't see him again.

'It turns out that Anita is a decent soul,' Theo continues to explain. 'When Glen started hanging around, I got worried he might break into her apartment. I felt I had to warn her, so I told her the whole story. I was so impressed by her reaction. It was the easiest robbery I have ever committed.'

'Why? What happened?'

'Once I showed her all the evidence, she agreed to give me

the picture. Just like that! I guess she is so stinking rich she can afford to be principled.'

'That's a bit harsh.' Valentina remembers something else Anita had said to her now, when they were talking about her grandmother and the erotic film: 'It changes who we are to learn the secrets of our ancestors.'

'Maybe, like you, she wanted to make amends for the actions of her grandfather,' Valentina suggests.

Theo shrugs. 'You're right. I guess I have no right to judge anyone after what my own grandfather did, selling off all those poor Jewish people's priceless treasures to the Nazis for a pittance.'

'But he had little choice, remember, Theo, and he has spent the rest of his life trying to retrieve all those pictures and return them to their rightful owners.'

Every family has dark secrets – skeletons in the closet. She is still astounded that her grandmother appeared in those early erotic films, and yet all the evidence seems to indicate it is true. And then there is the huge fat lie about her father . . .

'So, Valentina,' Theo says, carefully putting the attaché case back down on the floor, 'my career as an art thief has finally come to an end. Do you think you will still find me attractive when I am just a fusty old academic again?'

'Of course I will,' she says, kissing him on the lips. 'In fact, I can't wait!'

She pulls back all of sudden, feeling a clench of anxiety in her stomach as she remembers something. 'Theo, I forgot to tell you: there's more about Glen.'

Theo pulls her into his side. She puts her hands on his bare chest, her fingers in his soft hair.

'What is it, darling?'

'He followed me . . .' She pauses, deciding not to tell him that she and Glen first ran into each other outside Philip Rembrandt's house. She is not quite ready to explain all about her father to Theo. She wants some time, just the two of them, before she unleashes the mess of her family history on him. 'He said that, if you didn't give him back the money for Mrs Kinder's painting or let him have the Masson drawing, then he would take me.'

'How dare he!' Theo growls in disgust. 'He tried that on with me at the gallery and I told him to get lost. He claimed he'd already made an arrangement with Guilio Borghetti's son before I came along. I told him that, if he left us alone, it would be the last picture I ever took. He is welcome to every single piece of the lost Nazi hoard after last night. I thought that he was happy with that.'

'Well, I don't think he is,' she tells him.

'That's it!' he says, angrily. 'I don't care about the consequences; if he turns up again, we'll just report him to the police.' Theo looks so deadly serious that she has no doubt he will do just that.

'But couldn't you get into trouble?'

'No, not really; not now I'm finished with it all. Remember, none of the paintings I have taken are actually officially reported stolen.' He pulls her even tighter to him, so that her chin is resting on his chest and she can breathe in his delicious scent. 'And, furthermore, I am not letting you out of my sight now. Not until I return the painting to Guilio Borghetti's son in Sorrento.'

She is breathless at his words. He doesn't want to let her out of his sight. So their reunion is not just momentary, it has a future. She cuddles into him, pressing her lips against his skin, feeling more satisfied and safe than she has felt her whole life.

'Theo?' she whispers into his chest. 'When did you know that you wanted me back?'

'I have never stopped wanting you, Valentina. Although I didn't realise that until I saw you again, that first time in the Lexington.' He takes a breath. 'God, it was all I could do not to take you into my arms, but Anita was there and I was at a delicate stage with her in my negotiations for the Masson . . .'

She twists around to look up at him. 'Why didn't you tell me in the Tate what was going on with Anita? Why did you put me through all that uncertainty?'

'Because I had already laid my heart open to you.' He pauses. 'You were the one who needed to be sure of your feelings, not me. I told you to trust me. That's what you had to do.' He continues to speak, all the while stroking her hair. 'In a way, it was providential that Anita was around because, although I never would have said it of you, maybe it forced you to show me your feelings . . . it threatened you.' He looks at her questioningly and she blushes.

'I am surprised, even at myself,' she admits. 'I thought I was a true libertine but, when it came down to it, I wanted you all to myself.'

'I am quite happy about that, Valentina, because I don't think I want to share you anymore, either.' He kisses her forehead.

'So we are lost to each other?' she asks him.

'Yes, we have both of us stepped over the edge into that dangerous abyss called love.'

He begins to unwrap her dressing gown, so that it falls open. She climbs up on to his silky lap and looks down at him, drinking in his face, committing it to her heart.

'So, will you come with me to give back the Masson to Borghetti? I'm flying to Naples tomorrow morning, early.'

'But I'm supposed to go back to Milan this evening,' she protests, weakly.

He pulls her down to him and kisses her. 'Oh no, Valentina, this afternoon you are going to be very busy making love to me. I am afraid you are going to miss your flight . . .'

'If you say so,' she says, not even pretending to resist.

She leans back and strokes his balls through his silk pyjamas. She slips her hand underneath the waistband and feels his cock rising in her hand, the urgency of its need to be within her again. She kisses him deeply, drinking his love into her as sweet as honey on her heart.

'Theo?' Valentina pulls away for a second, feeling strangely bashful.

He looks up at her expectantly.

She is so nervous of his response to what she is about to ask him that she drops her gaze, stares down at the tiny folds in his stomach. 'Can I be your girlfriend now?' Her voice is barely above a whisper.

'No, absolutely not,' she hears him say, so fast, with no reflection whatsoever.

She feels a lump form in her throat. It is hard to disguise her disappointment. So, he has not forgiven her, then.

'Valentina,' he says, lifting her chin with his fingertip and gazing into her eyes.

She looks into a blue ocean of possibility.

'I don't want you to be my girlfriend, because I want you to be my wife.'

Maria

BACK IN THE HOTEL ROOM IN PARIS, SHE OPENS UP THE
case that Felix had given her. It is half empty, filled with
clothing and trinkets that Felix had bought her. She wrenches
the red cape off, rips her ivory evening gown from her and
kneels down, tipping the contents of the case on to the floor.
Stockings, silk chemises, gloves and scarves fly everywhere in
a carnival of colour. The bottle of L'Heure Bleu clatters on to
the floorboards. The glass shatters into thousands of tiny
bright crystals. Its rich perfume assaults her. The images that
arrive with its scent begin to make her tremble. Finally, after
the stony silence of her return drive to Paris, René's offer of
help and her rejection of him, the self-control it took not to
wail like a baby and take refuge within his chubby arms, after
all this, she cries. It is not just a young girl with her first broken
heart who is crying, it is also the gut-wrenching sobs of a
woman betrayed. Tears streak down her face, off her chin and
roll between her naked breasts, on to her quivering belly and

between her legs. She empties the case and, when she has done so, she climbs into it. The red silk of its lining is cool against her fevered skin. She lies on her side, raises her knees to her chest, and folds in on herself. She tucks herself up in the great big suitcase, and closes her eyes.

In her dreams, she becomes a tiny feral thing. She is in hibernation. The case suddenly slams shut. She is in darkness, the only sound the beating of her heart. Yet she is not frightened. It is comforting to be invisible to the light of day. She holds herself tight as she feels the case being lifted. Who is carrying her? Where are they taking her? The case sways back and forth and it is like being rocked in a cradle. She has little space and yet she is comfortable, as if she fits perfectly in this place. It surprises her, for she was always afraid of confined spaces. Yet it is as if being locked in a piece of luggage is where she belongs. She feels so safe that the rocking lulls her and she falls asleep.

When the case is opened, the first thing she tastes is salt on her lips. She opens her eyes, blinking in the bright light of day. She looks up at a wide cerulean sky and sees a seagull circling above her. She hears the sea crashing against the shore, a regular beat against the rocks, never stopping, on and on. She waits for the tide to come in and carry her away in her suitcase. She sees herself bobbing forever upon the ocean, until it finally swallows her up and she can be nothing. The crashing of the sea against the rocks becomes more and more frantic, urgent – and then she hears a voice.

'Maria!'

She opens her eyes. Above her stands Vivienne, looking down at her in the suitcase, her expression, for once, grave.

'Maria, what are you doing in there?'

She shakes her head. She doesn't have the energy or will to speak. She just wants to be nothing, to fade away.

'Come on,' Vivienne says, kneeling down by the case and picking up her limp arms, pulling her up. 'Get out of that suitcase. There you go,' she says gently. 'Let's get you dressed.'

Vivienne escorts her out of the little hotel bedroom in Saint-Germain-des-Prés, propping her up by the elbow. She leaves behind the empty suitcase, all her dresses and jewellery, all of her mistress's things.

Her friend guides her through the chaotic streets of Paris and back to her own apartment in the seventh arrondissement. Maria is oblivious to all the life around her. She feels numbed to the core. She feels as if she is dead.

Once inside her tiny apartment, Vivienne bustles around her. 'Have you eaten?' she asks her.

Maria shakes her head, biting her lip and trying not to cry again.

Vivienne lays the table with bread and cheese, and pours them both a glass of red wine. 'Come on; get that down you,' she says, handing Maria a glass of wine. 'You'll feel better.'

Maria takes a sip. It is true, the wine fortifies her a little, but she is still unable to speak. She is too ashamed.

As if she reads her thoughts, Vivienne speaks first. 'You don't have to tell me what's wrong,' she says. 'René told me.' She doesn't look at Maria, but concentrates on tearing off a hunk of bread. 'I cannot believe that Felix is protecting *that* woman,' Vivienne says, passionately. 'She is scum. All those women are whores who slept with the German bastards.'

Maria can hear the loathing in Vivienne's voice.

'But what if some of those women who you call horizontal collaborators fell in love with Germans?' Maria says, tentatively. 'Surely you cannot help who you love? And, besides, Matilde did not love the German she slept with. She did it to save Felix's life.'

'In times of war, I believe you must stick to your principles; you have to make sacrifices, Maria,' Vivienne says, sternly. She leans forward, gently brushing a stray of Maria's hair from her cheek. 'You are very young and think that love can rule you, but, you know, if it does . . . Well, then it's not a good kind of love.'

Maria thinks about what Vivienne says. Her love for Felix had completely taken her over. She had given up her dancing, Jacqueline, even to a certain extent her mammas because of him.

Felix. She sees his face for a moment, when he is telling her he loves her and how he feels like a young man again. Yet he is not. He is a married man, over twice her age. And now she sees him as she saw him last night: asleep within Matilde's arms. She shudders and closes her eyes.

'He tricked me,' she whispers to Vivienne.

'No, no, my darling,' Vivienne says. 'Felix loves you, I am sure about it, but . . . you know, he still has feelings for Matilde, as well.'

'He said he despised her.'

'Yes, but if he really did then he would turn her out . . .'

Maria had not told René why she made him drive her back to Paris in the middle of the night, and she wonders now whether he guessed and whether he had told Vivienne. She is too ashamed to tell her that she saw Felix and Matilde in the same bed together. She hopes her friend doesn't know.

Vivienne leans forward in her chair. 'You don't know what they did to him,' she says, picking up Maria's hand and squeezing it.

'During the war?' Maria asks.

'We all thought Felix was dead,' Vivienne continues to explain. 'He was subjected to severe torture in Lyon. No one had survived before.' Vivienne drops her hand, her eyes filling with tears. 'You know about my Marcel, don't you?'

Maria nods. 'I am so sorry,' she whispers.

'Well, now you know why I hate Matilde . . . Although I would not be responsible for her being hurt, either.' Vivienne wraps her arms around her waist and sits back. 'I am not like that. I could not do what she did. I loved Marcel,' she cries, wiping the tears from her eyes. 'Matilde made me feel like I failed him . . . I hated her for it.'

'It's not who she is that is the problem or the fact he was

married, it's that he never told me,' Maria says. 'And last night . . . I . . . saw . . .'

Vivienne leans forward and puts her hand to Maria's lips. 'I know; I guessed that's why you ran away,' she sighs. 'But I still believe it is you that Felix loves. Life is different now.' Vivienne offers her a cigarette.

'What do you mean?'

'War has made a mockery out of all that we held sacred before: life . . . and love. We cannot expect to live within the same moral codes anymore.'

'So do you think I should be his mistress?' Maria asks her, shocked that Vivienne could accept such an idea.

'That depends on you, my dear,' she says, softly. 'But I would not judge you for it. The love and passion you and Felix share is too rare a find to give up easily, even if there are other complications.'

'But . . . but . . . what if there was a child . . . ?' Maria asks her. She knows what it is like to grow up without a proper father. She doesn't want that for her children – to be seen as different, to be illegitimate.

Vivienne puts out her cigarette. 'You would manage. It would be worth it.'

Maria thinks of Vivienne's two dead daughters. She feels a wave of compassion for her friend. How can she be so selfish to talk about herself when Vivienne has been through so much?

'I am sorry,' she says, putting her hand on Vivienne's arm, 'about your girls.'

Vivienne looks at her for a moment, and Maria sees such raw pain in the other woman's eyes that it takes her breath away.

'I thought I could live in Paris again,' Vivienne says, quietly. 'I mean, it is the city for writers, especially for women writers. And yet I think I should have left when Felix did. I don't know why he came back.' She inhales deeply on her cigarette. 'Maria, remember all this tragedy has nothing to do with you. None of it. You have brought hope and sunshine into our lives.'

Maria balances her cigarette between her shaking fingers. 'I am just an ordinary girl.'

'And that is precisely why you are so special,' the other woman says, stroking her hair, tenderly, as tears trail down her cheeks.

'What were their names?'

Vivienne doesn't need to ask Maria who she means. 'Lucille and Tina,' she says, burying her face in her hands, her voice breaking down.

Maria wraps her arms around the older woman.

Outside, Paris is burning under a midday sun while Vivienne's apartment ticks in shadowed silence and the two women cry in each other's arms for all that they have lost.

Later, after they have dried their tears and sobered up with coffee, Vivienne asks her if she wants to go out. They could go to a jazz club and listen to some music, get drunk together and drown their sorrows, but Maria turns her down. She wants to sleep now; she needs to block out her heartache.

'Why don't you come to America with me?' Vivienne suggests as she applies her lipstick, looking in her compact mirror as she speaks.

'America?'

'Yes; I am moving to New York. I have been offered a writing job with *Harper's Bazaar*, and I think I shall take it. I need to say goodbye to Paris for a while, lay a few ghosts to rest . . .' She pauses, unscrewing the lipstick and slipping it into her purse, clicking it shut. 'So?' Vivienne asks, turning to her with falsely bright eyes. 'Will you come to New York with me?'

'I don't know anyone there. What will I do?'

'You know me . . . and haven't you made some American friends since you've been in Paris? There are so many of them here. It is nearly impossible not to have a few Yankie admirers, especially a pretty young thing like you.'

She thinks of Richard, and blushes at the memory of what nearly happened between herself, Felix and that man. 'No,' she tells Vivienne. 'I don't know any Americans at all.'

'Well, think about it,' Vivienne says. 'It could be a new beginning, for both of us.'

That night, when Vivienne returns and gets into bed with her, Maria wraps her arms around the older woman and breathes in the scent of Vivienne after a long night out: Chanel, alcohol and tobacco. She promises herself that she will cut all ties from her brief life in Paris, and go with Vivienne to New York. Maria will start all over again. She will leave Felix and her love for him behind in France. Her heart is broken but she must survive. Her mammas would expect nothing less from her.

$\mathscr{V}$alentina

SHE HAS SAID YES. SHE CAN HARDLY BELIEVE IT WILL happen, that the man in the car beside her will soon be her husband. Their rental open-top Mercedes twists and turns along the Amalfi coast road and she looks out at the jewel blue Mediterranean ocean. Despite her dark glasses and the scarf tied around her head, the sun is still glaring, beating down upon them relentlessly. Yet she feels like a lizard, happy to soak in its warmth and let the hot breeze flow through her as Theo drives them towards Sorrento. It is good to be back home in Italy, where they both belong. Theo may not be Italian by birth, but he is Italian by nature. Like her, he is an advocate of living in the moment and tasting the sweetness of life in the present.

The hotel in Sorrento is beyond all her expectations. It is situated right in the centre of the town, hidden from view by a luxurious garden of orange and lemon trees. Inside the hotel, all is old-style grandeur. They walk through salon after salon until they come out on to a terrace overlooking the bay of Naples and the island of Capri.

She and Theo look at each other. She knows he is thinking the same thing: what a perfect place it would be to spend their honeymoon.

They sit in sacred silence, enjoying a glass of Prosecco each as they watch the sun sink slowly, blushing the sky flamingo pink as it departs. She is happy. It is almost impossible to believe this feeling will last. She can't help thinking that something will go wrong. She blames it on the pessimistic side of herself: her mother's voice, or maybe it is the voice of her mystery father, Karel, the Czech cellist. She still hasn't told Theo about him.

Her lover reaches out and puts his hand on hers. 'Do you want to come with me tomorrow when I drop off the painting?'

'I don't mind. Do you want me to come with you?'

Maybe on the twisting drive down the Amalfi coast she can tell him the story of her father. She wonders what Theo will think of it all, if he will encourage her to go and find her blood father, although how she will do it, she has no idea.

However, Theo says, 'I think it's better if you don't come.' He brings her hand to his lips and kisses the back of it. 'Ricardo Borghetti, Guilio's son, is a little bit neurotic about keeping this all very quiet, even though Anita gave the picture back rather than me stealing it.'

'OK,' she says, a little disappointed. 'Well, in that case, I'll go to Pompeii. I've never been there and I've always wanted to see it.'

After dinner, they stroll through the gardens and along the side of the swimming pool. It is unlit, still early enough in the season that the pool is not in use at night. Yet, to Valentina, even at this time of night the air is still balmy, especially in comparison to the damp spring climate of London.

Theo is holding her hand. She locks her fingers tightly within his. She is thinking about her life with him. She is finally ready for commitment. She thought it would feel like a sentence to her and yet it doesn't. Instead, she feels like she has finally been liberated. Again, she considers telling him about her father, and yet she is enjoying the companionship of their silence.

'Would you like some sex on the edge?' Theo speaks softly beside her.

'Excuse me?' she asks him, a little taken aback by his question.

'I think that, now we are going to be man and wife, we must make a solemn vow to introduce as much random sex, in as many inappropriate places, as we can . . . without getting caught, of course,' Theo says, a mischievous glint in his eyes.

'I see,' she says, mock serious. 'So, what is sex "on the edge"?'

'It involves getting a little wet,' he explains. 'Hence the need for a swimming pool.'

'What if someone catches us?'

'We can just pretend we are skinny dipping.' He starts unbuttoning his shirt.

'Isn't it a little cold to be getting undressed at this time of night?'

'Come on,' he cajoles her. 'Remind me of my intrepid Valentina, the girl I fell in love with.' He drops his trousers and pants, and pads over to the pool and slips in.

She doesn't hesitate, unzipping her skimpy summer dress and pulling it off over her head. She walks over to the side of the pool in her underwear.

'Don't actually get in,' he says.

'Do you want me to take off everything and then stand here, naked?' she asks him, incredulously.

'No, don't stand, either. I want you to take your underwear off and to sit on the edge of the pool, right in front of me.'

She does as she is told, curious what he has planned for her.

'OK,' he says, standing before her in the pool, his hands on her waist, as she sits with her legs dangling in the water. 'Lie down and, as you do so, lift your legs in the air, like you are in a perfect L shape.'

She looks at him suspiciously. 'What exactly are we going to do?'

'I told you, sex on the edge.'

She smiles at him and he flicks some water at her.

'I love it when you smile, Valentina,' he says. 'It is so rare.'

She lies down and raises her legs, resting her feet on Theo's shoulders. He pulls her towards him so that her bottom is touching the water and her cheeks are resting in his hands. The cool water laps against her, and she can feel him just pressing two of his fingers very, very gently against her clitoris. The pressure is so slight, yet it builds and builds, rippling out and into her. She wonders why he doesn't enter her. It is as if he is waiting for her to be right on the edge, metaphorically as well as literally, before he will do so.

Instead of closing her eyes, she stares above her. It is a moonless night, pitch dark and yet all around her are hundreds of fireflies, effervescent balls of light. They are charged like her, burning with life. She begins to caress her own breasts, stroke her hot belly, all the while aware of the growing intensity where Theo is touching her. She is pulsing inside her vagina and, as if he knows by instinct her need to feel him, Theo pushes inside her, water lapping against her bottom as he does so. He withdraws and cold water rushes up her, causing her to spasm in response. In he goes again, slowly, surely, further up inside her. Every particle of her being is reaching out for him. It is an incredibly erotic experience. She knows it is not just because they are so exposed, the risk they are taking at being caught, but also because of the depth of their feelings for each other. Theo plunges in and out, building the pressure up inside her, the cold water stimulating her. She hears herself panting from deep down inside her belly. She raises her hands above her head, her arms flung in surrender as her lover comes inside her, and she receives his seed rapturously, orgasming herself in a delirium of her love for him.

Valentina is in the Villa of Mysteries at Pompeii, looking at the frescoes. Considering they had been buried under ash for hundreds of years, they are in amazing condition. She circles the Initiation Room, intrigued by what she is looking at. She has read that there are various interpretations of what is happening in these strange pictures. One is that they depict the initiation of a woman into a special sex cult of Bacchus. The second and most popular theory is that they show the soon-to-be-wed young woman undergoing a series of mysterious sacraments, parallel to the sacred union of Bacchus and Ariadne, ending with a confrontation with Eros, the god of love.

She looks at one image of a young woman kneeling, her head on the lap of a man, her backside exposed, while a woman nearby is holding a long branch with a thatch of leaves at its end, and another dances wildly, showing off her ample behind as well. All of it is painted on to a scarlet background, as if the very colour of the paint is a comment on its passionate content. Red: the colour of sex. It strikes Valentina that the fresco could be some kind of early depiction of not only sadomasochism, but also orgiastic activity with three women and one man present. The bacchanalian cults were famous for their popularity among young women in first-century Rome and, in particular, the practice of orgies. Even then it was something covert, a cult that was condemned as perverse. She considers the very fact that, because something is prohibited, it becomes seductive. Society in general brands the practice of orgies as depraved. She has never wanted to be involved in one herself . . . The closest she has been to it was when she, Theo, Leonardo and Celia were together last year. But that was with two men she knew and trusted. She is not sure if she could join in an orgy with strangers.

Valentina walks back out into the sunshine. Now that she and Theo are going to be married, she has no interest in sleeping with any other man or woman. She supposes her days of erotic explorations will be over. And yet, once they have been together a few years, maybe they will want to investigate other sexual adventures together, such as orgies or fetish clubs. It has always existed, the erotic needs of man. She wonders when sex became more than just instinct, when it entered the realm of spirit and pleasure.

Valentina wanders back into the ruins of Pompeii. There is no shade and she can feel the early summer sun beginning to burn her pale face. She should have brought a hat. It is such a sad place, she thinks. All of this life, arrested within a second. She looks up at the distant silhouette of Vesuvius. Against the backdrop of a sunny day, it appears even darker and more ominous than ever. She tries to shake a sense of foreboding, but she can't help it. She doesn't want any clouds on the unblemished blue of her love for Theo. It is in this moment that she decides to let the whole father thing go. She has found Philip Rembrandt, after all. He was more of a father to her than her real father ever was. It is surely enough that he regrets walking out on her, all those years ago, and that he wants to get to know her now. Can she not pretend, like her mother has for years, that he really is her father? Is that not a simpler story to believe in? She feels a sense of relief at the decision. No more soul searching about the past, and no more ghosts, she promises herself. Yet, even so, she feels as if the presence of that black volcano is tugging at her, like a dog nipping at her heels with its sharp teeth. Her sense of foreboding cannot be shaken. In fact, it grows as she gets on the train to go back to Sorrento. It is as if she is being followed, watched, despite the fact that, whenever she looks behind her, she can see no one.

Maria

SHE WANTS HER RED GERANIUMS. THAT IS HER FIRST thought the next morning as she wakes in Vivienne's bed. She sees the three flowers in her mind's eye, jammed into the narrow stem of the wine bottle, no longer scarlet but the colour of dried blood. They are sitting on the windowsill of their hotel room in Paris, part of the vista of her memory. She doesn't want any of the grand clothes or jewellery that Felix bought her, but she wants those dying flowers.

Maria slides out of the bed, gently dropping a kiss on the sleeping Vivienne's forehead. She gets dressed and slips out the door without even making coffee first. She walks briskly along the broad boulevards of Paris, the leaves of the plane trees glinting green and fresh. It is late August and finally the weather has cooled slightly. The energy of the city feels different around her: less fervid, more at peace. She walks past Notre Dame and across the Seine, back into the narrow streets of Saint-Germain-des-Prés.

Madame Paget is away from her desk. There are new arrivals in the lobby, ringing her bell: two young girls, much the same age as Maria, bubbling with excitement at the beginning of their Parisian adventure. She wants to warn them. *Don't lose your heart in the maze that is this city, for you may never find it again.* Yet she walks past them, head bowed low. She is not noticed.

Maria takes the stairs this morning. She cannot take the lift, for it reminds her of their nights of abandonment, of how much she still loves Felix.

The hotel room is unlocked and she knows before she opens the door, before she enters, that he is inside, waiting for her.

They stand facing each other. He is holding his hat in his hands, and is staring at her intently. She traces the outline of his face slowly, looks at those melting brown eyes, his thick black and grey hair, the story of his face. She tries to commit it to memory.

'Maria,' he speaks first. 'Where were you? Why did you run away?'

She comes straight out with it. 'I saw you together, Felix.' She grips her purse to her chest as if it will protect her heart. 'You were asleep in each other's arms.' She gives a little hiccup of grief. She wants to be calm, controlled, yet her emotions are fighting to be let out. She doesn't want him to see how much she is hurting.

'But, my darling, we were only sleeping,' he assures her.

'Yes, but you were in the same bed.'

'Matilde had a nightmare. I lay down next to her until she fell asleep, but I must have fallen asleep too.'

'You were under the covers with her, Felix.'

'Well, then, I got into the bed,' he says, sounding almost a little annoyed with her. 'I was tired.'

She says nothing, staring back at him fiercely.

'Nothing happened,' Felix says, emphatically. 'You must believe me.'

She does. Yet still it bothers her. She cannot bear the thought that he shared a bed with Matilde. 'I thought you hated her, so why did you get into bed to comfort her?' she insists.

He looks away from her, out of the little window of their love nest. 'I do hate her . . . at times . . .' he stumbles. 'I wish she had let me die . . .'

'Because you also love her,' Maria finishes the sentence for him, her voice a resigned monotone.

He turns to her with blazing eyes. 'When she slept with that German to save my life, well, actually, it killed me inside. I was so ashamed of what she did. And it broke my heart, Maria . . . It twisted my love for her into this two-faced emotion. I can't completely cut myself away from her, and yet I despise her . . . I . . .' He stops suddenly, examining the expression on her face, how she has stepped back, retreated towards the door. He takes a step forwards and grabs hold of her hands. 'But when I met you, Maria . . . everything changed for me; I began to feel things again. I never thought it could happen that I could love again, but you did that to me. And more . . .'

'How can you love me when you still love your wife?' Her voice trembles with emotion.

'Because the feelings I have for Matilde are different. It is like I have to take care of her. It is a duty. There is no passion between us anymore. But with you . . .' He pauses, sweeping his hand through his thick hair. She watches it flop back down on to his forehead. He has never looked more beautiful to her than in this moment. 'Oh, my darling,' he gushes, 'you have inspired me so. Despite your innocence, you have opened me up in a way I never expected . . .'

He tries to pull her to him, but she holds her ground, her heart in tumult. She knows what he means: the flagrancy of their passion, how she knows that it would take just a brush of his hand on her cheek, a kiss to ignite them right now. She remembers Vivienne's words from the night before: 'The love and passion you and Felix share is too rare to give up easily.' Maybe she is right. Maybe their love is so great that she shouldn't walk away from it. Can she be Felix's mistress?

'Maria,' Felix begs her, 'please don't leave me.'

Yet Maria knows she is the kind of woman who cannot share. Felix loves her, but he also still loves Matilde; his open hatred of his wife proves that. Felix's shunning of Matilde in front of others, his inability to forgive what she did – for the woman did act out of her love for him – all these aspects of her lover frighten Maria. His passion is split between the two women. Maria will always be living to please him, afraid that he will tire of her, cast her aside. She is afraid his love will turn to hatred, just as it had with Matilde. And then what will she be? A failed dancer *and* a fallen woman?

Somehow, she manages to walk away. Now all she wants is to go home to Venice. She promises Vivienne she will come to New York one day, but for now she needs her mammas.

That night, Maria boards a train for Milan. She cries all the way from Paris to Milan, curled up on her seat, like a child lost in the woods. She cannot forget the look on Felix's face as she turned away from him. It is etched upon her heart. His incomprehension, followed by his devastation. He had thought her so completely his. And yet he didn't run after her. The fact that he let her walk out of the hotel room on her own and down those stairs, and he did not try to stop her, tells her she is right. He loves her, but not enough. He was the centre of her world, but she was never his.

Maria returns to Venice in the clothes that she stands in. She bears the secret of her love for Felix as a scar upon her heart. She never tells a soul how close she came to becoming his mistress. Not her free-spirited mother, Belle, nor her darling Pina, and, in the years that come, not her husband nor even her own daughter. She tells no one that once she was a dancer who traded her calling in life for the love of a married man. She had gambled with her heart, and she had lost.

Maria remains in Venice. Two weeks after she returns, Jacqueline writes to her and tells her that Lempert has offered for her to return to her dance studies, but Maria writes back, turning her down. She could never go back to London, for what if she was to meet Felix again? She could never trust herself if she were in his company one more time, for, deep down, she comes to regret her decision. Even worse, she couldn't bear it if he no longer loved her. For surely one day he no longer will?

Yet, sometimes, love returns to us in the most unlikely way. Six weeks after she is home from France, the very day she knows for sure that she must be pregnant, Guido Rosselli walks back into her life. The young Italian had heard through Jacqueline of her return to Venice. He had never forgotten her. For Guido had fallen in love with Maria the day she had arrived in London, when he made her coffee with shaking hands. He had never stopped loving her, despite the fact she had run away with Felix. He blames the Frenchman for corrupting her, but he does not judge Maria, for he sees how pure she is, and this purity is what made her so beautiful to him. His love is so great for Maria that he cares not that she has loved another man.

Guido courts Maria studiously. At first she is indifferent. As the weeks pass, she begins to grow used to his company. He seems happy just to float down the Canal Grande in a boat with her, neither of them speaking. He doesn't touch her or try to win her over with pretty words. He just waits.

It is one such day, about three weeks after Guido arrived in Venice, that Maria feels she should tell him his attentions are to no avail.

'Guido,' she says, as they drift down the canal, her eyes flickering over the activity along the quays, her heart, as always, restless. 'I have to tell you something.'

'All right,' he says. He stops rowing and brings the oars inside their boat, so that they are dripping on their feet.

She turns to face him and she is surprised to see that Guido no longer looks so ridiculous to her. She notices how big his eyes are, and how kind. In fact, if he shaved off his moustache, he could be rather handsome. She shakes the thought from her mind and steels herself for his reaction to her news.

'I have to tell you that I am going to have a baby.' She squeezes her eyes shut and tilts her face to the skies. 'So you see, you are wasting your time. I am damaged goods.'

For a moment, Guido says nothing. Maria listens to the sounds of Venice: the call of the stallholders, the splash of oars upon the canal, the lap of water and, in the distance, the toll of a church bell.

'Maria,' Guido says. 'Maria, look at me.'

She drops her head and opens her eyes. He is looking at her with such an earnest expression that she realises he must love her. And, for the first time since she left Paris, there is a small stirring in her heart. He is a good friend, Guido. She knows that he will not abandon her, despite her circumstances. She wants her child to have a father. And thus his next words are no surprise to her, for she has already decided she will accept him. She cannot bear to be alone another day.

'Marry me?' Guido says.

After the wedding, amid the tearful hugs and kisses of her darling mammas, Maria and Guido say their goodbyes and move to Milan. She becomes a loyal wife and a devoted mother. She even takes up knitting, and dedicates her life to cooking and nurturing her husband and daughter. This is the grandmother that Valentina has been told about: a gentle woman, with a strong faith, who sought a quiet life.

Maria never left Milan, not until over twenty-five years later she surprised her husband by telling him she wished to go to New York to visit an old friend from her time in Paris: a woman called Vivienne, who was now the editor of the magazine *Harper's Bazaar*. This information her daughter Tina had always been quite astounded by. How on earth had her mother known such a woman? Yet she never got the chance to ask her, for her parents never returned from their trip to America. Their plane crashed somewhere over the Atlantic Ocean and Maria's secrets lay buried, apparently, forever. That is until the day Theo found the dance film of her, and Anita unearthed those old erotic films and used them in her own art. And so she lives on, Maria, the lithe, sensual lover, the wild-spirited young woman, the believer in the power of love. She lives on in the films, and she also lives on in Valentina.

Only once during their whole marriage – in fact, it was on their very wedding night – did Guido ask Maria to dance for him. Yet Maria had remained seated, her hands pressed together demurely in her lap, the slight dome of her belly visible beneath the white dress.

'Never ask me to dance again,' she chided him. And he never did.

Yet, that night, she showed her husband her erotic self. It deepened and enriched his love for her so that he remained faithful to the day they died. And, for Maria, she came close, so close, to what she had once felt with Felix . . . yet, not quite.

$\mathcal{V}$alentina

THE DAY BEFORE THEY PLAN TO LEAVE SORRENTO, Valentina and Theo take a ferry to the island of Capri. Not even when they first got together in Milan had she seen Theo so buoyant. She guesses he is relieved that his days as an art thief – or 'art retriever', as he would call himself – are over. His family has finally made amends. He is free from all obligations to the past.

They sit on the deck of the ferry and talk about their wedding plans. Venice is the perfect location – just the two of them. Theo wants to take her to America to meet his parents. She finds herself agreeing, almost excited at the prospect of being introduced to them now. She looks forward to hearing stories about her lover when he was a little boy, of seeing pictures and being taken to all the places he knew as a child. She wants to get to know New York, like he knows Milan. She even considers mentioning the possibility of visiting her mother, and Mattia.

As soon as the ferry docks in Capri, Theo leads her to a huddle of boats on the quays, all advertising trips to see the famous blue grotto.

'Shall we go?' he asks her. 'It's supposed to be stunning.'

'Sure,' she says, although, for some reason, she is feeling reluctant.

They sit on the small fishing vessel as it chugs around the island of Capri. Their skipper shows them the ledge where Emperor Tiberius would hurl his enemies into the ocean. He brings them through the opening in Lovers' Rock, instructing them to kiss as, if they do so, they will be together forever. Theo and Valentino need no encouragement. They wrap themselves around each other. Their kiss is so lingering that eventually the skipper has to call over to them to tell them that the Lovers' Rock is long past.

Valentina and Theo sit side by side in perfect silence, listening to the boat cresting the waves and looking out at the open blue of the sea. She imagines she sees herself dancing upon the water, spinning in the hazy light. It makes her think of her grandmother, Maria. She really wishes she had known her – even as a child. She had always believed that Maria was different from the rest of them – from her mother, her great-grandmother, Belle, and herself – but now, with the revelation of the old movies, it seems that Maria had been as much a free spirit as any of them. Yet why did she deny who she was? Why never dance again? It fills Valentina with such a deep sadness that Maria lived the rest of her life without being who she really was. She promises herself that marriage will not change her essence, that her love with Theo will only strengthen her sense of self, for she has, after all, found a man who knows her through and through, all her flaws and all her heart.

The boat grinds to a halt. The engines are cut as it bobs upon the sea. They are told that they can row to the blue grotto from here. The skipper offers to take them in the little rowing boat but, with a wink and a nudge, Theo gets him to agree to let them row out alone. Valentina clambers down into the little boat and sits in the bow, and Theo rows them back in towards the island.

'Apparently, the seabed is so white that it reflects the colour of the sea on to the ceiling of the grotto,' Theo tells her. 'It is supposed to be the purest blue you have ever seen.'

They reach the grotto, but the entrance is so low that they both have to lie down in the boat as Theo pushes them inside. They remain lying in the bottom of the boat, looking at the walls of the grotto. Theo had not been exaggerating. They are enveloped in blue – a Virgin Mary blue, the blue of hope. It sings to her soul and, when she turns on her side and looks into the face of her love, she sees he has the same colour blue eyes. With no words, they speak to each other in the language of their bodies:

I love you with all my heart and soul.

I love you always.

The sea rocks them gently inside their grotto sanctuary. She closes her eyes and imagines that they are making love at the bottom of sea, entwined like swirling seaweed, the seeds from his loins filling her like luminescent pearls inside her belly. She finds herself wishing for their child. They roll on the bottom of the boat, and now he is above her, framed against the ceiling of the blue grotto, and pushing deep within her. They roll again and she is above him. She pulls away from him and turns around, lying with her back pressed against his firm belly. She raises her back, her knees, and guides him into her, her hands pressed into his as she lifts herself up, her head tipped back and her eyes closed. Their foreheads touch, as if they are blessing each other. He lifts himself into her and they writhe together in unity, the boat rocking on the water, intensifying their union further. He is so deep within her, and she feels her power and strength as she brings him into her. She wants to hold him forever. He is her heart. She cries out, confident that no one can hear them. They are buried deep within the blue grotto as they climax together, and she falls back down upon him, melting into his body, as if they are one.

Afterwards, she sits within his embrace, the water lapping at the sides of the boat, the two of them looking out through the tiny entrance of the grotto, out at the endless breadth of the Mediterranean Sea. There is no need to speak. The moment is perfect, their joy complete.

* * *

Just as they are about to push the boat back out of the grotto, Valentina sees another rowing boat outside, about to enter.

'Wait!' Theo calls out to the boat. 'We have to come out first.'

The person in the boat is either stupid or deaf, because it continues to slide through the tiny entrance, its occupant unseen, obviously prostrate in the bottom of it. The two boats knock together and Valentina's mouth goes dry in horror, her fists clenching, as she sees the occupant of the other boat is Glen.

'What the hell are you doing here?' Theo speaks first.

'You wouldn't return my phone calls, and it was obvious that the pretty lady either didn't pass on my message or you both decided to ignore it. Very unwise,' Glen says, sitting up.

'Glen, I am sick of this,' Theo tells him. 'It's over, right? I told you. The Masson was the last picture. I am never going to get in your way again.'

Glen stands up in his boat, pointing his finger at Valentina. 'And I told her that that was not good enough for me. You owe me a lot of money, Theo. And I want some kind of compensation. I want the picture.'

'It's too late. Ricardo Borghetti already has it. I gave it to him yesterday.'

Glen looks furious.

Valentina doesn't like this – the two boats bashing against each other in the little blue grotto. She is beginning to feel claustrophobic. 'Let's go,' she whispers to Theo.

'Get out of our way,' Theo barks at Glen. He propels their boat forward aggressively. As it dashes against Glen's boat, it causes the other man, who is still standing, to stumble and fall backwards into the water. 'Shit!' Theo exclaims, pivoting their boat around and leaning over the edge so that he can help Glen. 'Take my hand,' he says to him.

However, instead of taking his proffered hand, Glen swims around to Valentina's side of the boat. For an instant, he looks right into her. She sees the menace in his eyes, the hatred that comes with the jilted, and she tries to push him away. Yet he has a hold of her, and he pulls her over the side of the boat and into the water.

How surprisingly deep the sea is in the grotto! He pulls her down and down. It feels as if his arms and legs are the tentacles of an octopus. He has her in a death grip. She struggles to free herself, but it seems that Glen is so intent on drowning her that he doesn't even care about his own life. She tries to speak, water rushing into her mouth, making it worse. She desperately needs to call out for her man.

Suddenly, she is released. She sees Theo in the water with them, pulling Glen away from her. He is calling to her in the watery depths. She knows he is telling her to swim. A force outside of her – could it be his love? – is pushing her skywards, and she emerges spluttering, bobbing beneath the roof of the blue grotto. She pulls herself up into the little rowing boat, shivering, despite the fact it isn't cold. She peers over the edge into the water and, as she does so, both

Glen and Theo come to the surface, water spraying everywhere.

The two men climb into the other rowing boat, coughing up water, unable either to speak or fight.

She sits, frozen with dread, in the second boat.

Finally, Theo manages to catch his breath. 'Valentina,' he orders her, 'go back to the fishing boat and wait for me there. Glen and I will follow.'

'No,' she says. 'I don't want you to stay with him.'

Glen is still coughing up water; his face is red, his blue eyes bloodshot, his chest heaving.

'Look at him,' Theo says. 'He's done in. Go. NOW!' he commands her.

Yet her instincts tell her not to leave him. 'Promise me you'll be right behind me,' she begs him.

'I promise, Valentina.'

She looks long and hard at Theo, then over at Glen, who is still in a heap on the floor of the boat. She supposes he needs to go to hospital – and then what? Will they charge him with assault? She looks back at Theo.

He nods at her. His blue grotto eyes making her trust him. 'Go on, Valentina,' he says, softly. 'I won't let you down.'

Reluctantly, she picks up the oars of her boat and uses one of them to guide her out of the grotto, lying back as she does so. Out on the open sea, she rows as fast as she can back to the small fishing vessel. The skipper helps her aboard, asking her where her husband is.

'He is just coming,' she tells him. 'There's another man and he fell in the sea.'

'As did you?' the sailor asks her, handing her a towel, which she wraps around herself.

They wait patiently. She stands in the prow of the boat, like a sentinel. She stares at the entrance to the blue grotto, but the two men never come out.

In the end, the skipper of her boat rows her back out to see what is taking so long. Yet, when they enter the grotto, neither Theo nor Glen is anywhere to be seen. Glen's boat is still there – empty. She hunts the clear water. She can see right down to the pristine white seabed. She can see nothing. She tries to shake this terrible moment from her head. It has to be a bad dream. But, when she pinches herself, her nails draw blood. The men are gone. It seems impossible. They can't just have disappeared, and yet it is undeniable. The blue grotto is empty of life and she has lost Theo again, maybe this time forever.

Acknowledgements

My deepest thanks to my agents, Marianne Gunn O'Connor and Vicki Satlow, for their support, faith and encouragement, and to Pat Lynch for his ever listening ear. Thank you to my editor, Leah Woodburn, who has guided me so skillfully yet again and to all the team at Headline Publishers for their hard work. Thank you to Suzy and Robert Wilson for providing me with a writing sanctuary and to Kate Pengelly for being the perfect writing companion. In Maria's story, the Ballets Jooss is real, although Jacqueline, Lempert and his school are fictional. Thank you to my mother's friend, Claire Warner, for showing me her dance notes during the time she and my mother were both students of the Ballets Jooss.

The passage describing Anita Chappell's video installation is an homage to *Story of O* by Pauline Réage. Thank you to Clara and Manoushka Gold for bringing me to Réage's house all those years ago. I also refer to Anaïs Nin's erotic short story, 'The Hungarian Adventurer', in her short story collection, *Delta of Venus*. Anita Chappell's photography is inspired by the erotic photography of the German artist, Nora Ness.

Thank you to Monica McInerney, Katrine Tilrem, Carol O'Connor, Donna Ansley, Tracey Ann Skjaeråsen, Bernie McGrath and to all my other wonderful friends who have helped me so much. Thank you to Clara Rose for letting me quote the lyrics from her song 'Girl' from the album *A Portfolio*. Thank you to my brother, Fintan, and his wife, Eimear, and my new-found siblings, Jane, Paul and Jed, my Aunty Joyce, my cousin Maria, and to my mother-in-law, Mary Ansley. Thank you to my two gems, Corey and Helena, and to my darling Barry, who is, of course, my one and only S.L.

Have you been seduced by Valentina?
Her story continues in the third addictive book
in the Valentina series,

Valentina Unlocked

Coming soon from Headline

Valentina

Evie Blake

Milan, 2012. Photographer Valentina Rosselli is living with her lover of one year. Theo Steen, but refuses to commit to anything more. When she is offered an intriguing photography assignment, taking pictures of those who indulge in the darker side of desire, she's drawn into a shadowy world that reveals a part of her she never knew existed . . .

Venice, 1929. Belle is the alter ego of a well-to-do socialite, trapped in an unhappy marriage and constrained by society. As Belle, she plays out her fantasies by leading a secret life as a courtesan – but she will only truly be set free by finding the man who will love her.

Though decades separate them, Belle and Valentina's lives are intertwined. Both will experience an awakening of their latent desires, but will they discover the connection between physical passion and true love?

978 0 7553 9887 4

headline

Because You Are Mine

Beth Kery

IT STARTS WITH THAT FIRST LOOK, WHEN YOU
KNOW YOU HAVE TO HAVE HIM . . .

It's at a cocktail party in her honour that she first
meets him – and the attraction is immediate for
graduate student Francesca Arno. It's also bewilder-
ing. She's not used to such a wholesale sexual reponse
to a stranger. Enigmatic, darkly intense, with a commanding presence, billionaire Ian Noble completely
unnerves her. And she likes it.

For Ian, Francesca is the kind of woman he can't
resist – one that comes all too rarely: a true innocent.
But he can sense in her a desire to open up, to
experiment, to give herself to the fantasies of a man in
control. The first kiss, the first caress, the first
challenge for a woman who craves what she's never
had – a man who gets what he wants . . .

978 1 4722 0066 2

headline

Exposed to You

Beth Kery

All it takes is . . . ONE NIGHT OF PASSION

Reserved art teacher Joy will never forget being hired to paint a body tattoo on a total stranger at a Hollywood film set. Certain she'll never see her sexy subject again, she gives herself to him completely in a moment of passionate desire.

Little does she know the man is film star Everett Hughes. For Everett, women and sex come as easily as fame. How can he convince the guarded Joy that beneath the hard body and sexy façade of celebrity is a real man who wants only one, real woman?

In the heat of an intoxicating affair, Everett endeavours to break down her barriers and gain her trust. But can Joy do the same, and reveal to him the vulnerable woman who longs to be loved, wanted, and desired for ever?

978 1 4722 0057 0

headline

ETERNAL
ROMANCE

Release Me

J. Kenner

He was the one man I couldn't avoid. And the one man I couldn't resist.

Damien Stark could have his way with any woman. He was sexy, confident, and commanding: anything he wanted, he got. And what he wanted was me.

Our attraction was unmistakable, almost beyond control, but as much as I ached to be his, I feared the pressures of his demands. Submitting to Damien meant I had to bare the darkest truth about my past – and risk breaking us apart.

But Damien was haunted, too. And as our passion came to obsess us both, his secrets threatened to destroy him – and us – for ever.

An irresistible, erotic, emotionally charged romance for fans of FIFTY SHADES OF GREY and BARED TO YOU of a powerful man who's never heard 'no', a fiery woman who says 'yes' on her own terms and an unforgettable indecent proposal . . .

978 1 4722 06053

headline